ALSO BY LAURA JOH ROWLAND

Shinjū

Bundori

THE WAY OF THE TRAITOR

VILLARD

NEW YORK

THE WAY OF
THE TRAITOR

A Samurai Mystery

LAURA JOH ROWLAND

Library of Congress Cataloging-in-Publication Data
Rowland, Laura Joh.
The way of the traitor: a Samurai mystery/by Laura Joh Rowland.
p.   cm.
ISBN 0-679-44900-0
1. Japan—History—Genroku period, 1688–1704—Fiction.
I. Title.
PS3568.0934D47   1997   813´.54—dc20   96-41706

Random House website address: http://www.randomhouse.com/

Printed in the United States of America on acid-free paper
24689753
First Edition
Book design by Tanya M. Pérez-Rock

To Marty Rowland

THE WAY OF THE TRAITOR

JAPAN
GENROKU PERIOD, YEAR 2, MONTH 5
(June 1690)

PROLOGUE

LIKE A PALE moon, the sun's white globe rose in a mesh of drifting clouds above the eastern hills beyond Nagasaki, the international port city on Kyūshū, the westernmost of Japan's four major islands. Mist clung to the forested slopes and shrouded the city clustered around the harbor. Bells echoed from hillside temples, over the governor's stately mansion, the townspeople's thatched houses, and the foreign settlements. In the harbor, a salt-laden summer breeze stirred the sails of Japanese fishing boats, Chinese junks, and myriad vessels from the exotic, faraway lands of Arabia, Korea, Tonkin. A patrol barge glided down the corridor formed by the harbor's high, wooded cliffs, past the watchtowers, toward a calm sea. On the western horizon, the silhouettes of distant ships appeared as dawn gradually pushed back night's curtain.

On a steep road leading away from town, a low, anguished moaning heralded a solemn procession. First came Nagasaki's highest officials—mounted samurai dressed in black ceremonial robes and caps —then four hundred lesser dignitaries, attendants, servants, and merchants, all on foot. Last marched a small army of soldiers armed with swords and spears, guarding the terrified prisoner in their midst.

"No," whispered the samurai between his moans, which grew louder as the procession climbed higher into the hills. He had been stripped of his swords, and all clothing except a loincloth. He tried to break free, but heavy shackles hobbled his ankles; ropes bound his wrists behind his back. Spears prodded him up the path. "This can't be happening!"

Amid the lower ranks of officials, one witness fought back fear and nausea. He hated watching executions, but his attendance at this one was mandatory, along with that of everyone else who had dealings with Nagasaki's foreign community. The *bakufu*—the military dictatorship that ruled Japan—wanted to remind them all of what would happen to anyone who violated the nation's harsh antitreason laws, to warn them against any allegiance with the foreigners, no matter how innocent, or any act of disloyalty toward the government. Here, in the only place where foreigners were allowed in Japan, an ambitious man might gather powerful allies and launch a rebellion against the Tokugawa regime. To prevent this, the *bakufu* enforced the laws more rigorously than anywhere else in the country, devoting immense effort to identifying and punishing traitors. Even a minor infraction would inevitably lead to death.

"Why are you doing this?" the prisoner pleaded. "I beg you, have mercy!"

No one answered. The march continued relentlessly, until at last the members of the procession gathered on a plateau overlooking the city and harbor. None spoke, but the witness sensed their emotions, hovering in the moist air like a malignant cloud: fear; excitement; disgust. He watched, terrified and appalled, as the army bore the captive into the center of the plateau.

There waited four grim, muscular men with cropped hair, wearing ragged kimonos. One, hammer in hand, stood beside a newly erected frame composed of two wooden pillars joined by a crossbeam. Two others seized the prisoner's arms and forced him to his knees beside the man holding a sword; the sharp blade gleamed in the dawn light. These were *eta*, outcasts who served as executioners, and they were ready to cut off the prisoner's head and mount it on the frame as a warning to would-be criminals.

"No!" the prisoner screamed. "Please!" Straining away from his captors, he entreated the audience. "I've committed no crimes. I haven't done anything to deserve this!"

The witness longed to clap his hands over his ears and shut out the screams, to close his eyes against the sight of the panic-stricken samurai whose courage had fled before this ultimate disgrace, to deny his terrible sense of identification with the condemned prisoner.

Hoofbeats clattered as the governor of Nagasaki urged his horse forward. "The prisoner, Yoshidō Ganzaemon, is guilty of treason," he announced in grave, ceremonial tones.

"Treason?" The samurai ceased struggling, his face blank with shock. "I'm not a traitor. I've served the shogun well all my life." His voice rose in disbelief. "I'm the hardest-working officer in the harbor patrol. I always volunteer for extra duty. I risk my life in rough weather. I practice the martial arts so that I can someday bring my lord glory on the battlefield. I've never acted against the shogun or his regime. Whoever says so is lying!"

But the governor's voice drowned out his plea. "Yoshidō Ganzaemon has cravenly denounced the lord to whom he owes his ultimate duty and loyalty. He has called His Excellency the Shogun Tokugawa Tsunayoshi a weak, stupid fool."

The witness knew that Yoshidō had insulted the shogun during a party in the pleasure quarter, where the courtesans flattered and the sake flowed freely, removing men's inhibitions and loosening their tongues. Nagasaki boasted more spies than anywhere else in Japan, all alert to the slightest transgressions. They'd overheard Yoshidō's careless words and brought him to this sorry fate as they had many others.

"I didn't mean it," Yoshidō protested. "I was drunk; I didn't know what I was saying. A thousand apologies!" He tried to bow, but the two *eta* held him firmly. "Please, you can't kill me for one little mistake!"

No one spoke in his defense, not even the witness, who knew of the man's exemplary record and character. To take a traitor's side would mean sharing his guilt, and punishment.

"For his dishonor, Yoshidō Ganzaemon is hereby sentenced to death." The governor nodded to the executioners.

Now the prisoner's fear turned to rage. "So you condemn me as a traitor?" he shouted at the silent, watchful assembly. "When there are much, much worse criminals in Nagasaki than I?" Harsh, bitter laughter exploded from him. "Just take a look around Deshima, and you'll see!"

The crowd stirred; murmurs swept the plateau like a troubled wind. The witness gasped at the accusation, for Yoshidō spoke the truth. By unfortunate accident, the witness had discovered shocking activity on Deshima, the Dutch trade colony. He'd observed clandestine comings and goings, illegal transactions, forbidden collusion between foreigners and Japanese. Even worse, he believed he knew who bore the primary responsibility for the crimes. Now his bowels loosened; he swayed dizzily. If an underling like Yoshidō knew about the crimes, then who else did, or would eventually find out?

The governor held up a hand, arresting all sound and motion. "Proceed!" he ordered.

The *eta* seized the looped knot of hair at Yoshidō's nape and yanked, forcing his head high, holding it immobile. The witness's heart thudded; his limbs went numb and cold in horrible empathy. He saw himself in Yoshidō's place, ready to die not in glorious battle, or honorably by his own hand in ritual suicide as befitting a samurai, but in disgrace, a convicted traitor.

Then he pictured the person he suspected of the Deshima crime, kneeling beside the executioner whose sword now rose in a high, deadly arc. A person to whose fate his own was inextricably bound. Would they die together like this, someday? The penalty for a crime of such magnitude was death not just for the criminal, but also for his whole family and all close associates. *Please,* the witness prayed in mute terror, *let it not happen!*

"Oh, yes, there are bigger villains than I, who are probably committing their evil, treasonous deeds even now. Punish them instead!"

Yoshidō's hysterical voice echoed through the hills, in vain. Panic sharpened the witness's senses. He heard the crowd's simultaneous intake of breath, smelled anticipation mingling with the salty sea breeze. Under the sun's blind, merciless eye, and over the hammering of his own heart, he heard Yoshidō scream: "No, please, no no no NO!"

The executioner's sword slashed downward. In a great red fountain of blood, the blade severed Yoshidō's head, forever ending his protests and accusations.

But the witness's terror lived on. If matters continued along their present course, the danger would escalate. There would be more violent death, more mortal disgrace . . . unless he stopped the crimes before someone else did.

1

THROUGH THE DESOLATE streets of nighttime Edo marched Sano Ichirō, the shogun's *sōsakan-sama*—Most Honorable Investigator of Events, Situations, and People. A storm had cleared the Nihonbashi merchant district of pedestrians. Rain pelted tile roofs, streamed from eaves and balconies, dripped off the brim of Sano's wicker hat, and drenched his cloak and trousers. The moist air saturated his lungs with the odors of wet earth and wood. Beside him walked his chief retainer, Hirata, and behind them ten other samurai detectives from the elite corps Sano led. Their sandaled feet splashed along the narrow, muddy road. Spurning shelter and comfort for the sake of their mission, they forged ahead through the downpour.

"This is the place," Sano said, halting outside a mansion surrounded by a high stone wall. Black mourning drapery hung over the gate; lanterns inside sent a shimmering glow up into the rainy night. Under the balcony of a shop across the street, Sano and his men gathered to review their strategy for the climax of a long investigation.

Since early spring, a rash of bizarre crimes had plagued Edo. Thieves had been stealing corpses from the homes of the deceased and the sites of accidents, or intercepting coffins on the way to funerals. Ignoring class distinctions, they'd seized dead peasants, merchants, and samurai—nine in all. In addition, eight religious pilgrims had been murdered on highways outside town, with abandoned baggage and fresh blood found at the death scenes, but the victims gone. None of the corpses had been recovered. The crimes had terrified travelers and deprived families of the right to honor their dead with proper funerary rituals.

Sano, ordered by the shogun to capture the body thieves, had placed agents around town. Disguised as itinerant peddlers, they'd loitered in teahouses, entertainment districts, gambling dens, and other places frequented by the criminal element. This morning an agent had overheard a servant boast that the thieves had paid him to help steal the body of his dead master, during the funeral vigil tonight. The agent had followed the servant to the home of a rich oil merchant and reported the location to Sano.

"If the thieves come, we follow them," Sano reminded Hirata and his men now. "We have to catch their leader and find out what happens to the corpses."

The detectives surrounded the merchant's house, while Sano and Hirata hid in a recessed doorway across an alley from the back gate. They waited for a miserable, wet hour, breathing the weather's humid warmth. Still the streets remained silent and deserted. Sano's urgency grew.

The son of a *rōnin,* he'd once earned his living as an instructor in his father's martial arts academy and by tutoring young boys, studying history in his spare time. Family connections had secured him a position as a senior police commander. He'd solved a murder case, saved the shogun's life, and been promoted a year and a half ago to the exalted position of Tokugawa Tsunayoshi's *sōsakan-sama.* By capturing the Bundori Killer, who had terrorized Edo with a series of grisly murders, he'd won the shogun's greater favor. Since then, he'd solved many other cases, seen his income and personal staff grow, and achieved a satisfying sense of professional accomplishment. His socially and financially advantageous marriage to Reiko, daughter of the rich, powerful Magistrate Ueda, would take place in the autumn. Yet a dark cloud shadowed Sano's existence.

He'd grown increasingly disillusioned with the *bakufu,* a corrupt, oppressive dictatorship. Under its orders, Sano had to spy on citizens who'd criticized government policy or otherwise offended the Tokugawa. Distorted and embellished, his findings were used to discredit honest men, who were then exiled or demoted. And the shogun was no better than the regime he commanded. Tokugawa Tsunayoshi indulged a weakness for religion, the arts, and young boys, while neglecting affairs of state. He also sent Sano on fruitless searches for ghosts, magic potions, and buried treasure. Yet Sano had no choice but to pursue such immoral or ridiculous activities. The shogun commanded his complete loyalty, and his future. And his personal life offered no consolation.

While time and self-discipline had exorcised the worst of his heartbreak over losing Aoi, the woman he loved, he couldn't relinquish her memory. He'd delayed his marriage for more than a year, but not just because it would finalize their separation. He didn't want to become close to anyone again, to risk the pain of hurting—or losing—someone else who mattered to him. Hence, he rejoiced at every assignment that was worthy of his effort and allowed him to postpone the wedding yet again, and to maintain his emotional isolation.

Now Sano raised his head, straining to hear. "Listen!" he said to Hirata.

From up the alley came the sound of brisk footsteps splashing through puddles.

"A palanquin," Hirata said as the sedan chair, carried by four hooded and cloaked bearers, emerged from the dripping darkness. The bearers laid down their burden at the merchant's gate. They were all samurai, with swords at their waists. The gate opened, and two of the men hurried inside. Soon they reappeared, stowed a long bundle in the palanquin, lifted the sedan chair, and trotted away.

Imitating a dog's bark, Sano signaled his men. He and Hirata followed the palanquin, darting in and out of alleys and doorways, through the rain's relentless clamor. Shadows moved through the night as the detective corps joined the pursuit. The palanquin led them deeper into Nihonbashi's twisting maze of streets, past closed shops and over canals. Finally it stopped outside one of a row of thatched buildings on the edge of the swordmakers' district. A sign over the door bore a circular crest and the name MIOCHIN. And Sano guessed the fate of the stolen corpses.

The bearers vanished inside the building with their bundle. Behind the paper windowpanes, lights burned and shadows moved. Sano gathered the detectives beside the abandoned palanquin and said, "Surround the house, and arrest anyone who comes out. I'm going inside."

He drew his sword, but Hirata whispered urgently, "The thieves are dangerous killers. Please stay here, where you'll be safe." Beneath his hat, his wide, boyish face was tense with concern; his earnest gaze beseeched Sano. "Let us handle this."

A rueful smile touched Sano's lips as he started toward the door. Twenty-one years old, Hirata took very seriously his role as chief retainer and primary protector, opposing Sano's determination to fight battles alone and reserve the worst risks for himself. He didn't know that his master's unspoken fear of loss and guilt outweighed the fear of death. And he didn't understand that Sano needed danger, and confrontation with evil. Bushido—the Way of the Warrior—taught that a samurai's sole purpose was to give his life to his lord's service. Duty, loyalty, and courage were its highest virtues, and together formed the foundation of a samurai's honor. But Sano's personal concept of Bushido encompassed a fourth cornerstone, as important to his honor as the others: the pursuit of truth and justice. The exhilarating quest for knowledge, the satisfaction of seeing a criminal caught and punished, infused his existence with a deeper purpose than serving a gravely flawed regime.

"Come on, let's go," Sano said.

With Hirata beside him, he stole up to the building, quietly slid open the door, and looked into a large room lit by hanging lanterns. Mounted on wall brackets were many sheathed swords, and gleaming steel blades with the hilts removed. Characters etched on the tangs certified that these blades had cut human bodies during *tameshigiri,* the official method of testing swords. In the back of the room, near sliding doors that opened onto a wet courtyard, stood seven men: the four thieves in dripping cloaks, the hoods thrown back from their coarse faces; two peasants in cotton headbands, loincloths, and short kimonos; and an older man dressed in a formal black surcoat and trousers stamped with the Miochin crest. In his pale, aquiline face, deepset eyes burned.

The thieves unwrapped the bundle on the floor, baring the corpse of a stout man shrouded in white silk funeral garments. Gazing down at it, Miochin said, "A perfect specimen. Many thanks."

According to Tokugawa law, the bodies of executed criminals could be used to test swords, but murderers, priests, tattooed individuals, and *eta* were taboo. A recent shortage of suitable traitors, thieves, and arsonists had reduced the supply of raw material for sword testers. When the *bakufu* sold the few available corpses to the highest bidders among the hereditary testing officials, the wealthy Yamada, Chokushi, and Nakagawa families bought up the precious commodity, forcing minor clans such as the Miochin to use straw dummies. However, the cutting of human flesh and bone was the only true test of a blade's quality. Since swords tested otherwise fetched lower prices and commanded less respect, Edo's swordsmiths and samurai avoided testers who couldn't certify their weapons at the highest level of strength. Miochin, unwilling to accept the loss of income, had hired *rōnin* to procure corpses by theft and murder.

"We'll test the blades from swordsmith Ibe," Miochin told the peasants, who had to be his sons. "I shall perform *ryōkuruma* and *o kessa.*" The most difficult cuts of all: across the corpse's hips, and through the shoulder girdle. "You will use the arms and legs for lesser blades."

The thieves stirred nervously. "I think someone followed us," one said. "Hurry up and pay us, so we can get out of here."

Miochin gave a string of coins to the thieves. Outside, Sano and Hirata drew their swords, then burst into the room.

"Tokugawa Special Police Force. You're all under arrest!" Sano cried.

Amid exclamations of dismayed surprise, the thieves unsheathed their swords; Miochin and sons grabbed weapons off the wall. Aware that the penalty for theft and murder was death, the criminals advanced on Sano and Hirata, blades drawn, faces taut with desperation.

"The building is surrounded," Sano said. "Drop your weapons and surrender."

Miochin laughed. "When oxen fly and snakes talk!" he jeered. "You shan't execute me for trying to earn my rice!"

The criminals assaulted Sano and Hirata, who fought back, blades flashing. The detective corps, hearing the commotion, stormed into the room. Sano battled Miochin. The sword tester's blade lashed the air like a whirlwind. Gradually he drove Sano backward, into the courtyard. Sano returned cut for cut while he skirted a mound of sand upon which bodies would be tied to bamboo stakes for the testing of swords. He stumbled over a pile of charred bones and turned a backward somersault over a stone furnace where Miochin evidently destroyed the remains of his ill-gotten corpses. Landing on his feet, Sano lunged at Miochin. In the streaming downpour they clashed in mortal combat. The sword tester was fighting for his life and liberty. In a way, so was Sano.

Now he entered a plane where the corrupt regime that held him captive disappeared. He forgot the shogun; he forgot Aoi, and his self-imposed loneliness. He spared a last, worried thought for his men, who expertly battled the thieves and Miochin's sons. Their shouts and movements soon faded from his consciousness. All that mattered was his victory over this evil criminal.

A heady euphoria heightened Sano's perception. Quickly he saw that Miochin's strength lay in his feint and recovery. He lowered his sword, apparently intending a cut across Sano's stomach. Then his blade suddenly changed direction. Sano parried the sword tester's diagonal chest slice almost too late. His counterstrike slashed Miochin's thigh. Miochin gasped in pain, but didn't falter. Then Sano took a risk he would have once instructed his students to avoid.

When Miochin hoisted his sword in both hands for a deadly vertical slash, Sano gambled that this was another feint. Resisting the instinctive urge to raise his weapon and shield his torso, he lowered and swung his blade.

It gashed Miochin's belly from side to side. The sword tester howled in horrified surprise. Reflex carried his arms out of the feinted downslash and sideways for the crosscut he'd really intended. The light went out of his eyes before he hit the ground.

Sano stepped back. He saw his men, all alive and well, hurrying to his rescue. The other criminals lay dead in the shop. Releasing the tension from his body in a series of deep gasps, Sano let the rain wash Miochin's blood off his sword, then sheathed it. Although killing and death were a samurai's natural domain, he hated taking lives. The act placed him uncomfortably close to the murderers he hunted. But this instance he could justify as necessary.

"*Sōsakan-sama.*" Hirata's voice cracked as he addressed Sano, his face stricken. "*Sumimasen*—excuse me, but that was a dangerous thing to do. You could have been killed. It's my duty to serve and protect you. You should have let me take Miochin."

"Never mind, Hirata. It's over now." *And, merciful gods, with no casualties on his side!* Still gasping for breath, Sano said, "We'll report the raid to the local police. They can close down the shop, clear away the dead, and return the stolen corpse." His heart still pumped the exhilarating tonic of victory through his veins. Miochin's thieves would no longer prey on travelers or grieving families.

Hirata tore the hem from his cloak and bound Sano's left forearm, which bled from a cut he hadn't noticed. "You'll need a doctor when we get back to Edo Castle."

Back to Edo Castle. The four words deflated Sano's spirits. At the castle, he must report to the shogun and face again the fact that a weak, foolish despot owned his soul. Glumly Sano looked forward to resuming his place in the corrupt Tokugawa political machine, and his bleak existence in an empty house haunted with memories of Aoi.

Until another search for truth and justice again gave his life honor and meaning.

IN THE MORNING, after a long night of giving orders and filing reports at police headquarters, Sano, Hirata, and the other detectives arrived at Edo Castle, which perched on its hilltop above the city, beneath low, ominous storm clouds. At the castle gate, a massive, ironclad door set in a high stone wall, guards admitted Sano and his men into the maze of passages and security checkpoints.

"I'll meet you at home," Sano told Hirata, referring to the mansion in the castle's Official Quarter where he and his retainers lived.

He followed a passage that wound up the hill between enclosed corridors and watchtowers manned by armed guards. He entered the inner precinct, crossed the garden, and stopped before the shogun's palace, a vast building with whitewashed plaster walls, carved wooden doors, beams, and window lattices, and a many-gabled gray tile roof.

"*Sōsakan* Sano Ichirō, reporting to His Excellency," he told the guards stationed outside.

They bowed and opened the door without asking him to leave his swords or searching him for hidden weapons: He'd earned the shogun's trust. "You may proceed to the inner garden," the chief guard said.

Sano walked down cypress-floored corridors past the government offices that occupied the building's outer rooms. A sliding door, manned by more guards, led him outside again, where he followed a flagstone path through Tokugawa Tsunayoshi's private garden. The pine trees' densely fringed boughs hung still and heavy in the humid heat. Lilies filled the air with a cloying sweetness; bees buzzed lazily; dead maple leaves lay motionless on the pond's glassy surface. Above the castle, a dark storm front bled across the gray sky like an ink wash on wet paper. Distant thunder rumbled. The oppressive atmosphere intensified the trapped sensation that Sano always felt in the castle. He prayed for the shogun to assign him a new criminal investigation, not another ghost hunt or spying job. Then, as he neared the thatch-roofed pavilion, he stopped, disconcerted.

Chamberlain Yanagisawa Yoshiyasu—the shogun's second-in-command—occupied the center of the pavilion's raised wooden floor. Dressed in a cool silk summer kimono patterned in blue and ivory, he knelt before a large sheet of white paper, his slim hand holding a brush poised over it. A servant waited beside him, ready to replenish the ink, refill the water bowl, or supply him with fresh paper from a thick stack. In two rows flanking Yanagisawa knelt the five men who comprised the Council of Elders, the shogun's closest advisers and Yanagisawa's flunkies. More servants circled the pavilion, flapping fans to create an artificial breeze. But Tokugawa Tsunayoshi himself was nowhere in sight.

In a series of rapid, graceful curves and slashes, Yanagisawa swept his brush over the paper, writing a column of characters. "*Sōsakan,*" he murmured. "Won't you join us."

Sano climbed the steps onto the pavilion, knelt, bowed, and offered formal greetings to the assembly. "Honorable Chamberlain, I've come to report to the shogun." Apprehension tightened Sano's chest: Yanagisawa's presence during an audience with the shogun boded ill for him.

Chamberlain Yanagisawa contemplated the verse he'd written. He frowned, shook his head, and motioned for the servant to remove the page. Then he looked up at Sano. Thirty-two years old, he'd been the shogun's lover since his youth. Tall and slender, with fine features and large, liquid eyes, he possessed an arresting masculine beauty at odds with his character.

"I'm afraid His Excellency is unavailable at the moment," he said. "Whatever you have to say, you may say to me."

His suave tone barely concealed a massive hostility. From Sano's first days as *sōsakan,* Chamberlain Yanagisawa had viewed him as a rival for Tokugawa Tsunayoshi's favor, for power over the weak lord and thus the entire nation. He'd tried to sabotage Sano's investigation of the Bundori Murders, and have Sano beaten to death. Sano had survived, and succeeded anyway. Unfortunately he'd also caught Chamberlain Yanagisawa in a trap he'd set for the killer, who had taken Yanagisawa hostage, terrifying and brutalizing him before Sano could come to the rescue. Chamberlain Yanagisawa would never forgive this unintentional offense.

"His Excellency ordered me to report directly to him upon my return to Edo Castle," Sano said. He knew Yanagisawa was deliberately blocking his access to Tokugawa Tsunayoshi. Long ago he'd abandoned the submissive manner that demeaned him without appeasing the chamberlain. Now he refused to back down. "I will speak to him."

Sano understood Yanagisawa's anger, but all sympathy had fled when the chamberlain's retaliation campaign began. For the past year, Yanagisawa had spread vicious rumors about Sano, ranging from alleged drunkenness, sexual perversion, and embezzlement to violent abuse of citizens and disloyalty toward the regime. Sano had been forced to waste much time and money battling the slander and bribing cooperation from people whom Yanagisawa had ordered not to help him. Yanagisawa's spies dogged him constantly.

Yet so far, the chamberlain's efforts to discredit Sano had failed, as had the covert assassination attempts: a horseman nearly running him down in the street; arrows fired at him while he was in the woods on the shogun's ghost hunts. Sano continued to enjoy the favor of Tokugawa Tsunayoshi, who had latched on to him with uncharacteristic steadfastness, requiring his constant service and company.

But now he experienced a sinking feeling as Yanagisawa said, "His Excellency has a fever that requires a strict regimen of rest and quiet. He can see no one now—except myself, of course." Yanagisawa's finely modeled mouth turned up in a malevolent smile. "I shall relay to him the news of sword tester Miochin's death: According to official sources, he and his thieves were captured and slain by special troops sent by me."

Anger flared inside Sano, but seeing the elders waiting in veiled anticipation for him to make a scene, he controlled his temper. "You can't hide the truth forever, Honorable Chamberlain," he said evenly. "When the shogun recovers, I'll tell him what really happened."

Chamberlain Yanagisawa dipped his brush into the ink. Across the fresh paper that the servant had placed before him, he quickly wrote three characters. Sano read them upside down: *success, wind,* and *tree.*

"I regret to say that you won't be here when His Excellency recovers." Chamberlain Yanagisawa pushed the paper away, accepted another from the servant, and reinked his brush. "Because I have an assignment for you. One that will take you far, far from Edo."

Away from the shogun, who would be angry at his absence, and into

Yanagisawa's power. Dread stole over Sano; nervous sweat dampened his kimono. The elders stirred. Sano stood his ground. "You can't do that. I report to the shogun alone. My duty is to him, not you."

Yanagisawa laughed, as did the elders. "With His Excellency indisposed, I am in charge. I can do anything I choose. And I choose to send you on an inspection tour of Nagasaki."

"Nagasaki?" Sano echoed, horrified. The western port was two months' journey from Edo. The trip there and back, plus the work itself, could consume a year—a year during which Yanagisawa could destroy Sano's reputation, turn the shogun against him, and deprive him of his position. Yet Sano foresaw even more serious consequences than these.

"You seem displeased, *sōsakan.*" Chamberlain Yanagisawa fairly shimmered with amusement. "I can't see why. Nagasaki is a prestigious posting. All you need do there is document the state of the government, the economy, and the citizens."

On the blank paper, he practiced the same characters again—*success, wind, tree*—then signaled the servant for a clean page. "You needn't work very hard, and you can exact a portion of the revenue from foreign trade, while enjoying a leisurely life on the beautiful Kyūshū coast."

Sano didn't want money, leisure, or a trivial job. And he knew the dark side of the rich paradise that was Nagasaki. There, the most innocent behavior, wrongly interpreted as treason, could condemn a man to death—especially a man set up by his enemies for a fall from grace. Sano could guess why Yanagisawa was sending him to Nagasaki. The chamberlain knew his propensity for breaking rules and offending important people during his investigations. The chamberlain hoped that, in Nagasaki, Sano would get in enough trouble to destroy himself once and for all. And Yanagisawa's far-reaching power could virtually guarantee it.

"Really, *Sōsakan* Sano, you should thank me for this splendid opportunity." Chamberlain Yanagisawa held his brush over the new sheet of paper. "I believe I'm ready to write the entire verse now," he told the elders.

"I'm sure you'll do it beautifully, Honorable Chamberlain," said Senior Elder Makino Narisada, who was Yanagisawa's chief crony. The sinews of his ugly skull face flexed in a sly grimace at Sano.

"I have to stay in Edo for my wedding," Sano protested, though he didn't welcome marriage and had few personal ties to keep him home.

Chamberlain Yanagisawa smiled smugly. "I'm afraid your plans will have to be postponed indefinitely."

Sano stood and bowed. He had nothing to gain by agreeing, and nothing to lose by refusing. "With all due respect, Honorable Chamberlain. I'm not going to Nagasaki."

Yanagisawa laughed. Taking a deep breath, he wrote swiftly, covering the paper with flowing characters. He contemplated his work with a sigh of satisfaction, then laid down his brush. "Oh, but I think you are, *Sōsakan* Sano."

He fingered the fine scars on his lip and eyelid: souvenirs of his traumatic experience with the Bundori Killer. Leveling at Sano a gaze filled with vengeful glee, he clapped his hands. Five guards rushed up to the pavilion.

"See that *Sōsakan* Sano is on the ship that leaves for Nagasaki tomorrow," Yanagisawa told them.

Furious at this blatant coercion, Sano could only stare.

"And oh, before you leave to prepare for your trip, *Sōsakan* Sano," Chamberlain Yanagisawa said, eyes alight with cruel mischief, "what do you think of my poem? I composed it specifically with you in mind."

With a graceful flourish, he turned the paper around to face Sano. Thunder rumbled; raindrops pelted the pavilion's roof. Sano read the characters:

In this difficult and uncertain life
Success often requires many endeavors—
Ah! But the wind can fell a tree
From more than one direction.

"WHERE IS THAT miserable Nagasaki harbor patrol? They should have seen us by now, and come to welcome us." Regal in his many-plated armor and horned helmet, the captain stomped angrily around the deck of the ship. "This is a disgraceful slight against the shogun's envoys. Someone will pay!" To the crew, he shouted, "Prepare for landing, and discharging our passengers."

He sneered at Sano and Hirata, who stood in the bow, hands shielding their eyes from the sun as the ship approached Nagasaki Harbor.

Hirata sighed in relief. Due to frequent seasickness, he was pale, shaky, and thinner than when they'd left Edo. "I sure will be glad to get off this ship."

"You're not the only one," Sano said.

When Chamberlain Yanagisawa had banished him, he'd dreaded reaching Nagasaki. Yet after two months at sea, sailing along the coasts of Honshū, Shikoku, and Kyūshū, he rejoiced at the thought of stepping onto land. Beyond the sparkling water, the green landscape of their destination looked like paradise, for the journey had been a terrible experience.

Like all Japanese craft, the ship, whose square sail bore the Toku-gawa triple-hollyhock-leaf crest, was unseaworthy because the government wanted to discourage citizens from leaving the country. With its shallow draft, the awkward wooden tub pitched at the slightest wave. Sano and Hirata had experienced nerve-racking passages through reefs, shoals, and ferocious summer storms. They'd shared the tiny cabin with the officers, while the sailors slept on the roof, and eaten a monotonous diet of salt fish, pickles, and rice cakes. The journey's relentless pace told Sano that Chamberlain Yanagisawa had ordered the crew not to stop for bad weather, hoping Sano might die in a shipwreck. Hostilities within the *bakufu*'s upper echelon were no secret to the lower ranks, and the crew had treated Sano resentfully, knowing the chamberlain would sacrifice their lives to destroy an enemy. And Sano had never ceased worrying about how the hiatus from Edo would affect his future.

Thuds and crashes erupted from the stern, where the crew was bringing baggage out of the hold.

"I'll make sure they don't ruin your things." Hirata ran down the deck, shouting, "Hey, be careful with those!"

Before leaving Edo, Sano had postponed his wedding again, angering his prospective in-laws and jeopardizing the match. He'd left his detective corps behind to serve the shogun in his absence, but knew it couldn't substitute for his personal attention; he might not have a post when he got home. He seethed with anger at the regime that rewarded his accomplishments with virtual exile. Surely Chamberlain Yanagisawa was sending the governor of Nagasaki instructions to ruin him.

But now Sano's relief at surviving the journey inspired a burst of optimism. As he neared Nagasaki, his interest stirred. He'd never been this far from home. What unknown challenges awaited him in this land of troubled history and exotic foreign influences?

The ship moved down a wide, convoluted channel in the Kyūshū coastline. Coves adorned the shores; woodlands topped high cliffs. Terraced rice fields ascended gentler inclines. Over small islands, seabirds soared and shrieked. Fishing boats dotted the calm water. In the distance, the city of Nagasaki cascaded down the lower slopes of steep hills.

"Look!" Returning, Hirata pointed to a glint of light on a clifftop. "And there's another. What are they?"

"The sun reflecting off spyglasses," Sano answered. "They're used by guards who watch for foreign ships and warn of any threat to national security."

Nagasaki, the center of overseas trade, received merchants from many nations—some with hopes of military conquest as well as financial gain.

The ship passed a large island that rose like a mountain in the channel. "Takayama," Sano said. "During the Christian persecutions a hundred years ago, foreign priests were thrown off it and drowned. And that smaller island must be the Burning Place, where hostile ships are set on fire."

Remembering these facts, Sano felt the resurgence of a buried passion. While a young pupil at the Zōjō Temple school, he'd sneaked into a forbidden section of the library. There he'd discovered scrolls documenting Japanese foreign relations over the past two hundred years, and read with fascination of the white barbarians . . . until the abbot caught him. Sano's back still ached when he recalled the beating he'd received. But his curiosity about the barbarians had persisted, despite much discouragement. Laws barred everyone except the most trusted individuals from contact with Europeans, whom the *bakufu* feared would incite rebellion, as they had in the past, and ultimately conquer Japan. Foreign books, and books about foreigners, were banned. Now Sano saw an advantage in his status and his unwanted trip to Nagasaki. At last he would see the legendary barbarians with golden hair, eyes the color of the sky, and bizarre customs. And hidden under his sash was a document that would bridge the language barrier between them.

Sano's closest friend was Dr. Ito Genboku, a physician sentenced to lifetime custodianship of Edo Morgue as punishment for practicing forbidden foreign science. Dr. Ito had assisted Sano with murder investigations and continued his studies, using foreign books obtained through illicit channels from Dutch traders in Nagasaki. Sano, kept under house arrest by Yanagisawa's men during his last hours in Edo, had sent Hirata to convey his farewells to Dr. Ito. Hirata had returned with this message:

Sano-*san,*

It was with great regret that I learned of your imminent departure. To make your stay in Nagasaki more interesting, here is a letter of introduction to Dr. Nicolaes Huygens, my trusted, confidential source of information about foreign science. I believe you will enjoy his company as I have his correspondence. I hope that fate will soon allow your safe return to Edo.

Ito Genboku

Folded inside this letter was a paper inked with scrawls that Sano assumed to be Dutch writing. Yet any encounter with foreigners could provoke accusations of treason.

"I wonder what's going on up there," Hirata said, breaking Sano's line of thought.

Following his retainer's gaze, Sano saw running figures atop the cliffs, shouting to one another in inexplicable frenzy. Toward the ship sped a long barge, rowed by teams of oarsmen and crammed with samurai.

"Ah, the harbor patrol. At last." The captain called out to the barge: "The shogun's envoys wish an official escort into harbor. Wait, where are you going? Stop!"

The barge raced past. Two more followed; none stopped. The faces of the crews reflected the urgency of men on some strange life-or-death mission.

"Something's wrong here," the captain declared.

The ship neared Nagasaki, which formed an irregular crescent around the harbor. A jumble of tiled and thatched rooftops climbed the hills; crooked streets ran between them. Three rivers flowed through the city to the sea. The red pagodas of temples studded higher slopes, with the towers of watch stations above. On the waterfront, more patrol barges circled anchored ships and herded fishing boats toward shore. Sano could see no reason for the commotion. Was this some peculiar military exercise, or preparation for an unknown natural disaster? Another barge rowed straight for Sano's ship and drew up alongside.

"It's about time," the captain huffed.

The barge's chief officer called, "Our apologies for the tardy welcome, but we've got big trouble. The Dutch East India Company's director of trade has disappeared."

Sano, joining the captain and crew on deck, heard their mutters of consternation. Beside him, Hirata whispered, "Why is one man's disappearance such a problem?"

"Because any security breach in Nagasaki means death for everyone responsible," Sano whispered back, understanding the reason for the mysterious panic he'd witnessed. "The missing barbarian might foment dissension and war, or spread Christianity throughout Japan."

The second threat went hand in hand with the first. Christianity had come to Kyūshū about a hundred and fifty years earlier, with Jesuit missionaries who traveled on Portuguese merchant ships. For a time, it had spread unchecked across Japan, welcomed by poor peasants who embraced this doctrine that promised salvation, and by daimyo— samurai warlords—who converted in hopes of luring the lucrative Portuguese trade to their domains. Fifty years after its arrival, Christianity had boasted some three hundred thousand followers.

But the foreign religion had later posed serious problems. Peasant converts destroyed Shinto and Buddhist temples, creating civil unrest. Missionaries supplied arms to Christian daimyo and conspired with them to overthrow the government. From overseas came news of Christian crusades against the Muslims; of Portuguese and Spanish conquests in the East Indies and the New World; of the pope's plans to seize the lands of non-Christian rulers. Finally Ieyasu, the first Tokugawa shogun, issued an edict banning Christianity and deporting the missionaries. During the seventy-five years since, the *bakufu* had rigorously suppressed the dangerous foreign creed. Now the escape of a single Dutchman had revived the threat to national peace and independence.

"Follow us, and we'll see you safely ashore," the harbor patrol officer told the captain.

The ship sailed after the barge, into increasing chaos. From patrol barges, soldiers boarded Chinese junks with many-battened sails like insect wings and smaller ships manned by dark-skinned sailors, searching for the lost Dutchman amid loud protests in foreign languages. More troops swarmed the white stretch of beach and the docks and piers outside warehouses. From the starboard deck, Sano watched the activity with a mixture of excitement and fear, for a sudden thought had taken hold in his mind.

"Stop here, or you'll run aground," the harbor patrol officer called when they reached a point some distance from the city.

The crew dropped anchor. From the beach, small ferryboats rowed out to carry passengers and baggage ashore. Sano moved astern, where the sailors raised and turned the rudder so it formed a gangplank. He was not only the shogun's *sōsakan-sama,* but also Chamberlain Yanagisawa's designated Nagasaki inspector. Despite the ignominious circumstances of his arrival, didn't he have a tacit charge to locate the missing trader? Sano experienced a not unpleasant thrill of danger. As he climbed over the railing and walked down the wet, slanting rudder, the old fascination tugged. He looked toward the middle of Nagasaki's crescent, and saw the subject of many of the scrolls he'd eagerly perused as a boy.

"Deshima," he said to Hirata as they settled into a ferry.

Deshima: the fan-shaped island, some three hundred paces long, whose inner curve faced the Nagasaki shore; where the Dutch East India Company officials lived like prisoners in a heavily guarded compound. From the water surrounding the island's rocky foundation rose tall poles bearing placards that read, ABSOLUTELY NO BOATS PAST THIS POINT! A high wooden fence, topped with sharp spikes, enclosed the compound. Sano craned his neck, but saw only thatched roofs and pine trees within. He could see nothing of the barbarians who had captured his youthful imagination, but his disillusionment with his own country only intensified his desire to know about the outside world.

The ferry bobbed over the waves, then glided up on the beach.

Sano climbed out and saw troops fanning toward the city and hills in search parties. Commanders barked orders. One, arms waving wildly, berated a group of kneeling samurai.

Behind Sano, the captain laughed nastily. "The Deshima guards. They should be executed for letting the barbarian escape."

One guard, apparently wanting to avoid this fate, drew his sword. With a blood-chilling yell, he plunged it into his belly. Hirata gasped. Sano looked away, shaken.

"Welcome!" Through the crowd, a black-robed official hurried toward them. Porters, guards, and palanquins followed. Bowing deeply, he said, "A thousand pardons for this inconvenience. We'll take you to the governor now."

THROUGH THE WINDOWS of his palanquin, Sano watched the sights of Nagasaki move past. He rode like a visiting dignitary, with Hirata and the captain in palanquins behind him, while their Nagasaki escorts walked ahead to clear the way. Sano might almost believe he wasn't a prisoner of the captain, who would soon transfer him to the governor's custody and deliver Chamberlain Yanagisawa's orders concerning him.

The palanquin tilted as the bearers ascended Nagasaki's narrow, crowded streets. Crammed closely together, the shops and houses of the merchant district clung precariously to the hillside. Stone staircases were built alongside the steepest roads. People scurried up and down these, and through the mud from a heavy rain last night. Merchants and peddlers hawked sake, food, and housewares; children gathered around a juggler; an old woman told fortunes. A fishy tang laced the bright morning air. And through the normal everyday bustle, Sano saw news of the Dutchman's disappearance spread.

Mounted samurai in full armor barked questions and orders at pedestrians: "Has a foreign barbarian passed this way? Report any sightings at once!"

Footsoldiers ransacked houses and shops, shouting, "Anyone caught harboring or aiding the barbarian will die!"

Sano feared they might begin slaughtering innocent townspeople if the missing trader wasn't found soon. Trapped in his cushioned vehicle, he longed to run off and join the search. But the captain would kill him if he did, then probably collect a reward from Chamberlain Yanagisawa. And without the governor's sanction, Sano had no right to interfere. Clenching his teeth in frustration, he forced himself to sit still for the ride.

The palanquin crossed a wooden bridge over a river that flowed between high stone embankments. Here, above the merchant district, the streets were wider, less crowded, and populated mostly by samurai. Tile-roofed mansions, enclosed by long barracks with barred windows, lined the streets. Sano saw the crests of Kyūshū daimyo on guarded gates. Troops streamed through these, searching for the Dutch barbarian. Finally the procession stopped before an ornate portal with a double tile roof. From beyond the barracks came men's angry shouts, and the stomp and neigh of horses.

"I've brought the shogun's envoys to Governor Nagai," Sano heard the Nagasaki official announce.

Guards admitted them into a courtyard jammed with men. Mounted troops and footsoldiers marched past Sano as he stepped out of the palanquin. A commander issued orders to his squadron: "Search the hills. If you find him, capture him alive. We don't want an international incident."

In a stall by the gate, guards checked men in and out, hanging a wooden name plate on a board to indicate someone's entry, or taking one down when someone else left.

"If you will please come this way?" Sano's escort led him, Hirata, and the captain into the rambling, two-story mansion with half-timbered walls and latticed windows. They left their shoes and swords in the entryway and walked down a corridor past chambers where officials argued loudly as they pored over maps and secretaries drafted reports about the disaster. At the corridor's end, by the open door to a garden, stood two men.

One was perhaps fifty years of age. Broad across the shoulders and chest, he exuded an air of elegance even as he paced in agitation. Two ornate swords hung at his waist. His rust-colored silk kimono, patterned with gold ginkgo leaves, emphasized his ruddy complexion. The graying hair drawn back from his shaved crown was glossy with oil.

"It will be very bad for us if we don't find him at once," he fumed. Despite his anger, his voice had a mellow, melodious tone—like that of an actor feigning emotion in a Kabuki drama. He wiped his sweating forehead with his sleeve. "What a fiasco!"

The other man was a spare, plainly dressed samurai with ashen hair and a stiff posture. Sano, approaching with his party, heard him mutter, ". . . never would have happened if . . ."

"And what's that supposed to mean?" The first man's smooth voice tightened. "You—" Then he spied his visitors.

"Governor Nagai, may I present the shogun's envoys." Deftly the escort managed the introductions.

"I'm here to perform an inspection of Nagasaki, Honorable Governor," Sano said when his turn came.

Shrugging off his agitation like a discarded robe, Nagai bowed in a relaxed, courteous manner. The lines of his face smoothed into a pleasant expression. His coarse features—broad, porous nose, thick lips, and fleshy jowls—had an agile mobility that lent him a semblance of handsomeness.

"Welcome to Nagasaki. You had a pleasant journey, I hope? Yes. Well." The words issued from Governor Nagai in a honeyed flow. "I apologize for the temporary state of confusion. But everything is under control."

Sano had heard Nagai mentioned in Edo. His admirers praised the administrative skills that had raised him from lowly provincial inspector to commissioner of finance, then won him Tokugawa Tsunayoshi's favor and a prestigious Nagasaki governorship. His detractors said he abused his power to enrich himself, and got away with it because of his talent for pleasing the right people.

Governor Nagai gestured to his companion. "This is Ohira Yonemon, chief officer of Deshima. He was just leaving to make sure no more barbarians disappear."

Ohira wordlessly bowed his farewells. On him would rest the major blame for any problem on Deshima, Sano knew. His square jaws were clenched, his pale lips compressed, and he looked physically ill. His skin had a blanched pallor, with purplish pouches under the eyes as if he hadn't slept in a long time. As he walked away, his rigid shoulders trembled.

The captain stepped forward. "The Honorable Chamberlain Yanagisawa's orders," he said, handing Governor Nagai a scroll case.

Governor Nagai read the enclosed document with a neutral expression, and his geniality didn't waver when he addressed Sano again. "Yes. Well. Come, let's go to my private office and discuss your plans for the inspection," he said.

After ordering an assistant to give the captain quarters in the barracks, he ushered Sano and Hirata upstairs to a bright, spacious room. Sliding doors opened onto a balcony, below which the city's rooftops spilled down the hill in a picturesque clutter. In the distance, sky and sea were azure; the harbor looked deceptively peaceful. Faint street noises drifted in on the warm breeze. Governor Nagai knelt behind the desk, his back to shelves filled with ledgers. Sano and Hirata knelt opposite on silk cushions. The room held the usual cabinets and chests found in any official's chambers, but one curious feature caught Sano's attention.

In the alcove stood a table with long, spindly legs. On this sat a peculiar wooden box the size of a man's head, with a white enamel circle on its upright face. Twelve strange symbols, inlaid in gold, rimmed the circle, from whose center extended slender gold pointers. The box emitted loud, rhythmic clicks.

"I see you've noticed my European clock." Governor Nagai regarded the object fondly. He offered refreshments, ordering them from a servant who appeared at the door. "It and the table were gifts from the Dutch barbarian who has disappeared: East India Company Trade Director Jan Spaen."

"Remarkable," Sano said. He recalled Chamberlain Yanagisawa mentioning the wealth that a Nagasaki official could reap from the overseas commerce. Apparently it came from both Japanese merchants as taxes, and from foreign merchants as presents intended to facilitate trade relations. But more intriguing than the possibility of riches was the thought of meeting the men whose culture produced such wonders as a mechanical timekeeping device.

"Your reputation precedes you, *sōsakan-sama*," Governor Nagai said. "The last time I was in Edo, I heard about your capture of the Bundori Killer."

To ensure that no individual commanded too much power over the international port, Nagasaki actually had three governors, who took turns ruling the city. While one was in Edo, reporting to the shogun—and visiting his family held hostage to his good behavior—the others served alternate shifts. Fate had saddled Governor Nagai with the Dutchman's unfortunate disappearance. But he'd surely benefited from his trips to the capital, testing the political climate there. Sano guessed that the courteous treatment he was receiving meant Governor Nagai knew he enjoyed the shogun's albeit unreliable favor. Yet the governor, though subject to Tokugawa Tsunayoshi, also had Chamberlain Yanagisawa's orders, and would know of his animosity toward Sano. However, perhaps Sano could use Nagai's conflicting loyalties to his advantage.

"His Excellency took a special interest in the Bundori Murder investigation," Sano said, mentioning the shogun to make Governor Nagai think he was secure in Tokugawa Tsunayoshi's protection, which he'd earned by solving the case. He must survive his stay in Nagasaki and return to his proper post.

"Yes. Of course. Well." Governor Nagai acknowledged the ploy by sucking his lips. "I shall be happy to lend you and your retainer a fine mansion, servants, and horses."

This concession was a good sign, even if it wasn't what Sano really wanted. "Thank you, Nagai-*san*." The servant brought tea and cakes, which he accepted, tasted, and praised according to polite convention. "These cakes have a unique and delicious tang." He suppressed a smile as he saw Hirata, seasickness gone now, eating hungrily for the first time in days. "What is the seasoning?"

"Mace and cinnamon," Governor Nagai answered between bites, "from the Indonesian Spice Islands. Here in Nagasaki, foreign traders bring us all the flavors of the world."

This was the opening Sano needed. "Perhaps I should begin my inspection with an assessment of the current state of foreign commerce. Starting with the Dutch trade." If he must carry out the charade, he would at least realize his dream of seeing the barbarians.

"Yes. Well." Governor Nagai smiled and sipped his tea. "I'm afraid that the current state of Dutch-Japanese relations is hardly typical." He looked out the window. Down the hill, troops filed through the streets, still searching. "If you inspect Deshima now, you'll carry an inaccurate report back to Edo—and Chamberlain Yanagisawa."

Was the governor asking Sano not to criticize his administration, or implying that Chamberlain Yanagisawa would back his refusal? Whatever his reason for invoking the chamberlain's authority, Sano couldn't afford to yield. His status in Nagasaki was ambiguous enough that losing this power play would establish him as the governor's inferior, rather than approximate equal.

"I'll help restore conditions to normal so that my inspection of the Dutch trade may proceed," he said.

A speculative gleam lit Nagai's eyes. "Are you offering to assume charge of the hunt for Trade Director Spaen?" His bland tone didn't quite hide his eagerness. "Yes. Well. That's very kind. But you needn't trouble yourself. Still, if you insist . . . ?"

Sano saw the trap. By taking over the investigation, he would relieve Governor Nagai of an onerous burden—and play right into Chamberlain Yanagisawa's hands. Failure to locate the Dutch barbarian would mean his death. But if he refused the task, he might spend the next six months accomplishing nothing of value, growing increasingly bitter toward the *bakufu*, missing Aoi, and worrying about his future.

"I insist," Sano said.

Governor Nagai relaxed with an audible sigh. A reckless exhilaration filled Sano. Now he would be doing real work, pursuing truth, if not justice, and following the Way of the Warrior as he perceived it. He would see the barbarians. And success could bring a political bonus as well as personal satisfaction: owing him a favor, Governor Nagai might agree to ignore Chamberlain Yanagisawa's orders. Sano glanced at Hirata, whose mouth dropped: From what he'd seen and heard today, he guessed the danger Sano courted.

"Hirata-*san*, I won't be needing you for this investigation," Sano said. To shield his retainer from the consequences of possible failure, he must keep Hirata at a distance from this dangerous task. If his actions caused his own ruin, then so be it; but he would not—could not—endure the pain of harming his faithful companion. "When we leave here, see the baggage safely to our lodgings. Then you may amuse yourself in town."

"Amuse myself," Hirata echoed, not quite managing to conceal his hurt at the dismissal, or his fear for Sano.

"Governor Nagai, I would appreciate any details you can give me about the barbarian's disappearance," Sano said. "When was it noticed, and by whom?"

The governor offered more tea and cakes, eager to cooperate now. "Just after daybreak, during a routine inspection by Chief Ohira and the guards."

"How many other Dutchmen are on Deshima? Has anyone asked them where Trade Director Jan Spaen might have gone, or why?" As Sano stumbled over the strange name, his pulse quickened in anticipation of encountering much more that was unfamiliar.

"There are presently six barbarians in Japan, who came two years ago and have stayed to protect the goods in their warehouse and pay homage to the shogun and *bakufu* officials. However, three of them are away visiting various daimyo. The Deshima guards have questioned the other two. They claim ignorance regarding their superior's whereabouts, but may be lying to protect him. To induce cooperation, I've ordered them confined to their quarters without food or water."

Governor Nagai was a strong administrator, not afraid to act quickly and decisively, Sano thought. The prompt search effort also attested to that. And, unlike many bureaucrats, he displayed ready knowledge about his domain.

"Your efforts are commendable," Sano said. "I'll go to Deshima and see if the Dutch will talk, while the troops continue their search. Is there an interpreter who can assist me?" He spoke no Dutch, and knew that the barbarians were kept ignorant of the Japanese language so as to discourage relations with citizens.

"Yes. Well. Certainly," Governor Nagai said. "But first, you and your retainer must take the oath that is required of everyone who has contact with foreigners."

He clapped his hands and gave orders to the servant who appeared. The servant fetched two officials and a tray bearing two scrolls, a roll of discolored cloth, a dish of ink, and a long, sharp needle. The officials knelt on either side of Governor Nagai, while the servant laid the scrolls open before Sano and Hirata, setting the tray between them.

"With myself and my aides as witnesses, you will read the scroll aloud," Nagai told Sano.

"I hereby promise to deny foreigners all communication, service, or friendship that could conceivably promote foreign interests over those of Japan," Sano read. "I also promise never to practice the Christian religion. If I fail to uphold these promises, may the gods, the *bakufu*, and His Excellency the shogun wreak their vengeance upon myself, my family, and all my associates."

"Trample the Christian icon," Governor Nagai instructed.

The servant spread the cloth on the floor: a portrait of a long-haired, bearded barbarian with a circular golden aura around his head. Sano stood and trod on the image, over the scuffs and cracks that already marred its surface.

"Now sign the scroll, if you please."

Sano knelt. From the pouch at his waist he took his personal seal, which he inked then pressed against the scroll. He picked up the needle and plunged it into his finger. The pain underscored the oath's gravity. The drop of blood he squeezed onto the scroll represented the blood that would flow if he broke his oath.

Just as Hirata finished taking his turn, a guard burst into the room. "Honorable Governor," he blurted, falling to his knees and bowing. "Please forgive this interruption, but a Dutch ship has been sighted approaching the harbor!"

"Yes. How inconvenient. Well." Governor Nagai turned to Sano. "The Dutch cannot land now. All the security forces are busy searching for Director Spaen; there's no one left to escort the ship. It would be dangerous to let a horde of barbarians enter Japanese territory unsupervised; the law forbids it. You must immediately tell the captain to wait outside the harbor until Spaen is found."

Sano guessed from Nagai's suddenly sharp gaze that this wouldn't be an easy task. A kernel of fear took root in his chest. What had curiosity and the desire for personal fulfillment gotten him into?

But it was too late to reconsider his decision. He'd committed himself, and duty called.

"My personal barge will take you to the Dutch ship," Governor Nagai said, hearty in his relief at no longer being responsible for matters concerning the missing Dutchman. "Chief Interpreter Iishino will translate for you." After telling the guard to convey the orders, he smiled at Sano. "I wish you good luck, *sōsakan-sama.*"

3

SANO GRIPPED THE railing of Governor Nagai's barge as twenty oarsmen propelled him up the harbor channel toward the yet unseen Dutch ship. During the journey from Edo, he hadn't been seasick once. Now his stomach churned, and he felt cold despite the hot sun that blazed down on him. The sight of the tossing waves and passing cliffs made him dizzy while he prayed for courage.

Like most of his fellow Japanese, he had no experience of the outside world. He instinctively distrusted and feared foreigners—especially the white barbarians, subject of much hearsay: The Dutch were monstrous giants who stank of the cow's milk they drank; they had huge, round eyes like a dog's, and wore high-heeled shoes because the backs of their doglike feet didn't touch the ground; they worshipped wealth, and would kill for it. None of this had bothered Sano when he'd imagined interrogating a mere two Dutchmen on Deshima, but soon he must face hundreds aboard a merchant ship, with only a small squadron of guards as backup.

"*Sōsakan-sama, sōsakan-sama!*" Chief Interpreter Iishino hurried up to him. "Why don't you sit in the cabin? It's more comfortable in there, much more comfortable."

"I want fresh air," Sano said, fighting nausea.

"But the sun, the sun will make you too hot."

Interpreter Iishino was near Sano's own age of thirty-one. He had a large head on a scrawny body, his face tapering from a broad brow to a pointed chin. Wide-open eyes gave him a perpetually alert expression, and he wore an ingratiating smile full of big, healthy teeth. Yet his most prominent feature was his restlessness. When he moved, as he did now, seeking a cool place for Sano to stand, he bustled. After he'd ushered Sano into the shadow of the barge's cabin, his sandaled feet tapped the deck; his fingers fiddled with his swords and drummed the cabin wall. Sano could almost hear a buzz of nervous energy coming from Iishino. Now he desperately missed Hirata's calming presence.

"There, isn't this better?" Interpreter Iishino smiled into Sano's face, anxiously seeking approval.

"Yes, thank you," Sano said. Ashamed of his irritation, and even more irritated with Iishino for shaming him, he resigned himself to the interpreter's company. Perhaps Iishino could supplement his knowledge of the Dutch.

From the old scrolls, he knew they came from a small European nation located on marshy lowlands whose barrenness drove them to sea in search of food and supplies. For generations they'd traded with France, Germany, Norway, Poland, the Mediterranean, and the Ottoman Empire, but they hadn't stopped with the western hemisphere. Merchants had formed the United East India Company, a private concern that held a monopoly on the lucrative spice trade. During the eighty-some years of its existence, the company had made a fortune by selling nutmeg and mace from the Banda Islands, pepper from Java and Sumatra, cinnamon from Ceylon, cloves from the Moluccas. The company maintained a permanent force of twelve thousand men in the East Indies and sent twenty ships there each year. Eighty-nine years ago, the merchants had reached Japan. Because they'd consented to trade without trying to spread Christianity, they'd supplanted the Portuguese. Now they were the only white barbarians allowed in the country.

Sano knew these bare facts, but needed to learn more in a hurry. "Interpreter Iishino, tell me about Dutch customs," he said. "How does one address them?"

Iishino beamed, fairly hopping in his pleasure at having his advice sought. "The barbarians are very different from Japanese, very different. The merchants fight wars, like samurai. But they are misers with no dignity. Excuse me, *sōsakan-sama*, but you're standing in the sun again. Please, get back in the shade."

Sano had moved to get away from Iishino's jittering. He disliked the way the interpreter bossed him around. His annoyance must have shown, because Iishino said reproachfully, "I'm only trying to help."

"All right. Thank you." Sano hid his exasperation. "Now about the Dutch . . . ?"

Iishino's smile returned. "Call them by their titles and their last names, which are their family names. They hate formality, and it's funny to watch them get impatient during ceremonies." He laughed, a loud, braying hoot. "They're very coarse and inferior. But when they're in our country, they must follow our customs. It's the law."

The Dutch barbarians sounded utterly alien. As the barge navigated around Takayama and several other islands, Sano's trepidation increased.

"If you'll permit me to speak frankly, *sōsakan-sama*, I'm sure you're very competent. But since you have no experience with barbarians, it would be foolish for you to handle the Dutch in a grave situation like this. And I've heard—"

Iishino jittered closer to Sano. "I've heard that you've displeased Chamberlain Yanagisawa, which shows a lack of the diplomacy one needs in foreign relations. When we reach the ship, let me handle things. You talk, and I'll pretend to translate what you say, so you don't lose face. Oh, and you really should stand here in the shade, where it's comfortable, more comfortable."

"I'll stand where I choose, if you don't mind," Sano snapped. He was astounded by the pushy Iishino's tactless insults. As chief interpreter, Iishino would have many junior interpreters working under him. In addition to his salary, he would collect translation fees from both Dutch and Japanese merchants. How had such an obnoxious man gotten such a coveted position?

"Tell me something," Sano said. "Was your father chief interpreter before you?"

"Why, yes."

"I might have guessed." Many posts were hereditary, with less importance attached to ability or character than to lineage.

Iishino's smile dimmed. "You're angry, aren't you? I was only—"

"Trying to help." Now Sano felt guilty for rejecting Iishino's solicitude.

The barge cleared the harbor. Across the waves Sano saw the Dutch ship's tall, curved hull and many sails. Fear solidified in his gut as he realized that he couldn't depend on Iishino for anything except translation. The interpreter's offensive personality and derogatory attitude toward the Dutch made him the least suitable bearer of bad news. Sano would have to rely on his own judgment.

"When we reach the ship, you'll translate exactly what I say," he ordered with more confidence than he felt.

The Dutch ship loomed upon them like a majestic, mobile castle, dwarfing the barge. The uppermost deck crowned two interior levels. Three main masts and a long, canted bowsprit supported a complex web of rigging. Flaring quadrangular sails bellied with the wind. Atop the masts fluttered colorful flags: the yellow Dutch state flag, emblazoned with a rampant red beast holding a curved broadsword and a fistful of arrows; the United East India Company's standard, striped horizontally in red, white, and blue, bearing a circle and a semicircle with an arrow-shaped mark superimposed. An upward-curving extension protruded from the bow, framed in ornate railings and culminating in the figure of a snarling lion. In this stood three barbarians. Others hurried about the deck or climbed the rigging. Shouts carried across the water: The Dutch had sighted the barge. Anticipation nearly overcame Sano's fear.

"Tell them to stop," he instructed Iishino.

The interpreter yelled something Sano hoped was his command in Dutch. Then the sails let out and began to flap. Sano told his oarsmen to position the barge beside the ship's head. He stared at the men who stood there. All had hair that fell past their shoulders—not gold, as Sano had expected, but still shockingly fair. The center man had red locks that glowed like fire in the sunlight. The open neckline of his white upper garment revealed matching hair on his chest, like an animal's pelt. The others had brown hair and wore long black cloaks and wide-brimmed black hats.

When these barbarians raised hands in greeting, Sano bowed. "Iishino. Introduce me, and say that I welcome them to Japan," he said, speaking loudly so the Dutch would know he was in charge. He gazed in awe at their faces, which were not actually white, but ruddy pink, as though the blood flowed beneath transparent, tanned skin. But all had the round, pale eyes Sano had expected, and the biggest noses he'd ever seen. "Tell them to drop anchor."

Iishino loosed phrases of guttural gibberish. His linguistic skills obviously compensated for his personality, because the red-haired barbarian replied promptly in syllables that sounded much like Iishino's. The others chimed in. Although they seemed to Sano like members of another species, he could tell by their shaking heads that they were puzzled.

"The one in white is Captain Pieter Oss, and the others are East India Company officials," Iishino said. "They want to know why you ask them to stop here, instead of at Takayama, where they usually moor."

Sano's neck was getting stiff from looking up, and whatever the differences between Dutch and Japanese cultures, he suspected that they shared one similarity: The man who stood below lost the advantage to the man above.

"Captain Oss," he called, pronouncing the name as best he could. He was glad for the barbarians' distinctive costumes and hair color, for their facial features looked identical to him. "I request permission to come aboard."

Iishino gasped. "*Sōsakan-sama*, you can't. The barbarians are dangerous, very dangerous. Just tell the captain that if he doesn't obey, we'll sink his ship."

Sano saw no reason for hostility, and with the harbor security forces out searching for Director Spaen, any threat of military aggression would be an empty one. Also, though he feared the barbarians, the ship exerted a powerful attraction on him.

Once Japanese had traveled the world. Embassies had ventured to Rome and Spain to foster trade and learn about the West. Monks made pilgrimages to Russia, India, Persia, Portugal, and Jerusalem. Traders settled in China, Tonkin, and the New World. Mercenaries fought in Malaysia, the Philippines, and Indonesia; exiles were sent to Cambodia. But fifty-five years ago, the *bakufu*, fearing that its citizens would ally with foreigners, had forbidden them to go abroad. As a boy, Sano had yearned to sail the seas, while knowing he never could. Now, seeing the Dutch ship revived his youthful dreams and increased his resentment toward the regime that curtailed his freedom and knowledge.

"Do as I say, Iishino-*san*," he ordered.

Iishino conveyed the request. Captain Oss nodded, motioning for the barge to pull alongside port deck.

"*Sōsakan-sama*, please be careful," Iishino hissed.

Sano gazed in awe at the ship as they circled it. The hull bore the scars of a long journey: gouges from rocks and reefs; repaired holes; barnacles clinging near the waterline. The square stern, crowned by bulbous lanterns, was like the facade of some bizarre temple, with gilded garlands dividing two rows of mullioned glass windows. The unbleached linen sails were seamed and patched. The Dutch had come from the other side of the world, braving other dangers besides the elements. Square outlines in the hull defined the gunports: The ship was prepared to defend itself against human threats as well.

An order from the Dutch captain brought sailors swarming onto the ship's deck to help attach the barge. They seemed even more bestial than he, with shaggy fair hair on their heads, faces, and bare limbs and chests.

"Who is the leader?" Sano asked Iishino urgently.

"Oh, the captain rules the ship. But the officials are partners in the East India Company, which owns it."

This ambiguous reply didn't bolster Sano's confidence. He ascended a ladder attached to the ship's hull, thankful for the presence of the guards who followed. Then he stepped onto the ship's deck, and as far into the outside world as he would ever go.

The smooth planks were solidly stable under his feet, but the masts and yards creaked; the sails flapped; the rigging groaned. The ship seemed alive, like a great beast. Then Captain Oss and the two East India Company officials came to meet Sano, and their smell hit him: a foul, animal reek of sweat, urine, dirty hair, and a rancid scent he attributed to their diet of milk. From his two months at sea, he knew the discomfort of bathing on board ship, in cold salt water. Yet he'd done it daily, and so had Hirata and the crew. The barbarians stank as though they hadn't washed since leaving home! Sano's stomach roiled.

"Captain Oss." Feeling awkward and intimidated, Sano decided to accept Iishino's statement that the Dutch disliked formality, and get straight to the point. "Permit me to explain why I'm asking you to delay landing."

As Iishino translated, at least a hundred sailors watched from the decks, the yards, and the rigging. They scratched themselves constantly. Studying the three leaders, Sano saw flea bites on their necks. Didn't the barbarians know that regular washing eliminated vermin? Oddly, their clothes seemed clean, down to their knee-length black trousers, black stockings, and shiny black leather shoes with square silver ornaments over the insteps—and high heels. To support their dog feet? They awaited Sano's explanation, regarding him with their eerie eyes, which were as clear and bright a blue as the ocean.

"I'm sorry to say that Trade Director Jan Spaen disappeared last night," Sano said. "Until we find him, no other Dutchmen can enter the country, so you must wait here." Sano hoped that Iishino would accurately convey his direct, courteous explanation. "I apologize for the delay, but it can't be helped."

An immediate outcry greeted Iishino's translation. Shouting sailors waved their fists and bared broken teeth. A thrill of fear clenched Sano's spine as he remembered that these dirty, bestial creatures were fierce warriors. The Dutch had resisted Spanish takeover of their homeland, then replaced the Spanish Empire as the world's greatest maritime power. More recently, he'd heard rumors that they'd scored victories over the English, who were challenging their trade monopoly. They had quelled native rebellions in the Banda Islands and now ruled the world's sole source of nutmeg. They'd secured the pepper monopoly by battling and defeating tribal kings and English rivals on Java. By seizing the colonies of Malacca and Ceylon, they'd ended Portuguese domination of the East Indies trade. Dutch relations with Japan had so far been peaceful—but the past guaranteed nothing.

Now Captain Oss quieted the crew with angry commands. He and his companions stood a head higher than Sano, who nervously eyed the long-barreled pistols at their waists. Knowing the ship's lower decks contained cannon and more guns—all powerfully superior to any Japan possessed—Sano felt tiny and vulnerable; his sword wouldn't protect him now. Again he longed for Hirata's company. But he'd made the right decision to face terror alone, with a clear conscience.

Iishino translated as fast as the barbarians spoke. "The captain says the ship has been at sea for a year, a whole year. They've braved storms and drifted for months without wind. They're out of food and water. The crew is desperate to go ashore."

Captain Oss's pointed incisors flashed. Combined with his red hair, these gave him the look of a fox—the animal reviled by Japanese as an evil prankster.

"The officials say this delay is a violation of the Dutch-Japanese trade agreement," Iishino continued. "They insist that the ship be allowed to proceed to Takayama, and the crew and cargo conveyed to Deshima immediately." He wrung his hands. "Oh, *Sōsakan-sama*, they're angry, very angry that their colleague is missing. But you must tell them that your word is the law, and they have no choice but to obey!"

The sea spread around Sano; Nagasaki and its troops seemed very far away. Twelve thousand Dutch in the East Indies, Sano thought, with at least twenty ships like this. Even one could ruin Nagasaki before he could mount a defense. He must placate the Dutch—fast. And beneath his revulsion, Sano felt a tinge of respectful sympathy for the barbarians who had sailed for an entire year to reach Japan.

"Captain Oss," he said, "I shall order provisions sent aboard, compliments of Nagasaki."

Iishino hissed, "That's against the rules, the rules! The Dutch receive nothing until their goods are inventoried and unladed. And they must pay for all their supplies."

Sano silenced him with a glance. Shrugging helplessly, Iishino spoke in Dutch. To Sano's relief, the captain and merchants nodded; conciliatory mutters rose from the crew.

"As soon as we find Trade Director Spaen, you may enter the harbor," Sano said, bowing.

The barbarians bowed, too, watching him warily through their strange, light eyes. Sano headed for the ladder, trying not to run like a coward. But Interpreter Iishino tugged his sleeve.

"*Sōsakan-sama,* you must disarm the ship. It's the law that all guns and ammunition be taken from the Dutch when they arrive in Japanese waters."

Sano inwardly cursed his inexperience, and Iishino for not telling him sooner. "Captain Oss," he said, "in accordance with Japanese law, I must order you to hand over your weapons."

This request provoked another controversy. Captain Oss shook his head violently. The merchants threw up their hands. Barbarian protests deafened Sano; the ship shuddered under hundreds of stamping feet. The captain shouted above his men's voices.

"He asks you to reconsider," Iishino said. "They've already been attacked by pirates three times this journey, three times. If you confiscate their weapons while they're outside the harbor and unprotected, you could be sentencing them to death. Let them keep the weapons, and he promises not to use them against Japan."

Sano's nausea turned into the even more sickening feeling he knew all too well. In the past, someone had always suffered as a result of his investigations. Guilt welled up inside Sano as he recalled Aoi, in particular. He didn't like the foxy gleam in Captain Oss's eyes, or his arrogant posture. This man seemed the quintessential Dutch trader of

Japanese myth: rashly adventurous, willing to exploit any situation to increase his own wealth. Sano didn't trust him. However, he couldn't endanger innocent human lives, alien though the barbarians seemed.

"You may keep your weapons," he said.

Iishino reluctantly translated these words, and Sano's farewells. They climbed down the ladder onto their own pitifully small, inadequately armed barge. As the oarsmen rowed them away, Sano leaned against the cabin. His lungs still thick with the reek of barbarian, he breathed deeply, praying that he wouldn't be sick and thus betray weakness. He watched the receding Dutch ship and contemplated the enormity of what he'd just done.

Opposite him, Interpreter Iishino drummed his fingers on the railing. "You were very brave out there, *sōsakan-sama,* very brave. But for your own good, I must tell you that you weren't firm enough with the barbarians. You shouldn't have let them keep their guns, and you shouldn't give them anything. People might get the wrong idea."

Sano could see the ugly aura of treason tainting his actions. Although he didn't know how he could have done otherwise, he already regretted the decision. By trying to protect the Dutch, he'd endangered his people by leaving an armed ship full of unruly barbarians off the Nagasaki coast.

To avert the potential threat of attack, he must find Trade Director Jan Spaen, soon.

4

THE MANSION THAT Governor Nagai had provided for Sano stood
at the lower edge of the official district. Hirata, arriving with porters
and the two guards who'd escorted him, said, "Leave the baggage at
the gate. I'll take it inside." Although he was a trained detective with
six years' experience as a police officer, he had nothing else to do. To
the guards, he said, "You can go now."

"Our orders were to stay with you," the tall, thin one said, opening
the gate.

His companion, a short, paunchy man, ushered the porters and baggage inside. Before following, Hirata eyed the house critically. What
he saw didn't improve the dark mood that had befallen him when
Sano cut him out of the investigation.

The two-story house had freshly whitewashed half-timbered walls,
a neat thatched roof, and a latticed balcony. Built like a rich merchant's dwelling rather than a fortified samurai residence, it was a security officer's nightmare. There were no enclosing barracks.
Intruders could easily climb the stone wall—or drop into the yard
from the roofs of adjacent houses—then snap the flimsy wooden bars

off the windows and enter the house. Guarded gates at either end of the street wouldn't keep out a determined evildoer. How was Hirata supposed to protect a master who spurned protection?

Gloomily he strode up the flagstone path beneath an arbor of flowering vines. The front door opened, discharging a horde of servants. "Greetings, new master," they cried, hurrying to take in the baggage.

Hirata shook his head as he entered the house, shadowed by the guards. Remembering the attacks on Sano, he deplored the abundance of strangers in the house. Undoubtedly Chamberlain Yanagisawa's influence covered Nagasaki as well as Edo. Inside, Hirata discovered more problems. In the kitchen, servants unpacked rice bales, vegetables, sake barrels, and fish. His stomach growled hungrily. But in the living quarters, where landscape murals decorated walls and clean tatami covered the floors, numerous windows afforded too many access points. Flimsy paper-paned lattice partitions divided rooms and corridors. In the reception hall, doors led to a garden full of shrubs, trees, and plenty of other places for an assassin to hide.

"Master, would you like a meal?" a servant asked.

Hirata started to say yes, then hesitated.

He'd been born into the police service, inheriting his father's job as a *doshin*—patrol officer—at age fifteen. He'd captured criminals and maintained order in one of Nihonbashi's roughest sectors. When assigned to help with the Bundori murder investigation, he'd won a permanent post as Sano's chief retainer by demonstrating his competence and loyalty. Ecstatic over leaving a corrupt police force, he thought he'd gained his heart's desire: a master whose character he could respect.

A year later, reality had set in. Bushido dictated that he provide Sano with protection, assistance, and counsel until his own death, which would ideally occur during battle at his master's side. But Sano refused Hirata's service when he needed it most, often leaving Hirata at home during crucial stages of murder cases, spying assignments, and the shogun's ghost hunts. Now he'd done the same thing again!

Upon leaving Governor Nagai's mansion, Hirata had begged Sano not to lead the search for the barbarian. "It's my duty to tell you that you're placing yourself in grave, unnecessary danger," he'd whispered as they walked out the gate. "Nagai and his men let the barbarian escape; they're the ones who should suffer if he's not found."

But Sano, waiting for the guards who would escort him to the harbor, had already withdrawn into his private world of inner compulsions and self-imposed challenges.

"At least let me help you," Hirata had persisted. "Delegate the investigation to me, so that if it fails, I'll die, not you."

Sano had said gently but adamantly, "Hirata-*san*, I appreciate your loyalty. But I've made my decision."

"Why must you always push me away and do things alone?" Confusion had made Hirata outspoken. "It's the same with the detective corps. They're supposed to serve you, yet you give them the safest, easiest tasks. It's as if you don't want them hurt, even though you've barely gotten to know them beyond their names and work records. What—"

The arrival of the guards had cut short their conversation. "You have your orders," Sano had said. "I'll see you later."

Now resentment kindled beneath Hirata's fear for his master. Sano was thwarting his fulfillment of Bushido and wasting his detective skills. Hirata couldn't loaf while Sano faced danger; but neither could he violate Bushido's most important tenet: unswerving obedience to his master. Yet Hirata was forced to acknowledge a more personal motive that exacerbated his dilemma. The present situation reminded him of a time when his character had been tried and found inadequate, an experience that had changed his life.

He'd been eighteen, a *doshin* for three years, with a growing reputation for courage and skill. Craving official recognition, he'd gotten it when Senior Police Commander Terukuni had singled him out of the ranks to help break up a crime gang, and become his mentor. Hirata had been a self-centered young man who had valued the relationship mainly because of what it could do for him. Ambitious for wealth and power, he'd aspired to a position in the shogun's court. When the gangsters had ambushed him and *Yoriki* Terukuni in a teahouse, Hirata had chosen to escape with his own life, letting his master die.

He'd repaid Terukuni's kind generosity with betrayal, forsaken samurai loyalty for personal gain. After much soul-searching, he'd seen the error of his ways and vowed to embrace the Way of the Warrior. Hence he could not abandon Sano, his present master, to stand or fall alone, regardless of orders to the contrary.

Fierce resolve inspired Hirata. Sano had told him to amuse himself in town, but hadn't specified how. "I don't need anything," Hirata told the waiting servant. "I'm going out for the rest of the day."

When he walked out the door, the two guards followed. "Governor's orders," the paunchy one said.

Hirata realized they meant to spy on him, the last thing he wanted. If Trade Director Spaen had thus far managed to evade capture, someone might be harboring him—perhaps a professional criminal. From his police experience, Hirata knew that the best way to find such a man was by unobtrusive means, which he couldn't use with two soldiers in tow.

Reversing his steps, Hirata said to the guards, "I've decided to stay home."

They eyed him skeptically, then stationed themselves beside the gate. Inside the house, Hirata reconsidered his clothes—silk surcoat and kimono printed with the Tokugawa crest, flowing silk trousers, and high clogs—the uniform of an Edo official, and not exactly one to inspire trust in the townspeople. Hurrying to the bedchamber, Hirata found two maids unpacking his baggage.

"Give me those," he said, grabbing a short cotton kimono, sash, leggings, old wicker hat, and straw sandals. Hastily he changed into the ensemble and rehung his swords at his waist. Feeling younger and freer, as if he'd stepped back in time to his police days, he ran out the back door to the stables for a horse. Then the back gate opened, and the paunchy guard appeared. Hirata dashed back into the house. Hearing voices in the corridor, he skidded to a stop.

"Where is your master?" the tall guard demanded.

"He changed clothes, then left," a maid replied.

Running footsteps came from the direction of the back door. Hirata swerved down another corridor as the paunchy guard called, "I saw him, he went that way."

Hirata bolted through the bustling kitchen and into a courtyard, where he came upon two men. Their furtive manner alerted his police instincts. A familiar warning buzz went off in his head, arresting his flight.

"One hundred *zeni* for a barrel of prawns, ten quail eggs, a jar of candied plums, and steamed rice buns?" The speaker was a shabbily dressed peasant. "That's robbery!"

The other man, who wore a neat blue kimono, stood beside the basket of provisions. "But these are the finest quality foods, bought especially for the shogun's envoys." About fifty years of age, he had a long face with protuberant eyes and pursed lips. Wispy gray hair straggled around his bald pate. "Why should I sell them for less, when they'll fetch twice that from the customers at your food stall?"

Forgetting his pursuers, Hirata seized the bald man's arm, demanding, "How dare you steal from my master? You're under arrest!"

The peasant scuttled over the wall, but the captive thief bowed and smiled. "Allow me to introduce myself, master," he said. "Old Carp, kitchen provisioner, at your service. Perhaps you're hungry?" He plucked a round bamboo box from the basket and offered it to Hirata.

Hirata laughed in spite of himself. With his bulging eyes and puckered mouth, the man really did resemble a fish. And how quick he was to bribe his way out of trouble—with stolen goods, yet! Then Hirata saw the two guards in the kitchen, coming straight toward him. Releasing Old Carp, he said, "I'll punish you later," and turned to flee.

The wily servant acted quickly. "Have this, master, with my compliments," he said, thrusting the box into Hirata's hands. Then he picked up the basket, ran toward the kitchen door—and collided with the guards as they ran out.

The basket crashed to the ground, spilling its contents. Amid streaming water and broken eggs, live prawns squirmed. The guards cursed as their feet slipped in the mess.

"A thousand apologies, masters!" Old Carp bleated.

"Get out of the way!"

Old Carp motioned for Hirata to run. The paunchy guard skidded on the eggs and fell flat on his back. The tall man dodged Old Carp, only to trip and sprawl facedown beside his comrade.

Hirata raced across the courtyard to the wall. He would have discarded the box Old Carp had given him, but for the delicious smell emanating from it. Tossing the box over the wall, he scrambled after it. He landed in the next yard, retrieved the box, ran out the gate, and sped down the street, dodging pedestrians. Ducking into an alley, he leaned against the wall and burst out laughing.

What a perfect getaway! Now he was free as the wind, his dinner in hand. He would overlook Old Carp's thievery just this once. With tears of mirth still wet on his cheeks, Hirata opened the box and found ten round white buns. Eagerly he ate them, savoring the prawns, soy sauce, and scallions in the filling. He licked his fingers and dropped the box in a wooden wastebin. Stomach full and humor restored, he cautiously emerged from the alley, looking both ways. No trace of his guards. He started downhill toward the waterfront in search of leads on the Dutch barbarian.

The streets grew narrower and more crowded as the mansions of Nagasaki's affluent merchants gave way to the modest quarters of humbler townsfolk. Keeping an eye out for the guards, Hirata passed open storefronts and the red torii gate of a Shinto shrine. As he descended a stone staircase, he looked over the rooftops and saw soldiers storming a pottery workshop. More soldiers rushed up the street. One grabbed Hirata by the front of his kimono.

"Have you seen the barbarian?" he shouted. "Speak up, *rōnin!*"

"No, master," Hirata said.

The soldier released him and turned to question someone else. Hirata continued on his way, pleased that the soldier had mistaken him for a masterless samurai. Where he intended to go, he would blend right in.

The sea's fishy smell grew stronger, the screech of gulls louder. Sentries patrolled the beach. The harbor had been cleared of all craft except for the patrol barges and foreign ships. Wooden shacks cluttered the hills' lowest reaches. Nets covered thatched roofs; buckets and ropes cluttered doorsteps and balconies. Interspersed between the shacks were tiny teahouses. Tattered blue curtains hung from the eaves, partially shielding patrons from streets thronged with fisher-folk. Hirata selected a teahouse at random.

Two patrons sat on the edge of the raised floor. Both were old men with wrinkled, weathered skin. Through eyes permanently narrowed against sun and wind, they peered at passersby while clutching sake cups in gnarled hands.

"Hello, Grandfathers." Hirata bowed. "May I join you?"

They regarded him with lively interest. Heads bobbed on frail necks; grunts arose from scrawny chests as they moved over to make room. Hirata sat in the middle. The proprietor came up behind him.

"A round of sake," Hirata said.

Eagerly the old men raised their cups, cackling, "Thank you, master." The proprietor filled their cups, and one for Hirata. They drank. Then the man on Hirata's left peered into his face. "Don't recall seeing you before." He had only three teeth, and his voice was too loud.

"I just arrived in Nagasaki today," Hirata said.

"Eh?" The man cupped his hand around a hair-filled ear.

Hirata repeated his words, then said loudly, "I just met some soldiers who were looking for a missing barbarian."

The man to Hirata's right snorted. He was so stooped that his chin almost touched his knees. The pipe between his lips shook with the constant tremor of his body. "They'll never find him."

Hirata asked, "Why do you say that?"

"Let me tell you this, young stranger." Pipe jabbed a bony elbow into Hirata's side. "There've been some very odd things happening around Deshima." He nodded sagely. "I'm not at all surprised that the barbarian disappeared."

"What kind of odd things?" Hirata signaled the proprietor for more sake.

Everyone drank, then Pipe, speaking loudly enough for Deaf to hear, said, "Everyone in town knows about the mysterious lights around the island at night. They're purple and green and white, and make a lot of smoke. They float over the water toward Deshima, blinking." He sketched a slow, drifting movement, knotty fist opening and closing to simulate flashes. "And then they disappear."

"What are these lights?" Hirata was intrigued.

"Ghosts." Pipe emphasized the word with a large puff of smoke. "Spirits of Dutch barbarians who died on Deshima and have come back to haunt their countrymen."

Superstitious peasant nonsense—or more? "Were the lights seen last night?" Hirata said, trying to relate them to the barbarian's escape.

"Oh, yes." Puff, puff. "And many other times during the past two years."

"Has anyone ever followed the lights?" Hirata asked.

"Oh, no. Ghosts kill men and eat their hearts. All the townspeople stay away from the harbor when the lights come."

Deaf broke in, "I'll tell you what the lights are, young stranger. They're a magic spell, cast by the Chinese priest. Abbot Liu Yun, his name is. Runs a temple for the Chinese sailors. Hates the Dutch, he does. Especially the one who disappeared. Conjured up a demon to take him away."

The mention of a name quickened Hirata's interest. Could this Abbot Liu Yun, by magic or other device, somehow have abducted Jan Spaen?

"It wasn't the Chinese priest," Pipe shouted.

"Oh, but it was," Deaf shouted back.

Pipe reached across Hirata and swatted Deaf with his feeble hand. "You old fool. It was the spirits of dead men who took the barbarian away."

"Ouch! No, the Chinese priest!"

Shouts and running footsteps drowned out the argument. Hirata looked up the street, then groaned. Hurrying toward him, red-faced and panting, came his two guards, their uniforms smeared with egg yolk and slime. "You don't go anywhere without us," the tall man said angrily. "Governor Nagai's orders."

Hirata said to Pipe, "Why does Abbot Liu Yun hate the Dutch barbarian? And where could he have taken him?"

But the soldiers' presence cowed the old men. Feigning exaggerated senility, Pipe blinked uncomprehendingly. Deaf said, "Eh? Eh?"

Hirata thanked them, paid the proprietor, and rose, only slightly discouraged. Perhaps these odd rumors reflected some truth about Deshima that, when exposed, might also reveal the barbarian's whereabouts. Walking up the street between the two guards, Hirata plotted how to escape them.

Somehow he would help Sano find Trade Director Jan Spaen. By doing so, he would achieve the highest expression of samurai duty and loyalty. He must not fail his present master as he had his first.

5

WHEN THE PATROL barge drew into Nagasaki Harbor, Sano noticed that the horde of troops on the beach had swelled. Townspeople poured from the steep city streets onto the sand. Shouts carried across the water as soldiers tried to maintain order and the mob surged around the focus of interest at the water's edge. Sano, Interpreter Iishino, and the barge crew leaned over the railing to watch.

"What is it, what is it?" Iishino said, hopping and craning his neck.

The barge docked at the harbor patrol station, a building with a square watchtower, mounted on stilts over the water. On the long pier waited a party of officers. A sense of foreboding stole over Sano. When the crew had secured the barge, he was the first one off.

"What's going on over there?" Sano asked. "Has something happened?"

The harbor patrol captain stepped forward and bowed. "*Sōsakan-sama*. The search for the missing barbarian is over. His dead body has washed ashore."

"OUT OF THE WAY! Let us through!" shouted the harbor patrol officers who had escorted Sano from the barge to the beach, where the Dutch trader's body had been recovered from the sea. They cleared a path through the crowd that had come to witness the anticlimax of the great manhunt.

Gritty sand cushioned Sano's footsteps as he walked past staring faces to the water's edge, with Interpreter Iishino close by his side. Both ends of the beach's long curve terminated at warehouses that jutted into the harbor. Beyond them to the right Sano could see Deshima's walled compound. Ahead waited a circle of soldiers and officials, their expressions grave. As Sano approached, his initial relief at hearing that Director Spaen had been found gave way to disappointment.

The investigation was over. He was out of danger. The Dutch ship and the Deshima barbarians were no longer his responsibility. He could simply document today's events, then spend the rest of his time in Nagasaki completing a cursory inspection and staying out of trouble until he could return to Edo. He and Hirata could visit scenic spots and relax at seaside inns. Yet Sano's spirit rebelled at the prospect of such meaningless leisure. He remembered his hunt for the body thieves: the painstaking investigation; the battle; his ultimate triumph. With an almost physical hunger, he wanted to experience it all again.

From amid the waiting officers, the commander came forward and bowed to Sano. "We left the body just the way we found it," he said uneasily. "It seemed the right thing to do, under the circumstances."

Before Sano could request an explanation, Hirata hurried up to join him, accompanied by two guards, one short and paunchy, the other tall and thin. Simultaneously Governor Nagai arrived with Chief Ohira and two other men.

"What circumstances?" Nagai demanded.

In answer, the circle of officers opened to admit Sano, Hirata, and Governor Nagai's party, then closed protectively around them. Everyone gazed down at the dead Director Spaen.

Tall and muscular, the barbarian lay sprawled on his back on the damp sand just above the waterline. His square jaw, firm chin, and jutting nose reflected the masculine vigor he must have possessed in life. But now his face was a stark, pallid white; death had leached expression from his eyes. His parted lips revealed a bloated tongue and strong teeth. Strands of his long, straw-colored hair stirred in the wind. He wore only a pair of knee-length black trousers. His bare feet, though pale and large, were nonetheless human: So much for the Dutch dog-feet story. Sano's stomach contracted when he looked at the corpse's midsection.

Wounds gashed Director Spaen's stomach and chest, the worst just below his left breast as if a wild animal had gnawed and slashed there, exposing pink tissue and splintered white bone. Snails and tiny crabs clung to the torn flesh. Flies buzzed and swarmed over the corpse; seaweed entwined the hair. But nature's encroachment hadn't yet obliterated the shocking signs of human malice. The wounds, narrow and clean except for the chest mutilation, had been inflicted with a sharp knife. Between them, bruises stained Director Spaen's skin with blotches of purple, green, and yellow. Faint red indentations encircled his wrists and ankles, while his neck had swollen around some sort of ligature.

Sano stooped to examine this, gingerly pushing aside the flaccid, cold flesh. Embedded there was a slender chain; from it dangled a small gold pendant. In meticulous detail, this portrayed a naked, bearded male barbarian suspended by his wrists from a cross. A wreath of thorns crowned his drooping head; a stake penetrated his chest.

"Gesu: the martyred Christian deity," Sano said.

"Contraband, which is forbidden in Japan." Governor Nagai shot a hard, questioning glance at Chief Ohira.

"All Christian relics were confiscated from the Dutch upon their arrival," Ohira said tonelessly, "as the law requires. Jan Spaen never wore a crucifix while in my charge. I can assure you that I don't know where it came from."

Sano walked to the water and washed his hands in the cold, foamy waves, cleansing himself of the spiritual pollution incurred by contact with death. Returning to Governor Nagai, he said, "Possibly the crucifix came from the killer."

There could be no doubt that this was murder, which meant that his troubles, instead of ending with Spaen's death, had just begun.

Crowd noises filled the drawn-out silence within the circle. Then Governor Nagai, belatedly following the social convention that must be observed even during a crisis like this, introduced his other companions to Sano. "This is *Yoriki* Ota." He was a stout, coarse man whose veinous nose glowed bright red, as if from drinking too much sake. "And Kiyoshi, the eldest of Chief Ohira's six children."

The two men bowed. Kiyoshi was a slender youth whose bare crown was several shades lighter than his tanned face, freshly shaven in the ceremony that initiated samurai into manhood at age fifteen. He had sensitive features, but his body was muscular, with an athletic grace. Old bruises shadowed his high cheekbones; healed cuts marked his forearms. His well-shaped hands were callused, and Sano glimpsed faint ink stains on the fingers: the mark of a scholar. This was how he himself had looked at that age, pursuing martial arts and academic learning with equal ardor. Watching Chief Ohira gaze at Kiyoshi, Sano's heart ached. His own father had looked at him the same way, not quite managing to conceal his love and pride. He envied Kiyoshi and Chief Ohira that important bond which he himself had lost with his father's death a year and a half ago.

Governor Nagai said, "I take a great interest in young men of talent. And Kiyoshi is my most promising protégé."

In the *bakufu*, samurai advanced by way of ability and connections. The governor's patronage would, Sano knew, guarantee Kiyoshi a good post in Nagasaki's administration.

"And Kiyoshi is studying the Dutch language with me, so that he can be an interpreter," Iishino added. "He shows great aptitude, great aptitude." For once Iishino stood perfectly still. The shock of seeing the corpse had blanched his face, and without his usual nervous motion, he looked like a wax effigy of himself. Nonetheless, he managed a weak grin. "Say something in Dutch, Kiyoshi."

"Not now, Iishino," Nagai said impatiently, while *Yoriki* Ota grimaced in disgust: It was apparent that neither of them liked the interpreter. Kiyoshi blushed. Chief Ohira frowned at his colleagues, as though resenting Iishino for calling unwanted attention to his son, and Nagai and Ota for some other, indiscernible reason. Sano detected between the men an alliance whose nature he couldn't grasp. Certainly Nagai, Iishino, and Ohira shared something more than an interest in Kiyoshi's future, and whatever it was bound them together despite mutual antagonism. Sano remembered his arrival at the governor's mansion and the exchange he'd overheard between Nagai and Ohira. He had a sense of secret tensions within Nagasaki's administration, an undercurrent of both discord and conspiracy. Did this relate to Director Spaen's disappearance—and murder?

"The person who killed Director Spaen must be found and punished," *Yoriki* Ota said. "The laws concerning murder apply even when the victim is a foreigner." Reluctantly he added, "So. I guess I'll begin the investigation at once."

But he made no move to go. Everyone looked at Sano. And waited. In the expectant hush, Sano heard the gusting wind and the shriek of seabirds; the clamor of the crowd; the ocean's hiss and smack. Then his own voice, saying what he knew his companions wanted to hear.

"The murder is related to Director Spaen's disappearance. Therefore, the responsibility for apprehending the killer is mine."

A reckless elation intoxicated Sano. Here was his chance to pursue knowledge and right a wrong. But the stakes were even higher than during the search for the missing barbarian. He faced his companions, both hoping and fearing that someone would challenge his right to commandeer the investigation.

No one did. *Yoriki* Ota nodded. Governor Nagai said, "As you wish." Behind their neutral expressions, Sano sensed relief. Hirata's face shone with the certainty that Sano couldn't possibly refuse his assistance now. Sano hated to disappoint Hirata, but it was more crucial than ever to protect the young retainer from harm, and prevent subsequent anguish for himself.

Chief Ohira kept his worried gaze fixed on Kiyoshi, who stared at the ground. Face pale, lips trembling, and Adam's apple bobbing, he looked as if he was trying not to vomit. Interpreter Iishino sucked air through his teeth as he studied the corpse.

"One of Director Spaen's comrades must have killed him," Iishino said. "Who else but a fellow barbarian could have hated him enough to tie him up, beat, stab, and strangle him? And who but a Christian Dutchman would leave a crucifix on him?"

"Yes. Well." Governor Nagai turned to Sano. "How fortunate for you that such is the case. If a Japanese citizen were found to be the killer, the Dutch could interpret Director Spaen's murder as an act of military aggression, and retaliate in kind."

Everyone looked seaward. Sano could almost see the Dutch ship riding at anchor beyond the bright waves.

"And incriminating a Japanese citizen could have other unpleasant consequences besides jeopardizing national peace," Nagai added.

Two more officers arrived, carrying a litter covered with a white cloth. "Take the body to Deshima," Governor Nagai ordered them. To Sano, he explained, "The law forbids the barbarians to administer Christian rites to their dead, but they are allowed to keep a funeral vigil and prepare the body for burial."

Placing Director Spaen's stiff form on the litter, the officers draped it with the cloth and bore it toward Deshima. "Go home! Nothing more to see!" they shouted at the townspeople. Sano was glad that the evidence would be preserved for a while, though he didn't know exactly what to do with it. How he longed for Dr. Ito's scientific expertise and wise counsel! Because Governor Nagai's circumspect remark had warned him of the perilous dilemma he might face.

"Chief Ohira," Sano said, "please confine the barbarians to separate rooms on Deshima." He wasn't ready to eliminate the staff as suspects, or overlook the possibility that Spaen had met his death at the hands of a stranger after escaping; but the Dutch were logical suspects. "Don't let them see Director Spaen's corpse, or tell them he's dead. I'll interview them right away, with Interpreter Iishino's help."

Ohira nodded distractedly, his eyes still on Kiyoshi.

To the harbor patrol officers, Sano said, "Take this message to the Dutch ship: 'I regret to inform you that your missing comrade has been found murdered.'" He added an explanation of the circumstances of Spaen's death, then continued, "'I am in charge of the investigation. Until I find out who killed Spaen and why, we must act on the assumption that the murderer poses a danger to all your people.

Therefore, your landing must be delayed until the murderer is caught and punished. With apologies, *Sōsakan* Sano Ichirō.' "

Sano feared that his plan would anger the Dutch captain, yet he couldn't do otherwise. The addition of hundreds more barbarians to Deshima would complicate his work, possibly destroying evidence and creating unrest. He wished he could deliver the news in person and placate Captain Oss, but he couldn't waste time on another trip offshore; he must concentrate on the search for the killer.

The troops resumed their patrols. Governor Nagai, Kiyoshi, and *Yoriki* Ota bade Sano farewell, then departed. Sano trudged up the beach toward Deshima with Hirata and the two guards, while Chief Ohira and Interpreter Iishino walked ahead. The wind seemed colder, the ocean's roar an ominous portent as Sano pondered the conflict that he feared would compromise his investigation.

Prudence and diplomacy required him to place the blame for the murder on a barbarian. If he didn't, he risked bringing war to his country—and charges of treason upon himself for passing over foreign suspects to condemn a fellow Japanese. Sano thought of the Dutch, imprisoned on Deshima, with ample time and leisure to foster mutual hatred. By incriminating one of them, he could save himself from death and disgrace.

But would he also be letting the real murderer escape punishment for the crime?

"SUMIMASEN — EXCUSE ME," Hirata said, trudging beside Sano up a flight of stone stairs leading from the beach to the waterfront promenade, a wide road built upon a stone embankment along Nagasaki Harbor. After a moment's hesitation, he blurted, "Catching a murderer in a strange city is going to be hard. You have to let me help!"

Sano had expected the ardent young retainer to renew his plea for a role in the investigation: For some personal, unspoken reason, he carried samurai loyalty and dedication to the extreme. Sensing that this wasn't all Hirata had intended to say, he waited. They passed warehouses and shops, patrolling troops, and fishermen carrying buckets of squid and octopuses before Hirata spoke again.

"I've had lots of detective experience," Hirata hurried on. Faint creases appeared on his forehead, as they always did when he was most serious, giving Sano a glimpse of how he would look as an older man. "I can identify suspects, and interrogate them, and check alibis, and—"

"Hirata!" Sano's raised voice silenced the young man. Then he said,

"I don't dispute your ability. But this case is dangerous. If I go down, I won't take you with me."

"But it's my duty to go wherever you go," Hirata argued. "I—" He paused, then took a deep breath. "Just now, when I was in town, I found out that there's something strange going on around Deshima. The townspeople have seen mysterious lights nearby, in the harbor. And there's a Chinese priest who hates the Dutch. He practices magic, and may be involved in Director Spaen's disappearance, or death."

This was interesting, possibly relevant information. But the news of Hirata's inquiries hit Sano like a fist to the stomach. "You had your orders," he said with an anger born of concern for his retainer. "You were supposed to amuse yourself, not conduct interviews, as if on my authority."

Humiliation suffused Hirata's face, but he spoke up bravely: "I just walked around and talked to people. I didn't disobey."

"You defied the spirit of my order, and you know it." The irony of the situation almost made Sano laugh. That he, who'd often disregarded orders for the sake of his own convictions, should now reprimand another man for the same offense! In many ways, they were two of a kind: honor-bound, enamored of the danger and challenge of detective work—and stubborn to the core. "Now, either you obey or I send you back to Edo."

Hirata's eyes widened in alarm. "You wouldn't."

They reached the Deshima guardhouse, a long building with plank walls, tile roof, and barred windows, situated in a gravel-strewn yard at the mainland foot of the bridge to the island. Interpreter Iishino waited outside; Chief Ohira must have already entered. "I will, if that's what it takes." Sano hardened his voice and heart. He couldn't let selfish desire for Hirata's companionship weaken his resolve. "Now go home and stay there."

"PLEASE GIVE ME your pouch, *sōsakan-sama*. Then stand with your legs and arms spread."

In the Deshima guardhouse, Sano untied the drawstring pouch from his sash, handed it over, and stood as requested. The guard placed the pouch in a cabinet for safekeeping. On a spiked board he hung Sano's wooden nameplate—the pass, issued earlier by Governor Nagai, that allowed him entry to Deshima. Another guard searched Sano's body for items that a traitor might pass to the Dutch: money, weapons, secret messages. More guards subjected Interpreter Iishino to the same procedure, because no one, not even a high-ranking Nagasaki official, was above suspicion.

The guard's searching hands reached Sano's sash. Sano willed himself not to tense when the guard touched the spot where he kept Dr. Ito's letter to the Dutch physician. Hopefully the thin, soft rice paper was indistinguishable from the cloth folds of the sash. With feigned nonchalance, Sano gazed around the guardhouse. On the walls hung ropes, iron shackles, and wooden staffs for restraining and disciplining Dutch escapees—or for conveying Japanese trespassers and traitors to the execution ground.

He suppressed a sigh of relief when the guard said, "You may proceed to Deshima."

Accompanied by Interpreter Iishino and two escorts, Sano left the guardhouse. A stone bridge arched over the sea, whose color had deepened to turquoise under the late afternoon sun. More guards, posted at intervals, bowed as Sano crossed. Ahead, the island's high, spiked wooden fence rose from vertical algae-covered foundations. The fan curve of Deshima seemed to beckon Sano toward all the perils beneath the thatched rooftops and swaying pines.

"*Sōsakan-sama,* I've worked with barbarians for nine years, nine years." Interpreter Iishino bustled along beside Sano. "Anything you want to know about them, just ask me."

Sano slowed his pace. He'd longed to see Deshima and the Dutch, yet he felt extremely unequal to the challenge of interrogating the barbarians. The confrontation on the ship had shaken his confidence in his personal strength and his country's, and he regretted the naïveté that had made him believe himself capable of this investigation in which he must succeed—or lose his honor, and his life.

They reached the iron-banded gate. At the guards' knock, it swung open. Inside stood Deshima Chief Officer Ohira, flanked by two more guards.

"*Sōsakan-sama.*" Chief Ohira bowed. "Welcome to Deshima." The stiff greeting conveyed no warmth, and Ohira looked even more miserable than he had at Governor Nagai's mansion earlier. The bones of his face seemed sharper, the cheeks more sunken, the pouches beneath his eyes darker. Oddly, the murder seemed to have exacted an even greater physical toll from him than Director Spaen's disappearance had. After all, the security threat to Japan had ended with the barbarian's death, as should the threat of punishment for Ohira and his staff. "I await your orders."

To buy himself time, Sano said, "Before I see the barbarians, I'll inspect the island." Perhaps he could find clues as to how Director Spaen had escaped, and who had killed him.

Ohira ushered Sano and Iishino through the gate. A short passage, bordered by high fences, led to Deshima's main street. Entering the world he'd often imagined, Sano found it disappointingly small, yet still intriguing. The street curved along the island's lengthwise axis, between two-story wooden cottages. On the ground floors of these, sliding doors faced the road; above, barred windows formed orderly rows beyond covered balconies. A sentry stood at each door; others patrolled the street or perched on the roofs. Chief Ohira had indeed made sure that no more barbarians escaped.

"These buildings have all been searched?" Sano asked.

"Of course." Annoyance tightened Ohira's features. "I can assure you that no corner was overlooked during the hunt for Director Spaen, and I would have reported any evidence of foul play. This incident wasn't caused by negligence on my part, and if the killer isn't caught, it won't be my fault."

"I'm not accusing you," Sano hastened to say, surprised at the chief's defensiveness. "If I've given you that impression, I apologize. But I'd like to look inside the houses and see everything for myself."

Resentment smoldered in Ohira's bloodshot eyes, but he nodded. At his command, the sentries opened doors, showing Sano large storerooms with shuttered windows, all empty except for one, which contained crates and bundles.

"Those came on last year's ship, but were not sold then," Interpreter

Iishino explained, head bobbing. "The law says they must be stored until the next ship arrives, then offered for sale again along with the new goods."

Sano examined the warehouses and the vacant rooms upstairs, but found nothing remarkable. Under Chief Ohira's glowering gaze, he proceeded to the street's east end. There stood a guardhouse with more sentries inside. At its doorway Sano saw buckets and ladders—firefighting equipment—and a short, cylindrical structure faced with stones.

"A cistern?" he guessed, moving closer to inspect the barbarian's possible escape route.

"Fresh water comes to Deshima through bamboo pipes, from the river." Chief Ohira tapped the cistern's wooden lid. "This is kept nailed down, except when the servants fetch water."

"Is there another access to Deshima besides the bridge?"

"Yes. The water gates."

Ohira led the way to the island's opposite end, past another guardhouse, and into a large corner compound where more sentries paced. This contained a house with a prominent entry porch and latticed balcony; two cottages; a long one-story building; and two small, square ones with plaster walls, ironclad doors, and tile roofs. Grudgingly Ohira named each building's function: "My office. The interpreters' office; the governor's deputies' office. The store where the barbarians sell their goods to Japanese merchants. Fireproof warehouses."

At his orders, two guards opened a wide double gate in the fence. Sano saw stone steps leading down to the sea, and, perhaps twenty paces beyond, the signs warning ships away from Deshima.

"Were the gates open last night?" he asked the guards.

Chief Ohira answered. "No. They're opened only when the Dutch ship's crew and cargo are ferried to or from Deshima. And I can assure you that the gates, and every part of the island, are under constant watch."

"Including last night?"

"Including last night."

Sano examined the steps, but saw no footprints or other signs that anyone had recently descended them. "Does the island have a drainage system?" he asked.

Chief Ohira tilted an exasperated glance skyward. "Underground pipes empty into the harbor below the sea. They're narrow and crooked; nothing except water can pass through." Obviously anxious to finish the tour, he said, "What do you want to see next?"

Interpreter Iishino chimed in, "Show him the perimeter of the island, and Director Spaen's rooms. Maybe he'll find something you missed."

"I don't take orders from you," Ohira snapped. "And how dare you suggest that I'm incompetent?"

Hands raised in supplication, Iishino grinned. "My apologies if I offended you, but I'm only trying to help."

"Well, don't!"

The chief's reaction seemed extreme, even considering how unpleasant it must be to work with Iishino on a regular basis. Sano knew he would worsen his already adversarial relationship with Ohira if he took Iishino's side, but he did intend to examine the areas the interpreter had suggested.

"Interpreter Iishino, wait for me at Spaen's quarters," Sano said. "I'll meet you there after Chief Ohira shows me the perimeter."

His attempt to defuse the conflict sent Iishino bustling off toward the main street, but didn't pacify Ohira, who told the guards to close the water gates, then stalked away.

Sano followed. "Would last night's storm have interfered with security on Deshima?"

Ohira gazed straight ahead as they followed a path that ran between high fences along the island's outer curve. "I maintain strict control over Deshima. The weather does not interfere with it."

Something must have, Sano thought. He saw no scratches on the fences' smooth, weathered boards, or anything caught on the spikes to suggest that a man had climbed over them. He wondered if Ohira's defensiveness indicated mere resentment of a challenge to his authority, or guilt. What had really happened on Deshima last night?

"When and where was Director Spaen last seen?" Sano asked as he and Ohira turned the corner and moved down the island's west side.

"At midnight. When the guards inspected his room, he was there. They locked him in."

Regardless of how Spaen had gotten out of his room, he could have been gone for hours before anyone discovered him missing. "You must be well acquainted with Director Spaen by now. Have you any idea where he went when he left Deshima?"

Halting abruptly, Chief Ohira faced Sano. "I don't fraternize with the Dutch." Fury whitened his nostrils. "I don't break the laws. And if I knew anything about Spaen's murder, I can assure you I would have said so."

Sano's doubts about Ohira increased. If the chief was as blameless as he claimed, wouldn't he be eager to cooperate with Sano? Stress sometimes affected people in odd ways, yet Sano couldn't trust someone so antagonistic.

"I'll speak to your staff," he said, "and see what they know about last night's events."

An unhealthy sweat glistened on Ohira's face, as if from a febrile illness. "I can assure you that I've already questioned all the guards, servants, and interpreters." He glared at Sano. "No one saw, heard, or knows anything. They're all trustworthy; you can believe they're telling the truth."

Sano believed that subordinates often knew things they didn't tell their superiors, but he didn't argue. Ohira couldn't deny him access to Deshima's staff, and the chief knew it. "Let's finish inspecting the perimeter, shall we?"

This they did, to no avail, then returned to the main street. "Are you satisfied?" Ohira asked, a gleam of righteous vindication in his eyes.

"For now. I'll examine Director Spaen's quarters next."

"This way, *Sōsakan-sama,* this way," Iishino called from outside one of the houses. He led them up a flight of stairs to the balcony and slid open the door.

The first thing Sano noticed when he entered the dim chamber was the rancid odor of barbarian. He opened the four shuttered windows—two overlooking the street, two above the rear garden—and noted the intact bars.

"We already checked those," Chief Ohira said from the doorway, where he stood with his arms folded.

This finding, combined with his observations on the rest of the island, forced Sano to conclude that if Director Spaen had escaped Deshima without leaving a trace, he must have had help from someone on the Japanese staff. Had that person killed him, too? Temporarily postponing speculation on this dangerous subject, Sano observed the room's unusual features.

In one corner, a quilt-covered futon sat upon a low wooden platform. So it was true that barbarians didn't sleep on the floor. A long-legged table held a carved ivory pipe and leather tobacco pouch, an oil lamp, a ceramic water jug and basin, and a crumpled rag—evidence that barbarians did bathe occasionally. Sano examined the straight razor, and a comb with yellow hairs caught in it. The mirror above the table reflected with amazing clarity his own surprised face. A flat, round gold case on a chain contained a miniature version of Governor Nagai's clock. Sano opened the cabinet that stood against the opposite wall.

Inside hung dark cloaks, trousers, and surcoats, and white shirts. A rack above held two broad-brimmed black hats. Below stood a pair of shiny black leather shoes. A chest beside the cabinet held black stockings and peculiar white pants, shirts, caps, and robes that Sano guessed were barbarian underwear and nightclothes and, oddly, three short lengths of rope, kinked and frayed as if once knotted.

"Why are these ropes here?" Sano asked his companions. "Is anything missing?"

From the doorway, Ohira made an irritated sound. Interpreter Iishino shrugged and said, "Barbarians have strange customs." He pawed through Director Spaen's apparel. "All here except for one suit of clothes, which he must have been wearing when he left."

So Jan Spaen had either planned a short absence, or had preferred to travel light. "What's in there?" Sano asked, indicating a door in the room's interior wall.

Iishino opened it and the windows in the adjoining chamber. "Director Spaen's office."

To Sano, accustomed to the bare austerity of Japanese rooms, the office seemed very full and cluttered. Papers littered a high desk; goose feathers with ink-stained tips served as writing implements. Ledgers stood piled around an open iron chest. Sano lifted the stiff leather cover of one volume and saw columns of scrawl. He examined the long-necked stringed musical instrument that leaned against the wall, and the high wooden seat whose back looked like a section of a ladder. He studied the strange objects on the windowsill, the materials mounted on the wall above the desk—and realized that, knowing little of Dutch culture, he could scarcely hope to glean information about Jan Spaen's character and motives from his possessions.

"Tell me what these things are," Sano said to Iishino. Chief Ohira had walked to the window, where he gazed down at the garden.

"This is Director Spaen's lute," Iishino said, tapping the musical instrument. "He played very well, and sang and danced, too. When he went to Edo to pay homage to the shogun, His Excellency was very impressed with his talent, very impressed."

Hurrying to the windowsill, Iishino held up a stack of cards with a colored picture of a female barbarian on one side and strange symbols on the other; two long, curved, pointed teeth; and a leathery conical object.

"Dutch playing cards—Director Spaen liked to gamble—tiger fangs, from India, and a rhinoceros horn from Africa. He was a great hunter." The interpreter's eyes misted with regretful admiration. He pointed at the wall above the desk. "Maps of the world, the whole world, with all the trade routes marked. These pins show the places Director Spaen had been." Iishino touched each one. "Japan, China, Taiwan, Korea, India, Indonesia, Africa, and all over Europe."

The maps were beautifully rendered in colored inks, with foreign script designating nations and cities. Sano, never having seen a map of the entire world before, felt a stab of surprise at how tiny Japan looked. How insignificant the Tokugawa empire must seem to the barbarians!

"This is Piet Hein," Iishino said, tapping a black-and-white drawing of a mustached barbarian. "He captured the Spanish silver fleet. Director Spaen admired him very much, very much. He said Hein inspired him to join the East India Company and fight his own battles for wealth. And this is a painting of a teahouse in Leyden, Director Spaen's home city."

Surrounded by a gilt frame, the miniature painting depicted a group of laughing male barbarians who toasted one another, played cards and musical instruments, or fondled huge-bosomed female barbarians, while dogs and fowl scampered underfoot. The work seemed vulgar and overcolored compared to Japanese prints, but the realism was stunning. One could almost step into the scene.

"Is anything missing from this room?" Sano asked.

"Not that I can tell."

"What do these papers say?" Preferring to interpret evidence himself, Sano hated the ignorance that left him dependent on another man's knowledge.

Iishino riffled the papers on the desk. "These are Director Spaen's calculations of profits on the sale of Dutch goods. He had to bring the accounts up to date before leaving Japan on the ship that just arrived. Another trader will take his place on Deshima, along with a new staff. None of the Dutch are allowed to stay more than two years, two years. Otherwise, they might get too friendly with Japanese citizens."

"The most recent sale of goods was a year ago, when the last ship came, wasn't it?" At Iishino's nod, Sano asked, "Then why did Director Spaen wait so long to prepare the accounts?"

For some reason, this seemed to bother Iishino, who dropped his gaze and sidled away from Sano. Chief Ohira spoke from the window. "The barbarians are not as diligent as the Japanese, *sōsakan-sama*. I can assure you that Spaen's procrastination was not unusual behavior for a lazy Dutchman, and can hardly have any bearing on his death." Sarcasm edged Ohira's voice. "Have you seen enough yet?"

Sano could have pointed out that traveling around the world and making a fortune in international trade belied Dutch laziness. Iishino's and Ohira's responses to an innocuous question intrigued him. But he had yet to discover how this trader, musician, gambler, warrior, and hunter had escaped, where he'd gone, or who had killed him. There were no weapons, blood, signs of a struggle, or any other evidence of murder in these rooms or any other place he'd so far inspected on Deshima.

"I'll see the barbarians now," Sano told Ohira, unable to put it off any longer.

INTERPRETER IISHINO AND Chief Ohira led Sano down the main street of Deshima, under mellow sunlight that had warmed the air with the deepening afternoon. "What are the names of the two barbarians presently on the island?" Sano asked.

"Assistant Trade Director Maarten deGraeff," Chief Ohira said, "and Nicolaes Huygens, ship surgeon."

Dr. Ito's source of information about foreign science! The letter beneath Sano's sash seemed to expand. To cover his eagerness, he said quickly, "What sort of relationships did the barbarians have with Director Spaen? Were they friendly? Did they have any disagreements?"

Ohira frowned. "The law prohibits my forming a close acquaintance with barbarians. I'm not in a position to know how they feel about one another. And I can assure you that they always behave civilly in my presence. I don't tolerate unruliness."

"The barbarians try not to let us interpreters overhear anything important," Iishino said. "But sometimes they fail." He pantomimed listening at a door. "I once heard Spaen and Assistant Director deGraeff arguing about 'private trade.' I don't know what that meant, because they saw me and stopped talking."

"And Dr. Huygens?" Sano said.

"He takes meals with the others and treats them when they're sick, but otherwise he keeps to himself."

"This is where Assistant Director deGraeff lives," Ohira announced.

Sano followed Ohira up to the balcony of a house near the west guard station, glad to learn of Spaen's acrimonious relations with at least one comrade. So much the easier to implicate a barbarian in the crime. Only the thought of the Dutch ship dampened Sano's rising spirits. How would the barbarian crew react to news of Spaen's murder?

Guards admitted Sano, Ohira, and Iishino to an office whose basic layout resembled Director Spaen's. But the walls were bare, the floor uncluttered. Stacked ledgers stood on the desk, edges perfectly aligned. The only personal item visible was a small framed picture, turned facedown. Two more guards and a servant kept watch over Assistant Director deGraeff, who sat at the desk, spine straight, writing with an inked goose quill. He wore a brown coat, black knee-length trousers, stockings, and shoes, and a wide-collared white shirt. His stench permeated the hot, stuffy atmosphere.

"The honorable investigator will speak with you now!" Chief Ohira barked at the Dutchman.

Interpreter Iishino translated. The guards yanked the barbarian out of his seat and shoved him onto the floor, shouting, "Bow down!"

The barbarian prostrated himself. Alarmed by the tone Deshima's staff had set for the interview, Sano said, "Please get up and return to your seat." This man was a representative of the powerful nation whose ship waited offshore, and Sano saw nothing to be gained from antagonizing witnesses. When the barbarian had resumed his place, Sano eyed him cautiously.

Tall and spare, Assistant Director deGraeff had lank gray hair that fell to his shoulders. Gray stubble shadowed his face, which was long and narrow, with a pointed nose, thin mouth, and deeply cleft chin. A craggy brow overhung his wary gray eyes.

Sano introduced himself, then said, "I'm sorry to bring you bad news. Director Jan Spaen is dead."

The barbarian looked to Iishino, who translated. Sano hated this te-dious method of communication. Uneasily he wondered whether he could trust the officious interpreter not to twist his words, or the bar-barian's.

DeGraeff clasped his hands and bowed his head over them, re-maining silent for a moment before he spoke.

"He thanks you for the information," Iishino said. "He will assume Director Spaen's responsibilities at once, so that trade may proceed without interruption."

Now Sano found an unexpected advantage in not knowing the sus-pect's language. Without the distraction of words, he could concen-trate on deGraeff's expression and tone of voice while the barbarian spoke. Before deGraeff averted his eyes in prayer, Sano had glimpsed an odd look in them: shock, or elation? Sano thought it significant that deGraeff hadn't asked the obvious question: *How did Spaen die?*

"Director Spaen was murdered," Sano said. "His killer must be caught and punished. Therefore, I must ask you some questions."

DeGraeff listened to the translation, nodded, replied. "He'll coop-erate fully," Iishino said. He spoke to deGraeff in Dutch, then said to Sano, "I told the barbarian that he should tell us everything he knows right now. If he refuses, he'll be beaten." Smiling, he waited for Sano's approval.

Resisting Iishino's attempt to lead the interrogation, Sano ad-dressed deGraeff. "I understand that you haven't eaten all day. I apol-ogize for your discomfort. Food will be brought to you soon." To Iishino: "Tell him what I said. And from now on, I'll ask the questions."

Iishino's mouth formed a circle of surprise. "But *sōsakan-sama*—"

"Just do it!" Sano said, exasperated by the constant interference. Would that he spoke Dutch, and could manage without Iishino! While the interpreter translated, Sano told the servant, "Bring the food, and be quick."

The servant rushed from the room. Ohira and the guards eyed Sano with disapproval. "You are very kind to the barbarian," Ohira said in an accusing tone. "Is that wise?"

Sano remembered the oath he'd taken, and wondered uneasily

whether feeding a hungry man could be misconstrued as promoting Dutch interests over Japanese. Another wrong step, so soon after placating the ship's crew? But he read in the barbarian's strange, pale eyes the relief that here at last was a reasonable, compassionate Japanese official. Perhaps deGraeff would cooperate out of gratitude.

"When and where did you last see Jan Spaen?" Sano asked.

The barbarian spoke, and Iishino translated: "At sunset last night, during our evening meal in the common room."

"What did you and your comrades do after the meal?"

"I went to my chambers, and assumed the others went to theirs. It was the usual routine. There was a bad storm, so I stayed in all night."

Even without understanding Dutch, Sano couldn't mistake the barbarian's weary, rehearsed tone: DeGraeff must have answered these same questions many times. "Did you see or hear anything unusual outside?"

"Nothing except the rain and thunder."

"Did you know Director Spaen had left Deshima, or where he was going?"

"No; he didn't tell me," Iishino translated as deGraeff leaned his head on his bony hand.

"How long had you known Director Spaen?" Sano asked, "and what was your relationship with him?"

The barbarian spoke, eyes devoid of emotion. "They met ten years ago, in Batavia, Indonesia," Iishino said. "DeGraeff was a clerk for the East India Company, and Spaen was an assistant trade director then. They traded European goods for spices, then sold the spices around the world. The company was pleased with their profits. They were promoted and assigned to Japan."

"Were you and Spaen on friendly terms?"

DeGraeff's smile bordered on a sneer. Beneath his courtesy, Sano detected a harsh, uncompromising nature, an antipathy toward people in general. "Of course. Otherwise, we wouldn't have asked the company to keep us together when we left Indonesia."

"What is 'private trade'?" Sano asked.

If this question surprised deGraeff, he didn't show it. His gaze re-

mained steady, his body still. "East India Company agents often buy
and sell goods independently when they go on voyages, financing the
ventures themselves. That is private trade."

"You use your employer's ships to transport these goods and its
trade networks to distribute them? Free of charge, while competing
with the company?" To Sano, this sounded highly dubious, if not illegal. "Doesn't this violate its monopoly on East Indies trade?"

"We must compensate ourselves for the low salaries the company
pays us."

Now Sano saw a possible motive for Spaen's murder. "Did you and
Director Spaen profit from your private trade?"

This time the barbarian paused between Iishino's translation and
his own reply, though his expression didn't change. "Yes. But I don't
see why it concerns you. Japan has no law against Dutch private trade.
Your merchants don't care whether they deal with the company or
with individuals. And your shogun doesn't care either, as long as he
collects his share of the revenue."

"Who inherits Jan Spaen's share of the profits?" Already guessing
the answer, Sano moved closer to deGraeff.

A flicker of emotion momentarily broke the barbarian's gaze. "I do.
I was his partner; he had no family."

Sano stopped as near deGraeff as the man's foul odor would allow.
"Is that why you killed him? For the money?"

DeGraeff shot out of his chair. "I didn't kill Spaen!" Gone was his
spurious courtesy; anger flushed his cheeks.

"Sit!" Sano ordered. Alarmed and frightened, he held his ground
against the towering barbarian. "You admit you broke your country's
law for the sake of profit. Why would you stop short of murder?"

With a sigh of exasperation, deGraeff sat, crossed his legs, and
folded his arms. He looked at the ceiling instead of at Sano or Iishino
when he spoke. "Jan Spaen had only ten thousand *koban* to his name.
He liked women and gambling. He speculated on ventures that didn't
always work out. He was better at spending than saving. I had more to
gain by continuing our partnership than by killing Spaen for such a
paltry sum. Now, may I please return to my work? The guards tell me

the ship has arrived. There's much to be done, and Spaen's death has left it all to me."

Sano didn't consider ten thousand *koban* paltry; in Japan, it could keep a man in comfort for a lifetime. "How exactly would you benefit from continuing your partnership?" he asked, hiding his fear of another unnerving face-off with a barbarian. "Why couldn't you use Spaen's money to buy more goods, then carry on alone?"

"Neither of us could have accomplished alone what we did as a team. We worked well together."

"But you recently quarreled about the private trade, didn't you?" Sano said.

The barbarian picked up the picture that lay on his desk, turning it over to reveal an oil painting of a cobbled street lined with stone houses. DeGraeff contemplated the image while he listened to Iishino's translation. Then he laid the painting aside—face up. "Spaen and I often argued. He had a quick temper, as do I. But we always settled our differences to our mutual benefit."

So you claim, Sano thought. The barbarian's odor had grown stronger from nervous perspiration. "Did Dr. Huygens also have disputes with Spaen?"

"My job is to ensure that trade proceeds smoothly. As long as it does, my colleagues' personal relationships are none of my business."

Was this evasive answer an expression of genuine ignorance, loyalty to comrades, or something else? Sano couldn't believe that after two years' virtual imprisonment together, quarrels hadn't arisen between the men, or that deGraeff would not know of them. Once again, he felt handicapped by his lack of knowledge about Dutch culture.

"What were you doing the night Director Spaen disappeared?" Sano asked.

"I worked, here. Then went to bed. The guards can verify that. They were outside my room the whole time."

Sano predicted that the guards would corroborate his story even if it wasn't true, for two possible reasons. To do otherwise would be tantamount to admitting negligence. And Sano couldn't imagine deGraeff disposing of Director Spaen's corpse alone. One or more Japanese must have played a role in the murder—at the very least, facilitating a coverup. With difficulty, Sano relegated this unwelcome thought to the back of his mind. DeGraeff had sufficient motive for murder. Sano just needed evidence to prove his guilt.

"I apologize for invading your privacy, but I must search your quarters now," Sano said.

"He says go ahead; he has nothing to hide," Iishino said after the barbarian spoke.

Sano went through deGraeff's office without finding anything except more ledgers, writing supplies, pipe, and tobacco pouch. There were no travel souvenirs; no hunting trophies such as Director Spaen had owned. What, besides a mutual desire for money, had bound these dissimilar men together? Sano moved on to deGraeff's adjoining bedchamber, where the same austerity prevailed. Cabinets and chests held a minimum of worn clothing.

"Those are everything he has, and it's all there, all there," Iishino said. "There's nothing that doesn't belong, either."

From the doorway, Assistant Director deGraeff and Chief Ohira watched, expressions stony.

"What are these?" Sano asked Iishino, holding up some papers he'd found in the bedside cupboard. All bore red censors' seals; the law required that foreign documents be inspected before entering Japan.

Iishino bustled over and scanned the papers. "Letters from Assistant Director deGraeff's father. He is dying, and begs his son to come home, become a priest, and take over his position in the village church."

The paucity of clues discouraged Sano, as did the absence of blood. He looked under the futon, bed, and other furniture; he examined floor and walls for secret hiding places. But he found no knife, which could have been dumped into the sea along with Spaen's corpse. Sano peered out the window into the yard. The ground looked hard and smooth, the grass kept short by the barbarians' grazing cow. The soil in the vegetable garden seemed undisturbed. Sano guessed that a search for buried evidence would prove futile.

DeGraeff spoke. Iishino said, "He asks if you're satisfied that he didn't kill Director Spaen."

Far from it, Sano thought, yet he was forced to admit temporary defeat. Identifying the killer—and incriminating the Dutch—wouldn't be easy. Keenly he regretted the inner drives that always endangered his life. What cruel god had endowed him with this fatal curiosity and desire for truth?

The servant returned with a tray of food, which the barbarian eyed hungrily.

"Well, *sōsakan-sama*," Chief Ohira said, "do you still think you can solve the mystery?"

With an effort, Sano kept his voice and expression untroubled. "That will be all for now," he told the Dutchman. He nodded to the servant, who set the tray before deGraeff.

"Watch the barbarian eat," Interpreter Iishino said, giggling.

Thoroughly tired of Iishino, Sano nonetheless couldn't help staring as the Dutchman devoured the food. Instead of sipping soup from his bowl, he slurped it out of a wooden spoon. Instead of using chopsticks, he crammed rice, fish, and vegetables into his mouth with his hands. Between bites, he swilled huge, noisy gulps of water and sake. Such crude table manners disgusted Sano, while intuition told him that the Dutchman knew more about Director Spaen's death than he'd admitted.

Accompanied by Chief Ohira and Interpreter Iishino, Sano descended the stairs and walked down the street toward the residence of Dr. Nicolaes Huygens: Dr. Ito's trusted friend and Sano's last Dutch suspect, upon whom his hopes for a quick, successful end to the investigation now rested.

THE DOOR TO Dr. Huygens's residence stood wide open and unguarded when Sano arrived there with Chief Ohira and Interpreter
Iishino.

"I can assure you that this negligence is atypical, and the sentries
will be disciplined for it," Ohira said grimly, preceding Sano and
Iishino through the door.

In the doctor's study, shelves held wooden boxes labeled in foreign
script; leatherbound books; a human skull; cases displaying seashells,
rocks, butterflies, and other insects; and clear glass jars in which
floated preserved specimens, including a two-headed newborn kitten.
On the floor sat shallow pans filled with water, in which lived crabs,
snails, and sea urchins. Potted plants stood on the windowsills, and a
samurai youth was watering them with a spouted pot. Two guards
leaned on either side of the desk beneath the window, watching the
Dutchman.

Dr. Huygens sat with his back to the door, his head bent over something he was working on amid a jumble of books and writing materials.

"What are we going to see now?" a guard asked him.

The youth spoke to the doctor in Dutch, then translated the reply as he tended the plants. "A drop of pond water."

Ohira stalked over to the guards; they looked up in dismay. "Fraternizing with a barbarian," he fumed. "Disgraceful! Get back to your posts. Now!"

The men fled.

"I'll take over here," Iishino told the junior interpreter, who scurried from the room.

The doctor turned and rose. With his bulky physique and disheveled appearance, he looked not at all like the Japanese ideal of a refined, elegant scholar. His skin was very pink; his round nose and cheeks glowed like cherries. He must have passed his fortieth year, for white hairs streaked the long, coppery waves that receded at his temples. On the bridge of his nose sat a pair of clear glass circles, joined with a loop of gold wire: the famed barbarian eyeglasses that miraculously improved vision. From behind these, the Dutchman's pale amber eyes regarded Sano with intelligent curiosity. His hands had thick, blunt fingers that seemed unsuited to delicate medical procedures. In the right one he held a small metal object. The sight of this raised an instinctive flare of alarm in Sano.

"Look out!" he shouted, drawing his sword. "He's got a weapon!"

Dr. Huygens shrank against the desk, his large, pink face aghast, eyes frightened behind his glasses.

"Guards!" Ohira shouted.

They burst into the room. Dr. Huygens fell to his knees, babbling in Dutch.

"He says it's not a weapon," Iishino said. "It's a scientific device. He begs permission to show you how it works."

"He's telling the truth," one of the guards said. With a nervous glance at Ohira, he added, "I've seen it myself."

Sano sheathed his sword, ashamed of his mistake and horrified at what had almost happened. Overreacting after too many unsettling encounters with barbarians, he might have slain an innocent man and provoked the war he was trying to prevent. Vowing to keep a tighter grip on his self-control, he nodded at Dr. Huygens.

"All right. Show me."

The doctor got clumsily to his feet, cradling in his palm the strange device. It consisted of two rectangular brass plates, sandwiched together by rivets at each corner. A clamp at one end held a long, threaded bolt parallel to the plates along their lengthwise axis. The bolt ended at a flat metal crosspiece with a tiny screw at one end and a pointed probe sticking out of its center. An even smaller screw pierced the probe at a right angle. Directly opposite the probe's tip, set into a hole in the plates, was a minute circle of glass. Sano almost forgot his troubles as he watched his first demonstration of foreign science.

Dr. Huygens sat at the desk and bent over a cleared space surrounded by pages of foreign script and beautiful ink drawings of sea life. He evidently occupied his days with the study of nature, when he wasn't acting as ship surgeon and his comrades didn't require medical care. Ceramic dishes held grains of dirt and other specimens brought to him by the Deshima staff. Dr. Huygens held the scientific device upright by the flared end of the long bolt. Into a dish of clear water, he dipped a pick and transferred a drop to the device's probe. He faced the window and brought the device to his eye. He looked through the glass while adjusting the screws on the probe and crosspiece. Then he turned to Sano, proffering the device.

Warily Sano grasped the bolt between his thumb and finger. The guards watched him with expectant smiles. Was this a joke? He raised the device to his eye, peered through the glass—and cried out in shock.

In the center of his field of vision squatted a lumpy green monster, rapidly spinning a wheel-like appendage. Around it floated long, undulating worms and prickly spheres.

Sano dropped the device and leapt backward. Dr. Huygens, with surprising agility for such a stout man, caught the instrument before it hit the floor. Sano snatched up the water dish and looked into it, but saw no sign of monsters. What kind of barbarian magic had he witnessed?

The guards and the doctor burst out laughing. Even Chief Ohira smirked. "The device is a magnifier, a magnifier," Iishino explained with a superior smile. "It works on the same principle as Dutch spyglasses, making small creatures in the water look big."

Embarrassment burned Sano's face. "Get out," he told the guards. Mustering his dignity, he glared at Iishino and Ohira.

The guards slunk away, hands over their mouths. The chief's and interpreter's expressions turned respectfully serious, but Dr. Huygens kept laughing. "Ho ho, hee hee, hoo hoo!" His belly shook; his face turned even redder.

"Shut up!" Sano commanded.

Then his eyes met the barbarian's, and saw there good-natured enjoyment and pride in the scientific miracle, but not spite. And Dr. Huygens's jolly foreign chortles were comical. Sano smiled, then laughed, too. Shared mirth formed a bond between them. Liking the Dutch physician, Sano regretted that Dr. Huygens was a murder suspect, whom he must incriminate if he could.

Chief Ohira frowned; Iishino shook his head in disapproval. Sano ended his laughter on a rueful sigh. "Honorable Doctor, I have bad news for you. And I must ask you some questions."

THE INTERVIEW REVEALED that Dr. Huygens had joined the East India Company twelve years ago, accompanying Jan Spaen as ship surgeon on voyages since. Huygens had spent the evening of Spaen's disappearance working in his study, and the night fast asleep. No motive for murder emerged, and Sano searched his quarters without result. Secretly Sano had hoped to clear Dr. Ito's friend of suspicion, yet by doing so he'd lost a chance to save himself.

Now, as Sano contemplated the barbarian, who sat meekly at the desk, an idea dawned on him. Inclined to trust this man because Dr. Ito did, he believed in Dr. Huygens's innocence. And he needed his help.

"Will that be all?" Interpreter Iishino asked. Chief Ohira waited impatiently.

What Sano wanted to do was dangerous, illegal—treasonous. But he wanted the truth about Spaen's murder. He wanted the personal and professional triumph of delivering the killer to justice. If he didn't solve the case, he would lose the shogun's favor and cause a war. And he wanted to know the barbarian doctor and explore the world of foreign science denied him by the Japanese laws he abhorred.

"I'd like a moment alone with Dr. Huygens," he said.

Ohira frowned. "This is highly irregular. The rules forbid me to allow it."

"Because it's dangerous to be alone with a barbarian," Iishino chimed in, "very dangerous. Why, people might think you were plotting against the government together! And how can you communicate with him by yourself?"

The doctor watched curiously, waiting for a translation.

"I'll take full responsibility for my actions," Sano said. "Go. I'll meet you at the gate when I'm done."

He watched from the balcony as Ohira, Iishino, and the guards descended the stairs and walked down the street. Then, with a sense of stepping ever deeper into jeopardy, he went back inside the study, closing the door behind him. Through the window, he surveyed the yard. Two guards patrolled there, safely out of hearing range. Sano turned to Huygens. Taking Dr. Ito's letter from beneath his sash, he handed it to Huygens, who looked puzzled, but adjusted his glasses, read silently, then smiled and nodded.

"Ito Genboku," he said, pointing to the letter, then at Sano. "Ito Genboku!"

They'd established their mutual acquaintance with Dr. Ito, but how to proceed? Sano spoke loudly in an attempt to induce comprehension. "I need your help examining Director Spaen's body. To see if the killer left any clues." He gestured in vague pantomime, then shook his head. "This is hopeless!"

Without an interpreter, the doctor would never understand what he wanted; he could never learn anything from Huygens. More than ever Sano missed Dr. Ito, who not only had the requisite scientific expertise but had also learned Dutch from forbidden books.

"I help Ito friend," Dr. Huygens said. "I look body." His pronunciation was strange, but the words intelligible. "I maybe see how die. Who kill."

Sano stared in amazement. "You speak Japanese!"

Glancing at the door, the doctor put a finger to his lips, then said, "Two years I here. People talk. I listen. Learn. Now I help friend. Yes?"

"Come on." Jubilant, Sano led Dr. Huygens to the house where Spaen's corpse lay. To the guards outside, he said, "The doctor will prepare his comrade's body for the funeral now. Bring it to his surgery."

The guards hesitated. "Chief Ohira told us to keep the body here, and the barbarians away from it," one demurred.

"I'll take responsibility," Sano said.

The guards brought out the corpse, now shrouded in white cloth. They carried it into Dr. Huygens's ground-floor surgery near the east guardhouse. The room ran the whole depth of the building, with large windows overlooking both street and back garden. Cabinets and shelves lined the walls; two long, waist-high tables with accompanying seats occupied the center. The guards unloaded the corpse onto a table. Servants appeared and started to open the shutters.

"No. Light the lamps." Sano wanted no witnesses. "Bring water and cloths."

The servants obeyed. Sano ordered the staff away. At last, he and the barbarian doctor were alone.

"Unwrap the body," Sano told Dr. Huygens. He had no intention of physically handling the examination if he didn't have to. Already he sensed death's foul aura seeping through the white shroud, suffusing the dim, hot surgery.

The barbarian seemed not to share the Japanese distaste for death. Gently, but without squeamishness, he uncovered Director Spaen's head, then peeled back the cloth to reveal the mutilated torso and stiff limbs. He didn't flinch at the nauseous odor of decay; he surveyed the killer's work with calm detachment.

Sano experienced a sudden qualm. Shouldn't the barbarian show surprise at Spaen's wounds, or display respect for his dead superior? Or had he known what to expect? Sano tried to dismiss these disturbing thoughts while he watched Dr. Huygens examine the crucifix around Spaen's neck, then the stab wounds. Perhaps the doctor had merely seen so many terrible deaths that he'd grown hardened to such experiences.

Dr. Huygens shook his head. "This not kill," he said, pointing to the crucifix's chain. "Body swell up in water. Then—" He pantomimed choking, then indicated the stab wounds. "I think this not kill, too."

Taken aback, Sano said, "What do you mean? Surely that alone"— he pointed to the hacked area below Spaen's breast—"would have been fatal. And he was badly beaten."

"No. No." Dr. Huygens waved his hands and muttered in Dutch, obviously frustrated by his lack of Japanese vocabulary. "Beating not enough kill. And see?" He raised an imaginary knife and pretended to stab Sano, who instinctively threw up an arm to shield himself and reached for his sword. "You protect, you fight. But Spaen—"

The doctor touched the dead man's unmarked arms and hands, where Spaen would have suffered defensive injuries during a knife attack. "He very strong. Good fighter. No let kill easy. He hurt after die."

"Wonderful." Sano expelled his breath in a gust of exasperation. The only thing about this case he'd been sure of was how Spaen had died. Now the Dutchman had dispelled that certainty. Thinking aloud, Sano said, "Maybe Spaen was killed while asleep. But there was no blood in his room. Maybe he was drowned. But why would the killer mutilate him after he was already dead? Why not let everyone think it was an accident? And why put the crucifix around his neck?"

Dr. Huygens bent over the corpse, probing with his finger the torn flesh around the worst wound, scrutinizing it over the top of his eyeglasses. Then he opened a cabinet, muttering in Dutch.

Sano's breath caught when he saw the cabinet's contents: saws, hammers, pincers, clamps, probes, shears, and knives of every description. Tools of the ship surgeon's trade. Could one of them have inflicted Spaen's wounds?

Dr. Huygens selected a knife and a pair of pincers and set them on the table. Clearly intending to perform a dissection, he opened the shutters.

"No!" Sano hurried over and slammed them shut.

"Need light. Need air," protested Dr. Huygens.

"We can't let anyone see. Dissection is a crime in this country." Seeing the doctor's blank look, Sano longed for a translator. But he couldn't risk letting Iishino or anyone else witness the dissection and report him for participating in the practice of illegal foreign science, for which the penalty was execution. Sano rephrased his statement. "Cutting a dead body is wrong in Japan."

Comprehension lit the doctor's face. "Not wrong in Netherlands," he said. "We look in body, learn how work. Learn cure sick. Everyone watch. No punish." He studied Sano with puzzlement. "Why bad here?"

In the simplest language he could manage, Sano explained how the government so feared the encroachment of foreign ways that it forbade even beneficial barbarian practices. "I think the laws are wrong," he finished. "We shouldn't let fear close our eyes to the truth, or try to shut out the world. There's so much I want to see and know, but can't."

Huygens nodded and smiled, and Sano knew the doctor grasped his meaning, and sympathized with his plight. He felt closer to this barbarian than to his compatriots who accepted the laws without question. An increasing sense of alienation frightened Sano. In his estrangement from lord and regime, could not the seeds of treason take root?

"You go school?" Huygens asked. At Sano's assent, he said, "What learn?"

"History," Sano answered. "Calligraphy; mathematics; military strategy; the Chinese classics; the martial arts. After I left school, I taught those subjects." But never science. Sano felt ashamed of his ignorance, and newly resentful of the laws that had restricted his education.

"Ah." Huygens bobbed his head enthusiastically. "You scholar, teacher." He thumped his chest. "Like me."

They smiled at each other. The tentative friendship between them deepened, and Sano gave in to an impulse to confide. "I would have remained a scholar and teacher for the rest of my life," he said, "but for family obligations." He described how his father, eager to improve their clan's status, had gotten him the job of police detective, which had led to his current position. "Have you any family?"

The cheerfulness vanished from Huygens's plump face. "Wife and son dead," he said somberly. "Father want me be scholar. In Nether-lands, I doctor. I teach and study there; Paris and Rome, too. But no more."

He paused, as if mentally translating an explanation into Japanese. Sano waited, intrigued at the prospect of seeing into the life and soul of a barbarian.

Then the doctor forced a smile and said, "We look Spaen's body now. We learn. Good, maybe. Yes?" He walked back to the corpse, took up the knife, and beckoned. "Bring lamp, please?"

Disappointed, Sano hesitated while other concerns took prece-dence over his wish to further their acquaintance. Witnessing a dis-section in the relative safety of Edo Morgue, which even the most conscientious spies avoided, was one thing; to do so with a barbarian on Deshima, with guards lurking nearby, after the solemn oath he'd taken . . . Madness! But Sano wanted the truth about Director Spaen's death. Without it, he might never identify the killer.

He picked up a lamp, joined Dr. Huygens at the table, and held the light over the corpse.

The doctor cut away pieces of torn flesh from in and around the chest wound. With the pincers, he lifted out blood clots, bone frag-ments, a snail that had lodged inside the opening. The odor of spoiled meat rose to Sano's nostrils. His stomach convulsed. To distract him-self and thus prevent sickness, he concentrated on unclasping the chain around Spaen's neck and removing the crucifix, an important clue that he didn't want buried with the body.

"What are you looking for?" he asked, suppressing a gag and hoping the procedure would be over soon.

Huygens spoke a word Sano couldn't understand. Deeper and deeper he probed, twisting the pincers, churning the flesh. Foul-smelling liquid oozed from the wound. Nausea kept Sano from press-ing for an explanation, and in the silence he heard the ocean lapping against Deshima's foundations, and voices in the street. He hoped the guards would stay away. Then, with a soft click, the doctor's pincers struck something hard.

"Ah!" Dr. Huygens exclaimed.

Failing to grasp the object with the pincers, he dropped them on the table, fetched a small saw, and cut away a bloody rib. Sano closed his eyes against the horrible grinding noise. When he opened them again, he saw Dr. Huygens reach into the wound.

"Ah!" Triumphantly the doctor pulled his slimy hand out of Spaen's chest. In a water bucket, he rinsed the pebble-sized metal sphere he'd found, then held it up.

Sano's heart began a slow descent as recognition struck him. "A bullet. Director Spaen was shot."

"Shot. Yes!" Dr. Huygens nodded and pantomimed firing a gun. In his excitement, he lapsed into Dutch, but Sano could guess what he was saying.

"After Spaen died, the killer tried to remove the bullet, and failed." Sano spoke reluctantly, delaying the inevitable conclusion. "So he cut up the area around the gunshot wound, to disguise the hole. He hacked and struck the body to make it look like Spaen had been stabbed and beaten to death. Perhaps he's a Christian, and attached the crucifix as a gesture of atonement. Then he threw the body in the sea, hoping it would never be found."

From outside came voices, moving nearer. The examination was over, and Sano almost wished it had never happened.

"Prepare the body for the funeral," he told Dr. Huygens.

The results had changed the focus of his investigation and placed him in the dangerous position he'd hoped to avoid. *Treason . . .* the word echoed in his mind as the threat of death and disgrace loomed closer.

The barbarians on Deshima had no guns; all their weapons were confiscated when they entered the harbor. Therefore, the killer was Japanese: a fellow citizen, whom Sano must pursue at the risk of his own life.

REFRESHED FROM A good night's sleep and armed with a revised plan for investigating Jan Spaen's murder, Sano returned to Deshima early the next morning. The previous day's balmy weather had fled. Sculpturesque clouds swirled across the sky; a chill wind blew in from the sea.

"I want divers to search the water around Deshima for a gun and knife," Sano told the officers in the guardhouse. "I want the names of everyone on duty and all visitors present the night Director Spaen disappeared." These were his prime Japanese suspects.

The chief officer showed Sano the duty roster, then opened the ledger where he'd recorded Sano's visit to Deshima yesterday. "There," he said, pointing to a single name.

"Peony?" Sano read, surprised. "A woman?"

"Director Spaen's courtesan," the officer explained. "She spent the night in his bedchamber. We found her there alone the next morning. She didn't know where Spaen had gone, so Chief Ohira sent her home."

Prostitutes were the only women allowed on Deshima. Could this one have killed Spaen? Guns were not common weapons; only high-ranking officers owned them. And though Sano hadn't asked about visitors earlier, it seemed odd that Chief Ohira hadn't mentioned Peony. She could be a crucial witness, if not a suspect.

"Where can I find Peony?" Sano asked.

"She lives at the Half Moon Pleasure House."

Despite his doubts about Peony's potential as a suspect, Sano's spirits rose. By attributing the crime to a low-class citizen, he might avoid treason charges. The *bakufu* wouldn't care what happened to a prostitute, or punish him for condemning her instead of a barbarian. However, the more probable suspects were Chief Ohira, who'd already withheld important information, and the guards.

"When does the second watch come off duty?" Sano asked reluctantly.

Through the seaward door of the guardhouse came the sounds of footsteps on the bridge, male voices, and laughter. "Here they are now," the officer said.

A group of perhaps forty samurai filed into the room. All wore identical leather armor tunics and shinguards, metal helmets, and swords at their waists. They carried spears, bows, and quivers. Sano believed that no barbarian could have left the island without Japanese assistance, or disposed of a corpse without it. And what better suspects than the men who controlled security on Deshima?

Sano introduced himself to them, then said, "Form ranks. State your names and positions."

A tall, lean man with hawklike features stepped forward. "I am Nirin, commander of the second watch." His subordinates lined up in pairs; each member of these shouted his name, then both voiced their shared position together. Sano could tell from their sullen expressions that they considered him an outsider who meant trouble for them.

"Were all of you on duty the night Director Spaen disappeared?" Sano asked.

"Yes, honorable master," they chorused.

"I'm going to ask you some questions," Sano said, already anticipating the problem Deshima's security system posed for him. He turned to the men assigned to guard Spaen, and asked, "Did you have any contact with the director between the last inspection and daybreak?"

"No, master," said one guard. "That's right," seconded his partner.

Sano next addressed deGraeff's and Dr. Huygens's guards. "Did you see your barbarians during those hours?"

A series of "No, master" replies.

"And what about you?" Sano asked the patrol guards. "Did you see any Dutchman with Spaen, or near his quarters?"

More negative answers. The Deshima watch was structured to protect the troops, as well as to ensure security. Each man had a built-in alibi should any question of wrongdoing arise. A guard exposed his partner's misdeeds only at the risk of sharing the punishment.

"Do the officers report to you during their rounds?" Sano asked the guardhouse captains, who assented. "At any time during the night, did anyone look like they'd been in a fight? Did they have blood on their clothes or weapons?"

The captains shook their heads. Nirin said, "Just what are you implying?"

Ignoring him, Sano addressed the gatekeepers. "Did you let anyone or anything out the water gates?"

Nirin stood between his men and Sano, feet planted wide, bow held upright like a spear. "We had nothing to do with the murder. We had no reason to kill Spaen, or cover up for the barbarians." Angry rumbles of agreement came from the guards.

Hand on his sword, Sano stared Nirin down. "There was a storm that night. Did your men really watch over the island as usual—or sit in the guardhouses and stay dry?"

"If you're accusing us of negligence, then you owe us an apology." Nirin spat on the floor just far enough away from Sano's feet not to constitute an open insult. "We're not layabouts." Like you Edo folk, said his scornful glance. "Or liars."

Someone was lying about something, Sano thought. If the Deshima guards had performed their duties properly, they couldn't have failed to notice a murder taking place. Their collusion seemed a more likely possibility. But Sano saw no immediate way to break the conspiracy of silence.

"Tell me about Director Spaen's courtesan, Peony."

Lewd mutters and laughter came from the guards, while Nirin frowned. "Why are you asking us all these questions anyway? We've already told your retainer everything."

"You have?" Sano experienced an unpleasant jolt of surprise. "When was this?"

"Yesterday. He came here when we were outside practicing archery before going on duty."

"I see." With difficulty Sano kept his expression neutral. While he'd been inspecting Deshima and questioning the barbarians, Hirata had disobeyed orders again! And he'd told Sano nothing of this illicit investigation. Last night they'd had a quiet dinner together at the mansion before retiring to their separate chambers. Conversation had been stilted; Hirata had seemed uneasy, and now Sano knew why. Angry with himself for not preventing the incident, Sano decided that he must find something to occupy Hirata's time. Perhaps Hirata could perform the inspection for which they'd come to Nagasaki.

"Well," Sano said, "tell me anyway."

With a sly smile, Nirin said, "Director Spaen treated Peony like dirt. He cursed her and called her names, and had the interpreters translate so she knew what he was saying. He would force her to carry away his chamber pot, then trip her and make her clean up the mess. And sometimes we heard noises coming from his bedchamber when she was there. Slaps. Blows. Screams.

"If you're looking for someone with cause to kill Spaen, you won't find better than Peony."

NAGASAKI'S PLEASURE QUARTER occupied the slope of a hill south of town, and was surrounded by a high wall that kept the women from escaping and the revelry contained. As Sano rode through the guarded gate and began searching for the Half Moon Pleasure House, he noticed many similarities between Edo's Yoshiwara and this smaller quarter. The brothels had barred windows in which courtesans sat like exotic caged animals, flirting with potential customers. From eaves hung red curtains printed with the name and crest of each establishment. Samurai and commoners thronged the streets, browsed the windows, and drank in teahouses. But Nagasaki's houses boasted balconies and roof terraces with a harbor view, where paper lanterns fluttered and shrubs bloomed. A procession moved past Sano toward the gate: mounted samurai, escorting ten palanquins. Through the windows, Sano saw plain-faced, gaudily dressed courtesans leaving the quarter as the Yoshiwara's never did.

"Chinamen's whores! Barbarian's whores!" a group of strolling samurai jeered at the women. "Give the sailors some fun in the foreign settlements tonight!"

The women hid their faces and wept in shame: Serving foreigners was a distasteful task reserved for courtesans so unattractive that Japanese men shunned them. Recalling the barbarians' foul odor, hairy bodies, and crude manners, Sano pitied the women. Many had been sold into prostitution by poor families, or sentenced to the quarter as a punishment for petty crimes. Being forced to consort with foreigners added to their disgrace.

Down the street, a familiar figure suddenly caught Sano's eye. Alarm stabbed him. "Hirata!"

The young retainer blanched when he saw Sano. He turned and darted into an alley. Obviously he hadn't come here for women or drink, but to pursue the lead he'd gotten from the Deshima second watch.

"You're going back to Edo," Sano muttered to his absent retainer. "Tomorrow, if not today."

He found the Half Moon Pleasure House, a small brothel near the quarter's back wall. Dismounting, he gave the reins to a stableboy, then introduced himself to the doorman.

"I wish to speak to Miss Peony," he said.

The doorman gaped. "But master, we have many prettier courtesans. Surely—"

"Maybe he likes ugly girls," called a woman seated in the window. Her companions giggled.

Sano had no time for argument or banter. "Take me to Peony," he told the doorman, "now."

Inside the pleasure house, an attendant manned the entryway. Two courtesans chatted with clients in the reception room, but the real festivities wouldn't begin until after sunset. A servant led Sano to a court-yard garden, where flower beds and stunted pines surrounded a tiny pond. Female voices shrilled like discordant birdsong.

"Peony, pour me some more tea." "Peony, fix my hair." "Peony, this bath is too hot. Add some cold water." "Peony, massage my back."

On a veranda sat three women, all in bright dressing gowns. One held up a tea bowl while she filed her toenails. Another frowned into a hand mirror, poking at her upswept hairdo. The third shed her robe and flopped facedown. Through the open door beyond them, Sano saw a fourth woman's face protruding from a wooden bathtub. They chattered and giggled together, interjecting more orders:

"Peony, my tea!" "Peony, my hair!" "Water!" "I want my massage now!"

Shuttling frantically among them was the witness Sano had come to question. As he approached, he saw that all the other women were beautiful and no doubt belonged to the Half Moon's first rank of cour-tesans. But Peony was one of the biggest, ugliest females he'd ever beheld.

Though no more than twenty years old, she was as dumpy as a middle-aged matron. The skirts of her plain blue cotton kimono, hiked up to allow easy movement, bared legs so bowed that she could have carried a rice bale between them. Her face was so flat it looked almost deformed, with sallow skin, narrow eyes, broad nose, and a puffy, loose-lipped mouth. Her only good feature was her hair—thick, luxuriant, and blue-black, piled untidily on her head.

Peony picked up a teapot and splashed tea into the courtesan's up-held bowl. Then she hurried to the next woman and plucked pins from her hair. Her movements were awkward, jerky. The bathing courtesan shouted, and Peony dumped a bucket of water into the tub. Then she squatted and gave the prone woman's back a few strokes before the others complained and she jumped up to serve them. Her loose mouth quivered; her eyes welled with tears. Sano pitied her, and al-most hated to cause her more trouble than she already had.

"What are you doing here?" demanded a loud male voice. "This area is off-limits to clients."

The women shrieked when they spied Sano. Peony dropped the

teapot; it shattered on the veranda. Turning, Sano faced a swarthy man with the pugnacious scowl of a carved temple dog, dressed in expensive silk robes. He berated first Peony for breaking the teapot, then the servant for bringing Sano inside.

"I'm Sano Ichirō, the shogun's *sōsakan*," Sano explained. "I'm here to ask Peony about the last night she spent on Deshima. Are you the proprietor?"

"Yes. Minami Hideo, at your service." The proprietor's manner turned obsequious. "But Peony has already been questioned by Chief Ohira. She didn't know anything, so he let her go. Isn't that right?" He bent a menacing gaze on Peony, who nodded mutely, ducking her head and clasping her big hands.

"Is there a place where she and I can talk in private?" Sano asked.

"Certainly. But you're wasting your time." Shrugging, the proprietor started across the garden. Peony shuffled after him, humble and downtrodden. Then Minami halted and stared at her bosom. "What have you got in there?" Boldly he thrust his hand down the front of Peony's kimono and pulled out a silk fan.

"That's mine!" shrieked the bathing courtesan. "I've been looking all over for it."

The other women watched avidly. The nude one sat up, not bothering to cover her breasts.

Minami slapped Peony's face; she cowered, whimpering. "Stealing again! That's what got you here in the first place, or have you forgotten? Well, there's a merchant in the Arab settlement who likes to hurt women. None of the other houses will accept his business, but I'll let him have you. That will teach you to behave."

Grabbing Peony's arm, he dragged her across the garden. Sano, though dismayed at this harsh treatment, didn't intervene. Brothel owners could do as they pleased with the women, who had no legal rights. Sano followed Minami and Peony to the veranda opposite, where Minami admitted them into an unoccupied guest room, sparsley furnished with a low table and a cabinet. Sunlight filtered through a latticed window overlooking a busy side street. The proprietor shoved Peony onto the floor, closed the door, and left. Sano exhaled in relief, glad to escape the other courtesans. Their beauty had evoked in him an intense sexual longing for Aoi. Since she'd gone, he hadn't taken another lover. Somehow the deprivation of celibacy kept her memory alive. But personal torments had no place in a murder investigation. Now he studied the witness—or suspect—who promised its possible success.

Peony lay motionless, a hand clasped to the cheek where Minami had struck her. Her hair, which had tumbled down, gleamed richly. Her silent misery filled the room like an audible wail.

"I won't hurt you, Peony," Sano said reassuringly. "Sit up."

She did, scooting backward to kneel in the corner, as far out of reach as possible. Sano glimpsed a spark of cunning in her eyes, a spirit not quite crushed.

"Now tell me everything that happened the last night you spent with the barbarian," he said.

"I already told Chief Ohira. I didn't see Spaen-*san* go. Don't know where he went." Face downcast, she spoke in terse mumbles, as if her puffy lips impaired her speech. "He was alive when I last saw him. I didn't kill him. I couldn't have." Harsh sobs wracked her body; she buried her face in her hands. "Because I—I loved him!"

Sano knelt beside her and placed a consoling hand on her shoulder. Suspicion cooled his sympathy when he felt hard muscles: She had the strength to maim a man's body.

Peony must have sensed his doubt, because she shrank away, weeping harder. Sano pulled her hands away from her face. He shook her until the sobs turned to gasps and she stared at him in fearful woe. Tears streamed down her cheeks; mucus oozed from her nostrils. Sano took a cloth from beneath his sash and wiped her face, feeling both pity and disgust. He sympathized with her suffering, but also understood how her ugliness invited abuse.

"Director Spaen was cruel to you," Sano said. "He insulted you. He beat you. How can you expect anyone to believe you loved him?"

His accusing tone restored Peony's composure. She held her head up and retorted, "It was a game. He would act mean to me in front of other people. Later, when we were alone, I would tie him up. Hit him. He would scream and cry, but he liked it. I liked it, too."

"You mean it was Director Spaen the guards heard screaming, while *you* beat *him*?"

"Yes!" Peony's slitty eyes dared Sano to disbelieve.

Sano knew that some people derived sexual pleasure from humiliation and pain. Peony's story explained the bruises on Spaen's body and the ropes in his room, as well as what the Deshima guards had observed. But was it a clever lie? Had she in reality suffered Spaen's abuse, then taken revenge?

In answer to his unspoken questions, Peony untied her sash and dropped her kimono, revealing a strong torso with small, pointed breasts and a thick waist. Her sallow skin was unmarked. She turned to display her back, also unbruised and unscarred. "He never struck me."

Yet shame could hurt worse than blows. "Cover yourself," Sano ordered, disappointed by the evidence that weakened his case against her. "I want to know everything you did from the time you got to Deshima until the time you left."

Peony's defiance faded under his stern gaze. Pulling on her kimono, she huddled inside it, face hidden behind curtains of hair. "The palanquin left me at the gatehouse. I went inside. The guards searched me and wrote my name in the book. They laughed and said I was lucky the barbarian wanted me, because no one else did."

"Did you take anything onto the island?"

"No." She sniffled, weeping again. "The police took all my things when I was arrested. To pay back the people I stole from. Minami checks to make sure I don't take anything from the house when I leave. And now that Spaen-*san* is dead, I have nothing left. Nothing."

Sano doubted whether anyone could have smuggled a gun and knife past the Deshima guards. But although Peony's grief seemed genuine, he couldn't imagine a Japanese woman loving a barbarian. Could the same person who'd helped dispose of the body also have furnished the weapons?

"What happened next?" Sano asked.

"The guards took me to Spaen-*san's* room. I went inside. He was there. We . . ." Sobbing, she gasped out, "We drank. Then we . . . pleasured each other. Afterward, I fell asleep. The next thing I knew, the guards were shaking me awake. Asking where Spaen-*san* was."

The last part of her speech sounded rushed, as though she'd glossed over important details. "So you slept all night," Sano said, "without hearing or seeing anything that happened in the room, or outside?"

"Yes."

The reply, muffled behind her heavy hair, was barely a whisper. Sano, sensing a new wariness about her, pressed the point. "Didn't the storm wake you? Peony. Look at me." Grasping her chin, he forced her head up. "Tell me what happened to Director Spaen."

Her features were blurred with weeping, her nose red and swollen, her cheeks blotchy. But her eyes darted slyly between their puffy lids.

"I had five cups of sake," she mumbled. "I slept very soundly. I didn't even hear the storm. But I wish it had wakened me. Because then I might have saved Spaen-*san.*"

Her face twisted, and she tried to turn away. Sano grabbed her shoulders. "Director Spaen treated you like filth. You didn't love him—you hated him. That night, you decided to take your revenge. You shot Spaen and mutilated his body to make it look like he'd been stabbed to death. But you couldn't have done it alone. Someone gave you the weapons after you were on the island. Someone opened the water gates for you." Much as he feared this, he couldn't ignore the obvious possibilities. "Who was it, Peony? A guard? Chief Ohira? Talk!"

"You're hurting me," Peony blubbered, writhing in Sano's grip. "I didn't kill him. I wouldn't. I loved him. I didn't see anything. I don't know anything." Pulling free, she crawled away and sat with knees hunched, head cradled in her arms. A high, keening moan rose from her as she rocked back and forth.

Sano sat back on his heels, frustrated and torn. If she was innocent, then he was needlessly brutalizing her. A Deshima guard might have conspired with deGraeff—or Dr. Huygens—to kill Spaen. However, if Peony knew something about the murder, he couldn't stop now.

"Who put the crucifix around Spaen's neck?" Sano demanded, standing over her. "You or your accomplice? And why? Because you're Christians?"

Abruptly Peony's moans stopped; she went still. "I'm not a Christian," she muttered. "It's against the law."

Either she hadn't known about the crucifix, or its mention had struck a nerve. "The Christian doctrine forbids killing," Sano said, "and requires people to love one another. Did you atone for your sin by putting the crucifix on Director Spaen and praying for his soul after you killed him? Do you love him now, because he can't hurt you any more? Did your hatred die with him?"

"I never hated Spaen-*san*." Peony raised her head, tossing back her hair. Her teary eyes glistened with new defiance and cunning. "But I can tell you who did. Urabe, the foreign-goods merchant. Because Spaen-*san* cheated him. And he was on Deshima that night, too."

"But yours was the only name listed in the visitors' ledger," Sano said.

She laughed scornfully. "Then the ledger is wrong. I saw Urabe with my own eyes. Not everything that happens on Deshima is recorded, you know." Then she looked stricken, as if she'd said more than she had intended. Ducking her head, she whimpered, "I'm tired. I have work to do, and Minami will starve me if I don't finish. Please, leave me alone. I've told you everything I know."

When questioned about the staff's and the other barbarians' relations with Director Spaen, she pleaded ignorance. "The guards don't let me see everything they do. And I can't understand what the barbarians say."

Finally Sano rose to go, more confused than ever. The scope of the investigation kept growing. How many secrets must he expose before discovering the truth about Spaen's murder? How did the Christian element fit into it? Sano didn't trust Peony's veracity any more than the guards'. She was hiding something; he could tell. But he must at least check out her story about Urabe, his latest Japanese suspect.

PEONY REMAINED IN the room, listening to the sound of the *sō-sakan's* receding footsteps. She heard him speak and Minami reply. Then their voices faded as they left the garden. Hurrying to the door, Peony looked outside. The courtesans had gone from the veranda. Maybe no one would miss her for the moment. As much as the forced sex with strangers, she hated the constant demands made upon her by the brothel's residents. But now a path to liberty had opened. Soon she would no longer be a prostitute by night, a servant by day, despised and scorned.

Wiping the tears from her face, Peony slid open the door leading to the corridor, looked both ways, and saw no one. She tiptoed down the corridor. Through the paper-paned walls, she heard courtesans chattering while they bathed and dressed for the night's festivities. She cringed, anticipating shrill voices calling her name. Miraculously, no summons came. She was free to plot her escape.

She lumbered down a narrow passage and up three steps to the privy, a small shed attached to the house, and slipped inside. The light from a barred window illuminated the cramped room with a hole in the floor. The stench of urine and feces enveloped Peony, but she was blessedly alone. She reached up, removed a loose board from the ceiling, and inserted her hand into the open space under the roof.

After she'd been convicted of theft and sentenced to the pleasure quarter three years ago, she'd continued stealing—money from clients, trinkets from the other women, food from the kitchen. At first she'd hidden the loot in her room, but Minami had found it and beaten her badly.

"You'll learn your lesson," he'd said when she pleaded for mercy.

Instead, Peony found a better hiding place in the privy, where no one would stay long enough to inspect the ceiling. Now she pulled out a black lacquer box, one handspan square. Lovingly she caressed the floral design inlaid in mother-of-pearl on the cover. This, stolen from a traveling merchant, was the most beautiful thing she'd acquired since arriving at the Half Moon. Yet the box had less value than what was inside: her passage to liberty.

As she anticipated a life far away from the pleasure quarter, Peony's excitement invoked the same sensations she always got from stealing. Her heart thudded; her breathing quickened. A thrilling sense of power flooded her. She had known and craved this feeling since childhood, when she'd stolen for the first time—a beautiful doll, taken from a peddler of toys. The pleasure derived from the ill-gotten items was secondary to the joy of stealing. She felt invincible. So had it happened with the prize concealed inside the lacquer box.

One sultry summer night last month, the revelry in the Half Moon had reached its bawdy zenith. Drunken clients sang and clapped to the music of samisen, flute, and drum.

"The river is rising, rising—"

"Lift up your skirts so they don't get wet!"

Forced to dance for the clients, Peony raised her skirt above her ankles. The other courtesans tittered; the men hooted and yelled. Tears of shame trickled down Peony's cheeks as she reluctantly hopped, spun, and exposed first her bowed calves, then her heavy thighs.

"Higher! Higher!"

Minami laughed with the crowd, but his eyes were hard when they met Peony's, his message clear: If she disobeyed the customers, she would suffer. Almost fainting with embarrassment, she hiked her skirts, revealing her huge, bare buttocks and shaved pubis.

The clients jeered, gagged, and held their noses. Peony fled, sobbing, down the dark corridor. The door to one of the guest chambers stood open. From it issued giggles and moans. Moonlight streamed through the window, illuminating two nude figures entwined on the futon, and an item that lay amid scattered clothing. Quicker than a breath and more quiet, Peony was inside the room, then out again with the thing hidden beneath her kimono, and triumph spreading a balm over her wounded pride.

Now, secluded in the privy, she smiled. She'd soon learned the significance of her treasure, and what crimes its owner had committed. The *sōsakan's* mention of the crucifix supported her other suspicions. In her excitement, she'd almost revealed Deshima's secrets to him, then caught herself just in time. The owner of the treasure wouldn't want such damning evidence to reach the Edo authorities. How much would he pay to get it back? Surely enough to buy her freedom from the pleasure quarter!

Quickly Peony stuffed the box back in its hiding place. She grabbed the coins also secreted there, replaced the board, and left the privy. Luck favored her; she met no one as she hurried out the back door and into the street. She scanned the crowds, yearning for the limited independence she'd once had.

At age fourteen, Peony had gone to work as a maid in a rich man's house. She'd cleaned and sewn, fetched and carried from dawn until late at night. Fearing her employer's wrath, she'd controlled her thieving impulses until the eldest daughter's wedding day, when she'd stolen a set of hair ornaments, gifts to the bride. If she'd hidden the loot right away, she might have escaped her sad fate. But vanity proved her downfall. She was inserting an ornament in her hair when her mistress walked into the room, saw the ornament in Peony's hands, and cried, "Thief! Thief!"

Soon the *doshin* arrived and took Peony to jail. At her trial, the police testified that they'd found other stolen goods in her room. Citizens came forward to report past thefts associated with places Peony had frequented. And her employer had considerable influence with the *bakufu*.

"You, Peony," said the magistrate, "will work as a courtesan in the Nagasaki pleasure quarter until you have repented of your crimes, made reparation to your victims, and repaid the cost of your keep while serving your sentence."

With her looks, she could never earn enough money to pay for all that. Peony wished the magistrate had sentenced her to death. Day after day she slaved at the Half Moon. Night after night she spent in the foreign settlements, bedding the only men who would have her: stinking Chinese, Arab, and Korean sailors and merchants. The high prices they paid were not enough to cover the costs Minami charged against Peony's earnings. Her continued thefts made life bearable, but extended her punishment. And the worst day of all had come two years ago, when Minami ordered her to service the Dutchmen whose ship had just arrived.

Crossing the bridge to Deshima, Peony had tried to jump into the sea, to drown herself and thus avoid the disgrace of bedding a barbarian. But the guards restrained her. They led her to the house where the Dutch trade director waited. Peony struggled and sobbed. The guards threw her into the barbarian's room and locked the door.

The barbarian rose from his seat. Peony shrank back against the door, fearing his strange blue eyes, light hair, and immense size. His odor sickened her. Helplessly she waited for him to assault her the way other foreigners did after long journeys without women. He would savage her with those huge hands and strong teeth. His huge organ would tear her insides apart. Peony suppressed a scream, fearing that resistance might provoke cruelty.

But the barbarian merely pointed to himself and said, "Jan Spaen." Then he pointed to her, a question in his strange eyes.

"Peony," she whispered, surprised. Clients never asked her name; she was just a convenience to them.

Jan Spaen went to the table and poured two cups from a flask. "*Een brandewijn?*" he said, offering one to her.

And clients never offered her a drink, as they did the prettier women. She accepted the cup, careful not to touch his hand. Maybe the liquor would give her courage. When Jan Spaen sat on his raised bed and motioned for her to join him, she perched as far from him as possible. He raised his cup to her, then drank. Hesitantly she followed suit. The potent foreign liquor burned her throat. Heat flushed her body. Suddenly light-headed, she giggled despite her fear.

Jan Spaen proffered the flask.

"Yes, please," Peony said eagerly.

They drank again, and she relaxed. The barbarian wasn't so bad after all. He didn't seem to notice her ugliness. His smell no longer seemed so awful, either. Though she knew he didn't understand Japanese, she began to flirt with him.

"Master is so kind," she cooed. "And so strong and virile."

The barbarian answered in his own tongue. Their attempts at conversation struck them both as hilarious; they laughed together. Peony, the usual butt of all jokes, marveled at the unexpected pleasure of shared humor.

Then Spaen set the cups aside. His expression turned serious. Peony saw the hunger in his eyes, and her fear returned. She fumbled at the knot in her sash. Maybe once they got the sex over with, they could drink and laugh again.

"*Nee!*"

Spaen's vehement negative stopped her. Puzzled, she watched as he walked to the chest and took out three ropes. Then he shed his coat and shoes, his shirt, trousers, stockings, and undergarments. Seeing his hairy, muscular body, Peony shuddered. She turned away from the sight of the bull-like genitals that hung from a tangle of wiry gold pubic hair. Hugging herself, she waited for the inevitable attack. But Spaen's voice was gentle.

"*Kom hier.*"

She glanced at him, curious now. Her mouth dropped.

He sat on his seat, binding his ankles to its legs. Then he spoke, motioning for her to tie his hands behind his back. Peony stood paralyzed with shock. She'd heard other courtesans whisper about such disgusting sex games. How unfortunate that the barbarians also knew them! Only the thought of Minami's anger enabled her to take up the rope.

When she tightened it around his wrists, Spaen groaned, a deep, wounded-animal sound. Quickly she let go and jumped back. "I'm sorry I hurt you, master!" she cried.

But he twisted in his seat, face dark with passion, and shouted for her to continue. Sweat beaded his skin; the rank smell grew stronger. Peony saw his organ swell upright. And strangely, she felt an answering response within her own body. Her heartbeat and breathing quickened the way they did when she stole. An unfamiliar warmth pulsed in her groin, tingled her nipples. She realized she wanted the barbarian as much as he did her, and in the same way. When he shouted more orders, she knew instinctively what to do.

She slapped his face, hard. He moaned, his eyes feverish with pain and lust. She punched his chest, and he writhed, his organ fully erect. As she struck him again and again, her moans joined his. She tore off her clothes and straddled Spaen, impaling herself on his erection. The heat and smell of his sweat-drenched skin fed her desire, as did the sight of his contorted face and straining muscles. She raised and lowered herself, nearly mad with pleasure.

He climaxed almost immediately, in a series of hoarse shouts and violent convulsions. She rode him until her own pleasure crested. She felt powerful, triumphant. This mastery of a wild barbarian was even better than stealing.

That was the first of many nights. The game grew more intense and violent. Sometimes Spaen made her threaten him with a knife or gun. Peony had wondered where he'd gotten the weapons. Now she knew. She'd seen and heard things on Deshima, and not just on the night Spaen had disappeared. Eventually they'd learned to communicate using a mixture of simple Japanese and Dutch words. Sometimes he told her interesting things. This was his legacy to her, a payment for the suffering she'd endured during their game's other phase.

She'd soon understood that for Spaen to completely enjoy sex, he must first abuse his abuser, mocking and mistreating her in front of other people. He derived extra pleasure from the reversal of their roles, the constant shift of power between them. This caused terrible anguish to Peony, who had told the *sōsakan* only half the truth about her feelings toward Spaen. She'd loved the barbarian for the power and ecstasy he'd given her; she honestly grieved for him. She'd accepted the rules of their private game. Yet she had hated the humiliation of cleaning up the dung he'd deliberately spilled, of enduring his insults. The besotted love slave in her wanted to die so they could spend eternity together, but the survivor rejoiced in his murder.

Through her lover's death, she would live, as an independent woman who need not steal to assert her power.

In the street she spotted a town messenger, a young man with the city crest painted on a flag attached to his back, and his kimono tied up around the waist to free his legs for running. She beckoned, and he trotted over.

"Deliver this message for me," Peony said. She whispered in his ear the name of the man from whom she'd stolen the treasure, then said, "Tell him Peony has the property he lost. She'll return it for ten thousand *koban.*" This sum would settle her debts and secure her future. "He must come alone to my room tonight, with the money, at the hour of the boar."

She explained what would happen if he didn't, then paid the messenger, who ran off to deliver the ultimatum. Peony smiled. She was sure the man would meet her demands. Yet even if he refused, she couldn't lose: She would simply sell her prize to the *sōsakan,* and win her freedom that way—with the added bonus that she need no longer fear being convicted for the murder of her lover.

"Peony!"

Minami's voice jolted her back to the present. "Get back in the house. Now!" Scowling, he grabbed her hair, dragging her inside. "You have work to do."

Peony's secret buoyed her heart. Hiding a smile, she murmured, "Yes, master."

He was her master now, but not for much longer.

11

BY MAKING INQUIRIES around town, Sano tracked down the merchant Urabe in Nagasaki's Chinese settlement. This occupied an area near the harbor and was surrounded by high wooden palisades, a moat, and fishermen's cottages. A continuous stream of Japanese merchants, porters, officials—and even a few women, accompanied by male escorts—passed through the gate, where guards searched them and recorded entries or exits.

Afternoon had begun its descent toward evening by the time Sano tied his horse to the moat's railing and joined the traffic entering the settlement. The sunlight had turned coppery, the sea cobalt. Wind-blown clouds, edged in violet, swept across a fading sky.

"State your name and business," a guard ordered when Sano reached the gate.

Sano complied, noting the perfunctory way the man searched him and recorded his name without asking for proof of identity. The Chinese were subject to the same basic restrictions as all foreigners—trade quotas; a separate residential area; limited contact with citizens—but China's centuries-old relationship with Japan accorded special advantages.

Entering the settlement, Sano found himself in a busy marketplace. Chinese merchants manned stalls decorated with red lanterns and heaped with porcelainware, bolts of raw silk, barrels of sugar, turpentine, camphor, and myrrh, Cambodian teakwood, Korean ginseng root, books, medicines, and other exotic goods. The merchants, dressed in cotton trousers, high-collared tunics, and cloth slippers, dashed about, queues waving as they bargained with Japanese buyers. Their fingers flew over abacus beads, calculating prices. Each Japanese merchant was accompanied by clerks, an interpreter, and porters carrying the goods he'd purchased or brought to trade. Government censors examined Chinese books and applied seals to those that passed inspection. The rapid singsong of Chinese speech lent the business a frenetic quality. The Chinese enjoyed freer trade privileges than the Dutch—seventy ships allowed each year instead of just one, and continuous sales open to a greater number of Japanese merchants. With the current peaceful state of relations between the two countries, security was looser; the Chinese merchants and sailors could even leave their residences to worship at their own temple.

Lifting his gaze, Sano saw the temple's red pagoda rising from its distant hillside. He recalled Hirata's story about mysterious lights and the abbot's grudge against the Dutch. The Chinese were allowed to keep guns on their ships. Sano must eventually question the abbot, whose mobility and access to weapons made him a viable murder suspect.

However, freedom of movement and trade didn't translate into other special privileges for the Chinese. Their quarters consisted of shabby, crowded barracks. Laundry flapped on the balconies, and the stench of sewage mingled with cooking odors. Still, none of the residents stayed long, and their profits made up for the discomfort.

A sudden disturbance broke out down the aisle of stalls along which Sano walked in search of Urabe. Two shouting Chinese merchants lunged at each other. Fists flew and feet kicked. Nearby Chinese flocked around the fighters, yelling and waving. Coins changed hands: Instead of stopping the brawl, the Chinese were betting on it!

"Break it up!" Wielding bamboo canes, Japanese guards delivered sharp blows to Chinese rear ends. "Fun's over. Go back to your business!"

The guards dragged away the two troublemakers. The audience scattered, howling unintelligible complaints. "Ouch, my behind hurts!" a passing interpreter translated.

Sano watched in amazement. As a scholar, he'd always viewed the great Middle Kingdom as the font of knowledge and civilization. From China had come many mainstays of Japanese culture: Buddhism; the Confucian system of education and government; herbal medicine; the formal written language. Chinese influence had shaped Japanese architecture, music, painting, and literature. Chinese scientists had invented steel, lacquer, paper, porcelain, matches, gunpowder, block printing, and the compass. But the Chinese whom Sano now beheld seemed like pure rabble. Disillusioned, he approached a guard.

"Where can I find the merchant Urabe?" he asked.

The guard pointed. "That's him at the lumber stall—in the green kimono, bargaining for all he's worth. His business isn't doing too well lately."

Sano worked his way over to the lumber stall, where Urabe was inspecting rough, fragrant boards through a small magnifying lens. Seeing the device, Sano uneasily remembered Dr. Huygens and their illicit collaboration.

"This wood has wormholes in it," Urabe announced. His voice rasped like a sliding door in a warped frame. He was in his mid-forties, and had a neck so short that his head seemed set directly upon his shoulders. His face wore a look of perpetual irritation, with frown lines on the low brow above his narrowed eyes, and tensely puckered lips. Urabe moved from board to board, peering through his lens, sharp chin jutting forward as if eager to get ahead of himself. "I won't pay more than fifty *momme* for this whole lot."

An interpreter translated the words into Chinese for the dealer, who erupted in angry disagreement. "He says that what you see are natural pores in the wood, not wormholes," the interpreter told Urabe. "He won't lower his price."

"Well, then, the deal is off. Let's go."

Urabe sauntered down the aisle past Sano, gesturing for his staff to follow. But Sano saw the hard, acquisitive gleam in Urabe's eyes, the nervous way he picked at a mole on his left cheek. He meant to get the lumber on his terms, but he was afraid he wouldn't.

The Chinese man hurried after Urabe. He entreated and gestured. "My final offer is seventy *momme*," Urabe rasped, chin thrust forward belligerently. "Take it or leave it."

Looking resentful, the Chinese merchant agreed. Money changed hands, and Urabe's porters loaded up the wood. Sano stepped forward. "Urabe-*san*. I'm Sano Ichirō, the shogun's *sōsakan*. I'm investigating the murder of the Dutch trade director, Jan Spaen, and I'd like a word with you."

The merchant's face took on a "what now?" expression. "Of course, master," he said. His gaze roamed, seeking other deals.

"What happened between you and Spaen when you met him on Deshima the night before last?" Sano asked.

"Sorry, you're mistaken." Urabe edged across the aisle to a porcelain dealer's stall. "Haven't been to Deshima since the barbarians sold their goods there last year."

Given that Urabe's name hadn't appeared in the visitor's log, Sano had expected a denial. "Are you saying you haven't seen Jan Spaen since then?"

The Chinese porcelain merchant came up to Urabe, smiling eagerly. "Ask him how much for these plates," Urabe told the interpreter. To Sano he said, "That's exactly what I'm saying. One hundred *momme* apiece!" he exclaimed when the interpreter translated. "That's robbery. Forty *momme*, no more." He turned back to Sano. "Who told you I was on Deshima the night before last?"

"A witness who saw you there," Sano said, reluctant to reveal his source.

Urabe chuckled. "Bet it was Spaen's whore, Peony. Ha, I'm right, aren't I? Fifty *momme*," he countered in reply to the Chinese man's offer of eighty. "Whatever Peony says about me is a lie. To get me in trouble."

Sano was tired of competing for his suspect's attention. "Stop the negotiations until we're done talking," he ordered the interpreter. "Urabe, why would Peony want to get you in trouble?"

The porcelain merchant turned away to greet another customer. "Come back!" Urabe called. To Sano, he protested indignantly, "I have a living to earn. Can't this wait?"

Seeing Sano's glare, he shrugged, his head sinking deeper between his shoulders. "Oh, all right. I was at a party at the Half Moon last month. Went to buy a drink; reached for my money pouch. It was gone. Looked around and saw that ugly whore sneaking out of the room. I guessed she'd stolen my pouch, so I reported her to Minami. He went after her and got it back, then beat her. So now she hates me. When you asked her about the barbarian, she pointed you toward me, out of spite."

The explanation sounded plausible, to Sano's regret. If he couldn't pin the murder on a prostitute, his next safest choice was a merchant. The *bakufu* might even welcome Urabe's conviction as an excuse to seize his assets. Yet there was still hope of incriminating him.

"I hear your business is in trouble," Sano said.

Urabe, who had turned for another look at the porcelain, snapped his head around, his expression suddenly guarded. "No, it isn't. Who told you that?"

"Made some bad deals lately?" Sano pressed, raising his voice. "Short of cash?"

Looking around to see if anyone was listening, Urabe put a finger to his lips. "Just a small setback, that's all. Please, I don't want rumors to get to my bankers."

"What kind of setback?"

"Ahhh." The merchant flapped a dismissive hand. "I thought the price of copper was going to rise. So I borrowed money and bought a lot. When the time came to sell, the *bakufu* set a lower price than I expected. But I'll make it up on other ventures. That's business: You win, you lose."

"The Dutch buy a lot of copper from Japan, don't they?" Sano asked. At Urabe's assent, he continued, "So the copper you bought at a high price, you sold to them at a loss. Is that how you got cheated in your deal with Jan Spaen?"

Urabe scowled. "I never get cheated," he rasped. "And certainly not by barbarians. The *bakufu* set the price. Spaen had nothing to do with my loss."

Sano felt someone watching them, and turned. Backlit by the sun, a woman stood in the aisle nearby. Sano's heart skipped, then drummed a joyful cadence when he saw upswept hair, the outline of a squarish face. *Aoi!*

Then she came nearer, and the illusion faded. She was a girl about fourteen years old, long hair pinned back at the sides, dressed in a pink kimono. Her resemblance to Aoi didn't extend beyond the shape of her face. Her nose was small and round, her lips were a pair of delicate, rosy petals. Totally lacking Aoi's serene self-possession, she hovered awkwardly, hands clasped at her small bosom, eyes shining with youthful innocence. A sour-faced woman and two male servants, presumably her chaperones, hovered behind her.

"Father," she began.

Urabe waved her away. "Not now, I'm busy."

"I'm sorry, Father." Her voice was shy and sweet. Blushing, she bowed, then quickly retreated.

"Sorry for the interruption," Urabe said. "That was my daughter, Junko. The youngest, and the only one yet to marry." He shook his head gloomily. "Four daughters and no sons. The gods have cursed me, to be sure. They could at least send me a rich son-in-law who's fit to be my business partner. But no—of the ones I have so far, one is a drunk, the second a wastrel, and the third a moron. Junko is my last chance to bring capital and talent into this family. I intend to get my money's worth for her dowry."

Sano watched Junko wandering about the market. His joy died, leaving behind a familiar ache in his spirit. Must he spend his whole life seeing resemblances to Aoi in every woman he met? Taking a deep breath, he forced his thoughts back to the investigation.

"You sell the Dutch other goods besides copper, don't you?" he asked Urabe. "Were those dealings with Spaen amicable?"

"Of course," Urabe said impatiently, but his fingers picked at his mole, belying his words. Dutch traders drove hard bargains. Had Spaen gotten the better of Urabe?

"If you weren't on Deshima the night before last, then where were you?" Sano asked.

Urabe thrust his chin forward, gaze defiant. "Worked late at the shop, then came home and slept. My clerks and my wife can vouch for me. I couldn't have killed Spaen even if I'd wanted to, which I didn't. The Dutch are important suppliers and customers, even if they are dirty animals."

Sano didn't give this alibi much credence, because self-interest bound Urabe's wife and employees to say whatever he ordered. Yet even if Urabe had a motive for Spaen's murder, it would be hard to establish his presence on Deshima.

From down the aisle came Junko's sweet voice, singing:

"Since the last autumn moon have I traveled,
Following the promise of love.
The rain is cold and the wind blows bitter—
I cry lest we fail to meet again."

Sano saw her lift and examine a vase from a stall, head tilted gracefully as she hummed. Against his will, Sano imagined Aoi in her place. He wrenched his gaze back to Urabe and, to stem a flood of memories, abruptly introduced another subject related to the murder case.

"I've heard rumors about mysterious lights in the harbor around Deshima," he began.

Junko's humming stopped. There was a loud crash. Sano looked over and met the girl's stricken eyes. Quickly she bent and began picking up broken pieces of the vase she'd been holding. The Chinese vendor assailed her with angry shouts.

"Clumsy girl," Urabe fumed. "Now I'll have to pay for that vase. What were you saying?"

Sano noticed a furtive, listening air about Junko. Why was she interested in this part of the conversation? He repeated his comment, then added, "Do you have any idea what's causing the lights?"

Urabe picked at his mole. "Never bothered to go look. I'm too busy to waste time on things with no profit in them."

Realizing he would get no further with Urabe at present, Sano took his leave. Outside the settlement, he pondered his next move. The day was drawing to a close. Smoke rose from chimneys; orange-robed priests filed uphill toward the temples for evening rites. But for Sano, much work remained. He must requisition Chief Ohira and the Deshima guards, confront Peony with Urabe's statement, and ask the barbarians about Spaen's relations with Japanese citizens.

He'd mounted his horse and started toward the harbor, when someone ran out the settlement gate past him. It was Junko. Pulling a shawl over her head, she dashed uphill.

Sano considered her odd reaction to his mention of the mysterious lights. Perhaps she knew something about Urabe's dealings with the Dutch. And, in spite of himself, he felt drawn to Junko because of her fleeting resemblance to Aoi.

He turned his horse and rode after her.

12

UP THE HILL Junko hurried, weaving through the crowds. Soon she began to pant. Unaccustomed to vigorous exercise, her slender legs ached. She dreaded the consequences should her father learn that she'd again defied his orders, but her yearning heart propelled her toward her forbidden lover.

Until recently, she'd accepted the idea of marriage to a man chosen for his wealth and business acumen. She'd endured countless meetings with unattractive potential husbands. Then, at the town's last autumn festival, she'd met a man with whom she'd fallen instantly and deeply in love.

"He's too young, too poor, and has no business experience," her father had scoffed when she voiced her preference. "And his family would never consent to your marriage anyway; they'll want him to marry into an important samurai clan. Forget him."

But Junko had cast aside fourteen years of proper upbringing and rebelled. They'd been meeting secretly for almost a year now, whenever his work schedule allowed and she could sneak away from home—until two months ago, when her father had caught her climbing out the window.

"I won't have my daughter whoring around," he raged, chasing her through the house, a bamboo cane in hand.

Junko sobbed as he rained blows upon her back. "Please, Father, I love him! We want to be married."

"You'll marry the man I choose!"

Afterward Urabe had hired a chaperone to watch Junko. He intensified his search for an appropriate match for her. Junko hid her heartbreak, praying that her father would reconsider her request. Today, desperation had forced her to approach him again. What she'd overheard between him and the *sōsakan-sama* had driven her to seek her lover. Escaping her chaperone, Junko had fled the Chinese settlement.

Now she ran past the walled daimyo estates above the merchant district. Soon she left behind the summer villas that clung to the hills, following a narrow, winding road up into the forest. The air grew cooler and thinner. Junko's heart thudded and her lungs heaved, but she didn't slow her frantic pace. Taking a shortcut through the woods, she scaled bluffs, climbing over rocks and tripping on fallen branches until at last she reached her destination.

A tall, thin structure with a pointed tile roof, the watchtower was one of several that crowned Nagasaki's hills. Narrow, barred windows pierced the weathered plank walls; from the room at the top, a larger, unobstructed window overlooked the harbor. There Junko saw a glint of light. Joy shot through her. He was there, watching through his spyglass for approaching ships.

Out of breath and belatedly cautious, Junko hesitated beneath the trees at the base of the tower. Evening's chill darkness seemed to rise from the loamy, fragrant earth, absorbing the daylight. Crickets and locusts shrilled; birds twittered; the cool wind rustled the leaves. But Junko detected no sign of human presence. Quickly she slipped through the tower doorway and ascended the stairs that spiraled upward into the shaft.

From the top, a young, male voice shouted, "Who goes there?"

"Kiyoshi, it's me!" Junko cried eagerly.

His footsteps pounded down the stairs. Almost sobbing with happiness, Junko climbed faster. They met halfway up, beside a window that admitted light into the narrow stairwell. Junko halted two steps below Kiyoshi. She drank in the sight of him.

He looked as beautiful as ever, but his sensitive face had somehow aged since they'd last met. New shadows in his eyes lent him a somber maturity far beyond his fifteen years. In his gray uniform, he seemed an unapproachable stranger. A chord of alarm reverberated in Junko's breast. Then Kiyoshi smiled, and the familiar youthful exuberance animated his features. Junko's alarm yielded to joy, and she smiled too.

"It's good to see you, Junko," Kiyoshi said, "but you took a big risk coming here. Your father will beat you if he finds out. There are hoodlums in the streets, outlaws in the hills. You could have been hurt. Promise me you'll be more careful in the future."

"I promise," Junko said happily, taking his hand.

This was what she loved most about him: the way he cared more for others than for himself. He defended peasants against bullying samurai, though his comrades mocked his compassion. He worked long hours in the watchtower and the harbor patrol, and studied martial arts and the Dutch language, not for personal advancement but to bring honor to his father, Deshima Chief Ohira; his patron, Governor Nagai; and his teacher, Interpreter Iishino. He could lose his position for neglecting his duties to receive a forbidden visitor now. But his first concern was her safety. Couldn't her father see that his kind consideration had more value than wealth? And couldn't Chief Ohira see that she would be a more loyal, devoted wife to Kiyoshi than any highborn samurai woman?

Together they climbed the stairs to the small, square room at the top of the tower. Beneath the window lay Kiyoshi's spyglass, his folded cloak and wicker hat, an oil lamp, and the Dutch dictionary he studied during his lonely shift. Suddenly shy in his presence, Junko walked to the window. City and sea glowed with the warm, diffuse radiance of late afternoon. Then a drifting cloud mass obscured the sun, rendering the landscape cold and colorless. Junko sensed a difference, a remoteness about Kiyoshi, who showed none of his usual eagerness to share his thoughts and experiences with her. Junko turned to him, anxious to reestablish their connection.

"Kiyoshi," she began hesitantly.

"What?" His brief smile didn't brighten his somber face. Now he looked away and said, "You can't stay long, Junko. The lieutenant will be coming by on his rounds soon. We'll both get in trouble if he finds you here."

For the first time, Junko felt insecure in Kiyoshi's love. Had absence weakened his affection for her? "What's wrong?" she asked, a tremor of fear playing along her spine. She reached for Kiyoshi, then dropped her outstretched hand. She didn't want to lose her dignity by pleading or clinging, so she sought another way to reassure herself that he still cared. She remembered what she'd come to tell him.

"The shogun's *sōsakan* talked to my father," she said. "He's interested in the mysterious lights. If we're to catch them before he does, we must hurry. Have you learned anything yet?"

At first Kiyoshi didn't speak. Then, still without looking at her, he said reluctantly, "I know what the lights are."

Joy burst like a bright fountain in Junko, washing away her doubts. "You mean you've seen the ghost? Oh, Kiyoshi, all our problems will be solved!" Gleefully she clapped her hands. Then, to her dismay, she saw sadness and pity in the gaze Kiyoshi turned on her. "What is it?"

He took her in his arms, holding her head against his chest so she couldn't see his face. "You must forget about the lights, Junko," he said. "Especially now that the *sōsakan-sama* knows about them."

Junko pulled away, puzzled. "But why? The fortune teller said they're the key to our happiness."

During their last rendezvous, they'd gone to consult Nagasaki's best fortune teller. The old crone had told them, "The strange lights in the harbor hold the key to your happiness. They're the ghosts of Dutch barbarians. Catch one, and it will pay you a fortune in gold to be set free."

"Enough gold to make our families agree to our marriage?" Junko had asked eagerly.

"Enough to make all things possible."

Now Junko tried to remind Kiyoshi of the fortune teller's advice. "The mysterious lights—"

"I said, forget them!" Kiyoshi shouted, eyes blazing.

He'd never before raised his voice to her in anger. Silently Junko turned away, blinking back tears.

"I'm sorry," Kiyoshi said. The anger had left his voice, and he sounded weary. "I didn't mean to hurt you. But this is what's best, you have to believe me."

The cold draft from the window made Junko shiver. Sniffling, she said, "But what about the money? Our plans?"

Kiyoshi hovered beside her, his hand clasping her shoulder. With a forced laugh, he said, "That old fortune teller was just repeating town gossip and saying what we wanted to hear. There's no ghosts or treasure. We were fools to believe it."

Disturbed by the forlorn note in Kiyoshi's voice, Junko glanced sideways at him. He was watching her with concern, but a part of him remained separate, preoccupied.

"If the lights aren't Dutch ghosts, then what are they?" Junko asked, loath to relinquish their dream.

Kiyoshi's hand dropped from her shoulder, leaving behind a fleeting warmth. "I can't tell you."

His recalcitrance destroyed Junko's fragile dignity. She whirled to face him. "Please, tell me what's wrong," she pleaded, clutching his sleeve. "I want to help!"

Holding her, Kiyoshi stroked her hair. She felt his hand tremble, his ragged breath on her forehead, his warm strength. But his body stayed rigid. "There's nothing you can do," he said hopelessly. "I have to handle it alone." After a long pause, he continued, though more to himself than her, "I have to decide whether to do what's right, even if it hurts . . . someone."

Then he released her. He swallowed hard, then said, "I don't want to say this, Junko. But . . . I think we should stop seeing each other."

"Stop seeing each other? Why?" Junko could no longer hide her insecurity. "Don't you love me anymore?" she cried. "Is there someone else?"

"That's not what I mean!" Kiyoshi seized her hands, crushing them to his chest. "I love you. There will never be anyone else for me. But this is for the best. Please, believe me."

"No!"

A sound paralyzed them both: footsteps on the stairs.

"It's the lieutenant," Kiyoshi said. He pushed Junko toward the window, where a ladder extended to the ground. "Go! Before he sees you."

"Wait, Kiyoshi," Junko pleaded. They couldn't part like this, with matters left unresolved.

The footsteps grew louder, closer. Much as Junko wanted to stay, she couldn't endanger Kiyoshi's career. She let him help her out the window. Her hands and feet found the ladder's rungs. As she descended, she peered upward through the rapidly fading daylight for one last glimpse of Kiyoshi.

After a quick wave and a brief, strained smile, he turned away from the window and vanished from sight.

"HELLO! IS ANYONE up there?" Sano called, ascending the stairs inside the watchtower.

Encumbered by his horse, he'd lost track of Junko in the forest. Still, the tower seemed the only place where she might have gone. He called out his name and title so the guard on duty wouldn't mistake him for an attacking enemy. Emerging through the opening in the floor of the room at the top of the tower, he faced a young man who stared at him in speechless dismay.

"It's Kiyoshi, isn't it?" Sano asked, remembering him from the beach yesterday. "Chief Ohira's son?"

Kiyoshi gulped. "I . . . was expecting the lieutenant," he said, then bowed hastily. "My apologies for this rude greeting, *sōsakan-sama.* Please allow me to be of service."

"I'm looking for a young lady named Junko," Sano said, wondering why Kiyoshi was so nervous. "She's the daughter of the merchant Urabe. Have you seen her?"

"No!" Kiyoshi backed toward the window and picked up a spyglass from the floor. He clutched the long metal tube as if eager for something to hold. "I mean, I haven't seen anyone."

"I heard voices up here," Sano said.

"That was me, talking to myself. I'm learning the Dutch language." Kiyoshi gestured to a book that lay on the floor. "I was just practicing."

From below came a muffled thump. Seeing the boy's worried glance out the window, Sano joined him there. He looked down and saw the ladder. A brief, fluttering movement disturbed the forest beneath.

"Do you know Junko?" Sano asked.

"No! That is, I may have seen her in town. But I'm not actually acquainted with her, no."

He lied bravely, looking straight into Sano's eyes, yet Sano easily pieced together the truth. Kiyoshi and Junko were illicit lovers who'd just stolen some time together here. Feeling the loss of Aoi, Sano pitied the young couple. He said, "I wanted to ask Junko what she knows about the mysterious lights in the harbor." Seeing panic flare in Kiyoshi's eyes, he thought he might learn something after all. "Do you ever work the night watch?"

"Sometimes." Kiyoshi's long-fingered hands toyed with the spyglass. "Not often. I usually work in the harbor patrol then."

"Perhaps you've seen the lights," Sano suggested. "Do you know what causes them?"

Kiyoshi stole a glance out the window. "No. I mean, I've never seen the lights. Actually, I don't believe there are any. I think a drunk must have imagined he saw something, then told his friends. Now everyone in Nagasaki thinks he's personally seen the lights, and has ideas about what they mean." His laugh was a sickly croak. "You know how it is."

Sano knew how gossip could spread and turn fantasy into apparent reality, but he couldn't see why Kiyoshi was so eager to deny that the lights existed, or discourage his interest in them. Looking out the window, he saw that the tower was a perfect place from which to monitor the vast panorama of sky, city, and sea.

"May I look through your spyglass?" Sano asked Kiyoshi.

"Yes, of course, *sōsakan-sama.*"

Obviously glad for a change of subject, Kiyoshi handed over the instrument and explained how to operate it. Sano aimed the long tube out the window, peering through the lens while scanning the landscape. He turned the focusing ring, and blurred scenes leapt into brilliant clarity. In a sky of cool, glowing azure that shaded to gold in the west, clouds drifted, every whorl and puff distinct. Birds soared over trees down the hillside; palanquins and tiny figures filed through the streets. Ships in the harbor appeared so close that Sano instinctively raised his hand to touch them. On open sea floated the Dutch vessel, masts and sails clearly defined. Sano experienced a pang of foreboding even as he admired the technology that had produced the spyglass. The ship's captain and crew must have received his message by now. What would be their response?

Sano trained the spyglass on Deshima. He saw guards patrolling the perimeter and main street. He could almost read the warning signs on the poles around the island.

"You have a wonderful view," he remarked, handing the spyglass back to Kiyoshi. "Tell me—were you on duty the night Director Spaen disappeared?"

The young man fumbled and almost dropped the instrument. Holding it across his chest like a shield, he said, "Yes. I guess I was."

"Did you notice anything unusual on Deshima then?"

Eyes wide and alarmed, Kiyoshi shook his head. His Adam's apple jerked.

"Any suspicious activity; any strange comings or goings? Any boats around the island?"

More negative responses. Then Kiyoshi blurted, "Please forgive me, but the harbor is very dark at night. It's hard to see what's going on from here, especially when there's a storm, like there was then. And I—I might have fallen asleep. Or gotten too interested in my studies. I'm sorry I can't help you."

Unconvinced, Sano probed harder for information, but met with more disclaimers. Finally he took his leave of Kiyoshi. The youth definitely knew something, his denials notwithstanding. Sano recalled how upset he'd seemed while viewing the corpse on the beach. He was beginning to believe that the lights were somehow linked to the murder, if only because the mention of either provoked similar reactions from Kiyoshi.

If other leads didn't point to the killer, Sano must question Kiyoshi again, and push him harder.

13

WHEN SANO RETURNED to town, the western sky was an intense orange. Framed by masses of lavender and pink clouds, the setting sun cast a lustrous red sheen upon the ocean, where ships floated as if in a sea of blood. In the streets, lamps flared above gates and behind windows. Hills and cliffs lost their definition, becoming lofty but insubstantial barriers against the oncoming night. Sano rode up to the Deshima guardhouse just as ten divers swam ashore.

"You didn't find the gun?" he asked, noting with disappointment their empty hands.

"No, and it's too dark to see anything now," said the leader.

"Resume the search in the morning," Sano said.

He'd intended to requisition Chief Ohira and the staff, but before he could dismount and enter the guardhouse, a strange spectacle drew his attention. He rode down the waterfront promenade for a better look.

In the harbor, a Chinese junk glowed with hundreds of lanterns that hung from its masts, golden sails fluttering like flames. On the deck, musicians played a dissonant melody on flute, drums, and cymbals.

Sailors danced, queues waving; their song drifted across the water. Down the hill came a procession of marchers carrying red lanterns and orange-robed priests bearing two litters. The first held the large gold statue of a fat, smiling god, surrounded by flowers and smoking incense burners. Upon the second litter rode a diminutive old man with a shaven head. He wore a multicolored brocade stole over his clerical robes. Other priests carried objects fashioned from gilt paper: houses, boats, furniture; animals; stacks of money. A boisterous crowd of Chinese sailors followed. Japanese guards, armed with bamboo canes, accompanied the marchers down a pier toward the junk.

Dismounting, Sano joined the crowd that had gathered to watch the procession. "What's going on?" he asked a soldier.

"This is a launching ceremony for the Chinese junk. The statue is their sea god. They pray to him for a safe journey."

"And the priest on the litter?" Sano asked, already guessing the answer.

"Liu Yun. Abbot of the Chinese temple."

Eager for a better look at this suspect, Sano gave the reins to the soldier, along with orders to mind his horse. He eased his way through the crowd of Chinese on the pier, where priests were helping Abbot Liu Yun off his litter. They handed him a flaming torch. Chanting in a deep, resonant voice, he set fire to an elaborate gilt-paper mansion. Smoke rose to the sky; ashes wafted over the water. From his litter, the golden sea god smiled benignly as the symbolic offering was sent heavenward. The sailors aboard the junk waved and shouted. The music played louder and faster. The audience cheered. Sano approached a guard.

"Is there anyone here who can translate Chinese and Japanese?" he asked, regretting that while he'd learned to read Chinese, he couldn't speak it. "I need to talk to Abbot Liu Yun."

"An interpreter is not necessary," interjected an oddly accented voice.

Turning, Sano saw that the other priests had assumed the task of burning the offerings, and Abbot Liu Yun stood beside him. The abbot's wrinkled skin had the thin fragility of ancient silk and the yellow color of old ivory. His head, supported by the feeble stalk of his neck, seemed too large for his body, but his features were delicate and precise, with a pointed chin and ears like tiny seashells. He bowed stiffly.

"You speak Japanese very well, Your Holiness," Sano said, impressed. Here was the elegant, scholarly refinement he'd expected of the Chinese and found lacking in the merchants. The abbot exuded a distinct air of class, wealth, and education. Sano was awed at actually meeting a citizen of the venerated Middle Kingdom, and curious to know more about him. This was as close as the hateful *bakufu* would let him get to that land of ancient knowledge and tradition. "How did you learn our language?"

"In my youth, I was an official in the Ming Imperial Court in Peking," the abbot said. "This was before your government forbade its subjects to travel abroad." Sano noticed that he slurred his *r* sounds and retained the musical cadence of his own tongue. "I studied with a Japanese tutor, and later served as a minister of foreign relations, receiving Japanese merchants, priests, and scholars who came to pay homage to the emperor. And I have been in your wonderful country for six years now."

Chinese priests, like their Japanese counterparts, often pursued other careers before entering the monastery, yet Sano was surprised to learn that Abbot Liu Yun had done so. He had the ethereal serenity that Sano associated with priests who'd taken their vows early and had limited contact with secular life. His voice carried a faint echo of shadowed worship halls. His tilted eyes, which did not quite focus on the same point, seemed to behold a landscape visible only to him. But Abbot Liu Yun was cognizant of city affairs, as his next words proved.

"I understand that you are investigating the murder of the barbarian. Is there some way in which I might assist you in this endeavor?"

Sano moved up the pier, separating himself and Liu Yun from the crowd. It was risky to speak to any foreigner alone, but Sano took the chance to further his investigation and indulge his curiosity. "I'm questioning everyone who had a connection with Jan Spaen and the Dutch. Your name has come up as someone with a grievance against them."

Placidly the abbot contemplated the festivities. The priests were setting fire to a paper barn full of paper animals, chanting as it flamed and smoked. The junk's crew had extended a long platform from the prow over the water. Upon this, an acrobat performed somersaults and handsprings.

"Ah, yes," Liu Yun said, nodding slowly. "Nagasaki, the great international port, is really just a small, gossipy town. My personal affairs, like those of everyone else, are grist for the local rumor mill."

"And exactly what is this grievance that has inspired the rumors?" Sano asked.

The priests lit the paper money and cast burning fragments into the sea. Liu Yun watched with benign detachment. "Jan Spaen was the man immediately but not solely responsible for the death of my only brother."

A series of booms rocked the earth as rockets shot up from the ship and burst in great showers of red, gold, and green stars. The crowd gasped and exclaimed. The colored light illuminated Liu Yun's serene face.

"How and when did your brother die?" Sano asked, surprised that Liu Yun could speak of the death with such equanimity. His own father had died a year and a half ago, but a part of him would never recover from the loss.

"The story of my brother is really the story of recent Chinese history," Abbot Liu Yun said. "I am seventy-five years old; he would have been seventy-three now. Thus we came of age during the decline of the great Ming dynasty. If you are familiar with Chinese history, you know that it follows a predictable cycle. A dynasty, founded by a strong leader, rises to power. The leader receives the Mandate of Heaven and becomes emperor. Eventually the dynasty loses its reigning vigor. The problems begin."

"Bankruptcy, famine, civil unrest," Sano said, remembering his lessons at Zōjō Temple. "And when government control over the country weakens enough, the emperor loses the Mandate of Heaven. Amid war and turmoil, a new regime rises to challenge the old. The cycle goes on."

"Exactly," Abbot Liu Yun said. "In this most recent instance, the challenge came from the northeast Manchurian nomad tribes. They conquered Fushun, Liaoyang, Mukden, Shensi, Honan, Shantung, Kiangnan, Kiangsi, Hupeh, Szechuan, Fukien, Chinchou, Amur, and eventually Peking. The chieftain proclaimed himself emperor and founded the Ching dynasty.

"Most of the population, including officials of the former dynasty, accepted Manchu rule. I was one of many who donned foreign costume and arranged my hair in a queue. But a few Ming loyalists would not concede defeat. A rebel named Kuo Hsing-yeh organized several thousand troops along the coast. They managed to take Amoy, Quemoy, Chinkiang, and the island of Taiwan. The Ching rulers recovered all the mainland territory, then hired the Dutch East India Company to help capture Taiwan. Taiwan fell seven years ago, in a fierce sea battle, after nearly two decades of war. My brother was one of Kuo Hsing-yeh's commanders—a broken old man and one of the last defenders of a lost cause. Jan Spaen was captain of the Dutch ship that destroyed his squadron. Spaen took my brother prisoner and tortured him to death. I suppose it's understandable that people who know this story would believe I bear a grudge against the Dutch in general, and Spaen in particular."

"You mean you don't?" Sano asked skeptically. A samurai would take the torture and slaying of a brother as a personal insult, and seek revenge. Were the Chinese so different?

Aboard the junk, the acrobat executed an impressive backflip, then bowed to the abbot. Liu Yun raised his hand in a gesture of praise before turning a condescending smile upon Sano. "When I entered the monastery, I freed myself from the pain, suffering, and complications of earthly life. I relinquished my diplomatic career, my wealth, and my family to seek spiritual enlightenment. Once I would have grieved over my brother's death. But in my present station, grief is an emotion that exists on a plane far below me. I feel only the joy of approaching nirvana—the eternal, ecstatic union with the cosmos."

"So you didn't blame Jan Spaen for killing your brother, or wish him dead?" Sano asked, still unconvinced.

The abbot's chuckle sounded like a cricket chirping inside a brass temple bell. "I did not, and would not have even before I turned my back on secular life. It was my brother's own stubbornness that really destroyed him—his refusal to accept that the Mandate of Heaven had passed to the Manchu rulers. Jan Spaen and the Dutch East India Company were merely agents of his fate."

More rockets exploded; the smell of gunpowder scorched the air. Smoke veiled the sky. Sano asked, "Were you personally acquainted with Director Spaen?"

"Before I came to Japan, I managed a temple in the Dutch trade settlement of Batavia, Indonesia, where there are many Chinese sailors, merchants, and laborers," Abbot Liu Yun said. "Jan Spaen was stationed there at the time. We met once or twice. But I did not know him well. My command of the Dutch language is far from perfect."

In view of the priest's fluency in Japanese, Sano couldn't help suspecting that this gifted linguist had achieved equal facility in Dutch. "When did you learn of Spaen's role in the conquest of Taiwan?"

"A year later. When a merchant ship brought the news to Batavia."

"And did you renew your acquaintance with Spaen when he arrived here?"

The abbot turned toward Deshima, where lamps burned outside the guardhouse. Sano couldn't tell whether Liu Yun's imperfectly aligned eyes saw the island, or some private scene, but his tranquil expression didn't waver. "I have not seen Jan Spaen since leaving Batavia. Chance brought us both to Japan, but there was no reason for us to meet again."

Sano knew he must check the visitor's log and question the governor's staff to verify this statement, but could he trust either Nagasaki's officials or their documents? Was it really a coincidence that both Spaen and Liu Yun had ended up in Japan, or had the abbot followed his brother's killer?

"How did you happen to get assigned here?" he asked.

"The previous abbot had died," Liu Yun said. "My superiors chose me to replace him because of my language skills and diplomatic background."

"I see. Do you own a gun, Your Holiness?"

The abbot chuckled again. "Certainly not. My Buddhist faith prohibits violence and killing. I have no need of weapons."

But he did have contact with his compatriots who owned them. Sano had seen the relatively lax security around the Chinese. It wouldn't be difficult for a merchant or sailor to smuggle weapons into the Chinese settlement, then pass them to the abbot during a ceremony such as this. A search of the temple might be necessary if the divers didn't find the gun off Deshima, evidence against other suspects didn't materialize, or if Sano found witnesses to acrimonious relations between Abbot Liu Yun and Spaen. For now, Sano turned the conversation to the subject that had brought Liu Yun to his attention.

"You've also been mentioned in connection with strange lights that have been seen around Deshima," he said.

The abbot nodded calmly. "I have heard this, certainly. The sailors bring me news of local events. But I have never seen the lights myself. Except on special occasions such as this, I retire immediately after evening rites at sunset, and do not venture outside my quarters until dawn. My attendants can confirm this, if you wish."

"Then you don't know the cause of the lights?" Sano said, disappointed. Even if the mysterious lights were indeed connected with Spaen's murder, he had yet to find an explanation for them. And Abbot Liu Yun had just presented an alibi for the night of Spaen's death.

A shadow of impatience crossed the priest's impassive features. "There are many curious phenomena in this world. In my travels, I have seen crackling lights flash up and down the masts of ships. I have seen a fireball hurtle from the sky and burn a house. I have seen a whirlwind destroy a town, and a great sinkhole swallow an entire team of oxen. Such phenomena, including the lights in Nagasaki Harbor, are surely manifestations of the spirits. Some men may be able to evoke them. I cannot, for I am no magician."

From the deck of the junk, the crew lowered two small boats into the water. Sailors rowed these up to the pier. The priests carefully placed the golden statue into the first boat. The sailor in the second boat called to the abbot.

"If you have any further questions, you can find me at the temple,"

Liu Yun said. "But now I must accompany the sea god to the ship so he can bestow his blessings upon it."

With a benevolent smile, he bowed to Sano, then allowed his subordinates to help him into the boat. Accompanied by chanting from the priests on the pier, bursting rockets overhead, and shouts from the waiting sailors, the boats glided toward the junk.

Sano didn't believe Abbot Liu Yun was as indifferent to his brother's death as he claimed. Chinese and Japanese cultures weren't completely dissimilar; Confucian family loyalty dominated both, and could seldom be completely erased by religious fervor. That same loyalty could inspire a priest's brethren to supply a false alibi for him. Liu Yun had access to weapons, and transportation available to carry him to and from Deshima by water. The Chinese, inventors of gunpowder, fireworks, and other magic, could surely create mysterious lights. Sano saw salvation in pinning Spaen's murder on a foreign subject. Yet he couldn't arrest Liu Yun on the strength of motive and rumor alone. Might he possibly locate witnesses who could place the abbot near Deshima the night before last?

The offshore commotion grew louder. A conch-shell trumpet blared insistently. Glancing up, Sano noticed that the new noise came from a barge docking at the nearby harbor patrol station. The crew disembarked, their panicky voices carrying across the water. A fearful premonition sent Sano hurrying up the pier. On the promenade, he caught a soldier who ran through the crowds toward town.

"What is it?" Sano demanded.

"Oh, good, it's you, *sōsakan-sama*." Gasping, the man said, "There's trouble with the Dutch ship. I have terrible news for you!"

14

"YESTERDAY WE GAVE the Dutch captain your message, and he was furious about the additional delay of the ship's landing," the soldier blurted. "Today he decided he doesn't trust you to conduct a fair murder investigation. He thinks Japanese are slaughtering his countrymen on Deshima and intending to punish innocent Dutchmen for the crime. He says that if you don't bring him the head of Jan Spaen's Japanese killer and allow the crew ashore in two days, he'll blast Nagasaki off the face of the earth!"

Speechless with horror, Sano looked out to sea. The Dutch had reacted as he'd feared; his distrust of Captain Oss had proved valid. The ambitious barbarian meant to use Spaen's murder as an excuse for the Netherlands to declare war on Japan, plunder its wealth, and subjugate the citizens. Sano remembered the tales of Dutch conquests. Should he go out to the ship and try to avert the threat? No: The barbarian's ultimatum left him no time for a long trip that might accomplish little anyway.

Hastily collecting his wits, Sano said, "Convey this reply to Captain Oss: 'My investigation indicates that a Japanese shot Director Spaen.

I shall do everything possible to identify the culprit and deliver him—
or her—to justice. You have my promise that I will not protect a killer,
regardless of nationality."

It was a vow that endangered his own life, but which he hoped
might placate the captain, especially since he now had even more reason to prevent the crew's landing. Until he either proved that the
Deshima guards were not involved in Spaen's murder or identified
and dismissed the guilty parties, he couldn't trust them to maintain security. He must keep the Dutch ship away.

"Tell Captain Oss that I will come to him in two days, with the head
of Spaen's killer. Until then, I respectfully request his patience."

"Yes, *sōsakan-sama*." The soldier bowed.

"I'll inform Governor Nagai about what's happened," Sano said. Re-
trieving his horse, he rode into town. Fatigue weighted his limbs; the
old wound in his arm ached, as did his head when he thought of all he
must do in the next two days: Force the truth out of Chief Ohira and
the Deshima guards; pursue the murder's Christian angle; and follow
up on his interviews with Peony, Urabe, Kiyoshi, and Abbot Liu Yun,
whose stories he needed witnesses to confirm or disprove. All this,
with the threat of war hovering over him. And he must discipline Hirata, whose help he desperately needed but could not accept.

The sun's fiery disk dropped below the horizon; the sky darkened
from bruise-red to black. As Sano passed tumbledown houses and
dark alleys, a sense of danger prickled his skin. At three hours till midnight, Nagasaki's early rising fisherfolk had long ago retired. The only
lights came from lanterns above neighborhood gates. The only pedestrians Sano saw were raffish-looking peasants and samurai. Wary of
bandits and outlaws, he kept his hand ready to draw his sword. He
forced his tired mind to stay alert and his horse to trot faster.

The road ascended the hills. At the top of an incline, Sano looked
back to see how far he'd come. In the sky above the harbor floated a
lopsided ivory moon whose radiance shimmered on the black water
and defined the silhouettes of anchored ships. Darkness cloaked the
waterfront, interrupted only by weak lights at the harbor patrol station
and Deshima guardhouse. As Sano scanned the scene, his heartbeat
suddenly accelerated.

Far out on the water, toward the eastern cliffs, a green light flashed rapidly five times. Then a flashing purple light took its place, followed by bursts of brilliant white. While Sano watched, the lights repeated their sequence, moving steadily toward Deshima.

Sano turned his horse and hurtled downhill. His meeting with Governor Nagai would have to wait. Here was a chance to investigate Nagasaki's mysterious lights, and determine their role, if any, in Jan Spaen's murder.

The twisting road led him on a roundabout path to the harbor. Sano looked across the water and saw the lights flashing from a point halfway to Deshima. He passed unguarded gates whose keepers must have fled in fear. Pedestrians had vanished. The night seemed unnaturally hushed, as if holding its breath until the danger passed. Sano reached the waterfront and found it deserted. Were the harbor police also hiding from the ghosts? A slither of dread crept into Sano's bones. As a veteran of the shogun's unsuccessful hunts for ghosts, he had good reason to doubt any existed, but now his ingrained superstition prevailed. To dispel fear, Sano sought a rational explanation for what he'd seen.

If the lights were a man-made device meant to scare people away from the harbor, then they'd certainly succeeded. Even if they were a natural phenomenon, as Abbot Liu Yun had suggested, any crime— including murder—could take place under their cover.

Sano rode down the promenade to the harbor patrol station, which stood dark and silent. "Hello! Is anyone there?" he called.

No answer. Sano abandoned the idea of alerting the authorities and getting help catching the lights. Slapping the reins, he sped down the promenade. Several hundred paces ahead, two sentries stood outside the Deshima guardhouse. Facing inland, they seemed unaware of the lights. Sano looked across the open firebreak and over the harbor to his right. The lights flashed brighter now, drawing nearer the island's water gates. He urged his horse to go faster.

A sharp hissing sound came from his left. Something whizzed past his face and landed with a clatter not far away. Sano ducked. His horse faltered, skidding to a stop. Heart hammering, Sano cautiously looked around. He'd recognized the sound immediately, from past attempts on his life. He didn't need to see the arrow to know someone had shot at him.

In the direction from which the arrow had come, shops and houses crowded close to the promenade's inland side. Amid the rooftops and firewatch towers, Sano saw a shadow move. Then he looked seaward. The lights floated up to the Deshima water gates. Black smoke drifted from them. Excitement leapt in Sano's throat. Instead of taking cover, he rode toward Deshima.

A second arrow soared just over his head. Sano rejected the idea of calling the Deshima guards. The archer might be someone who didn't want him near Deshima while the lights were there; someone associated with the staff, and perhaps involved in Jan Spaen's murder. Sano turned his mount in the opposite direction. He squinted at the rooftops, trying to locate the archer, but failed. After traversing a considerable distance without attracting more missiles, he hoped the assassin thought he'd changed his mind about going to Deshima. Yet when he doubled back toward the island, another arrow almost clipped his foot. Sano glanced over his shoulder and saw the mysterious lights flashing purple, green, and white at the Deshima water gates. He veered left, up a street leading inland through a neighborhood of closely spaced houses. He paused to look around.

The street was deserted. Jutting balconies obstructed the moonlight. Sano stiffened at a rhythmic tapping sound. Footsteps on a tile roof overhead? He relaxed when he saw a loose shutter flapping in the wind, but his extra sense detected a threatening presence. Staying in the shadows beneath the balconies, Sano continued inland, as if going home. He braced himself for another onslaught of arrows. None came. He scanned the surrounding rooftops and saw no one. Encouraged, he turned right, following a road that paralleled the waterfront.

Instantly an arrow hummed over his shoulder and hit the wall of a nearby building. The assassin had guessed his purpose, but Sano refused to turn back. The mysterious lights must be on Deshima now. He had to catch them and determine their cause.

Now Sano could hear footsteps pounding above him as he rode. He saw the archer, clad in black, long bow in hand, kneel on a roof and take aim. The arrow struck his right shoulder with a bone-shuddering impact. Tumbling off his horse, Sano landed hard on his hip. He cried out as horrible pain flashed down his arm and into his chest. He felt along the shaft to the head embedded at an angle just below the outer edge of his collarbone. Warm blood flowed over his hands. He didn't dare yank out the arrow for fear the bleeding would increase. Vigorous activity would worsen the damage. Yet he couldn't stay here for another, fatal shot.

Sano lurched to his feet. Then he heard the archer's steps, fleeing across the rooftops. A sudden fury gripped Sano. "Come back here!" he yelled, reaching for his sword.

The movement sent fresh agony shooting through his shoulder. In his condition, he would never catch his assailant. Without prompt medical care, the injury could prove permanently disabling, if not deadly. He hated to abandon his pursuit of the mysterious lights, but he had to get home, now.

Wincing, Sano remounted his horse, clasped a hand over his injury, then began the long, slow ascent through the hushed streets, wondering who had shot him—and why the person had left without finishing him off. He suspected an assassin sent by Chamberlain Yanagisawa, the rival responsible for past attempts on his life. How he hated the *bakufu* for allowing such crimes! But it could have been Jan Spaen's murderer, because he was getting too close to the truth. Or someone else who didn't want him to discover the secret of the mysterious lights.

REACHING HIS MANSION exhausted, weak, and soaked with sweat and blood, Sano collapsed outside the gate. The two guards stationed there helped him into the house.

"*Sōsakan-sama!*" Hirata came running to greet him in the corridor, accompanied by a manservant with bulging eyes and a puckered mouth. "What happened to you?"

"Shot. At the harbor," Sano gasped out as the guards carried him to his bedchamber. "Get a doctor."

The fish-faced servant spoke up cheerfully. "No need for a doctor, master. Old Carp, at your service. Better at healing than anyone else in Nagasaki, if I may be so bold to admit. A moment, please."

He shuffled off toward the kitchen. In the bedchamber, Hirata lit lamps and spread a futon on the floor. Gratefully Sano lay down on it. The pain was now a throbbing ache that consumed the upper right part of his body. He closed his eyes, fighting the fear that he'd lose the use of his sword arm.

Hirata knelt beside him. "*Gomen nasai*—I'm sorry, but I have to remove your clothes. I'll try not to hurt you."

With a sharp knife, he cut through Sano's cloak and kimonos. Sano winced when he saw all the blood on them. After Hirata peeled away the last layer of cloth, Sano nearly fainted at the sight of the arrow, protruding from the wound from which more blood oozed.

"Tell me what happened." Hirata's voice sounded as though it came from very far away.

Sano explained how he'd come to be shot, and his theories about why. The act of speaking helped him retain his grip on consciousness.

Hirata frowned as he gathered up Sano's ruined garments. "The Deshima guards practice archery. I saw them outside the guardhouse yesterday. Could one of them have shot you?"

"It's possible, if they're the ones behind Spaen's murder or whatever is happening on Deshima."

Sano's strength was spent. All he wanted was to have his wound treated, then rest before telling Governor Nagai about Captain Oss's ultimatum. Yet he couldn't put off dealing with Hirata's insubordination.

"You shouldn't have been anywhere near Deshima," Sano said, "or questioned the guards. And you shouldn't have gone to the pleasure quarter looking for suspects. I ordered you to stay out of the investigation. You disobeyed. Tomorrow morning, you leave for Edo."

Before Hirata could reply, Old Carp entered the room, carrying a water bucket in one hand and a laden tray balanced on the other. "I'll soon have you back in good health again, master," he said. Setting down his burdens, he knelt beside Sano. His mouth puckered tighter as he examined the wound. "Very shallow, and the arrowhead is small and thin. You are lucky. But I must remove the shaft and push the head through." From his tray, he picked up a knife. "This will hurt, I'm afraid."

"Just get it over with as fast as you can," Sano said, turning his face to the wall.

The servant touched the arrow, and the pain flared. Sano jumped. "Lie still, please," Old Carp said.

Sano gritted his teeth, holding himself rigid while the knife sawed through the cords that bound the arrow's shaft and head. Involuntary tears leaked from his closed eyes.

"Be careful," he heard Hirata say.

"Sorry, sorry," Old Carp soothed. "Almost done. Aha! Here we go."

A bolt of pure agony coursed through Sano as the arrowhead slid forward and broke through tissue and skin. Sano jerked violently. The pain tore a yell from his throat, then subsided. He opened his eyes to Hirata's relieved face, and Old Carp triumphantly holding up the arrowhead.

"Worst is over," the servant said. He pressed the wound with a cloth, stanching the flow of blood. "Now I make you feel better. Drink this, please."

Hirata lifted Sano's head, and Old Carp held a bowl of steaming liquid to his mouth. Sano swallowed, tasting spicy ginseng to calm the nerves, prolong life, and combat weakness; bitter honeysuckle to detoxify his system; musty turmeric to relieve pain and inflammation; the subtle flavor of saffron, used to prevent shock. He lay back and rested while Old Carp washed the blood off him and bathed the wound with a pungent extract of green onion, a remedy against festering and fever. His strength was returning, but melancholy dimmed his spirits. He remembered the night when soldiers had chased him through Edo Castle and beaten him, and Aoi treating his wounds with these same medicines. She had spread the cooked onion leaves over his skin, as Old Carp was doing now. That night, they'd loved for the first time.

To banish the familiar stab of longing, Sano addressed Hirata more sharply than he'd intended.

"You have my order. Can I trust you to obey this time?"

Hirata stood by the door, giving Old Carp room to work. "*Sumimasen*—excuse me, but you need my help. If I'd been with you, we might have caught the lights. And I could have protected you."

Old Carp, recognizing their need for privacy, said, "Young master, if you would please press your hand against the onion leaves like so, I will return soon."

Sano said, "Tell the groom to bring my horse. I have to go to the governor's mansion."

Old Carp sucked in his cheeks, increasing his resemblance to his namesake. "Must advise against riding in your condition, master. Bleeding has stopped, but will start again if you move around too much."

"Get me a palanquin, then."

"But . . . All right, master." Bowing, the servant withdrew.

Hirata pressed his palm gently against the onion leaves on Sano's wound. Sano felt warmth and concern flowing from his retainer's square, blunt-fingered hand. He resisted the urge to accept the implicit offer of comradeship, because it also carried the threat of pain and loss.

"If you'd been with me tonight, it might be you lying here instead of me," Sano said. "This investigation is dangerous. I don't want you involved." He paused, then added the selfish reason that was as important to him as Hirata's safety. "And I can't bear your death or disgrace, even if you can."

Above him, Hirata's face was an image of troubled uncertainty, though his hand maintained a steady pressure against Sano's shoulder. "I—please understand, but—I must . . ."

While he blushed and stammered, Sano waited, hoping to hear why he was so persistent in his disobedience. But Hirata, not given to personal revelations, finally shook his head and blurted, "It's my duty to face danger with you, or die in your place. If I don't, then I'm already in disgrace. I might as well be dead. A detective who doesn't detect is worthless." This obviously wasn't what he'd started to say, but he just as obviously meant every word. "And a samurai who doesn't serve and protect is no samurai at all."

Pinned under Hirata's hand, Sano stifled a sigh. Here in Nagasaki, all the buried tensions of the past year had surfaced. Hirata had placed him in an untenable position. He didn't want to deny another samurai the right to follow Bushido, but now his own role of master was at stake: He couldn't back down without losing face. Yet if he didn't offer a compromise, he would alienate Hirata even if they both survived this investigation. The dependable Hirata wouldn't leave him, but would serve without the spirit that made him a valuable second-in-command.

"Tomorrow you can verify Abbot Liu Yun's whereabouts the night of Spaen's murder," Sano said after telling Hirata about his interview with the Chinese man, "and also where he was tonight. Find out if he has, or ever had, a gun." He paused, then added with quiet emphasis, "And don't even think about going to Deshima, because if I catch you there, you leave Nagasaki."

"Yes, *sōsakan-sama*." Bitterness shaded Hirata's voice and expression: He recognized Sano's ploy to shield him by assigning him a suspect who was neither Dutch nor Japanese.

Old Carp returned, applied several more onion treatments to Sano's wound, then nodded in approval. "It should heal perfectly," he said, binding Sano's shoulder with white cotton pads and strips. "Are you feeling better?"

"Yes, thank you," Sano answered.

And for this he was glad. Because now he must deliver to Governor Nagai the news of the Dutch military threat. And tomorrow he must hurry to solve the murder case in time to save the city and his life, and prevent the rift between him and Hirata from becoming permanent.

15

AS NIGHT CREPT past the hour of the boar, Nagasaki's pleasure quarter sparkled with its usual gaiety. Parties adorned terraces and balconies; music and laughter floated from doorways. Through streets bright with lanterns, samurai, peasants, and merchants strolled past the window cages from which gaudily dressed women called and flirted. Boisterous drinkers filled every teahouse.

Like the other brothels, the Half Moon boasted a noisy gala of courtesans and clients. Peony could hear the music from her room, a tiny chamber at the rear of the second floor. Wringing her hands, she paced before the open window. The odors of liquor, cooking, and urine tainted the breeze that cooled her flushed cheeks. The lamp on the low table cast her restless shadow against bare walls. Peony prayed that her visitor would come before Minami noticed she wasn't serving drinks at the party and sent someone to fetch her.

All day she'd slaved in the house, hoping he would reward her obedience by not sending her to the Arab settlement. Fortune had favored her: Two maids had fallen ill, and Minami had kept her home to do their work. But if she didn't win her freedom tonight, she might suffer days of pain and degradation before another opportunity arose. The shogun's *sōsakan* might discover the truth about Deshima and Spaen-*san*'s murder before she could profit from the use of the evidence she possessed.

A sound outside halted Peony's nervous steps. Face pressed against the window bars, she peered down into the alley. She'd left the back door open and a lantern burning there for her visitor. Now her pulse fluttered as someone moved into the dim light. A man in a hooded cloak, coughing—the sound she'd heard. Stopping beside the door. Looking around to see if anyone was near. Lifting his garments, urinating against the wall . . .

. . . and walking away.

Clutching the bars, Peony sank to her knees and shut her eyes. Maybe he hadn't gotten her message. Maybe he couldn't get the money. Disappointment crushed Peony's heart. Rising, she looked out the window again.

The alley remained empty, enlivened only by noise from the streets beyond. Peony lumbered to the cabinet where she and her two roommates kept their possessions. She needed something to occupy her, to make the agonizing wait bearable. Among her bedding, clothes, and other personal articles, she found her comb and mirror. After a moment's hesitation, she took out the lacquer box containing her treasure. She'd meant to keep it safely hidden until she got the money, but she needed the hope it represented. She knelt and set the box on the table beside the lamp, then unpinned her hair. The gleaming mass cascaded around her shoulders. Holding the mirror before her face, she began to comb. The rhythmic motion and the sensuous feel of her hair lifted Peony's spirits. In the mirror's clouded glass, her ugly reflection smiled as she fantasized about the future.

She saw herself, money in hand, striding into the reception room. The crowd would jeer; Minami would scowl and say, "Where have you been, Peony? The guests want you to dance 'Rising River.' "

Peony would answer, "I'll never dance for you or anyone else again." Then she would throw the money in Minami's face and walk right out the door.

She imagined buying a house and hiring a maid; riding through the merchant district in a palanquin, shopping.

"I'll have this, and this, and this," she would say to the clerks as she selected the finest hair ornaments, clothes and food, household furnishings. Spending money would give her the power she'd once derived from stealing. But Peony knew that wealth alone wasn't enough. She also needed the kind of companionship she'd enjoyed with Spaen-*san*.

Her new bedchamber would be furnished with lacquer chests and tables, gilt murals, painted screens. Upon silk cushions she would recline, dressed in a lavish red satin kimono, watching a shy young man enter the room.

"Welcome," she would murmur.

The youth, chosen not only for his handsomeness but for his poverty and compliant nature, would gaze in awe at the luxurious surroundings. "I'm honored, my lady," he would say, kneeling and bowing as if she were the most beautiful woman in the world.

And she would bring out the ropes, the chains, the knives, the whip, the gun. "Don't be afraid," she would say as she initiated him into the way of love that she'd learned from her Dutch barbarian.

In the corridor outside Peony's room, the floor creaked under the pressure of footsteps that came from the stairs leading up from the reception room. Peony's fantasy evaporated; she dropped the comb and mirror, dismayed.

Minami!

Peony had to hide. She couldn't let him drag her back to the party, not now, when her visitor might still come. She leapt to her feet. In her awkward haste, she bumped the box on the table. Its loose lid popped off. Caught in a flurry of panic, Peony moaned. She must put out the lamp and get out, now. But she couldn't let Minami find the box and punish her for stealing it. She couldn't leave the treasure lying in plain sight. She couldn't think what to do first.

Her indecision doomed her. The door slid open. Helplessly Peony watched, wringing her hands. Then, when she saw him, a huge wave of relief broke over her.

"Oh, it's you!" she cried.

Her eagerly awaited visitor carried a cloth bundle under his arm. He entered the room and closed the door. Involuntarily she glanced at the open box on the table. His gaze followed hers; he saw. Quickly Peony stepped between him and his property.

"Give me the money, and you can have it back," she blurted, uneasy because things weren't going the way she'd planned. She'd wanted to tease him by withholding the property at first. She wanted to enjoy her power over him, but had lost the advantage.

Moving closer, he began unwrapping the bundle. He must have been at the party downstairs; Peony could smell liquor and tobacco smoke on him. Now a gleeful anticipation dispelled her uneasiness. She smiled and held out her hands. She started to thank him.

Then he flung the cloth aside. Instead of the money she'd expected, Peony saw a knife in his hand, and read the evil intent in his eyes. A gasp sucked the words back into her throat. Triumph turned to horror. She stumbled backward, raising her clasped hands in a plea for mercy.

"No, please, just take it and go," she babbled.

Unspeaking, he advanced until her back hit the wall. Then he lashed out at her.

The knife's long, gleaming blade slashed Peony's throat. Pain seared her vision. She tried to scream for help, but managed only a gurgle. A warm, salty liquid filled her mouth. She clutched at the wound; blood poured over her hands. A dizzying weakness flooded her muscles. She slid down the wall and landed in a crumpled heap. Through her terror, she saw him turning away, crouching to reach inside the box.

Then darkness obliterated external sights and sounds. Peony could hear the relentless thud of her heart, pumping blood out of her body. She was eight years old again, running down an alley with a stolen doll in her arms. She'd gotten away safely, then. But this time, a horde of furious soldiers, police, and townspeople pounded after her. She ran faster. Then strong hands grabbed her, pulling her deeper into darkness. She heard her heartbeat fading.

She, the nimble, clever thief, could not escape death.

16

SEDATED BY THE medicine Old Carp had given him, Sano slept until late afternoon the next day. Recalling the Dutch captain's ultimatum, he dressed hastily and ordered his horse saddled, anxious to make up for lost time. Then he rode out the gate, into a vastly altered climate.

The wind had died; the sun glared from a hazy sky. Upon the ocean's flat metallic expanse, anchored ships sat motionless, sails limp, while barges and fishing boats moved sluggishly. Moisture saturated the warm air, muting the street noises and enriching the odors of sea, fish, and sewage. The hills closed in on the city, shutting out fresh breezes. Yet more than the weather had changed for Sano. Overnight, Nagasaki had turned hostile. Someone had tried to kill him. Now Sano warily scanned the crowds as he rode, ready to draw his sword or dodge arrows. Beneath the bandages, his injured shoulder was sore, stiff, and incapable of maneuvering a sword with his usual expertise. Blood loss had drained his strength. And Nagasaki's administration had turned against him.

In response to Captain Oss's message, Governor Nagai had convened a meeting of top officials in his office last night. "Double the number of troops on duty," he told the harbor patrol commander. "Put everyone on extra shifts and draft more men from the daimyo estates. I want two barges watching the Dutch ship, and messengers to report to me every hour. Ready the warships. Build bonfires on the hills, and be prepared to light them and summon troops from other provinces."

To *Yoriki* Ota, he said, "Double the number of police on the street in case there are disturbances when the citizens hear the news."

Governor Nagai turned next to the armory captain. "What munitions do we have?" Upon hearing the quantity of cannon, arquebuses, powder, and shot, he said, "I hope that's enough. Transfer supplies to the warships and the harbor forts immediately."

He issued the magistrate orders concerning possible evacuation of civilians, then announced grimly, "We shall maintain this state of emergency until *Sōsakan* Sano meets the Dutch demands."

Everyone turned disapproving glances on Sano, seated apart from the others. "I expect to identify the killer within two days," he said, trying to infuse his voice with confidence. Unless he regained face with Nagasaki's officials, his investigation would suffer. And failure would destroy his career along with the city. Quickly he summarized his interviews with Peony, Urabe, and Abbot Liu Yun.

Governor Nagai frowned. "You wish to attribute the murder to Japanese citizens?"

"They had motive, opportunity, and more access to weapons than the other suspects," Sano said.

The audience exchanged unreadable glances, and the room's atmosphere changed. Sano sensed a pressure against his ears and skin, as if from an approaching storm.

"Yes. Well," Governor Nagai said. "I suggest that in your rush to incriminate your fellow Japanese, you don't overlook the barbarians on Deshima. Otherwise, you might suffer worse consequences than a superficial arrow wound."

Sano hadn't mentioned this. "Who told you about the attack?" he asked.

Nagai smiled briefly. "I have my sources."

Either Nagasaki's spy network was very efficient, or Nagai had some other way of knowing. "I haven't overlooked Deshima," Sano said, emphasizing the last word to tell them that he didn't mean only the Dutch. "The attack suggests that something is wrong there. Something that someone doesn't want me to know about."

When he explained about chasing the lights, his words dropped into a pool of silence. Then *Yoriki* Ota said, "You got shot while chasing ghosts? Ha, ha. You probably scared a drunk who thought *you* were a ghost, and fired at you."

His laughter sounded artificial, but the others joined in. "Think what you will," Sano said coldly. "But I mean to get to the truth about Deshima. When I do, I'll find Jan Spaen's murderer. And I should think it would be in your interest to support my efforts."

"Of course it is, *sōsakan-sama*," Governor Nagai said placatingly. "We must work together to save the city."

"I'm glad we agree on something." Still, Sano wondered whether Nagasaki's administrators wanted Spaen's murderer caught, or had reason to sabotage his investigation. Had they staged the attempt on his life? If so, why? Because Chamberlain Yanagisawa had ordered it?

Now Sano hoped that pursuing the murder's Christian angle would lead him to the truth he must find, in spite of the danger.

NAGASAKI JAIL WAS a complex of tile-roofed buildings set on multiple levels of a terraced slope near the edge of town. Guard towers rose from the surrounding high stone walls. In the adjacent neighborhoods, tumbledown shacks lined narrow alleys down which ragged peasants toiled and reeking open gutters flowed. Jails were places of death and defilement, where no one went voluntarily. Only the poor, who could afford no better accommodations, would live nearby.

As Sano dismounted outside the jail's ironclad gate, he surveyed the crowds and saw a familiar figure: the paunchy guard from his mansion. Coincidence might have brought the guard here, but Sano guessed that the man was spying on him.

Or waiting for a chance to kill him?

"I wish to see the official in charge of eliminating Christianity from Nagasaki," Sano told a gate sentry.

"That would be Chief Persecutor Dannoshin Murashige. I'll take you to him."

Sano secured his horse at the gate and followed his escort into a large compound, where more guards patrolled earthen paths between buildings with cracked plaster walls. Screams and groans issued from tiny, barred windows. The guard took Sano through passages, up flights of stone steps, and through other gates to the prison's uppermost level. Here, neat, freshly plastered barracks with dark woodwork and latticed windows surrounded a small courtyard. Sano's escort led him to the largest building, into a room where samurai knelt in rows before a dais. Upon it stood a low desk from behind which presided Chief Persecutor Dannoshin.

Stout and middle-aged, Dannoshin had pale, moist-looking skin and the soft flabbiness of a man accustomed to rich food and no physical exercise. Puffs of fat surrounded his narrow eyes; a double chin girded his neck. His mouth was full and red, the corners upturned in a perpetual smirk. Wearing a glossy cream silk kimono printed with mauve irises, he looked like an idle bureaucrat. Yet Dannoshin's authoritative manner imposed an air of military discipline upon the assembly.

"We must increase our efforts to banish Christianity from Japan." His voice, a heavy, deep monotone, brooked no resistance. To a group of men seated to his right, he said, "You shall administer the Anti-Christianity Oath to two hundred citizens a day instead of the usual one hundred."

"Yes, Honorable Chief Persecutor," the men chorused. They filed out of the room, taking portraits of the Christian deity for the oath takers to trample, and scrolls for them to sign.

Dannoshin addressed his remaining subordinates. "You will search fifty houses for Christian crosses, pictures, and holy writings. Leave no place or person unexamined."

The searchers left, carrying spears for threatening citizens and poking into small spaces. The chief persecutor bowed to Sano. "Greetings, *sōsakan-sama*. Have you come to inspect Nagasaki's anti-Christian operations? You'll find that we've been very successful in controlling the spread of Christianity. However, the rabble cling tenaciously to their faith. Total eradication will take time."

Dannoshin's sly smile hinted at his pleasure in harassing citizens. Sano immediately distrusted him, but he needed the chief persecutor's help. Approaching the dais, he opened his cloth pouch, took out the crucifix, and explained that it had been found on Director Spaen's corpse.

"I'm trying to track down the owner, who may be a member of Nagasaki's Christian community, and involved in the murder."

The chief persecutor took the crucifix from Sano. Their hands touched; Dannoshin's was repulsively warm and moist. As he examined the intricate carving, his pale, thick tongue slid over his lips, coating them with glistening saliva.

"A fine example of Spanish work," he said. "We don't see these often; most have been destroyed. The last time one turned up was in a raid on a secret Christian church ten years ago. I personally supervised the melting of all the gold and silver artifacts. So I must conclude that this crucifix belonged to a Dutch barbarian, who brought it with him to Japan and placed it on Director Spaen's corpse after killing him." He smiled, and his eyes creased into puffy slits.

"But it's my understanding that all Christian artifacts are confiscated from the Dutch before they enter Japan," Sano said, "and not returned to them until the ship leaves."

Dannoshin shrugged. "The barbarians are clever. They probably hid this crucifix so well that it wasn't discovered during the search. Nothing like it has survived the vigorous persecution that has reduced Japan's Christian population from over three hundred thousand to a few hundred." He handed the crucifix back to Sano with an air of finality.

Sano imagined searchers turning the city inside out, day after day, year after year. He understood the difficulty of locating every hiding place in the Dutch ship. However, he knew that the Japanese, too, were clever—and determined. Families who had preserved their traditions and treasures during wars, famines, and natural disasters could retain their religious faith and artifacts despite persecution.

"Are there any individuals whom you suspect of practicing Christianity?" Sano persisted.

The chief persecutor compressed his lips in irritation. "You shan't find the barbarian's killer among them. When a Christian cell is discovered, the members are jailed. Their associates are relocated in order to disperse any remaining evil influence. There are several people under surveillance now, and if any tried to approach Deshima, they would have been arrested. We exert great effort to prevent contact between Japanese Christians and foreigners. And the effort has been very successful. Come. I'll show you."

Rising, he led Sano outside and through a guarded gate. "Welcome to Nagasaki Jail's Christian compound."

Sano knew that Nagasaki, where Christianity had first taken root in Japan, had always harbored the largest concentration of converts and thus seen the most severe persecution in the country. During the Great Martyrdom some seventy years ago, churches had been destroyed and one hundred twenty Christians beheaded or burned to death. Subsequent regimes had carried out over five hundred more executions. Sano had heard that Nagasaki's current administration continued the relentless, brutal campaign against the few remaining Christians. But his first sight of the Christian compound didn't confirm this.

Within the fenced yard stood ten neat, thatched huts. Through the windows, Sano saw men and women placidly spinning yarn and sewing clothes; mothers nursing babies; families eating meals together; a doctor lighting herbal healing cones on a patient's chest.

"This is most of what remains of Nagasaki's Christian community," Dannoshin announced with a proud sweep of his pale, fat hand. "Sixty people, including children. Locked away so they can cause no harm."

In a larger building, residents bathed in wooden tubs or strolled around the room, watched by guards. More guards patrolled the yard; otherwise, the compound was a far cry from the jail's grim dungeons and torture chambers.

"The rabble are allowed to sell the things they sew, and keep the money," Dannoshin said. "Men and women have separate quarters, but families can visit freely. They can wash and take walks in the common house, and if they get sick, we cure them."

Sano was about to commend the chief persecutor for his humane treatment of the prisoners, and to ask if he might question them about fellow Christians outside the prison. Then Dannoshin added, "You might think we're too easy on them, but harsh punishment only makes them cleave more stubbornly to their faith. It creates martyrs, who attract more converts. We treat them well so they'll behave."

He licked his lips and smiled, a salacious leer. "I prefer to concentrate my efforts on a few favored individuals whom I believe will make good informants. As you will see."

Dannoshin ushered Sano into a small fenced enclosure. From a pulley attached to a pole, a man hung by a rope tied around his ankles. His head and torso dangled into a pit dug in the ground. His entire body was swathed in dirty hemp sacking, except for the right arm, which dangled free. Two guards awaited his confession. Sano stared, aghast.

"This torture method was devised by the governor who ruled Nagasaki seventy years ago," Dannoshin said. "He convinced a Jesuit priest to renounce his faith this way. He also forced Christian women to crawl naked through the streets, where they were violated by ruffians. Then he had them thrown into tubs full of snakes." Saliva welled at the corners of Dannoshin's smile. "When the snakes entered their bodies, the women were more than willing to give up."

Seizing the rope, he hauled the prisoner out of the pit. The man's face was purple and bloated, his eyes swollen shut. Blood oozed from his mouth, nose, and ears. His shaved crown and knotted hair marked him as a samurai; his lips moved in a cracked whisper: "God have mercy on my soul . . ."

"He's been here four days," Dannoshin said. He peered into the prisoner's face. "Tozō. Are you ready to renounce your faith and tell me the names of other Christians you know? If you are, then just raise your hand, and I'll free you."

The prisoner's arm remained limp. "God . . . Gesu . . . Maria . . ." he whispered.

Though conditioned to despise Christians and accept the *bakufu's* authority, Sano admired the prisoner's courage. He deplored torture, and the perversion that made Dannoshin enjoy such awful work. Sano remembered that Christianity was a tool of war, used by the barbarians to command loyalty and foment internal strife. Had it not been suppressed and its foreign proponents expelled, the Japanese might now be subjects of the Spanish crown. Sano had sworn a blood oath against Christianity, but he couldn't allow such terrible abuse of a helpless fellow samurai. All his anger toward the cruel, oppressive Tokugawa regime rose up in him.

"Take him down!" Sano ordered.

Dannoshin gaped. "But he hasn't cooperated yet."

"I don't care. Take him down. Now!"

"All right. If you say so." Shrugging, the chief persecutor let his minions lay the prisoner on the ground. He shot Sano a glance full of resentful insinuation. "Four days' work, wasted. One might think that even a naïve, thoughtless newcomer would know better than to sympathize with Christian rabble. There is such a thing as guilt by inference and association."

Sano didn't lower himself to answer the chief persecutor's insults or threats. He couldn't stand the sight of Dannoshin or the smirking guards. "Leave us," he said.

Once alone with the prisoner, he knelt by the man's side and loosened the tight sacking. Tozō's chest rose and fell in slow, barely perceptible breaths. His lips formed the names of his Christian deities.

"Tozō," Sano said. "Can you hear me?"

The swollen eyes cracked open. Blood filmed the whites. "God have mercy," Tozō whispered through the blood that burbled from his lips.

Sano grasped the man's free hand. "Your ordeal is over," he said. "You can die in peace now."

"Die . . . yes." Tozō smiled. "Enter . . . the holy Kingdom . . . of Heaven." He stared beatifically at the sky. "For God is the glory . . ."

A deep, wracking cough convulsed his body. Blood gushed from his mouth. He began to tremble uncontrollably. The death throes seemed to rob him of courage and faith, and the painful reality of dying to banish dreams of divine paradise. His gaze cleared, sharpening with terror.

"No! I don't want to die. I'm afraid!" His hand gripped Sano's with desperate strength. "Please, save me!"

Sano tried to quiet him; Tozō was beyond help. But the Christian refused to accept the inevitable. "Please, Honorable Chief Persecutor," he begged, mistaking Sano for Dannoshin. "I'll do anything you ask." Another cough produced a fresh outpouring of blood. "I renounce . . . the Christian religion. I spit on God . . . I swear eternal allegiance . . . to the shogun." He thrashed and shuddered.

"Quiet," Sano urged, hating to see a fellow warrior—even a Christian criminal—admit defeat. "Rest."

"I'll tell you anything you want to know. Just don't let me die!"

Sano was appalled. He badly needed information about Nagasaki's Christian underground, but how could he take advantage of this cruel torture? Tasting shame and anticipation, he held the crucifix in front of Tozō's eyes and said, "Where did this come from? Who owns it?"

". . . Barbarians . . . Deshima . . . secret network. Christian contraband . . . passed along a chain of couriers from the Dutch to my people . . ." Tozō coughed and gasped.

"Who leads the network?" Sano asked urgently.

"Uh . . . uh . . ." A massive convulsion spasmed Tozō's body. Blood gurgled in his throat. Then he became still. Disappointed, Sano bowed his head and offered a silent prayer for the man's spirit. Christian or Buddhist, everyone died eventually; everyone deserved a ritual to mark the end of life. Then Sano gently laid aside Tozō's limp hand and walked back to Dannoshin's office.

The chief Persecutor looked up from the dais. "Tozō is dead, then?" he asked, reading Sano's expression.

Sano nodded.

"Did he renounce his faith, or tell you anything before he died?" Dannoshin asked hopefully.

Without hesitation, Sano said, "No. Nothing."

However, Tozō's statement had given Sano an idea of what activities on Deshima might have led to Spaen's murder. And he could think of one way to prove it, tonight.

Then, after he'd left Nagasaki Jail and mounted his horse outside the gate, two soldiers approached him. "We have an urgent message from *Yoriki* Ota," said the spokesman, and Sano guessed that the paunchy guard he'd seen earlier had told the soldiers where to find him. "The courtesan Peony is dead. Please come with us."

17

ARRIVING AT THE Half Moon Pleasure House with his escorts, Sano noted the brothel's grim transformation since his last visit. Bamboo shades covered the window cages, although it was early evening and almost time for the festivities to begin. The crowds, evidently aware that a death had occurred, gave the Half Moon a wide berth. As Sano dismounted, he saw courtesans peering fearfully from the upstairs windows. A *doshin* and three civilian assistants guarded the doorway, where the proprietor Minami stood, his scowling temple-dog face livid with anger.

"I can't run my business with the house full of police," he raged. "And no one wants to come inside while she's still here. I want you to leave. Now!"

The *doshin* merely folded his arms with an air of weary tolerance. Minami jumped aside and glared as *Yoriki* Ota pushed past him out the doorway. "I'm losing money," Minami huffed. "I demand that you take your men and go, so I can clean up the mess and resume my business!"

"Be quiet, or I'll arrest you," Ota told him, then greeted Sano with a perfunctory bow. "So here you are. Come. I'll take you to Peony."

They entered the house. More *doshin* and assistants lounged in the lamp-lit reception room, smoking and talking. In the dim corridors, frightened servants shrank against the walls to let Sano and Ota pass.

"How did she die?" Sano asked.

"Suicide. You'll see."

Yoriki Ota led Sano upstairs to the courtesans' living quarters, a series of tiny chambers behind paper-paned walls. From somewhere came the sound of a woman's hysterical weeping.

"She's in there," Ota said, stopping outside a door where another *doshin* stood guard.

Gingerly Sano slid back the door. The fetid, metallic smell of blood and death poured out, polluting his skin, his lungs. Fighting nausea, he entered the room. The guard brought a lantern and hung it on the wall. Sano saw that the window had been opened to let in fresh air, but the cramped chamber was still hot and stuffy. Peony lay sprawled against the wall, knees bent, in the tangle of her blood-soaked garments. Flies alit on the thickly clotted gash that slanted down the left side of her neck and across her throat. More blood had dribbled from her mouth, caked her long hair into sticky strands, and fanned across the tatami. Her clouded eyes bore an expression of terrified shock. Her left hand gripped the plain wooden handle of a knife that protruded from the fatal wound.

Sano shook his head pityingly. "Who found her, and when?" he asked Ota, who stood in the doorway behind him.

"One of the maids. Around noon," Ota said.

Sano turned. "No one missed her until then?" Now he understood Minami's impatience to remove Peony, before the stench permanently tainted the house.

Ota shrugged. "Minami said she must have sneaked away from the party last night, come up here, and killed herself. There was a disturbance—some guests got in a fight and had to be expelled from the quarter. No one noticed that Peony was gone. Her chambermates were entertaining clients in the guest rooms. The maids didn't like Peony—she was a mean girl and a sloppy worker—so when she didn't show up for her chores this morning, they didn't bother looking for her. Then the cook noticed blood leaking through the pantry ceiling.

We kept her just the way she was found because we thought you'd want to see."

The explanation sounded reasonable, yet a sense of wrongness nagged at Sano's mind when he recalled Peony serving the other courtesans, and the meeting at Governor Nagai's office. He walked around the corpse to the table. It held a mirror, comb, lamp, and a lacquer box containing a sheet of thin paper covered with inked characters.

"Her suicide letter," Ota said as Sano picked it up.

Sano noted that while the table and other articles all bore spatters of dried blood, the letter was clean. It read:

> I must die to pay for killing the man I loved. It was an accident, but I blame myself.
>
> During our love games, Spaen-*san* often brought out a gun he'd hidden in his room. He would lie on the bed, and I would mount him and point the gun at him while we coupled. We both enjoyed this. But last time, I got too excited. My finger pulled the trigger. The gun went off: boom! Spaen-*san* screamed. And through the smoke, I saw him lying dead, with a bloody hole in his chest.
>
> I was so scared I didn't know what to do. I took Spaen-*san*'s knife and tried to cut out the bullet, thinking I could bring him back to life. My hands shook so much that I stabbed his chest many times.
>
> I knew I would be punished if anyone found out what I'd done, so I decided to make it look as if he'd run away. I dressed him in his trousers. I hung his crucifix around his neck and wrapped his body in bedclothes. I dragged him outside, to the water gates. It was raining very hard, and no one was around. I unbarred the gates and pushed Spaen-*san* into the sea. I threw the knife and gun in after him. Then I ran back to his room. I washed myself, made up a clean bed, and pretended to be asleep until the guards came in the morning.
>
> May the spirit of my lover forgive me for what I have done. May we meet again in paradise, and spend all eternity together.
>
> Peony

"So I guess this ends our problems," *Yoriki* Ota said. "I'll have her body wrapped up to deliver to the Dutch captain. I'll tell the harbor patrol to arrange the ship's escort, and Chief Ohira to prepare for its landing."

Sano didn't answer. The scenario Peony described seemed as believable as the apparent circumstances of her death. He could close the case and mend Dutch-Japanese relations. He and Hirata could begin the inspection of Nagasaki and restore their former harmony.

But he couldn't overlook the obvious discrepancies he saw. With much regret, but no less resolve, he turned to *Yoriki* Ota and said, "Director Spaen's killer hasn't been caught yet."

Ota's eyebrows shot up. "But the whore confessed. She killed herself out of remorse. What more proof do you need?"

"When I met Peony yesterday," Sano said, "she poured tea and combed another courtesan's hair—using her right hand. Don't you think it odd that she would stab herself with her left hand?"

Ota shrugged. "So people do strange things when their minds are troubled."

"The divers haven't recovered a gun or knife from the waters off Deshima. And about this letter." Striding over to Ota, Sano held it before the *yoriki*'s face. "Very nice and neat; it accounts for all the evidence. But Peony was a peasant girl. I'd be surprised if she could write at all, let alone this well."

"So she had someone write it for her." Ota stood his ground, but his ruddy complexion darkened. "She had a miserable life. Uglier than a pig; bedding dirty foreigners. Minami, the clients, the other courtesans, and even the servants treated her like dung. Death probably seemed better than all that. Killing her lover pushed her over the edge. I've been in the police service for twenty years. Are you telling me I don't know my business?"

Sano faced the gruesome tableau. "What if she came up here last night not to commit suicide, but to meet someone? He came; they argued. He stabbed her." Sano turned to *Yoriki* Ota. "Then, before he left, he put the letter—free of blood, because he'd kept it inside his clothes—in the box."

Ota guffawed. "That's ridiculous. The knife came from the kitchen downstairs—the cook identified it. Minami says Peony stole things all the time, including the box. And who would want to kill that ugly whore?"

"Jan Spaen's murderer," Sano said. "Peony was on the island with Spaen the night he disappeared. She might have seen something." Sano recalled her sly reference to things happening on Deshima that weren't recorded. "If she knew who the killer is, he couldn't let her live to tell. If he shot me, he wouldn't have hesitated to silence Peony."

"Any idea who this person might be?" Ota asked disdainfully.

"The merchant Urabe," Sano said. "Peony is the only witness to his presence on the island. He's having financial troubles, and might have killed her to avoid blackmail." Remembering Urabe's explanation for Peony's grudge against him, Sano added, "He's also a client of this house. He could have attended the party last night and sneaked up to the women's quarters."

Then another, more ominous possibility loomed in Sano's mind. What if Peony had also possessed dangerous knowledge about some-one in Nagasaki's administration—Chief Ohira, another Deshima staff member, or even Governor Nagai himself? Had this person arranged a "suicide" for Sano's benefit? Unfortunately there were many men in the *bakufu* capable of murdering a helpless citizen for personal gain.

Sano didn't voice his suspicions to Ota, who might be an accom-plice, if not the killer. Instead he fervently hoped that his plan for tonight would lead to the truth, so he needn't launch an investigation of Nagasaki officialdom and court the political danger it would entail.

"What about the barbarians?" Ota said with an exaggerated sneer perhaps intended to hide worry. "Are you going to tell me they es-caped Deshima and killed the whore?"

"No," Sano said. "But there's at least one other suspect besides Urabe who was free to move about town, and might have wanted Peony dead."

18

HIGH IN THE hills above Nagasaki, evening rites had ended at the Chinese temple. In his austere room, Abbot Liu Yun knelt on the floor to meditate. The lamp's mellow, soothing light warmed the plaster walls. Once this had been Liu Yun's favorite time of day, when peace filled his soul and spiritual enlightenment seemed within reach. But his brother's death had destroyed his serenity, and his faith. The past had returned to haunt him.

Liu Yun began to chant, willing the ritual to calm him, but the ceaseless lament howled in his mind: *Hsi! My brother. Gone, forever!* As he stared at the wall, scenes from another time and place appeared there.

Spring, sixty-five years ago, on the Liu family's estate in Shantung Province. The scent of flowers drifted through the window of the study where Liu Yun and Liu Hsi, aged ten and eight, took their lessons. Old Teacher Wu fixed his shrewd gaze on Liu Hsi. "What are the five cardinal virtues of Confucius?"

"The five virtues are, uh . . ." Hsi gulped, then blurted, "What good is school, when I want to be a soldier?"

"Don't talk back to teacher!" Liu Yun exclaimed, mortified because he was the good son who wanted to please his elders. Also, he'd coached Hsi in his lessons, and his brother's failure reflected poorly on him.

Teacher Wu pummeled Hsi's head and shoulders with his cane. "You will apologize for your rudeness!"

As Hsi sobbed, a wild, contradictory impulse seized Liu Yun. He'd often tried to beat sense into Hsi, but couldn't bear for anyone else to hurt his brother. An invisible cord—stronger than love, hate, or blood—joined them. Liu Yun shot out of his seat and jumped on Teacher Wu's back, shouting, "Leave him alone!"

Teacher Wu screamed and whirled and struggled, trying to dislodge Liu Yun, while Hsi laughed and clapped his hands.

"What a good fighter you are, elder brother!" he cried. "Let's run away together and become soldiers!" And Liu Yun, though horrified at his own behavior, roared in triumph.

Their victory was short-lived. Teacher Wu resigned; Liu Yun's father beat both sons for driving away their tutor. Still, the early pattern held. Liu Yun would coach, beg, and punish Hsi, trying to mold him into the Confucian ideal of scholarship and filial piety. Hsi would resist. Liu Yun would defend his brother, and they would both suffer. . . .

Now Abbot Liu Yun acknowledged the impossibility of meditation and sleep. Tonight other matters besides grief troubled his mind. The shogun's detective was investigating Jan Spaen's murder. Liu Yun feared that his alibi and statements wouldn't withstand close scrutiny. Furthermore, he'd recently embarked on a venture that could bring him great satisfaction—or disaster. He longed to know which.

He carried the lamp to his study, a chamber lined with shelves of holy texts and documents concerning the temple's administration. From the cabinet he took a cylindrical lacquer container, incense, writing materials, and a book wrapped in black silk. He would consult the I Ching—the Oracle of Change, which revealed the secrets of the universe, used by Chinese philosophers, statesmen, warriors, and scientists for some four thousand years.

Liu Yun spread the silk on the table. Upon it he laid the Book of

Changes, the ancient text that interpreted the oracle's messages, and bowed to it three times. He ground the ink and readied paper and brush. He lit incense in a brass burner. While the fragrant smoke rose to the ceiling, he sat at the table, opened the lacquer container, poured out fifty long, thin yarrow sticks, then voiced his question to the oracle:

"Should I proceed with my planned venture?"

He performed the elaborate ritual of dividing, counting, discarding, and grouping the sticks until he had three piles. On the paper, he inked a broken line, which corresponded to the numbers of sticks in the piles. Then he repeated the process. His hands moved automatically; his thoughts drifted. Once again, memory carried him into the past.

He saw himself and his brother as young men—Hsi, tall and robust; Liu Yun the slight, refined scholar—walking together down a country road beneath golden autumn foliage, returning home from the provincial capital where they'd taken the civil service exams that would determine their futures.

"I don't care about failing those stupid exams." Scowling, Hsi kicked a rock.

"But what will you do?" Liu Yun said. "You'll never get a government position now."

Hsi flung down his pack of books and clothing and glared. "Elder brother, how many times must I tell you? I don't want to be a bureaucrat. Anyway, it's over. You passed your exams—you be the family success."

"Repeat the exams," Liu Yun pleaded. Since childhood, he'd dreamed of their getting posts in the same government office. "I'll tutor you. Your score will be higher next time. Please—"

Hsi grasped Liu Yun's shoulders. "Listen. A war is coming. When we were in the capital, I heard that the Manchus have already conquered Shensi and Honan Provinces. Eventually they'll invade Peking. I plan to join the emperor's army and save our kingdom from this foreign scourge." His childhood dream—of being a soldier—hadn't changed, either.

Liu Yun had dismissed the news as gross exaggeration. "The Ming emperors have ruled China for almost three hundred years. The northern tribesmen will never take Peking. Father will never let you join the army. Nor will I!"

Hsi shouldered his pack and stalked down the road; Liu Yun hurried to catch up. "No regime is invincible, elder brother," Hsi retorted. "That much history I've learned, even though I failed the exam." Then he halted in his tracks and pointed. "What's that?"

From over the hill drifted black smoke. The brothers broke into a run. They reached the family estate to find the house and outbuildings on fire. Through the wreckage galloped mounted Manchu troops, clad in leather and fur, long queues waving as they carried away loot and trampled fleeing servants.

"Father! Mother!" Liu Yun cried.

The old couple lay at their door, throats slashed. Sobbing, Liu Yun knelt beside his parents. Hsi launched himself at the nearest horseman, yelling, "You'll die for this!"

The Manchu soldier laughed and drew his sword. Aghast, Liu Yun hurried to his brother's rescue. "No!" he shouted, pulling Hsi out of the blade's path.

The soldier rode off with the family silver chest. Hsi struggled in Liu Yun's restraining grip. "We must avenge our parents' death!" he cried. "We must save our lands."

"Don't be foolish, younger brother. There are too many of them, and we have no weapons. We must flee!"

Liu Yun dragged the reluctant Hsi to the village to seek shelter—only to discover that the Ming army had arrived. In the marketplace, commanders drafted local men to help fight the invaders. Hsi broke away from Liu Yun, pushed his way to the head of the line of conscripts, and enlisted.

"Good-bye, elder brother," he called from astride the horse the army had given him. His eyes, filled with dreams of glory, shone brighter than the blade of his new sword. "We'll meet again when the war is over." Then he galloped after his new comrades, leaving Liu Yun standing alone with tears in his eyes and a raw emptiness in his soul.

Now Abbot Liu Yun completed another round of the I Ching ritual. He drew a line on the paper, above the first. Through the old pain burned a fresh anger. Hsi's death had taught him what their parents' had not: the consuming desire for vengeance, which no amount of prayer or meditation could banish. He wanted to kill everyone connected with the massacre of Hsi's rebel band on Taiwan. Though his Confucian beliefs forbade him to punish the Chinese government, he hated himself for submitting to Manchu rule and not defending Hsi. His impotent anger, seeking an external target, had focused on the Dutch, who had slaughtered Hsi and the other rebels to gain trade privileges with China; on Jan Spaen, the ruthless adventurer who had tortured Hsi to death.

As Liu Yun counted and arranged the sticks, he hoped he'd managed to conceal his emotions from the shogun's *sōsakan*. Surely he had, after a lifetime spent perfecting the art of negotiation and manipulation . . .

Penniless and homeless, the young Liu Yun had traveled to Peking, which remained peaceful, unchanged. The emperor still resided within the Forbidden City's great complex of lavish palaces surrounded by bloodred walls; merchants, scholars, entertainers, and outlaws still sought their fortunes in this center of commerce and culture. Forced to support himself by begging, Liu Yun almost died of cold and hunger that winter. Then, when his exam score finally reached Peking, the government awarded him a clerkship in the Bureau of Foreign Relations, where he exhibited a talent for languages and diplomacy and began his climb up the civil service ladder. Over the next nine years, he heard distressing news of Hsi. The Ming army was losing ground; the Manchus had taken Szechuan and Fukien Provinces. Famines and peasant uprisings plagued the country. Hsi got wounded, recovered, and became a general. He went missing; was presumed dead. Then one day his prediction came true.

Forty-six years ago, peasant rebels had attacked Peking. The weak, corrupt Ming government was powerless to resist. The emperor hanged himself. In desperation, the bureaucrats asked the Manchus to quell the rebellion, ceding the capital to them as a reward. Manchu troops entered the Forbidden City, cutting down peasants armed with

sticks. As Liu Yun and other Ming officials, now under Manchu domination, rescued documents from a burning building, Liu Yun looked
up at the sound of a familiar voice. His heart lurched.

Into the courtyard rode his brother, leading troops resplendent in
Ming army regalia. "Hsi!" Liu Yun cried as gladness filled his heart.
"You're alive!"

Then he watched in horror while Hsi's troops attacked the
Manchus. "Younger brother, what are you doing?"

Bloody sword still raised, Hsi turned on Liu Yun. The battle raged
around them. "I could ask you the same question, elder brother." Hsi's
stern face showed no joy at their reunion. "How can you serve those
who slew our parents and stole our land?"

"Younger brother, your war is over," Liu Yun said, stung by Hsi's
hostility. "The Manchus have won. The Ming rulers have lost the Mandate of Heaven to them. Surrender."

"Coward! Fool! You're not my brother anymore!" As more Manchu
soldiers stormed the courtyard, Hsi launched another offense, shouting orders to his troops.

Within days, the Manchus had slain the last peasant rebel. They occupied Peking, completing their conquest of China. Liu Yun and his
colleages transferred their allegiance to the new rulers. China's civil
service machine ground on. Liu Yun rose to the position of minister of
foreign relations. He married; fathered children. Later, with his wife
dead and his sons grown, he took religious vows and began his second
career as an overseas priest. He tried to forget the brother who had
spurned him, whom he never saw again after that meeting at the be-
sieged palace.

Still, Liu Yun had secretly followed his brother's desperate exploits:
the renegade army's victories at Amoy and Quemoy; the raid on
Chekiang; the defeat at Nanjing and flight to Taiwan. Finally he'd received news of Hsi's death.

Then, two years ago, fate had brought him and Jan Spaen together
in Japan, where Abbot Liu Yun had conceived his plan. He knew
about Spaen's greed and ambition; he knew Japanese who shared
these traits. He provided the juncture at which they would come to-

gether and he could achieve his revenge. Yet Spaen's murder had failed to satisfy him. The invisible cord still pulled, even though there was no brother at the opposite end, and nothing except his own death could reunite him with Hsi. Therefore, he'd decided to proceed with his plan; to reap more vengeance.

Now Abbot Liu Yun finished the ritual, inking the sixth and last line on the paper. He drew a sharp breath of dismay when he saw the completed pattern, the oracle's decision:

Hexagram number twenty-nine. K'an, the Perilous Chasm, which presaged evil for him should he pursue his current course of action.

With dread clutching his heart, Liu Yun opened the Book of Changes. The oracle spoke in oblique references and vague allusions; a hexagram must not be interpreted too literally. Each line contained shadings that might modify the decision. Liu Yun turned the pages and located the K'an hexagram.

"Danger lies ahead like an abyss filled with rushing water," he read. "Your desired result may never come to pass." Liu Yun's throat constricted as he imagined two years of painstaking work culminating in his own destruction. Then he found fragments of cautious optimism inserted amid more warnings. Hope kindled.

"Progress can be made if obstacles are encountered with an attitude of sincerity and a sharp mind. Patience is essential. Eventually order will be restored."

Abbot Liu Yun smiled as he closed the book. He was deadly sincere in his purpose. Years of scholarship, diplomatic service, and meditation had honed his mind. He'd waited this long, and could afford to bide his time. The shogun's *sōsakan* would not thwart him in his drive to avenge his brother's death, thereby restoring order to the universe and peace to his soul.

19

AFTER A FRUITLESS search for witnesses to Peony's murder, Sano returned home at twilight, walking his horse because his sore shoulder could no longer bear the constant jolts of riding. A glowing apricot of a sun spread soft, pink radiance upon a teal blue ocean rent with waves like slits in wrinkled silk. Over the city, a long violet cloud mass advanced westward, resembling a mounted army with banners waving: the legion of night. However, Sano couldn't afford the time to admire the beauty of this imperiled place. This was the end of the first day of the two that the Dutch captain had given him to solve Jan Spaen's murder. He needed more medicine and a fresh bandage for his wound, a bath, and a meal before testing his theory about Deshima.

As he entered his street, he performed an automatic security check—and saw the paunchy guard strolling behind him. Uneasily he wondered whether the man had followed him all day. He must be more careful of spies tonight.

"Hirata?" Sano called down the corridor of his mansion.

Old Carp came to meet him. "Young master is out," he said. When

Sano asked where Hirata had gone and when he'd be back, Old Carp replied, "He didn't say, *sōsakan-sama*."

It was just as well, Sano decided while he ate a hasty meal, bathed, had his wound attended to, and donned clean clothes. He wanted to know whether Hirata had broken Abbot Liu Yun's alibi for the night of Spaen's disappearance, and to assign him the task of checking on Liu Yun's and Urabe's whereabouts at the time of Peony's murder. But tonight he intended to discover the truth about the mysterious lights. He didn't need Hirata's interference.

As Sano started down the street toward the harbor, the skin on his back tingled. Someone was following him—someone more adept than the paunchy guard he'd easily spotted earlier. Sano returned to his mansion and found Old Carp in the kitchen. "I need your help," Sano said.

A short while later, he watched from an upstairs window while bearers set down a palanquin outside the gate. Old Carp, wearing Sano's cloak stamped with the Tokugawa crest, a spare set of swords, and a wide-brimmed hat that covered his face, climbed into the palanquin. The bearers carried it off toward the hills. A shadowy figure slipped out of an alley and followed. Sano smiled. He left the house and headed for the harbor.

ABOVE THE WATERFRONT, the moon shone softly white, its edges hazy in the moist air. Lamps burned in the harbor patrol station and on a barge on the water. Nightwatchmen paced by the warehouses, their wooden clappers punctuating the ocean's murmur with sharp clacks: All was well. Patrol officers strolled the promenade and docks. Soldiers drove oxcarts laden with cannon and ammunition for a possible battle against the Dutch ship. Sano avoided notice by staying in the shadows beneath the eaves of closed teahouses and shops as he worked his way down the promenade toward Deshima. Not knowing who might be involved in illicit activities there, he couldn't trust anyone.

A hundred paces from the guardhouse, he sprinted across the road. He darted between two warehouses and followed a dank passage to the water's edge, where a dock jutted into the harbor. It was the last one before Deshima, and gave an unobstructed view of the island's water gates. Sano looked around. Seeing no one, he tiptoed to the edge of the dock.

A rowboat was moored to a piling. It appeared empty, except for what looked to be an old blanket spread on the bottom. Sano lowered himself into the boat. His feet had just touched the blanket, when suddenly it shifted under him. He bit back a cry of surprise and shot backward onto the dock. Sword drawn, he leapt to his feet. In the boat, a human figure sat up and threw off the blanket. The moonlight caught the man's face. Sano's relief turned to anger.

"Hirata, what are you doing here?" he demanded in a loud, furious whisper.

The young retainer bowed, clutching a *jitte* in one hand. "*Gomen nasai*—forgive me for startling you," he whispered back. "I'm waiting to catch the mysterious lights."

"I told you to stay away from Deshima." Sano jammed his sword back into its sheath. "Now get out of that boat and go home."

"But *sōsakan-sama*—"

A sharp clacking silenced his protest. Sano turned and saw a light between the warehouses. Instantly he was off the dock and in the boat with Hirata, who threw the blanket over them. They lay tense in suffocating darkness while the dock creaked under the watchman's footsteps. Sano inhaled the blanket's musty odor and hoped the watchman wouldn't inspect the boat. He didn't want a scene that might chase away the mysterious lights and suspend the events they signaled, or his actions reported to the authorities.

The watchman's footsteps retreated. Sano sighed in relief, then emerged with Hirata from beneath the blanket.

"I'm not leaving you," Hirata whispered. "I found witnesses who saw Abbot Liu Yun near the harbor the night Director Spaen disappeared. The townspeople say he's a powerful sorcerer who performs magic in the marketplace during festivals. He could be the one who makes the lights. If he's the killer, you mustn't face him alone."

Sano felt a spring of gladness at having new evidence against Liu

Yun, who might also have murdered Peony and left the fake suicide note. Yet he couldn't allow Hirata's continued presence in Nagasaki, especially if his own suspicions about the lights proved true. "No arguments, Hirata-*san*," he said. "You leave for Edo tomor . . ."

His voice trailed off as, across the water, lights blinked purple, white, green.

"Get out of here, Hirata!" Sano rasped.

"No!"

The lights drifted toward Deshima, growing larger and brighter. Sano resigned himself to Hirata's company. To send him away now might attract the notice of the culprits—or provoke an attack by the archer who'd wounded Sano last night. The lights drew nearer to shore, smoke wafting from them. A breeze carried a harsh, burnt odor toward Sano. Now he saw a dark shape beneath the lights, and behind it, a wake that gleamed in the moonlight.

"A boat?" whispered Hirata.

They watched the lights draw up to the Deshima water gates. In the colored flashes, they saw the gates open and dark figures descend the steps to the water.

"The Dutch?" Hirata guessed.

"Or the guards." Sano noticed that the barge he'd seen earlier had vanished.

Then the lights went out. Darkness enfolded the island. Sano cursed. "Let's get over there."

He cut the boat's mooring lines. Hirata stood in the stern, lifted the oar, and began to row. The boat sped across the moon-dappled black water. The wind blew chill and moist, but anticipation warmed Sano. He knew with certainty that he was on the path to Jan Spaen's killer. Then the lights reappeared, flashing upon the water south of the island, moving out toward the harbor channel. Hirata matched their speed to the lights' rapid pace. The tall, black forms of anchored ships rose around them, decks unmanned while the foreign crews slept—or hid from the ghosts.

"Take us closer," Sano told Hirata, softly so his voice wouldn't carry across the water.

Panting, Hirata labored to reduce the distance between their boat and the lights. Sano peered ahead. Did he see a boat under the lights, with an oarsman in the stern and a passenger in the bow? Were they human? Sano shivered involuntarily as his disbelief in ghosts wavered and his faith in his theory weakened.

"Maybe it's Urabe," he whispered, telling Hirata about his interviews with the merchant and Kiyoshi, and his ideas about Peony's murder.

The harbor channel narrowed. They headed seaward between wooded bluffs that sloped up to terraced fields. The lights angled right.

"They're going ashore." Sano's excitement grew. "Speed up, we'll catch them there."

Hirata turned their boat, but the lights suddenly disappeared, as if extinguished by the night that lay heavily upon the landscape. Only the faint smell of smoke remained.

"Row along the coast," Sano ordered.

The coastline was irregular, convoluted. Sano and Hirata navigated around partially submerged rock formations and jutting spits of land. Above them, the woods loomed like a windswept, rustling black wall. Waves lapped the shore. Ears alert for any guiding sound, Sano strained his eyes against the darkness.

Nothing.

Then, reaching the point where they'd seen the lights vanish, they came upon a narrow cut in the coastline.

"The lights must have gone in there." Hirata propelled the boat into the channel. There the darkness was almost complete, with only the faintest moonlight penetrating the overhanging foliage. The boat scraped against the sheer rock walls that lined the channel. The splash of the oars echoed. Not knowing what to expect, Sano gripped his sword, preparing for a clash with ghosts or men, while his heart drummed a quickening rhythm of anticipation.

Now the channel curved sharply left and opened into a circular cove. Moonlight illuminated a steep, rock-strewn shore with woods above and the mouth of a cave in the center. From within the cave's recesses, a purple light shone.

Hirata guided the boat to the right of the cave. Sano stepped out and helped his retainer lift the vessel ashore. With Hirata close behind, he tiptoed to the cave's opening, sword drawn, and peered inside.

Stone walls and an arched ceiling, purple in the light's eerie, smoky glow, enclosed a short passage. The sea filled its bottom; narrow ledges ran just above the waterline. At the rear of the passage, the floor slanted upward to form a landing. There sat a boat; the light shone from some sort of fixture on a pole in its bow. Otherwise the cave was empty. The boatman had vanished.

They cautiously sheathed their swords. Motioning Hirata to follow, Sano entered the cave. He crept sideways along the ledge, clinging to the rough surface of the wall. They stepped onto the landing and over to the boat.

The vessel, perhaps fifteen paces long, was heaped with wooden crates. Sano examined the light fixture, a pyramidal metal lantern of strange design, with a door on each face. One door stood open; inside, a metal cup attached to the support pole held a substance that burned a brilliant, blinding purple and emitted black smoke. Sano turned a crank on the side of the lantern and, by a clever system of gears, belts, and levers, the other doors opened and closed in sequence. Through them he saw two more metal cups, which held residues of what he surmised had once burned green and white.

"The mysterious lights," he said, his voice echoing in the cave. A man-made device—fashioned by Abbot Liu Yun, or by the Dutch?

Hirata pried the lid off a crate inside the boat. "Look at this!"

Nestled in layers of cotton batting were ten mechanical clocks like the one in Governor Nagai's office. Sano and Hirata opened the other crates. These held muskets and pistols; ammunition; Chinese porcelainware; Persian silks; Christian crosses and rosaries; bundled spices that filled the cave with the sweet odors of cinnamon and nutmeg.

"Smugglers' loot," Sano said grimly. Just as he'd expected. Jan Spaen had plied his illicit trade in Japan as well as in the Spice Islands, and it had survived his death. "The lights kept everyone away from Deshima while the smugglers moved the goods out of the warehouse and over here." Dismay seeped like cold water into his heart. "For an operation of this magnitude to succeed, a lot of people must be involved—the barbarians to supply the loot and the Deshima staff to transfer it; a merchant like Urabe to sell it; the harbor patrol, police force, and Governor Nagai to look the other way. One of the smugglers must have shot me last night, to keep me from catching them."

Sano knew he must expose and disband the smuggling ring, among whom he suspected he would find Spaen's killer. But could he stay alive long enough to do it? Such powerful adversaries wouldn't hesitate to destroy even the shogun's emissary to protect themselves and their operation, which must earn them huge, untaxed profits.

"Where did the boatman go?" Hirata said. "If he came out of the cave and went up the beach to the woods, we would have seen or heard him—we weren't that far behind."

In a niche in the cave wall stood an oil lamp. Sano lit it from the lantern's purple light and walked toward the back of the cave. He halted abruptly, looking down. A dark substance stained the cave's floor. Sano knelt and saw streaks, as if someone had tried to scrub the floor clean, but the rock had absorbed the color. He sniffed the substance and detected a faint, metallic sourness.

"Blood," he said. "Director Spaen was shot and stabbed here. That's why there was no evidence of his murder on Deshima, and why the divers couldn't find the weapons."

Now the barbarians rejoined the array of suspects. If Spaen had come here, so might have Assistant Director deGraeff or Dr. Huygens. The smugglers' cache proved that they did, after all, have access to guns. Sano's spirit quailed as he saw the investigation circle right back to where he'd started. He would have to reinterrogate the Dutch later. When he rose to continue his examination of the cave, he saw that Hirata had vanished.

"Here, *sōsakan-sama*," Hirata called, emerging from a crevice hidden behind a protruding rock formation.

Sano held the lamp to the crevice and saw an ascending passageway.

The lamp's flame wavered in a cool draft. "A tunnel. The smugglers must use it to carry the loot away. They have a head start on us, but maybe we can still catch them."

But before he and Hirata could enter the tunnel, they heard sounds outside the mouth of the cave: the rustle and snap of tree branches, then footsteps clattering over the rocky shore.

20

SANO PUT DOWN the lamp and crept along the ledge to the cave's mouth, Hirata behind him. The footsteps outside drew closer. Now Sano could hear the intruder's harsh, rapid breaths. A hand groped at the wall of the cave; a sandaled toe probed for the ledge. When the intruder's leg came into view, Sano grabbed it and yanked hard.

With a startled cry, the intruder thudded to the ground outside the cave. Sano lunged out and threw himself on the intruder, who shrieked and flailed. In a tangle of thrashing limbs, they rolled over the rocks. Sano banged his head and caught a blow to his jaw. His opponent struck his wounded shoulder, and he gasped. But the man was smaller and lighter than he. Sano grabbed the man's right wrist before he could draw his sword and quickly pinned him to the ground, faceup in the moonlight. Surprise shot through Sano as he saw handsome, youthful features, distorted with terror.

"Kiyoshi?" he said. Was Chief Ohira's son a smuggler—or Jan Spaen's killer?

In the woods above them, branches crackled; voices rumbled. "More smugglers," Hirata said. "I'll catch them." He scaled the rocks and disappeared into the dark forest.

Kiyoshi struggled. Sano kept a knee planted on his stomach and his hands immobilized. "Who sent you? Who are you working for? What do you know about the smuggling?"

The boy's chest heaved with panicky breaths. "Please, let me go," he begged. "I have to stop—I have to warn—I mean, I don't know anything."

Sano thrust his weight against Kiyoshi. "Who killed Jan Spaen? Was it you?"

"No, no!"

Bright light swept over them, and the sound of running footsteps echoed in the night. Sano tensed; Kiyoshi moaned.

"There they are!" male voices shouted.

Down a path from the forest tramped a band of samurai. The four leaders held flaming torches; their helmets bore the Nagasaki harbor patrol insignia. Then came two *doshin* armed with *jitte*, accompanied by assistants who carried clubs, spears, and ropes. Last strode *Yoriki* Ota. Quickly they surrounded Sano and Kiyoshi.

"So. Kiyoshi. And *Sōsakan* Sano." Ota glared down at them, his face ruddy in the torchlight. To his men, he said, "Arrest them."

Dazed, Sano released Kiyoshi and stood, raising an arm to shield himself from the torches and weapons pointed at him. Kiyoshi curled up, hands over his face, weeping. "What's the meaning of this?" Sano demanded, pulling away from the *doshin* who grabbed him. "Why are you arresting me? What are the charges?"

"Smuggling foreign goods," Ota said. "Take their weapons and tie their hands," he told the *doshin*, then turned to the harbor patrol officers. "Search the cave."

Sano struggled against the *doshin* and assistants, but they overpowered him, stripping off his swords and binding his hands behind his back. "I'm not a smuggler," he protested in vehement outrage. "I followed the lights here from Deshima, and found the cave. I caught Kiyoshi outside. I've done nothing illegal!"

The other police had seized Kiyoshi, who offered no resistance. He sagged between two captors, head bent. The sound of his sobs filled the cove.

"The real smugglers must have run away when they heard me coming," Sano said. "If we hurry, perhaps we can catch them. Now let me go!"

From inside the cave, an officer called, "We found it, Ota-*san*."

The *yoriki* smirked at Sano. "How can you deny your guilt when we've caught you here, with the loot and your partner in crime?" He jerked his chin toward the weeping Kiyoshi, then grimaced in disgust. "Fighting over the profits. Shameful behavior for samurai!"

"I've already explained," Sano insisted furiously, as a knot of fear tightened in his stomach. Were these men the smugglers? Had they come to pick up the loot, realized their operation had been discovered, and decided to protect themselves by incriminating him? "Untie me at once!" he ordered. "Why are you here, anyway?"

Yoriki Ota said impatiently, "We received an anonymous message saying that smugglers were using this cave. So where's your assistant?"

Sano's heart clenched. *Hirata!* If only he'd obeyed orders, or Sano had sent him back to Edo. "I don't know," Sano lied. *Merciful gods, this was a setup, and what would happen to them?*

A *doshin* said, "Hirata got away from the man who was watching him this afternoon. I bet he's out here somewhere."

The harbor patrol officers emerged from the cave. "Bring out the loot," Ota ordered two of them. "The rest of you go and find the *sōsakan-sama*'s assistant." The officers climbed the rocks and headed into the woods, torches lighting the way. *Yoriki* Ota said to the *doshin*, "We'll take our prisoners to Governor Nagai."

"You're making a big mistake," Sano shouted with desperate bravado as the police hauled him away. "You'll pay for this!"

Yoriki Ota snickered. "We'll see about that."

THEY TRAVELED BACK to town in an oxcart that Sano guessed had been brought by the police to transport the smuggled goods. At Governor Nagai's mansion, guards locked Sano and Kiyoshi in separate chambers until, hours later, the summons came. The guards untied Sano's hands and escorted him into the audience hall, where Governor Nagai, dressed in formal black robes, occupied the dais. At either side of him, aides sat behind desks that held the brushes, paper, and seals used for recording official proceedings. In a row in front of the dais, at Governor Nagai's right, knelt *Yoriki* Ota, Interpreter Iishino, and Chief Ohira. Facing them were three samurai Sano didn't recognize. Lanterns cast a menacing ocher pall over the assembly's grave faces.

"What is this?" Sano demanded as the guards pushed him to his knees. Hearing a scuffle behind him, he turned and saw more guards drag a trembling, white-faced Kiyoshi into the room. They dumped the youth beside him. "What's going on?"

No one looked directly at him. Governor Nagai kept his eyes on his desk as he said, "We are here to review your transgressions against the law, including your attempt at smuggling."

So it was a trial, and for what other alleged offenses? "Someone did smuggle foreign goods from Deshima," Sano said, forcing himself to stay calm despite the alarm that compressed his lungs, "but it wasn't me. I've already explained to *Yoriki* Ota that I followed the flashing lights to the cove and found the boat."

Nagai's thick lips formed a brief, skeptical moue; his hooded eyes avoided Sano's. "Yes. Well. We shall see what your partner has to say. Kiyoshi?"

The youth slumped wretchedly, shoulders hunched to his ears, his face almost touching his knees. In a barely audible mutter, he said, "The *sōsakan-sama* came to the watchtower when I was on duty yesterday. He ordered me to steal goods from the Deshima warehouse and bring them to the water gates. He said he would kill me if I refused."

Aghast at this unexpected treachery, Sano leapt to his feet and grabbed the young samurai's collar. "That's a lie! Kiyoshi, you know I never did any such thing. Why—"

"Silence!" thundered Governor Nagai. The guards pulled Sano away from the boy and pushed him back onto the floor. "Continue, Kiyoshi."

"I told the Deshima guards that my father wanted them to stay away from the warehouse. I got the goods and carried them to the water gates." Kiyoshi's voice quavered; his tremors shook the floor. He did not look at Sano or the assembly. Chief Ohira's face was a rigid mask that concealed all emotion. The aides wrote diligently. "The *sōsakan-sama* ordered me to help him and his assistant load the goods into a boat." Kiyoshi seemed reluctant, but determined, to speak. "He made me row to the cove. When I tried to run away, he attacked me. Then the police came."

Sano couldn't believe what he was hearing. "I was trying to catch the smugglers. I thought Kiyoshi was one of them."

Ignoring Sano, Nagai addressed *Yoriki* Ota. "Has Hirata been found yet?"

"No, Honorable Governor."

"Send out the troops," Nagai told one of his aides. "He must be punished for his part in the crime."

The aide bowed and departed. "We've committed no crime!" Sano argued vehemently, more worried for Hirata's sake than his own. When the troops caught Hirata, they might kill him. After all Sano's efforts to protect the young retainer! "The smuggling has been going on since before we came to Nagasaki. Jan Spaen was killed in the cave. The boat we used to follow the lights is still on the—"

At last Nagai met his gaze. "Any more such outbursts can only make matters worse for you," he said coldly. To Kiyoshi, he said, "Because you were forced to break the law, I shan't punish your family for your crime, as would be the usual penalty for smuggling." Chief Ohira's eyes closed briefly; otherwise his expression didn't change, and he made no move to defend his son. "But you must pay for allowing yourself to be coerced. You shall be held in Nagasaki Jail until your execution."

Supported by two guards, the weeping youth stumbled from the hall. Comprehension fed Sano's anger. Kiyoshi was not evil, just very young and frightened. Surely he'd incriminated himself and Sano to protect someone else. But who? His father, Chief Ohira, his teacher, Interpreter Iishino, or his patron, Governor Nagai—the men to whom he owed his greatest duty and loyalty? Which of them had he wanted to "warn"? Sano studied the faces of the assembly; all remained closed, giving nothing away.

"Now we shall hear the testimony of the other witnesses," Governor Nagai said.

In turn, they spoke. "I followed the *sōsakan-sama* on his inquiries in town," said one of the strange samurai. "He interrogated the merchant Urabe and the courtesan Peony, as if he was looking to punish a Japanese for the barbarian's murder, instead of the Dutch."

"I followed the *sōsakan-sama* to Nagasaki Jail, where he had a private conversation with a prisoner, who converted him to Christianity," stated the next stranger.

The last stranger said, "I observed a meeting between the *sōsakan-sama* and Abbot Liu Yun. The *sōsakan-sama* offered Liu Yun money to import Chinese troops into Japan."

Sano grudgingly admired the agents' efficiency even as their lies condemned him. The paunchy guard had been a decoy, meant to distract him from the real spies. And he'd fallen for the trick. Such stupidity!

Yet the most damning testimony came from Interpreter Iishino and Chief Ohira. "I translated conversations between the *sōsakan-sama* and the Dutch ship captain," Iishino said. "The food sent aboard by the *sōsakan-sama* was payment for weapons he agreed to purchase from the barbarians, the barbarians." Iishino slid Sano a grin that was at once apologetic and sly. "And I listened outside the door during his private interview with Dr. Huygens. The *sōsakan-sama* proposed an alliance between himself and the Dutch. If they would help him become shogun, he would grant them unlimited trading privileges with Japan."

In a remote, toneless voice, Chief Ohira said, "I observed how the *sōsakan-sama* favors the Dutch. He treats them with unnecessary mercy and seems generally infatuated with them. I can assure you that I did my best to discourage such fraternization, but he defied my efforts."

"Now that we have heard the evidence against you, *Sōsakan* Sano," Governor Nagai said, "you may speak in your own defense, or confess to your crimes and commit *seppuku* to preserve your honor."

Sano emitted a harsh, humorless laugh. "I will not confess! The evidence is false. The witnesses have twisted everything I've said or done. This trial is a farce!"

Nagai shook his head gravely. "Your objections are duly noted. But the evidence—presented by trustworthy witnesses—supports my own judgment of your poor character and evil motives. You have chosen the way of the traitor over the way of the warrior. Therefore I charge you with six counts of treason: running a smuggling ring; using a murder investigation to persecute Japanese citizens; conspiring with Dr. Huygens to overthrow the government; giving the Dutch captain supplies in exchange for weapons; enlisting Chinese military support through Abbot Liu Yun; and practicing Christianity."

Treason! A samurai's ultimate disgrace; punishable by death. Horror sickened Sano. "The charges are ridiculous and totally unfounded. I've been framed. I'm innocent!"

Too late Sano realized how perilously his negative attitude, his fascination with the Dutch, and his desire for truth and justice had jeopardized his life and Hirata's. His actions had landed him in the power of Governor Nagai, Interpreter Iishino, and Chief Ohira. Sano was sure that one or all of them were involved in the smuggling, and had framed him to protect themselves from the consequences of his discovery. Perhaps this had all been planned in advance, with Chamberlain Yanagisawa's sanction. Again Sano had a sense of strange tensions among Nagasaki's bureaucrats. He recalled his suspicion that they didn't want Jan Spaen's murder case solved. Had they killed Peony and shot him?

"However, because of your rank," Nagai continued, "you can't be imprisoned, or tried and sentenced immediately. A special tribunal, composed of magistrates from three provinces, shall convene to hear your case. It will take approximately three days to gather them in Nagasaki."

Sano could guess the outcome of his trial. The magistrates, like the local authorities, were undoubtedly Chamberlain Yanagisawa's minions; he needn't expect fairness or leniency from them. He could already feel the weight of iron shackles around his wrists and ankles; he could see soldiers leading him to the execution ground, and hear the hiss of the sword that would sever his head. . . .

"I won't tolerate this charade!" he burst out.

"Yes. Well." Governor Nagai's heavy shoulders lifted in a shrug. "I regret to say that you have no choice. Also, I am relieving you of responsibility for the murder investigation."

"But I'm making progress on it," Sano protested. "If the Dutch captain doesn't receive the head of Jan Spaen's killer in two days, he'll attack Nagasaki. I must be allowed to—"

Nagai cut off the interruption: "That no longer concerns you, and the subject under discussion is your fate. Until the tribunal convenes, you will enjoy the temporary freedom due a man of your samurai status and high position under these circumstances. But do not misbehave, or try to leave town. We will be watching you."

As the guards escorted Sano from the hall, he turned for a last outraged glare at Nagai, Iishino, and Ohira. "You're not going to get away with this!"

The door slid shut on the three men who were now his enemies, and his prime suspects in the murder of Jan Spaen.

21

AT DAYBREAK, SANO, escorted by Governor Nagai's men, returned home to find troops stationed outside his mansion. More troops swarmed the corridors; in the reception room, the commander had lined up the frightened servants.

"Where is Hirata?" he barked at them. "Has he been here? Speak up, or die!"

A mixture of relief and concern filled Sano as he hurried to his chambers. Hirata was still free. But for how long, and would he survive?

Sano thought of what he might have done to avoid this catastrophe. He should have ended the investigation after Peony's confession and ignored the mysterious lights. He shouldn't have boarded the Dutch ship, or sought acquaintance with Dr. Huygens and Abbot Liu Yun. He should never have taken the job in the first place! Now he rued the inner compulsions that had inspired his rash actions. Yet there seemed nothing to be done except continue as he'd begun.

He grabbed the wooden pass that would admit him to Deshima. Fortunately he hadn't been carrying it at the time of his arrest. He hated to risk more treason charges by associating with the barbarians, but he saw only one way to exonerate himself and Hirata: He must defeat the enemies who had framed them. He must prove to the tribunal that his motives were proper and his investigation was legitimate by exposing the smugglers—the real traitors—and Director Spaen's killer. Only then would he regain his freedom and honor. Also, Sano felt responsible for averting the threat of war. Now he must reinterrogate the Deshima barbarians, who were once again murder suspects and surely involved in the smuggling.

"Master, master!" Old Carp rushed into the room. "Is it true that you and Hirata-*san* are accused of treason?"

"Falsely accused," Sano corrected. Tucking the pass inside his cloak, he said, "If Hirata contacts you, tell him . . ." To give himself up, and face execution? Resist arrest and die? Or run away to live as a fugitive outlaw? "Tell him to hide and pray."

Sano hurried to the kitchen for a quick meal of rice cakes and dried fish, washed down with water, to fill his empty stomach. Then he rode out the gate, hoping to evade any secret pursuers.

The sun's hazy scarlet disk rose over the city like a battle standard, pouring a sullen, ruddy glow over buildings, streets, and morning crowds. A warm, damp wind blew. The sea was opaque, colorless, and edged with whitecaps. Huge, dark storm clouds smudged the sky. At the Deshima guardhouse Sano presented his pass.

"This is no longer valid," the guard said.

"On whose orders?" Sano demanded.

"Governor Nagai's."

He should have expected the governor to revoke his access to the island, Sano thought bitterly. Nagai didn't want him to gather evidence against his accusers, or clear his name. Then an alternative plan occurred to Sano.

"When is Director Spaen's funeral?" he asked.

"This morning. At the hour of the snake."

According to custom, the Dutchmen would leave Deshima and accompany their dead comrade's body to the burial ground, offering Sano a chance to find out what Assistant Director deGraeff and Dr.

Huygens knew about the smuggling. For now, perhaps a talk with Chief Ohira would reveal the criminals' identities, enabling Sano to appease the Dutch captain before tomorrow's deadline, and prevent a war.

IN ADDITION TO his duties as commanding officer of Deshima, Chief Ohira was responsible for upholding law and order and resolving civil disputes in the street that led to the island's bridge. His mainland headquarters consisted of a shopfront beside the gate. Sano reached it just as rain began to pelt the city in windswept bursts, clattering on the tile roofs. Umbrellas sprouted; pedestrians took cover. Sano dismounted and left his horse beneath the building's deep eaves. Barred windows gridded the plaster walls; blue curtains printed with the Ohira family crest covered the doorway. Through it Sano followed two samurai, who dragged between them a peasant whose hands were tied behind his back.

The sparsely furnished office smelled damp from the rain. Flanked by two sergeants, Ohira knelt behind a desk on the dais before an assembly of townspeople. The two samurai dumped the captive peasant on the floor. Curious about the stoic man whose son awaited execution, Sano knelt to watch the proceedings, which evidently concerned minor crimes that fell under Ohira's jurisdiction.

"Who is this person, and what is his offense?" Chief Ohira asked the sergeants.

"Yohei, a servant on Deshima. He tried to enter the island without a pass."

Ohira frowned. "What have you to say for yourself, Yohei?"

The servant bowed. "Honorable Chief, I had my pass when I left home." He was a meek-looking man with dazed eyes. "But it was gone when I got to Deshima; I must have lost it along the way. If I'd known, I would have come straight to you and reported the pass missing. I never would have tried to enter the island, I swear."

Sano expected Ohira to let the servant off with a warning and send him to Governor Nagai's office for a replacement pass. But the chief's frown deepened. "Attempting to enter Deshima without a pass is a serious offense," he said sternly. "As a punishment, you shall spend the rest of the day chained to the gate; your shame and disgrace will deter would-be criminals. Dismissed."

"No, please, I beg you!"

The servant prostrated himself before the chief, whose unyielding expression didn't change. From the back room the sergeants fetched iron chains and shackles, fastened them around the servant's wrists and ankles, and dragged him outside. Sano wondered whether Ohira's personal troubles had occasioned his extreme punishment of an honest mistake. Was the chief venting his anger on the unfortunate servant—or might he actually approve of cruel justice, even for his son?

Chief Ohira turned to Sano, and his guard went up, as if an invisible suit of armor had suddenly grown on him. He said to his sergeants, "Clear the room, then see that no one disturbs myself and the *sōsakan-sama.*"

Unflinchingly he held Sano's gaze while the sergeants obeyed, then said, "I should have thought you'd be meditating on your wrongs, cleansing your spirit, and preparing to die like a proper samurai." Bitter antipathy roughened his tone. "What do you mean by coming here now?"

"What do you think?" Sano strode up to the dais, hot with fury at this man who had incriminated him.

Then a closer look at the chief unexpectedly awakened his pity and admiration. Ohira's ashen skin was so taut that Sano could see every brittle bone in his face. The shadows rimmed his eyes like bruises; his emaciated body seemed little more than a skeleton beneath the folds of clothing. Ohira must be mortally ill with grief for Kiyoshi; yet, like a true samurai, he continued to perform his duties. Sano spoke more politely than he'd intended.

"I want to know why you framed me for treason."

Ohira glared. "I can assure you I don't know what you're talking about," he said through clenched teeth. "Your accusation is ridiculous, though criminals often try to shift the blame for their misdeeds. What I fail to understand is how you could corrupt a decent, honorable youth like my son. When you arrived in Nagasaki, I knew you would be trouble. But I've underestimated your evilness."

Sudden doubt arose in Sano. Maybe Ohira wasn't part of the smuggling ring and had nothing to do with Spaen's murder, or Peony's. Maybe, truly believing that Sano was a villain who had destroyed Kiyoshi, he wanted revenge. Maybe Governor Nagai had simply exploited this desire in order to create more evidence against Sano. Now Sano changed tactics.

"I don't think Kiyoshi is guilty," he said. "By telling the truth, you may be able to save him."

Ohira rose and stepped off the dais. As he walked to the window, his wasted muscles quaked with the effort. "Of course Kiyoshi is guilty," Ohira said, turning his back on Sano to look outside.

In the rainy street, the servant stood chained to the gate, his head ducked in shame while a crowd jeered and threw horse dung at him. "Kiyoshi was caught in the act; he confessed," Ohira said. "He must endure his punishment: It's the law. No one can save him now."

Yet Sano detected a fissure of hope in his stony voice. "Are Governor Nagai and Interpreter Iishino involved in smuggling? Or are you and they following Chamberlain Yanagisawa's orders to ruin me?"

"Your accusations against Governor Nagai and Interpreter Iishino are slanderous." Ohira gazed steadily out the window. "And I'm not privy to the chamberlain's orders."

Outside, a band of ruffians set a dog upon the chained captive, whose pleas for mercy chimed plaintively between the animal's barks. Ohira silently watched the consequences of his actions.

"Which barbarian helped Spaen import goods illegally?" Sano asked. "DeGraeff?" Or Dr. Huygens, whispered his inner voice, which he ignored. "Who on your staff helped moved the goods off the island? Who piloted the lantern boat? Who killed Jan Spaen?"

Slowly Ohira turned. The opposing forces of honesty and fear warred on his face. Sano spoke quietly, nudging the balance to his own advantage. "Only the truth can salvage Kiyoshi's honor."

At the sound of his son's name, the indecision in Ohira's eyes froze to solid, impenetrable resolve. "You lost your authority in Nagasaki when you broke the law," he said coldly, "and I am under no obligation to answer to you." His mental armor shimmered almost visibly.

Sano's doubts about Ohira's guilt wavered. "You relaxed security on

Deshima," he accused. "You ordered the guards to remove goods from the warehouse, open the water gates, and let the lantern boat approach. The police and harbor patrol are your accomplices. The townspeople didn't interfere; they're afraid of the mysterious lights because of the ghost stories you spread. You let barbarians leave Deshima because they insisted on accompanying the goods and collecting payment from the customers."

The audacity of the scheme awoke fresh outrage in Sano. He suddenly remembered the overheard conversation between Governor Nagai and Ohira on his first day in Nagasaki, and the chief saying, "This never would have happened if . . ." Meaning "Spaen wouldn't have disappeared if you hadn't ordered the smuggling"? Was crime the basis for the alliance Sano had sensed within Nagasaki's administration?

"And then you incriminated me to save your own corrupt skins," he finished bitterly.

"You destroy my son, and now you dare insult my honor?" Ohira's eyes burned in their reddened sockets as he choked out the words. "I've devoted my life to upholding the law. I would never break it, and I'll tell you why.

"The summer I was ten, I had three best comrades. One day we formed a scheme to dive for pearls, then trade them to the Chinese merchants for fireworks. Even though this is illegal, there was little risk involved. Security is weak around the Chinese settlement, and deals are often made over the walls.

"As it happened, my grandmother died and I couldn't leave home, so my friends went without me." Memory darkened Ohira's face. "One drowned while diving for the pearls. The other two, who were brothers, sold the pearls to the Chinese. The next night they burned to death when their house caught fire. Only I, who had no part in the scheme, was spared. I took this as a sign from the gods that it should thereafter be my vocation to obey the law and deter others from doing wrong. And I can assure you that I've fulfilled my vocation. Anyone who says otherwise will pay in blood!"

He reached for his sword. Sano grabbed Ohira's hand before the chief could unsheathe the blade. The conviction in Ohira's voice made him wonder again whether Ohira might be innocent. The chief was strict with his staff, his civilian subjects, and the Dutch. Sano knew that clever subordinates often worked illicit schemes right before an unsuspecting superior's eyes. Still, he didn't believe that Ohira, who seemed able and intelligent, could have been totally unaware of what was happening on Deshima.

Sano tightened his grip on Ohira. The chief's bony, feverish fingers possessed a determination that compensated for physical weakness. Locked together, their hands shuddered on the hilt of the sword.

"Where were you when Jan Spaen disappeared?" Sano demanded.

Ohira strained to pull the sword free. "Let go, and fight like a samurai!"

Sano grabbed Ohira's other hand before it could reach his short sword. "Did Peony see something that made her dangerous to you?" He shoved the chief against the wall, savoring the release of anger. He was sick of his countrymen's treachery, which made them no better than the barbarians they despised and with whom they had conspired. "Did you kill her?"

"Peony committed suicide." As Ohira struggled, his breath exuded the sour reek of illness. "And I never go near that disgusting pleasure quarter."

"Did you order the Deshima guards to shoot me? Where were you last night?"

"Traitor! Coward! Are you afraid to fight without your foreign allies to help you?"

Goaded by the worst insults anyone could inflict upon a samurai, Sano felt combat lust assail him like a typhoon. He wanted to draw his sword and do battle. Then he saw the sick, gloating triumph in Ohira's eyes: The chief wouldn't mind dying in a duel, ending his misery. However, killing one of his accusers would land Sano in jail for murder, depriving him of the chance to exonerate himself and Hirata, to serve truth and justice.

Sano tore the swords from Ohira's waist. He threw them across the room, and the chief to the floor. "Answer me!" he shouted while he fought his anger. One more day until the Dutch captain's deadline; two more days of freedom. Could he keep temper from overcoming wisdom for that long?

Ohira fell with a crash that must have hurt, but when he rose, his icy dignity betrayed no pain and acknowledged no defeat. "I was in my office on Deshima on the occasions you mention, surrounded by my staff. And I can assure you I gave no orders to shoot you."

Just then the curtains parted. In walked the Deshima second watch commander. "Honorable Chief," Nirin said, "we must talk." He did not appear to notice that his superior wasn't alone; the room was dim, and Ohira stood between Sano and the door. "What happened last night changes everything, and I need new orders about—"

"Can't you see I'm busy?" Ohira snapped. "Get out!"

Nirin glanced at Sano and frowned, then said, "Sorry to interrupt, but this can't wait. We have to tighten Deshima security at night to prevent future thefts. I need your permission to assign more troops to the warehouses." He touched his sword. "Is the *sōsakan-sama* giving you trouble?"

"I was just leaving," Sano told them.

As he walked out the door, a sense of vindication energized him. The second watch commander had dissembled quickly, but Sano guessed that what he'd really meant to ask Chief Ohira was how they would continue smuggling now that their operation had been exposed.

Then despair eclipsed Sano's elation. He mounted his horse and stared at the rain.

Even if Ohira was guilty of treason as Sano now believed—and possibly of murder, too—he would never confess, because it wouldn't save Kiyoshi. The law demanded that a criminal's entire family share his punishment for these serious offenses. Should Ohira admit his crimes, he would condemn himself, Kiyoshi, his wife, and five other children to death. Without hard evidence, Sano would never break Chief Ohira.

Therefore, he must try to break the other Japanese suspects—or the Dutchmen.

22

FROM THE HOUSE on Deshima where Jan Spaen's body had lain since its recovery from the sea, guards brought out the plain wooden coffin draped with black cloth and set it in the street. Across the bridge milled gawkers waiting to see the barbarians' funeral procession, and the officials who attended all diplomatic functions. The rain had diminished to a drizzle. A holiday atmosphere belied the solemnity of the occasion.

Dutch East India Company Assistant Director Maarten deGraeff watched the scene from the roof of his residence, where he went whenever he couldn't bear the prison of his rooms. For years he'd longed for Jan Spaen's death, yet the murder of his partner had not freed him as he'd hoped, but only multiplied his troubles. He should have known he could never escape the evil inside his soul, though he'd tried since his nineteenth year, when he'd joined the company.

He'd left the Netherlands, abandoning his parents, university studies, and a future career in the church not for money or adventure, but because of his crimes: the profane desire that prayer could not banish; sordid encounters with sailors in Amsterdam's alleys; and an affair with a fellow student that had ended when the other youth, torn by guilt, hanged himself in their dormitory. If his true nature was ever exposed, deGraeff wanted to be far away, so his family needn't witness the disgrace of a son executed for the sin of forbidden love.

Now a bitter laugh caught in deGraeff's throat. What had he achieved by his self-imposed exile? Here he was, half a world away, still a sinner, and a murder suspect besides.

A noise from below interrupted his glum reverie. Someone was ascending the ladder from the balcony to the roof. Then Dr. Nicolaes Huygens's worried face appeared over the eaves. "May I join you?" he said.

DeGraeff groaned inwardly as the stout doctor sat beside him. Since Spaen's death, he'd avoided Huygens. But they needed to talk.

Panting, Dr. Huygens took a handkerchief from his pocket, wiped his sweaty brow, then folded the cloth with meticulous care before putting it away. He clasped and unclasped his plump hands. "It's almost time for the funeral," he said at last. "Aren't you coming?"

His hesitancy indicated that this wasn't what he'd come to say, but deGraeff, preoccupied with his own concerns, didn't care. "Nicolaes," he said, "please, I beg you not to tell anyone what I've done."

He should have realized that he couldn't keep a secret on this tiny island. At first he'd used male whores dressed as women to hide their true gender from his comrades. Then he'd begun a foolish liaison with a junior interpreter. Huygens had accidentally walked in on them. Jan Spaen, who had learned of his sins years ago, was gone. Now deGraeff's fate lay in the hands of Dr. Huygens. He waited in cold terror as the doctor turned to him.

"You and Spaen were partners for a long time," Huygens said, as if he hadn't heard deGraeff's plea. "He probably confided in you."

"What?" deGraeff said in confusion. "Nicolaes—"

Blushing a deeper red, Dr. Huygens spoke urgently, eyes searching deGraeff's face. "Did he tell you things about—about the rest of us?"

Comprehension elated deGraeff. Spaen must have possessed compromising information about Dr. Huygens, too. DeGraeff had no idea what this could be; Spaen had hoarded knowledge and the power it conferred. Yet deGraeff saw that his salvation depended on hiding his ignorance from Huygens.

"Yes, Jan did talk," deGraeff said, striving for nonchalance, stalling for time.

Huygens's body seemed to shrink with defeat. In a strained voice he said, "So you know about me."

DeGraeff merely raised an eyebrow. He had an advantage now, and he intended to use it.

"If you turn me in to Investigator Sano or the Dutch authorities, I'll tell them what I know about you," blurted Huygens, desperation evident in his feverish eyes, the reek of his sweat. "And I'll tell them I heard you and Spaen arguing before he died, too. You wanted to leave the company, go home, and enter a monastery. But Spaen couldn't manage without you. So he threatened to report your sin if you quit. You would be tied up and thrown in the sea to drown. That's why you wanted Spaen dead—not for his share of the money you made together, but because he could destroy you. You hated Spaen and wanted to be rid of him."

Oh, how deGraeff had! Because Jan Spaen had not only held him captive through blackmail, but also destroyed his hope of redemption.

Upon joining the East India Company, deGraeff had planned to forsake his sordid life and purify himself through work, hardship, and prayer. At first it seemed he would succeed, though his job presented myriad dangers: long ocean journeys that provoked forbidden intimacies among the all-male ship crews; foreign ports where heathens pandered to every sexual perversion. By avoiding contact with other men, deGraeff had resisted temptation. Scurvy, tropical fevers, and other illnesses suffered by overseas travelers reduced his desire. For fifteen years he remained celibate, while discovering in himself a talent for trade. He rose from clerk to secretary, and finally attained a position as functionary in Batavia, the Dutch stronghold on the Java coast. He decided to work a few more years, save some money, and return home to his religious studies.

His dreams had died the night he delivered his life into Jan Spaen's hands.

Now memory transported deGraeff back to that time, four years after he'd arrived in Batavia. He could see his small, sparsely furnished room, and feel the terrible moist heat that weakened the body and mind. Sleepless and lonely, he'd left the trade compound to walk the streets of town.

Batavia's exotic glamor enchanted deGraeff. Along the canals, parties enlivened the balconies of the houses and lanterns shimmered upon the water. Dutch men and women strolled the lanes and bridges; Asian merchants, sailors, and laborers jammed the drinking houses and gambling dens. A blend of languages rose above music from Dutch mandolins, Chinese flutes, Indonesian drums and cymbals.

"Sir! You seek pleasure? Come in, come in!" Outside a row of tumbledown buildings in the native sector stood a smiling young Javanese man who beckoned deGraeff into a room where naked native girls paraded before a crowd of men. "I sell you beautiful woman, good price."

"No, thank you." DeGraeff walked away, but the procurer followed.

"You no like woman, sir? Then come with me—I give you what you want."

Every sane, pure instinct demanded deGraeff's refusal. His soul was at stake. The threat of exposure loomed large in this small colony where everyone knew everyone else's business. Yet deGraeff's need for physical release and human companionship outweighed his yearning for salvation. The roar of his own blood drowned out the voice of caution. He followed the procurer through dark, fetid alleys, over rank canals, to the river. The tropical night pulsed with insect songs and smelled of jungle flowers. A moon like a huge gold florin lit the footpath down which the procurer led deGraeff, past moored boats with bamboo roofs and ragged curtains sheltering the long hulls. Aboard a few, lamps flickered. The procurer stopped beside one of these.

"Here, sir," he said, parting the curtains.

Upon heaped cushions inside sat a beautiful native youth with sleek, dark skin, sculpted muscles, and lustrous eyes. A loincloth covered his sex.

DeGraeff's breath caught. *May the Lord have mercy on my soul . . .* "How much?" he asked hoarsely.

A short while later, deGraeff emerged from the boat, more shamed than satisfied. There was no hope for his soul; he was damned. Then he saw, standing on the footpath nearby, the figure of a Dutchman, his broad-brimmed hat clearly outlined by the moonlight. The glow from his tobacco pipe illuminated the handsome features and golden hair of Jan Spaen. He must have been at the brothel, heard the procurer proposition deGraeff, and followed them here. Horror paralyzed de-Graeff. He imagined strong hands forcing him into a hemp sack; heard his own screams as the sea enveloped him. Then Spaen nodded and sauntered away.

DeGraeff spent the next days waiting in terror for the police to arrest him. Then Spaen came. "I hear you're one of the best men in the business," he said. "I need a partner. I've already spoken to your superiors, and they've agreed to assign you to me. You'll get the same salary for your regular duties—and a percentage of whatever we make on the side. I guarantee you'll find it worth your while."

He never mentioned what he'd seen, but his knowing smile brooked no refusal. Thus deGraeff had accompanied Spaen through the jungles in search of new spice supplies, to India and China to purchase silks for the European trade. While Spaen's daring and charm had opened new markets and secured lucrative deals, deGraeff's financial acumen had built their profits into a fortune. Yet deGraeff found the partnership unbearable. He abhorred Spaen's drinking, gambling, sexual excesses, and combative nature; he was nearly killed during Spaen's raid on Taiwan. And Spaen encouraged his vices, procuring men for him wherever they went. "I always reward good performance," he would declare.

DeGraeff, having once yielded to sexual hunger, couldn't withstand the constant temptation. Thus Spaen bound him tighter even as his desire for freedom increased. In Japan, deGraeff had told Spaen they were through. They'd had the argument Dr. Huygens had overheard. Now, though the extent of Huygens's knowledge unsettled deGraeff, the doctor was a much weaker adversary than Spaen.

"You hated and feared Spaen, too," deGraeff replied to Huygens's clumsy attempt at blackmail. "If I had a motive for murder, then so did you. You hold a threat over my head, but it's no worse than the one I hold over yours."

How completely he'd misjudged the doctor, who had always seemed a paragon of stolid, bourgeois virtue! Whatever Huygens had done, it must be bad, for him to worry so. "As far as the Japanese authorities are concerned, either of us could be a smuggler," deGraeff continued, though he knew that his history as Spaen's private trade partner counted heavily against him. "We had equal access to the goods. Oh, but you're the one who speaks the native tongue, aren't you?"

Huygens buried his face in his hands and uttered a mournful curse: "*Verdomme!*"

DeGraeff smiled. "So it seems that we must unite for our mutual protection," he said. "If you keep my secrets, I'll keep yours." And not only the ones under discussion, but also their whereabouts last night and when Spaen had disappeared—and what deGraeff planned to do before they sailed. "If we both stand firm, no one can ever lay the blame for Spaen's murder on either of us. We'll be safe."

The doctor looked up, nodding eagerly in pitiful relief and gratitude. "Yes, yes. That's what we'll do." He clasped deGraeff's hands in his hot, sweaty ones. "Thank you, Maarten."

In the street, guards surrounded the three other Dutchmen, who had returned from their trip this morning. Interpreter Iishino waved, calling, "Assistant Director deGraeff! Dr. Huygens! Time for Director Spaen's funeral."

DeGraeff stood up and headed for the ladder. "And I thank you, Nicolaes."

His soul might be damned to burn in hell for all eternity, but with luck neither the Japanese nor the Dutch authorities would punish him for Spaen's murder or any other crimes. The danger would soon be over; he would return to the Netherlands a wealthy, free man.

He wondered what Huygens's guilty secret was, and whether the good doctor was capable of murder.

23

JAN SPAEN'S FUNERAL procession ascended the steep streets of Nagasaki toward the Dutch burial ground in the hills. Sano, dressed in his ceremonial garb of white under-robe, black silk kimono, trousers, and surcoat, with black cloth covering his swords as a gesture of respect for the dead, rode near the end. Mounted troops cleared a path through the crowd that had come to see the barbarians. Spectators trailed the procession and jammed balconies or rooftops along the route, cheering. Refreshment vendors did a brisk trade, but ordinary business had halted. The drizzle continued, yet no one sought cover.

"Get back!" shouted the footsoldiers who ran alongside the procession, pushing away gawkers who got too close. "Anyone who touches or speaks to the barbarians will die!"

In contrast to all this fanfare, the funeral party itself seemed insignificant, lacking the splendor of a Japanese ritual. There were no flowers; no lantern bearers; no priests, chants, incense, bells, or drums; no white-robed mourners. Six Deshima servants, wearing everyday kimonos, carried the black-draped coffin. Behind it walked Assistant Director deGraeff, Dr. Huygens, and the three other Dutchmen, who had returned from paying homage to the Kyūshū daimyo, all dressed in somber black. Chief Ohira, Interpreter Iishino, Nirin, and twenty guards followed, also clad in ordinary garb. Just ahead of Sano rode *Yoriki* Ota and other Nagasaki officials. After them trailed four peasants carrying ropes and shovels.

Sano knew that the anti-Christianity laws forbade the Dutch to practice their customary death rites. For the first time he pitied Jan Spaen, dying in a foreign land, his funeral a public spectacle for curious strangers. However, Sano's thoughts soon drifted from Director Spaen as he covertly scanned the crowds. Upon going home to dress for the funeral, he'd learned that Old Carp had received no word from Hirata. He'd seen troops searching buildings and questioning residents and pedestrians, but no sightings had been reported. Sano hoped Hirata would lie low until the charges against them were dropped, yet he knew the odds against that. He kept imagining he saw Hirata's face among the horde.

At last the procession reached the burial ground. Tall cedars bordered the grassy, windswept plateau where rows of wooden stakes marked barbarian graves. The funeral party grouped around these, with troops keeping away the gawkers. Chief Ohira avoided Sano's gaze, while Nirin stared insolently. But Sano wasn't concerned with these suspects at the moment. Dismounting, he started toward the barbarians.

"Sorry, you can't go over there."

Guards stepped between Sano and the Dutchmen, forcing him back. Sano despaired of ever speaking to the Dutch suspects again. Yet perhaps this trip would still prove to be valuable. He took a place next to a grinning, nervous Interpreter Iishino.

Chief Ohira announced, "We are gathered here to bury the earthly remains of Trade Director Jan Spaen." He nodded to the gravediggers, who began shoveling a hole in a bare patch of ground. The bearers set the coffin nearby. "Director Spaen's comrades will pay their last respects." Frowning at the Dutchmen, he added, "Any references to Christianity will result in a severe reduction of trade privileges."

Interpreter Iishino darted over to the grave, obviously eager to get away from Sano. He translated Ohira's words, beckoning to the Dutch. The barbarians stood beside the coffin, heads bowed, hats in their hands. DeGraeff spoke first. The clink of shovels, the rustling of the trees, and the horses' stomps accompanied his expressionless monologue.

"Jan Spaen was a brave, talented trader," Iishino translated, hunching his shoulders against the damp wind—or Sano's scrutiny? "He opened new markets and generated high profits for the East India Company. He was my partner for ten years, and I very much regret his passing."

Sano paid minimal attention to the rest of this positive eulogy from a murder suspect who wouldn't want to air his grievances against the deceased. He studied Iishino, trying with difficulty to imagine him as a murderer. Had this buffoon shot Jan Spaen? If the mere sight of Spaen's corpse had shocked the jitters out of him, how could he have stabbed Peony?

Yet perhaps Iishino's reaction to the corpse had been caused by fear of betraying guilt. He had access to Deshima's warehouses. He had the language skills necessary for colluding with the Dutch. He'd seemed worried when Sano asked why Director Spaen had been updating the account books so long after the official sale of Dutch goods, maybe because he knew Spaen had recorded the smuggling transactions and didn't want Sano to find out. And Iishino was the person most responsible for creating false evidence of Sano's wrongful behavior toward the Dutch. Sano's dislike for the interpreter deepened into loathing.

Iishino finished translating the assistant director's recitation. Then it was Dr. Huygens's turn to speak.

For a long time, the doctor remained silent, head bowed over the coffin. Drizzle misted the air. Dirt flew from the hole where the gravediggers worked chest deep. Then Huygens spoke two short phrases.

"May all our sins be forgiven. Rest in peace," Iishino echoed.

The doctor's ambiguous words seemed to imply that he himself was guilty of some offense. Distracted from his speculations about Interpreter Iishino, Sano again feared he'd trusted Huygens too quickly. Had he ignored clues during their meeting? Could the doctor have murdered Spaen?

The other Dutchmen spoke their pieces. The gravediggers placed ropes under the coffin and lowered it into the hole. Each barbarian cast a handful of dirt onto the coffin. Then the diggers shoveled earth into the grave. Sano's skin crawled at the thought of the corpse slowly rotting underground. How much cleaner and more final was the Buddhist custom of cremation. But Sano had no time to ponder the differences between Japanese and Dutch funerary rites, or Dr. Huygens's possible guilt. Interpreter Iishino was edging toward the road leading down the hill.

Sano cut through the circle of troops, pushed past spectators, and hurried after Iishino. The interpreter ran down the road, shoulders hunched, sandals flapping. Sano caught up with him, seized his arm, and swung him around.

"Not so fast, Iishino," he said.

Grinning, Iishino shrugged. He let out a high, nervous titter, and said, "Excuse me, *sōsakan-sama*, excuse me." When none of these ploys broke Sano's hold on him, he whimpered.

"Why did you tell those lies about me?" Contempt roughened Sano's tone. He flung Iishino up against a tree. "I never asked the Dutch captain for weapons, or conspired with Dr. Huygens to overthrow the government, and you know it." When Iishino cringed and trembled, Sano shouted, "Speak up! I want an answer, now. Why did you lie?"

Surprisingly, the interpreter's toothy grin reappeared. "I didn't lie, *sōsakan-sama*, I didn't lie," he said. "I only told my version of the truth, which is different from yours. The tribunal will decide which version to believe."

Of all the incredible nerve! "There's no one here but you and me, so you might as well drop the act," Sano said, locking a hand over Iishino's throat and pinning him to the tree. "You're going to explain why you lied. Then we're going to Governor Nagai so you can retract your statement."

Iishino kicked, thrashed, and managed to choke out, "My statement has already been entered into the official record. I couldn't retract it even if I wanted to. And if you kill me, it will only convince the tribunal of your guilt."

Much as Sano hated to admit it, the interpreter was probably right on the first point as well as the second: If Governor Nagai and Chamberlain Yanagisawa intended to destroy him, they wouldn't let Iishino change his statement. Reluctantly Sano released the interpreter, who collapsed to the ground with a moan of relief.

"Where were you the night Jan Spaen disappeared?" Sano demanded.

Clambering to his feet, Iishino made an exaggerated show of wiping mud from his garments, avoiding Sano's gaze. "I went to the governor's mansion in the afternoon to translate some Dutch documents. By the time I finished, it was so late that the city gates were closed, and I couldn't go home. I slept in the office, and didn't know the barbarian was missing until I reported for work on Deshima."

Sano thought that Iishino must be confident that the governor's staff would confirm his story, either because he really had been there, or because they had orders to protect him. "What about the night before last?" Sano asked, curious to see what alibi Iishino would present for Peony's murder and the attack on himself.

"I was at home with my wife." Iishino beamed. "She is Governor Nagai's niece."

And the unimpeachable source of another unbreakable alibi. "And last night? Were you on Deshima?"

Iishino sidled up the road. "I should go back to the funeral," he said. "My services might be needed. Of course I was not on Deshima last night. The junior interpreters cover the late shift. I was at home until the governor's messenger summoned me to your hearing."

"I'm not through with you yet," Sano said, blocking Iishino's path. "What was your relationship with Jan Spaen?"

Iishino tried to step around Sano, failed, then grimaced in resignation. "I know you're thinking maybe I killed the barbarian, *sōsakan-sama*. But I didn't. I liked Spaen the way I do all the Dutch—they're my friends." At Sano's surprised look, he amended hastily, "Oh, not in any improper way; I never favor barbarians. But I enjoy being with them. You see, they have no choice but to accept my company. They have to listen to me and talk to me. They can't run away when they see me coming, or brush me off the way other people do."

He sighed, and his face took on a mournful cast. "All my life I've had difficulty making friends. When I was young, the other boys at the temple school shunned me and played cruel jokes on me. One night they carried my bed outside while I was sleeping and put it beside the river. When I got up, I fell in the water and almost drowned. Learning the Dutch language was my salvation, my salvation. If not for the barbarians, I would be a very lonely man. And Jan Spaen was nice to me. He told me about his adventures. He followed my advice when I taught him how to behave in this country. I would never have done anything to hurt him."

Hearing the pained sincerity in Iishino's voice, Sano felt an unexpected rush of pity for the interpreter. He hadn't realized how much Iishino minded being disliked; some obnoxious men were unaware of the antipathy they inspired, or indifferent to it. How sad that a Japanese should turn to foreigners for friendship because his countrymen shunned him.

"You might be more popular if you stopped being so bossy and critical," Sano suggested.

The interpreter's wide eyes blinked in surprise. "But it's my duty to correct people when they're doing something wrong," he said with self-righteous pomp. His head bobbed emphatically. "If they don't appreciate my advice, it's because they're too sensitive or proud to benefit from my superior wisdom."

"Maybe you shouldn't always assume that your wisdom is superior," Sano said, though he saw the futility of trying to change Iishino's attitude. The interpreter seemed destined to remain friendless. "You can't be right all the time."

"I beg to differ—at least in your case, *sōsakan-sama*." Iishino grinned smugly. "Because you should have heeded my warning against getting too close to the barbarians. Maybe then you wouldn't be in all this trouble."

He dodged around Sano and scurried up the hill toward the burial ground. As Sano watched him go, he glimpsed other possible motives for Iishino's actions. Did the interpreter so greatly resent the universal rejection of his advice and friendship that he'd taken revenge on Sano, a convenient target? Were both Iishino and Ohira pawns of Governor Nagai and Chamberlain Yanagisawa?

Or was Iishino a criminal, trying to hide his guilt by destroying a man who might expose and destroy him?

Sano retrieved his horse and started down the road toward town. It was afternoon now; Kiyoshi would have had plenty of time to reflect on his dire situation. Perhaps he was ready to tell the truth about why he'd been in the cove last night, and supply answers that the suspects had not.

24

"YOU CAN SEE Kiyoshi if you want, but don't expect him to talk," said the warden, leading Sano through Nagasaki Jail. "He hasn't spoken a word to anyone since he arrived."

In the prison's dim corridors, ironclad doors studded dingy plaster walls. From behind these issued the wails of inmates, most of whom were convicted criminals awaiting execution. The air reeked of excrement, rotten food, and sickness. Patrolling jailers banged on the doors, ordering the inmates to shut up and behave. Sano tried not to picture himself and Hirata as prisoners. He would clear their names, and Kiyoshi was going to help him.

"He's in here," the warden said, unbarring a door. "Just call when you're done, and I'll come let you out."

Sano entered the cell; the warden secured the door behind him. Except for a wastebucket in one corner, the room was unfurnished. Rain streaked past the single window at ceiling level and dashed the tile roof. A tray of rice and pickles sat beside Kiyoshi, who knelt in the middle of the dirty floor. Stripped of his swords and shoes, he wore a ragged muslin kimono and didn't react when Sano spoke his name.

Sano squatted across from the youth, shivering in his wet garments and the unpleasant chill exuded by the prison walls.

"Kiyoshi?" Sano repeated. "Can you hear me?"

The boy's face seemed made of ivory, the handsome features sharp, pale, and devoid of animation. A split lip and bruised cheekbone added touches of livid color. His eyes focused inward; his hands lay motionless, palms down, upon his thighs. Yet Sano perceived an aura of agony radiating from Kiyoshi. All thought of using verbal or physical aggression to force the truth out of him fled Sano in a rush of sympathy. The boy's lies had incriminated Sano, but also condemned himself to a disgraceful death.

"How are you feeling, Kiyoshi?" Sano asked quietly. "Are the jailers treating you well?"

No answer. The youth's expression registered no sign that he even knew anyone was in the room with him. Sano, seeking a way to reach him, turned to the tray of food.

"It doesn't look as if you've eaten," he said. "Would you like to now?"

Then, seeing the condition of the food, he grimaced in disgust. The rice was burnt, the radish pickles moldy. A stale, sour smell arose from the mess.

"Warden!" Sano shouted. The man opened the door so fast that Sano guessed he'd been eavesdropping outside. "Take this garbage away and bring something better."

The warden frowned. "He's supposed to be treated the same as the other prisoners—he eats what they eat; no special privileges of any kind. Governor Nagai's orders."

How quickly and completely the governor had withdrawn favor from his former protégé, Sano thought. Did he really believe in Kiyoshi's guilt, or want to distance himself from an accomplice turned scapegoat?

"Bring hot soup, fresh rice, and sake," Sano told the warden. "I'll take the responsibility."

"Suit yourself." Shrugging, the warden took the tray and left.

When the new provisions came, Sano set them in front of Kiyoshi, but the youth made no move to eat. Sano held a spoonful of soup to Kiyoshi's mouth.

"Drink this," he coaxed. "You'll feel better."

The soup trickled down Kiyoshi's immobile lips and onto his kimono, as did the liquor Sano offered next. Sano wiped the young man's face with his own sleeve, then spoke in a calm, quiet tone, feeling his way.

"From what I can tell, you're a dutiful, hardworking samurai. And you must be intelligent to learn Dutch."

Sano paused, waiting for a response, but Kiyoshi didn't even blink. Sano continued, "I don't believe you would ever want to break the law, or intentionally hurt anyone. Isn't that why you're suffering now? Because even though you didn't commit the crime you confessed to, you've hurt so many people. Not just me, but the people to whom you owe your highest loyalty: your father, Governor Nagai, Interpreter Iishino . . . and Junko."

Though the young samurai's face retained its icy pallor and stillness, Sano detected a faint reaction to Junko's name: The atmosphere around Kiyoshi vibrated like a taut samisen string when touched too lightly to make a sound.

"Junko must love you very much, to disobey her father by meeting you secretly," Sano said. "She would be heartbroken if you should die—especially for something you didn't do."

Seeing Kiyoshi's throat contract, Sano continued, "I'm sure Junko must be desperate to know how you could sacrifice your honor and betray her love this way." Sano hated exploiting the boy's weakness, but his own life and honor, as well as Hirata's, might depend on what he learned from Kiyoshi. "If you tell me what happened last night, I'll deliver a message to Junko so she'll know you're innocent, and that you still love her."

The blank surface of Kiyoshi's gaze rippled like water during an earth tremor, but he kept his silence. Had he lost the ability to speak?

"I'll tell you what I think happened," Sano said, hiding his hope and worry. "You needn't talk; just nod if you agree, and shake your head if you don't. All right?"

No reaction. Sano persisted: "You somehow discovered the smuggling when you went to Deshima to practice conversing with the Dutch. Or did you see it from the watchtower? Maybe you followed the mysterious lights, the way I did—ghost stories wouldn't frighten a brave samurai like you, would they?

"You tracked the smugglers to the cove. Last night, did you try to catch them and become a hero? Or was there another reason you were in the cove? Kiyoshi. Answer me!"

Sano expelled his breath in a gust of frustration. The young samurai hadn't responded to any of his statements or questions. Yet Sano felt sure he had at least the framework of the truth. With increasing desperation, he tried to build it into a structure that would support his defense before the tribunal.

"Whom did you expect to find in the cove, Kiyoshi? The Deshima guards? Iishino—or your father?" Of the possible culprits, Chief Ohira was not only the one with the easiest chance to smuggle, but the closest to Kiyoshi. This factor supported Sano's belief in Ohira's guilt. "Did you incriminate yourself and me to protect him? Do you know who killed Jan Spaen?"

This was useless. No matter how logical an explanation Sano offered the tribunal, it wouldn't save him or Hirata without confirmation from Kiyoshi . . . who apparently intended to take his knowledge to the grave.

Then Kiyoshi's lips moved in a hoarse whisper so quiet that Sano had to move closer to hear him over the rain. "The death march begins. At first, everything is just the way it really happened. It's dawn, and the soldiers are leading the condemned man, Yoshidō Ganzaemon, into the hills. He's been convicted of treason for insulting the shogun. I'm in the procession with the other witnesses. Executions frighten me . . . but I don't have anything to worry about. I've done nothing wrong."

His eyes took on a haunted look, as if beholding the grim vision he described; his whisper quavered. "But when we reach the execution ground, suddenly I'm not in the audience anymore . . . I'm the prisoner." Sweat dripped off his forehead; the stink of terror wafted from him. "I can feel the ropes cutting into my wrists . . ." Slowly he moved his hands behind his back and held them there as if bound. "I feel the heavy shackles around my legs. I see everyone watching me. My father is there. So are Governor Nagai and my comrades from the harbor patrol. . . . They despise me, because I'm a traitor."

For the first time, Sano doubted Kiyoshi's innocence. Surely this fantasy meant that he suffered from extreme guilt. But for what misdeed?

"The soldiers make me kneel before the executioners," Kiyoshi whispered. A steady tremor shook him, gradually building in intensity. "I beg for mercy, because I'm innocent. I've served the shogun loyally all my life. I'm the hardest-working officer in the harbor patrol." His voice cracked on a high, plaintive note. "I always volunteer for extra duty. I practice the martial arts so I can someday bring my lord glory on the battlefield. . . . I spend my nights in the watchtower, looking out for foreign warships. . . . I study Dutch so I can understand the barbarians whose military power threatens our land." His voice rose to a wail. "I've never acted against the shogun or his regime. Whoever says so is lying!"

From the corridor, the warden called, "Is everything all right in there?"

"Yes," Sano replied hastily, fearing that the interruption would silence Kiyoshi.

But Kiyoshi, mesmerized by his hallucination, seemed unaware of external distractions. "Governor Nagai states the charges against me," he said, whispering again. " 'Ohira Kiyoshi has placed his personal gain before the interests of the shogun and nation, thereby committing treason against both. He has blood on his hands. Therefore, he must die.' "

Personal gain? Blood on his hands? Maybe the youth really was a smuggler, acting on orders from his father, Nagai, or Iishino—or on his own initiative, to get money to marry Junko. Had he conspired with Jan Spaen, then killed the barbarian during an argument? Had he later killed Peony because she knew what he'd done? Then, when caught last night, had he framed Sano in an attempt to excuse his own behavior and receive a lighter sentence?

Had the two surviving barbarians been involved in the crimes?

Sano couldn't dismiss Assistant Director deGraeff's possible involvement. And, with a sudden qualm, he thought of how Dr. Huygens's language skill would enable him to communicate with Japanese members of a smuggling ring. He'd probably acquired his Japanese speech through conversations with students, including Kiyoshi—his accomplice? Sano didn't want to believe the worst about either Huygens or the boy in whom he saw his younger self, but if it was true, he must know.

Moving closer, Sano grasped the boy's slim, muscular shoulders. Their tremors resonated through his fingers. "Kiyoshi. Was it you who took Dutch goods to the cove last night? Whose blood did you spill? Did you make a deal with a barbarian? Which one? Why did you lie about me? Answer!"

"Please, let me go!" Kiyoshi's eyes rolled in terror. "Don't bring that sword any closer. You must listen. I was just trying to stop—I didn't want anyone to find out about—no. Please. NO!"

The boy wrenched free of Sano and leapt to his feet. Sano lost his balance, falling hard on his tailbone. But he barely noticed the pain, because Kiyoshi's self-control had shattered. He rampaged around the cell, howling like a madman, pounding the walls. His frantic movements upset the meal tray and wastebucket, spilling food and filth all over the floor. Sano lunged after Kiyoshi, fearing he would hurt himself if not restrained immediately. But Sano was no match for the youth's wild energy. Kiyoshi dodged him again and again. Sano's feet slipped on the messy floor. From outside the cell, he heard cries, thuds, and the warden calling, "What's going on in there? Quiet down, you're disturbing the other prisoners!"

"I only did it out of duty," Kiyoshi shouted. "And loyalty. And—and love. You must let me go. I have to stop it, I have to stop it. . . ."

He made a frantic leap toward the window. Sano grabbed him, but he broke free, ran to the door, and battered it with his fists and head. "Let me out! Please, let me out!"

Throwing his arms around Kiyoshi, Sano forced him away from the door just as the bolt outside slammed back. "Calm down, Kiyoshi." With all his strength, he wrestled the young samurai facedown onto the floor. He sat on Kiyoshi's arching back and pinned the flailing arms. "Be still." Sano spoke between gasps of exertion as Kiyoshi's howls and struggles subsided. "Everything's going to be all right."

But was it? Kiyoshi's words could be interpreted as an admission of smuggling and murder, punishable by death even if he'd acted in a misguided attempt to please, protect, or control someone else. A madman's ambiguous testimony wouldn't clear Sano or Hirata. And if Kiyoshi was innocent, Sano couldn't pin the crimes on the boy, even to save his own life and honor.

Sano released his hold on the limp, trembling body beneath him. He laid a soothing hand on Kiyoshi's head. "Kiyoshi, you must tell the truth. It's the only way you can help yourself, or the people you care about."

Silence. But when Sano gently turned Kiyoshi over, he saw that the boy's expression, though still frightened, had lost its crazed panic.

The door banged open, and the din outside increased as other prisoners clamored in their cells. The warden and two guards rushed into the room. "You'll have to leave now," the warden said. "He's started a riot, and he'll make things even worse if you don't leave him alone."

"Just a moment longer," Sano pleaded. To learn the truth, he must break Kiyoshi's loyalty to whomever he was protecting, whether it be Chief Ohira, Interpreter Iishino, Junko, or Governor Nagai. "He's calm now; maybe he'll talk."

But the warden shook his head. "Come back later."

The guards firmly escorted Sano out of Kiyoshi's cell, and the warden bolted the door. "Wait," Sano protested.

Suddenly a huge boom rocked the prison. Sano's heart lurched; his ears rang. Fragments of plaster rained down from the ceiling as a shocked silence fell over the jail. Then the prisoners began shouting again, louder, pounding on the doors and begging, "Let us out!"

"What in heaven was that?" the warden said. "Thunder? An earthquake?"

Dawning comprehension horrified Sano. "The Dutch ship," he said, and bolted for the exit.

25

SANO'S GUESS PROVED unfortunately correct. From outside the jail, he saw the Dutch ship moving down the harbor channel with ominous majesty. Black smoke drifted out of cannon protruding from the lower decks. Flames blazed aboard a nearby patrol barge whose stern tilted below the water. The Dutch captain had entered the harbor before the two days were up, firing on troops who had tried to stop the ship. Sano's worst fear had become reality: His failure to resolve the barbarian's murder had brought war to Japan.

He leapt astride his horse and galloped downhill toward the harbor. Past him streamed noisy crowds seeking shelter, while braver, curious souls ran for the waterfront. Gawkers peered from balconies and roofs. Foreign merchants, concerned for their anchored craft, poured out of the settlements in raucous hordes accompanied by frantic Japanese guards. Shouts and cries filled the streets.

"The barbarians will kill us all!"

"Run for the hills!"

Doshin tried vainly to maintain order. Troops, armed with bows, arquebuses, swords, and spears, rode and marched toward the harbor.

Then a second boom shuddered the sky and echoed across the hills. A fountain of smoke and water burst from the sea near the wrecked barge. Another wave of panic rose.

"Move," shouted Sano, maneuvering his horse through massed bodies and trying not to trample anyone. He must somehow undo the harm he'd caused. The Dutch captain might be rash enough to risk dying in battle against Japan's more numerous forces, and with his superior firepower, he could ruin the city.

The waterfront promenade was already awash in troops when Sano reached it. Sentries manned small boats around Deshima, preventing contact between the Dutch crew and their imprisoned compatriots. Beyond the beach, survivors of the wrecked barge swam for shore while waves swallowed their craft. From the harbor patrol station, more barges, packed with troops, sped toward the Dutch ship, which loomed larger and closer. Scarlet war banners fluttered on the clifftops above the harbor. Sano hastily secured his horse outside the station and rushed down the pier.

"Wait!" he cried, waving at the last departing barge.

No one heeded his plea. Then, farther down the coast, he saw sailors preparing to launch Nagasaki's three warships. They raised masts, mounted oars and cannon, unfurled sails and banners bearing the Tokugawa crest. Sano reached the largest warship just as gunners and archers assumed positions on deck and the high command started up the gangplank.

Governor Nagai, wearing a magnificent suit of armor with red-lacquered breastpiece, chain-mail sleeves, a many-plated tunic laced with red silk cord, and a helmet crowned with golden antlers, led a group of aides. Interpreter Iishino, looking scared and uncomfortable in his armor, dawdled behind. When Sano arrived at the gangplank, Nagai was on deck, arguing with the ship's captain.

"Under no conditions shall we fire on the Dutch ship yet," Nagai said.

"But Honorable Governor," said the captain, "the barbarians have already attacked Japan. To accept such an insult would be an admission of cowardice. I can cripple the Dutch ship. The gunners on the cliffs can finish her off." His face blazed with zealous patriotism. "This is our chance to demonstrate Japan's military strength!"

The aides loudly seconded him, but Governor Nagai shook his circular gold war fan. "Our defense preparations are incomplete. At present, we can't guarantee a quick victory over the Dutch or minimal damage to Nagasaki. And think of the consequences of a battle.

"Even if we make sure the barbarians don't leave Japan alive, there are thousands of other foreign witnesses to today's events. We can't silence them all without inviting retribution from their governments, which would eventually realize that an entire international fleet of ships had failed to return home. The traders will carry tales to ports frequented by the East India Company. The Dutch will send more ships. Our nation cannot survive a full assault by the company fleet without massive destruction. Even if we escape total defeat, the battles will kill legions and disrupt foreign trade, costing us a fortune. I'll not bring full-scale war on Japan just to satisfy a fool's desire for glory!"

With an air of finality, Nagai turned to his chief aide. "Does everyone have orders to stand by unless they receive the signal from me?"

"Yes, Honorable Governor."

"Then let's be on our way. I must negotiate a truce with the Dutch before matters escalate to the point where war is unavoidable."

Nagai started toward the bow; his retinue followed. The captain shouted the order to set sail. Sano dashed up the gangplank, calling, "Governor Nagai! Wait!"

Troops seized Sano, locking him in a vise of chain-mailed arms. Nagai turned; a frown darkened his face. "What are you doing here?" he demanded, striding toward Sano. To the troops he said, "Throw him overboard, and let's go."

"Wait," Sano called as the soldiers started to hoist him over the railing. "Governor Nagai, you must let me go with you and speak to the Dutch."

"*Bakarashii*—ridiculous!" Nagai's thick lips twisted in annoyance, though his curt headshake arrested the soldiers' overboard thrust. "Haven't you caused enough trouble already? You failed to disarm the Dutch ship when you had the chance. You could have accepted the whore's confession, closed Spaen's murder case, and allowed the barbarians to land peacefully. Now your folly and ineptitude have endangered the entire nation."

The angry sweep of his war fan encompassed the harbor, where the fishing boats now clustered at the docks, the other foreign vessels had moved as far inland as possible, and the Dutch ship reigned triumphant. Yet Sano saw a familiar shrewd glint in Nagai's eyes: He realized that if Sano conducted the negotiations with the Dutch, Governor Nagai could not be blamed in the event of failure.

"The Dutch captain knows me," Sano said, hastening to help Nagai reverse his decision without losing face before his men. "When he hears about the efforts I've made toward catching his countryman's killer, he may consent to a truce."

After a moment, Nagai nodded. "Release him," he ordered the soldiers. To the captain, he said, "Proceed."

To the accompaniment of the rowers' chants and the splash of oars, the warship left the dock. Sano joined Governor Nagai in the bow, where they watched the Dutch ship, now ringed by patrol barges that looked puny in comparison. The moist, salt-laden drizzle chilled Sano, tightening muscles already stiff with anxiety; his shoulder ached. Not until he faced Captain Oss could he know what approach would best achieve peace. But he now had a chance to establish Nagai's role in the murders and smuggling, and convince the governor to drop the charges against him.

With a sidelong glance at Sano, Governor Nagai said, "My clan has a long tradition of military leadership. Even in peacetime, we consider the strategy of warfare an important field of knowledge, because war and politics are much alike—don't you agree?"

Sano nodded, unsure of where this was leading.

"Yes. Well. During my youth I studied the writings of my ancestor, General Noriyama, who lived more than three hundred years ago, under the Ashikaga shoguns. He had a saying: 'Attack the branches; weaken the tree.' He applied this theory in his campaign against a rival general. Instead of killing his rival, he took the man's family hostage, rendering him powerless to act against Noriyama. A bold move whose genius lay not only in concept, but also in execution. You see, General Noriyama didn't take the hostages himself; he had his lieutenants do it. This way he avoided any adverse personal consequences should the ploy fail, or displeasing his lord with an overt quest for power."

"I see," said Sano. He'd just been warned that if he attacked the governor, his mother, aunts, uncles, and cousins would suffer at the hands of Nagai's minions. Also, the governor, like General Noriyama, had covered himself in the event that the frame-up should fail and the *bakufu* ever challenge his handling of Sano's case. If the tribunal should find Sano innocent, Nagai could blame his subordinates, and thereby escape punishment.

"I find it difficult to understand why you take such an active interest in the problems of the nation," Governor Nagai said, "since your own days upon this earth are numbered."

Of all his enemies, the one Sano hated most was Nagai, symbol of everything wrong in the *bakufu's* upper echelon. He got a firm grip on his temper, knowing he could exploit Nagai's weaknesses to his own advantage, but only if he kept his main goal in sight. "I wouldn't be too sure of that if I were you, Honorable Governor." As the warship breasted the gray, choppy waves, Sano matched Nagai's bland tone. "I've spoken with Kiyoshi, Interpreter Iishino, and Chief Ohira today. The more closely one examines your case against me, the weaker it seems. After all, none of the witnesses are totally unbiased, credible, or beyond impeachment. The tribunal can't fail to notice."

"Oh?" Nagai's expression remained impassive.

"Take Kiyoshi, for example," Sano said. "His testimony links me to the smuggling, but he's gone mad. The magistrates will doubt anything he says. And it's not hard to draw the conclusion that he lied to protect someone with whom he has strong professional or personal ties."

Like you, Governor, Sano let his tone imply. "Then there's Iishino. He was the only interpreter present when I spoke with the barbarians. His statement about what happened between them and me can't be confirmed. And because Iishino speaks Dutch fluently, he's the person most able to conspire with the barbarians, and engage in conflicts strong enough to provoke violence."

"Yes. Well." Governor Nagai's warrior costume lent a menacing edge to his familiar geniality. "Interpreter Iishino and Chief Ohira are witnesses of great fortitude. They also have excellent records."

This meant that they would stand firm by their statements, thereby upsetting any claim of bias or perjury Sano made against them. Furthermore, their credentials weighed in their favor, while Sano, the accused, must battle the presumption of guilt, from which neither his rank nor accomplishments could shield him.

"Ohira is the most dubious witness of all," Sano said, fighting desperation. Only moments remained until his confrontation with the Dutch. "Who else is in a better position to move barbarians off Deshima and murder them? And anyone can see why he wants me condemned as a traitor and corrupter of innocent youth: That would excuse his son's behavior and lessen the family's disgrace, wouldn't it?" Sano described the hint of conspiracy he'd observed between Chief Ohira and Nirin. "As far as I'm concerned, Ohira is the prime suspect."

"But what would be his reason for killing Jan Spaen?" Nagai asked impatiently.

Lack of motive was the only weak point in the case against Ohira. "I don't know, but I intend to find out," Sano said. Nagai shrugged, keeping his eyes on the Dutch ship. Sano could now see its crew on deck, ready to attack again. With increasing urgency, he hurried on. "This tribunal convenes at considerable trouble to the magistrates and expense to the *bakufu*. The magistrates will resent being summoned to hear a fabricated case. The *bakufu* frowns upon anyone who abuses the law for personal gain. And I have allies in Edo. You could save yourself a lot of trouble by dropping the charges against me before matters go any farther."

Governor Nagai's expression turned cautious, but he shook his head. "I realize it's in your interest for me to discredit the witnesses and dismiss the evidence. But that's impossible."

Nagai must have more to lose by freeing him than by mounting a fraudulent treason case, Sano thought. Did this indicate the governor's complicity in the smuggling or murders? Was he afraid of what Sano's investigation might reveal about him?

"The law requires that I prosecute traitors without exception or mercy," continued Nagai. "And the proceedings have been set in motion; no one can halt them now."

Through the cloud of ambiguities, Sano sensed one awful certainty: The long arm of Chamberlain Yanagisawa, reaching all the way from Edo to Nagasaki. Whatever Nagai's motives, the chamberlain would support the campaign against Sano—and punish the governor if it failed. Nagai, the canny politician, knew this.

The warship was nearing the ring of patrol barges. Governor Nagai leaned over the rail, shouting commands. The ring opened, allowing the warship to pass through. Sano saw Captain Oss, his red hair swirling like windblown flames, standing on the upper deck. Surrounded by armed troops, he aimed a musket directly at the Japanese warship. Sano knew that behind the rows of jutting black cannon, barbarian gunners waited in the lower decks, flaming torches in hand, poised to fire more deadly mortars. As the only man aboard his craft not wearing armor, Sano felt naked and vulnerable.

"Iishino!" he called. "Get up here!"

Iishino hurried into the bow, his face ghastly white. The warship came within a length of the Dutch vessel, and Oss shouted into the gusting wind. "He says don't come any closer, or they'll shoot." Iishino trembled so hard that his shoulder plates rattled. "Oh, Honorable Governor, I think we should obey!"

Nagai leveled an icy stare at Sano. "You are in charge now."

"Stop this ship," Sano told the captain. They could never withstand an assault by the barbarian vessel.

The rowers lifted the oars. The slackened sails flapped in the rainy wind. With a great splash, the anchor hit the water; the ship stopped. Sano offered a mental prayer to the gods, drew a deep breath, waved, and shouted:

"Captain Oss! Do you remember me?"

Iishino crouched on the deck, his head barely clearing the railing. In a quavery yell, he translated Sano's words.

"You gave me two days to catch Jan Spaen's killer and provide safe

accommodations for your crew," Sano continued, hoping his voice—
and courage—wouldn't fail. "Why have you changed your mind?"

Oss didn't lower his gun, but he craned his neck to peer at Sano and
rapped out an angry reply.

"He says he's tired of waiting," mewled Iishino.

Sano realized that the barbarian had forced this confrontation because he knew Japan didn't want a war. Oss hoped to extort trade con-
cessions and advance himself. "Captain Oss, please order your men to
hold their fire. Go back outside the harbor until we're ready to escort
you ashore." Sano hated the thought of ever allowing the ambitious
barbarian and his wild horde onto land, but what mattered now was
removing the immediate threat to national security.

No sooner had Iishino finished translating, than the Dutchman's
gun muzzle flared. An explosion cracked through air, tore across
water. The bullet splintered one of the warship's yards. Sano dropped
to the deck. Cries erupted and armor clattered as Iishino, Governor
Nagai, and the crew followed suit. Then the captain was shouting orders, and the Japanese troops were back in position. Along a hundred
bows, arrows rested poised to fly. The smell of hot flint and charred
cloth rose as gunners lit the wicks that would ignite powder and speed
bullets and cannonballs toward the enemy.

"No!" Sano shouted. Merciful gods, the war had begun. He would
be among the first casualties. "Don't shoot!"

Governor Nagai bellowed threats at his captain and crew. Then,
when no additional shots came from the Dutch ship, the captain reluctantly signaled to hold fire. Yet bowstrings remained taut, guns
aimed, while, from across the waves, came the barbarian's wild rant-
ing.

"Translate!" Sano ordered, hauling Iishino to his feet.

The interpreter whimpered, "He says there's a fortune in goods in
the ship's hold, and he wants us to buy them now, for the price he will
set. Oh, sōsakan-sama, you must also bring him the corpse of Jan
Spaen's killer and allow them ashore, or they'll destroy Nagasaki!"

Sano sensed the Japanese troops' growing restlessness, but Captain
Oss's mention of money gave him an opening. And he saw terror on

the faces of the barbarian crew: They didn't want to die. Only fear of their leader compelled their obedience.

"Ten silver pieces for you if you cease fire and leave the harbor, Captain Oss," Sano called, "and one for each of your men."

A collective gasp rose from Sano's comrades. Diplomatic protocol forbade the practice of bribing barbarians, which could be used to court military allegiance. Sano saw Governor Nagai's faint smile and knew he'd just compounded the treason charges. Yet after Iishino translated the offer, he watched with jubilation as his ploy achieved the desired effect. Oss shook his head and roared a defiant negative, but his men turned on him, abandoning their posts to argue and gesticulate. Elation burst the iron band of worry around Sano's chest. His offer to Captain Oss had been a token bribe; it was the crew he'd meant to reach. Dutch seamen earned a pittance; to them, even one silver coin represented a small fortune. For a moment, mutiny seemed likely. At last Captain Oss nodded, conceding defeat. He shouted at Sano. Iishino translated.

"He'll hold fire for two more days, two more days."

Murmurs of cautious relief swept the warship's crew. Sano's spirits lifted.

"But he refuses to leave the harbor until he's satisfied that the true killer of Jan Spaen has been punished."

No amount of negotiation would induce Captain Oss to capitulate. The Japanese warship turned back while barges still surrounded the Dutch ship, the troops remained on the waterfront and cliffs, and Sano prayed that the tentative truce would hold.

"We'll pay the bribe, but maintain all forces on alert," Governor Nagai told his men. "When the Dutch ship fires, they are to destroy it; we have no choice now." Evidently he trusted neither Captain Oss's promise nor Sano's abilities. Turning to Sano, he said coldly, "This could be the beginning of the greatest catastrophe our land has ever known. How fortunate for you that you'll not live to suffer the consequences of your foolhardy actions . . . traitor."

The insult enflamed Sano's anger even as his conscience acknowledged his culpability—after all, hadn't he promoted Dutch interests above Japanese by leaving the barbarian ship armed? He should never have indulged the curiosity that had drawn him to the barbarians. How much was he compelled by the demands of honor and right; how much by the thrill of adventure?

"We'll soon see which of us is the traitor," he retorted, turning his anger at himself on Governor Nagai. "I intend to learn your role in the smuggling, and in Director Spaen's murder. When I tell the tribunal magistrates, they may decide to remain in Nagasaki for another trial—where I shall give evidence against *you,* Honorable Governor."

Nagai's laugh poured over him like poisonous oil: smooth, rich, corrosive. "You'll never find any evidence, or anyone willing to testify against me."

Rain and wind cloaked Sano in chill misery as he beheld the approaching shore with its massed troops, and the red war banners in the hills. Governor Nagai was smart enough to cover his tracks and powerful enough to command unfailing loyalty. Who among his subordinates would dare accuse him?

Nagai added, "In case you still harbor any illusions about your detective talents, let me relieve you of them. Two days before Director Spaen's disappearance, the Deshima guards reported a violent argument between Spaen and another barbarian—the doctor, Nicolaes Huygens."

Sano's stomach recoiled from the shock; his mind went numb. Then, as Nagai continued, hurt outrage flooded him.

"The guards heard angry voices coming from Spaen's office. They entered and saw Huygens lunge at Spaen and start choking him. When Huygens saw they had an audience, he ran out of the room. The guards didn't know what the fight was about, but they claimed that Huygens looked angry enough to kill Spaen." Governor Nagai laughed again. "Yes. Well. If you were a competent investigator, surely you would have discovered the animosity between your Dutch friend and Jan Spaen before you conspired with Huygens."

The story had the ring of truth. Yet far from doing him a favor by relating it, Sano knew the governor had done so just to torment him because he couldn't get onto Deshima to confirm it. But Sano's anger at

Nagai paled in comparison to the rage he felt toward Dr. Huygens. If Huygens had lied about his relationship with Spaen, what else had he lied about? Had he pretended to help examine Spaen's corpse, all the while falsifying the results of the dissection? Bitterly Sano wondered whether their friendship had been a sham, meant to deflect his suspicion.

"Now if you'll excuse me," Governor Nagai said, "I have a city to defend."

He gathered his aides into the cabin for a strategy session. Iishino had vanished; Sano was alone with his fears and doubts. Had he risked treason and compromised the investigation by unknowingly collaborating with the killer he sought?

26

IN THE DUTCH traders' common room on Deshima, Dr. Nicolaes Huygens sat with Assistant Director deGraeff and their three colleagues. They'd been there for six hours, since the East India Company ship had entered the harbor. Now the remains of their noon meal littered the table; the air was foul with tobacco smoke, burning lamp oil, and the stench of a wastebucket in the corner. The guards stationed outside wouldn't let them leave the room. As Huygens watched deGraeff get up to pace the floor, dread sickened him; sweat drenched his clothing.

"Why must they keep us locked up like this?" the trade secretary whined for what must have been the hundredth time. "When are they going to tell us what's going on? What was that big bang a while ago? What will become of us?"

DeGraeff snorted. "As I've said before, it's safe to assume that our ship entered the harbor without permission and fired on the Japanese. We can also assume that we're prisoners of war."

At times when Huygens couldn't ease his homesick misery with nature studies, he drew comfort from the past. Now, to calm his fear of what was to happen, he pictured his old laboratory at Leyden University, the world's greatest institution of learning, with faculty and students from all over Europe. He envisioned walls lined with shelves of books, anatomical models, and preserved specimens; the glassware, lamps, microscopes, and other scientific apparatus; caged animals; his research notes on the pathology and treatment of diseases. The laboratory was always crowded—Huygens's reputation attracted scientists who came to consult him, and scholars seeking tutorials.

Next Huygens conjured up the great, echoing Anatomical Theater, its tiers packed with doctors, medical students, and curiosity seekers. He recalled lecturing on the physiology of the dissected corpse on the table beside him, answering questions spoken in German, English, French, Swedish, and Hungarian accents.

For last he saved the image of his narrow stone row house beside a tree-shaded canal. On fine summer evenings, he and his wife Judith relaxed on a bench by the door. At their feet played Pieter, aged eight. Tiny-eyed, thick-featured, he acted like a toddler; he couldn't speak clearly, or dress and feed himself. Huygens, with all his scientific expertise, could find neither explanation nor cure for this malady, and he'd worried about Pieter's future. But Pieter's angelic nature had given his parents a joy that compensated for the sorrow. . . .

Today the happy memories seemed faded and remote. Like a medicine taken too often, they'd lost the power to ease pain. Now Huygens's thoughts carried him back farther, to the youthful days he kept sealed off in a corner of his mind.

He was the son of a wealthy Amsterdam merchant who'd paid a fortune to send him to Leyden University. But the seventeen-year-old Nicolaes Huygens had cared nothing for studies. He drank in taverns with a gang of rowdy comrades. They ravished maidens and brawled in the streets. When Huygens bothered to attend class, he heckled his teachers. The university threatened expulsion; his father raged. Yet Huygens continued his debauchery, until it culminated in the act that had bound him to Jan Spaen.

This had happened during *kermis*—the Dutch annual rite of celebration. Beneath colorful tents, vendors sold food and trinkets; acrobats and clowns entertained; gypsies told fortunes. A curiosity show boasted two-headed pigs and limbless men; a theater troupe presented plays. Revelers led a flower-wreathed ox to the marketplace to be slaughtered, roasted, and served at an outdoor banquet. Musicians fiddled; men, women, and children danced. Drinkers filled every tavern.

Through the crowds swaggered Huygens and his friends, drunk and boisterous. In search of a rival student gang, they carried pocketsful of flour and crocks of melted wax to smear on the offenders' faces in proper *kermis* tradition.

"Come out, Franz Tulp, you coward," Huygens called to the rival gang's leader.

His comrades hooted. "We need another drink!"

They piled into a tavern. And there, among the patrons, sat Franz Tulp, a burly blond lout with a scornful grin, his friends clustered round him.

"Get them!" Huygens shouted to his gang.

They assaulted their rivals, hurling flour and wax. The opposition flung the ale from their cups. Then suddenly, somehow, the fun changed to serious combat. Fists flew; sticks flailed. Laughter turned to cries of pain. Huygens, mad with rage, chased Tulp outside, cornering him alone in an alley. Drunken bloodlust swept Huygens's mind clear of reason. He reached for the short clay pipe he always carried in his pocket. . . .

Suddenly the Deshima common-room door slammed open. Huygens snapped back to the present. The hawkfaced second watch commander burst into the room, breathless and agitated, directing an order to the guards. To Huygens's dismay, it sounded like, "The doctor's services are needed." Had Investigator Sano learned about his argument with Spaen and returned to question him about the murder again?

When the guards protested, citing the governor's orders to keep the barbarians locked up together, Nirin ignored them and hustled Huygens from the room. This didn't surprise him; on Deshima, rules were frequently broken, by both staff and residents. He should know, with his learning of the native language, his clandestine work with the Dutch-Japanese underground, his illicit trips off the island. . . .

Huygens fought panic while Nirin led him through the drizzly twilit street, which was guarded by twice as many sentries as usual. On the mainland, he saw red banners in the hills. Japan and his country must indeed be at war. Silently Huygens rehearsed the statements he must convince Sano to believe: *I didn't kill Jan Spaen. I know nothing about any smuggling. I'm not the enemy; I'm innocent!*

They reached the surgery. Lamps burned in the windows. Nirin opened the door and shoved Huygens inside, ordering, "Save him, barbarian!"

Instead of Investigator Sano, four guards and a scared-looking junior interpreter occupied the room. Huygens experienced a rush of relief. Then he saw, lying on the table, the still, blanket-covered body of a young samurai. His face was white, his eyes closed.

Speaking too fast for Huygens to understand, Nirin whipped the blanket off the boy. Huygens's heart jumped when he saw the deep gash on the naked thigh, still oozing blood despite the tourniquet someone had applied.

"His son," the interpreter translated. "Hurt when Dutch ship sink barge. Please, honorable doctor, you heal?"

The Deshima staff often defied the rules and came to Dr. Huygens for medical treatment. Now Huygens forgot Jan Spaen, Sano, and the past as his professional self took command. Hurrying over to the youth, he touched the cold neck and felt only a weak pulse.

"Bring hot water," he said.

The interpreter translated; the guards obeyed. Washing the blood from the injury, Huygens saw that it was deep and serious. A slit artery leaked precious blood into the mangled tissue. Cauterization—the usual method of burning a wound shut with a hot poker—wouldn't work. From his medical kit, Huygens took a thin needle and a long human hair. Using a technique he'd developed at Leyden University, he sewed the cut artery with tiny stitches. He closed the flesh around it with a thicker needle and a strand of horsetail. The Japanese murmured in awe. Huygens removed the tourniquet, then cleaned and bandaged the wound.

"Your son has lost a lot of blood," he told Nirin. "To live, he'll need more. You must bring me a dog."

Suspicious queries greeted the interpreter's translation: The men wanted to know if Huygens meant to violate the Dog Protection Edict, their bizarre law that favored animal life over human.

"I don't have time to explain," Huygens said impatiently. "Get the dog, or the boy will die."

The guards ran out the door. Huygens, Nirin, and the interpreter stood around the patient. Glancing from the son's deathly white face to the father's grim one, Huygens experienced a thrill of fear. If he failed to repair the damage done by his people, would the Japanese kill him for revenge? Beneath his fear rose the hope of release from a life worse than death. . . .

Into the aftermath of his confrontation with Tulp had walked Jan Spaen. Yet despite the experience they'd shared, they didn't meet again until after Huygens's life had totally changed.

The Tulp incident had shocked him to his senses. Dreading the arrival of the police, he'd hidden in his rooms, physically ill with fear and guilt, and expecting some sort of demand from Spaen. But when weeks passed and nothing happened, he dared to believe he'd escaped punishment. He had another chance.

He'd spent the next twenty years atoning for his sin. Dropping his gang, he quit drinking, studied hard, and graduated first in his class. He won a coveted professorship at Leyden University; he also taught in Rome and Paris. At his private clinic, he treated both prominent citizens and charity patients. He married Judith, the rich girl his father had chosen for him, and fell in love with her. As time went on, Huygens gave less and less thought to his past evil, or the man who'd colluded in it.

Then, while attending a medical conference in Amsterdam, Huygens had left the lecture hall one evening with a group of colleagues, and spied, standing in the vestibule, a ghost from the past. Shock burst like a geyser of cold, foul water in Huygens's chest. He stopped dead in his tracks.

Jan Spaen smiled. "That was a brilliant lecture you just gave, Dr. Nicolaes Huygens," he said.

His features were still handsome, his body strong, his hair still golden, his gaze bold and knowing. Huygens would have recognized him anywhere. Now he was horrified to hear Spaen's use of his name and title: Though Spaen hadn't known his identity on that long-ago day, he did now. And Huygens realized that Spaen had at last come to collect on his debt.

"After all this time, we have much to talk about." Spaen led Huygens outside to a deserted street. "I'm a trader with the East India Company, in town until my ship sails again. I could use a good medical man on my staff. From your lecture, I know you're an expert on traumatic injuries and tropical diseases. How about it?"

An awful rushing sensation came over Huygens, as if an invisible tide were receding from him, taking along everything and everyone he cared about. "But I can't go to sea," he protested. "My work; my family . . ."

"The *Gertje* sails for the Spice Islands next week," Spaen said. "I'll see you then."

Huygens had no choice but to comply. If what Spaen knew about him became public, he would be ruined anyway. He resigned his professorship and closed his clinic, over the protests of his family and colleagues. Afraid of losing their love and respect, he let them think he'd developed a sudden wanderlust. On the cold, bleak day of his departure, he waved from the ship's deck at the rapidly diminishing figures of his wife and son.

"I'll be back soon," he called. Somehow he would break Spaen's hold on him.

Life at sea was worse than Huygens could have imagined: storms, pirates, rotten food, disease; the constant threat of mutiny; countless accidents that maimed and killed sailors; frequent military skirmishes. Yet Jan Spaen thrived on all forms of danger—including the company of men who served him against their will. Day after day, Huygens endured his jovial conversation at mealtimes, seething with bitter resentment. Two years later, a Dutch traveler brought him the news that Judith had died in an epidemic. Pieter, his cherished, mentally deficient son, was put into Leyden's squalid insane asylum and died soon afterward. These were tragedies Huygens might have prevented, if only he'd been there! His hatred for Spaen grew. By changing his ways and healing the afflicted, hadn't he atoned for his crime? Professional ethics forbade Huygens to take a life; still, he'd dreamed of killing Spaen. The unbearable torment of incarceration together on Deshima had made him desperate enough . . .

Loud barking outside signaled the guards' return. Into the surgery they hauled a frisky black hound by a rope around its neck. Huygens said, "Tie the dog in the yard. Then wait here."

The interpreter translated; the guards obeyed. Dr. Huygens went alone to the yard, carrying a club and a scalpel. The dog pranced and wagged its tail. "May God forgive me," Huygens whispered. One hard blow on the skull, and the dog fell dead; several quick cuts to its neck, and Huygens held a long, white vein, still dripping warm blood, in his hands. He hurried back into the surgery and rinsed the vein in a water bucket.

"Sit on the table," he told Nirin, "and roll up your sleeve so I can transfer some of your blood to your son."

Looking apprehensive, Nirin did as the interpreter told him. Huygens took from his medical kit two canulas: tiny silver tubes, each with one end blunt and one cut at an angle and sharpened to a point. He prayed that the operation wouldn't fail. Taking donor blood from the recipient's near kin increased the chances of success, but while some patients revived and flourished, others died.

Huygens fingered the youth's cold, flaccid arm and found a vein. When he pierced it with the sharp canula, the boy didn't even flinch. Huygens turned to Nirin.

The commander bravely proffered his arm at Huygens's request. He winced as the canula entered his flesh, and blood trickled out. Huygens slipped one end of the dog's limp vein over the canula's blunt exposed portion. The other he attached to the canula protruding from the boy's arm.

"Open and close your fist," he told Nirin, demonstrating.

The dog's vein reddened as blood flowed through it. From outside drifted the voices of the guards, who had gone out to hide the dog's corpse—another of Deshima's many secrets. A waiting silence pervaded the surgery. Nirin watched his son's face. Huygens felt the pulse in the boy's neck gradually strengthen. Color returned to his skin; his eyelids fluttered open.

"Father," he whispered.

Nirin's hard features softened; he touched his son's cheek. The interpreter cheered. For a moment Huygens felt the elation that saving a life always brought him.

Then dread and misery returned. Even medical miracles didn't compensate for everything lost when he'd joined the East India Company. Spaen's death couldn't restore what was gone forever, or end the hatred that Huygens still felt for him. If Investigator Sano learned the truth about Huygens, he would look no further for the killer of Jan Spaen.

27

THE RAIN-DRENCHED cityscape of Nagasaki blurred past Hirata as he trudged through wet streets, down fetid alleys, and up slippery staircases. Cold and exhausted, he yearned for a hot bath, food, and sleep. But he had no money, and he had to keep moving to evade capture by the troops who still combed the city in search of him, despite the threat of war.

Last night, while hunting for the smugglers, he'd heard noises in the cove and returned just in time to see the police arrest Sano and Kiyoshi. Then the harbor patrol had stormed after him. More troops had later joined the chase. He'd spent the night running through the forest, climbing hills, crawling over fields, and wading across streams in a desperate attempt to escape. If he didn't remain free, who would save Sano? Toward dawn, exhausted to the brink of collapse, Hirata had snatched an hour's rest in a tree. Yet sleep had brought no peace, because he'd dreamed of his former mentor, the ambush in the teahouse, and his own cowardly flight, which had given him a second chance to prove his worth as a samurai.

Hirata had sneaked back into the city just as the gates opened. Now he was glad that he wore the costume in which he was most comfortable: his old *doshin* uniform of short kimono, cotton leggings, wicker hat, short sword, and *jitte*. As long as he kept his face hidden, he could pass for a Nagasaki police officer. And for a while, his disguise had served his purpose.

First he'd found out what had happened to Sano. All over town, newssellers hawked broadsheets: "The shogun's *sōsakan* is a traitor. Read all about it!"

Hirata snatched a paper. Dismay flooded him as he read the outrageous charges against his master, followed by relief upon learning that Sano would remain alive and free until the tribunal convened in three days. Hirata had time to gather evidence against the real criminals and exonerate Sano.

He'd begun with a visit to Urabe. Outside the merchant's foreign goods shop, he'd met Urabe's daughter, Junko, who had begged Hirata to save Kiyoshi.

"Kiyoshi is innocent. You must tell your superiors, so they'll let him go!" In her agitation, Junko had pounded delicate fists against Hirata's chest, sobbing. "Please, I don't want him to die!"

"If Kiyoshi isn't a smuggler, then what was he doing in the cove?" Hirata had asked.

Junko related a tale about how Kiyoshi had chased the mysterious lights, trying to catch ghosts who would give them enough gold so they could afford to marry. "My Kiyoshi is a good samurai. He would never break the law." Weeping, she said, "He's so kind, obedient, and loyal!"

Enough to sacrifice his life to protect someone else? Hirata remembered Sano's suspicion that Urabe had aided Jan Spaen in the smuggling, perhaps by selling the goods on the black market. Had Kiyoshi lied to save Junko, who would share her father's punishment for the crime?

While pretending to search Urabe's establishment for the fugitive, he'd questioned the merchant regarding his whereabouts on crucial nights. Urabe had claimed that he'd been working late, alone, in his store at the time of the smuggling, Peony's murder, and Jan Spaen's disappearance. However, two events weakened his shaky alibi and strengthened his motive for smuggling.

Three raffish-looking peasants had come to the shop, their tattooed arms marking them as gangsters. When they accepted from Urabe a bulky package in exchange for strings of coins, Hirata had smelled a crooked deal. Then a moneylender had seized Urabe's goods as payment for a bad debt. The merchant was obviously in dire financial straits. And if those gangsters were black marketeers, he had the contacts to dispose of smuggled goods.

Then troops had arrived to search the shop; Hirata had barely escaped. Since then, hours ago, he'd accomplished nothing except mere survival, which didn't help Sano.

Marching footsteps heralded danger again. Hirata fled into the marketplace. Stalls sheltered vendors, merchandise, and customers from the rain. The smell of frying food made his mouth water. Famished, he walked to a stall that sold skewers of grilled seafood and vegetables.

"Give me five of those," he told the vendor, "and a large bowl of rice."

The man set the food on the narrow ledge that served as a table. "That will be ten coppers, master."

"I am the law!" Hirata said, waving his *jitte*. "I don't have to pay."

The frightened vendor went meekly back to his grill. Hirata wolfed the food while shame tore his spirit and he remembered the words of his father: "An honorable *doshin* does not abuse his power, because that would make him no better than the criminals he is supposed to discipline."

Now Hirata convinced himself that his mission justified thievery, and duty to his master overrode all other concerns. Finishing the food, he went to a tea seller and extorted a drink. With hunger and thirst slaked, his strength and inspiration returned. Avoiding the troops and police, he headed toward the waterfront.

A TALK WITH residents of Chief Ohira's street revealed nothing about Ohira except that he lived frugally and had a reputation as a strict, law-abiding leader. Hirata found no evidence that he profited from smuggling Dutch goods. When asked for information about Interpreter Iishino, the residents had told him, "You ought to go see Madam Ki-

hara, the wife of the city treasurer. She's the go-between who arranged
Interpreter Iishino's marriage, and she always investigates prospective
spouses very thoroughly."

They'd directed Hirata to the hillside below the governor's mansion. In the broad avenues, clerks and messengers dodged palanquins;
mounted administrators and diplomats passed through the gates of
the walled estates of Nagasaki's officials; merchants conversed about
prices, profits, and taxes on imported and exported goods. Neither a
citywide manhunt nor the threat of war could halt foreign trade, or the
bureaucratic machine that regulated it.

Hirata navigated the district with an air of purpose, as if on legitimate business. But his extra sense blared a continuous warning siren
in his head; glances from passersby stabbed him like knives. He told
himself that his uniform was adequate disguise, and no one would expect a fugitive to stride boldly into Nagasaki's seat of power. The
troops were fewer here. Yet only Hirata's desire to save his master kept
him from bolting.

He located the estate with the square crest above the gate and told
a guard he wanted to see Madam Kihara. The guard, assuming he was
a marriage client, summoned a servant who led him through the garden and into the house's entry porch.

"Your shoes and weapons, master?" the servant reminded him politely.

Every instinct in Hirata rebelled against removing his sandals, *jitte*,
and sword as custom required. What if troops should search the house
while he was inside? Reluctantly he slipped off his sandals, donned a
pair of guest slippers, and placed his weapons on the shelf, knowing
that refusal would arouse suspicion. The servant escorted him into the
house. From down the corridor came a deep, cracked voice, saying:

"I need a complete dossier on the Ono boy's family. Canvass the
shops and moneylenders and find out what debts they owe." A
phlegmy cough interrupted the orders. "Check the pleasure quarter
and see if the boy has a mistress there. Visit his superior and ask if he's
likely to rise any higher. Then find out who his friends are, and if
they've ever been in trouble with the law."

Hirata's spirits lifted with anticipation. If that was Madam Kihara speaking, she must know everything there was to know about people whose marriages she arranged. He followed the servant to the reception room. Its paper wall glowed with yellow lamplight. A samurai wearing the Kihara crest came out. The servant ushered Hirata inside and announced, "Master Watanabe Monemon to see you, Madam," using the alias Hirata had supplied.

The room was very bright, very warm, and filled with smoke. Oil lamps burned on a low table, and charcoal braziers radiated heat. Hirata's wet clothes began to steam. A squat, sallow woman perhaps sixty years of age, Madam Kihara knelt amid heaped cushions, sewing supplies, and a half-finished silk embroidery showing quail in a meadow. Her round face was wrinkled like a salted plum. The smoke came from her long silver pipe, which she held clenched in one corner of a smile from which several of her cosmetically blackened teeth were missing.

"So you're looking for a bride, young master?" Madam Kihara rasped. Bowing, she motioned for Hirata to kneel opposite her, which he did. "Some refreshment?"

Along with the lamps, tobacco container, and matches, the table held a teapot, cups, and a plate of rice cakes. Though both tea and cakes tasted of smoke, Hirata ate and drank gratefully, comforted by Madam Kihara's presence. She reminded him of his aunt, who also smoked and sometimes acted as a matchmaker. Hirata wondered sadly if he would ever see her, or his other relatives, again.

Madam Kihara regarded him quizzically. "I don't believe we've met," she said, puffing on her pipe. "Usually I only arrange marriages as a favor to people I know. What is your family?"

To avoid having to create a fictional background and direct the conversation to his real purpose, Hirata said, "Even though you're not acquainted with me or my family, there is a connection between us. I knew Chief Interpreter Iishino when we were young. We—studied with the same tutor for a while," he improvised, not wanting to claim too close a relationship. He also hoped Madam Kihara would overlook the ten-year age difference between him and Iishino, which weakened the story. "I understand you arranged his marriage, so I came hoping you could help me."

"That's funny; I don't recall your name turning up during my investigation of Iishino." Madam Kihara squinted at Hirata through the haze of smoke. Already too warm, he began to sweat. Could she tell he was lying? Then Madam Kihara coughed and shrugged. "Ah, well . . . I can't track down everyone a man has ever known, and it doesn't matter, as long as I don't miss any important contacts. And the negotiations did turn out well."

She preened. "Interpreter Iishino married the governor's niece. And the Nagai clan got rid of a girl who was born in the year of the horse—very unlucky." Madam Kihara refilled her pipe. "Now, tell me, young master: Have you any references who can vouch for your character?"

Hirata was growing nervous, trapped in this stuffy room, unarmed, while the troops scoured the city for him. He wondered what Sano was doing. He thought of the Dutch ship sitting in the harbor like a bomb ready to explode, and the tribunal magistrates who would arrive in Nagasaki in two days. And to continue the charade would only increase his chance of exposing his fraud.

"Before we talk about me," he said, "I need to know what kind of information you give clients about prospective matches. For instance, what did your investigation turn up on Interpreter Iishino?"

Madam Kihara frowned. "The results of my investigations are confidential." She paused, and Hirata waited, hoping that the enjoyment of learning and reporting facts about people was why she arranged marriages instead of idling away her time like most rich old ladies. ". . . However, since you're an old acquaintance of Iishino, it can't hurt to use him as an example of what I can do for you.

"Interpreter Iishino's service record was spotless." Madam Kihara picked up her embroidery and began to stitch. Hirata's heart dropped, then swelled with hope as she continued, "His salary is twenty *koku*— higher than usual for a man of his rank—but he often takes out loans." She named last year's total, a sum almost equal to the cash equivalent of his rice-based government stipend. "He always pays the money back promptly, though. He frequents the pleasure quarter but has no regular courtesan; he likes variety."

Hirata wondered why Iishino merited a high salary. Because he performed dubious tasks—like smuggling—at his superior's behest? Why did he need loans, and how did he repay them? Did Iishino patronize the Half Moon Pleasure House, where Peony had died?

"Iishino's prospects were very solid," Madam Kihara went on. "Dutch is a valuable skill. His only real fault is his personality—he's the most irritating man I've ever met!" She stitched, puffed, and grimaced. "Do you know what he said to me?

" 'Madam Kihara, I must tell you something for your own good, your own good.' " Head bobbing, eyes and smile wide, she did an excellent imitation of Iishino. " 'You shouldn't smoke; it's unfeminine, and the pipe draws attention to your missing teeth.' The gall of that man!" Madam Kihara jabbed her needle into the cloth. "During the *miai*, I had to burn his arm with my pipe whenever he started to speak, so he wouldn't offend the Nagai family."

Hirata laughed at this amusing picture, despite his burgeoning need to reclaim his weapons and be gone. "But you couldn't have hidden Iishino's problem forever. And surely the Nagai could have found a better match for the girl, even if she was born unlucky. Why did they accept Iishino's proposal?"

"For the same reason Governor Nagai and other officials tolerate him: He buys the favor of people he wants to impress, with gifts."

That might explain why Iishino needed loans. Perhaps Iishino borrowed money to cover his purchases, then paid his debts when he received a share of the smuggling profits. Maybe Peony had seen him remove goods from Deshima. But the interpreter had no apparent motive for killing Jan Spaen; there was no evidence to tie him to Spaen's murder, or Peony's. And without this, the tribunal wouldn't believe he'd framed Sano.

"Please excuse me for rambling on so long," Madam Kihara said. "Let's talk about you now. Who are your people? What is your income? Do you expect to inherit any property? Speak up, don't be shy. Any

good family will require this information before they consider a proposal from you."

Just as Hirata was wondering how to make a graceful exit, he heard
heavy footsteps in the corridor, and men's voices: ". . . fugitive . . . reason to believe he's posing as a *doshin* . . . possible sightings reported
. . . headed this way . . ."

Aghast, Hirata bolted toward the outer door, reaching automatically
for his *jitte* and sword—which were still sitting on the shelf in the entryway.

"What's wrong, young master?" The pipe fell out of Madam Kihara's
gaping mouth. "Where are you going?"

"Forgive me, madam," Hirata stammered, sliding open the door.
Panic arced through him when he saw three samurai searching the
garden. One was the paunchy guard from Sano's mansion. Hirata leapt
back into the house, but too late.

"There he is!" shouted the guard.

All three men rushed Hirata. At the same time, four more entered
the reception room, swords drawn, trapping him.

"How dare you attack my guest?" Madam Kihara demanded. "Get
out!"

"This man is a fugitive from the law," the leader told her. To Hirata
he said, "Come along easy, and you won't get hurt."

As the soldiers converged on him, Hirata's scattered thoughts focused into a white-hot sun of determination: He would not be locked
in a cell while his master's enemies went free. He lifted a charcoal bra-
zier and spun around, flinging hot coals and ash at the soldiers.

They fell back, howling and clutching their faces. Madam Kihara
shrieked. Over hot embers that burned through his cloth guest slippers, Hirata dashed to the door, then froze at the sight of more troops
swarming into the garden. He ran back into the room, where the
wounded soldiers blocked his path to the main exit.

"Stop!" they cried, grabbing at him.

The room's side wall was translucent paper divided by thin wooden
mullions. Hirata hurtled straight at it. With a splintering tear, he burst
through the fragile partition. Then he was running through parlors

and bedchambers, down passages. Frightened servants leapt out of his way. The troops stampeded after him. His body filmed with sweat, his heart thumping, he shot through a door and into a narrow courtyard inside the estate's back wall. In the open gate stood the paunchy guard, long sword drawn, eyes red from the ash Hirata had thrown.

"I've got you now," he said, glaring at Hirata in angry triumph.

The wall was too high and smooth to climb. Troops filled the mansion. Laughing, the guard lunged. Powered by desperation, Hirata grabbed the guard's sword arm, then punched him in the eye. The guard yowled. Hirata slammed him against the wall and wrenched the sword away. The guard recovered, drew his short sword, and staggered between Hirata and the gate. Hirata heard the troops coming, their shouts echoing down the corridor behind him.

"Surrender," the guard gasped out. "You can't escape."

He lunged again. Hirata lashed out with the captured sword. Its blade evaded the guard's parry and slit his throat from jowl to Adam's apple. He collapsed in a squealing, gurgling geyser of blood. Hirata dropped the soiled weapon, which would brand him a murderer to anyone who saw him carrying it. He leapt over the body and ran out the gate. As he raced down the alley, he heard the troops' cries fade and saw no one pursuing him. He was free.

But an overwhelming sense of doom quickly eclipsed his relief. He'd killed a man. The search for him would intensify. He was unarmed, his disguise useless. How could he save Sano now, or atone for past mistakes?

28

BY THE TIME the warship docked and Sano descended the gang-plank, evening was deepening into night. Patrolling troops carried flaming metal lanterns that smoked in the moist air. Townspeople, their backs laden with belongings, trudged uphill, evacuating the city. Over the blustery sea wind, Sano heard a strange, rhythmic pulse emanating from the hills. With mingled dread and excitement, he identified it as the beating of war drums. His samurai spirit would have rejoiced at the thought of serving honor and fulfilling his destiny by dying in battle for his lord—had he not borne a grievance against the regime nor felt responsible for courting a disaster that could lay waste to the country.

Now, as a tentative plan formed in his mind, Sano rode back toward Deshima. If the smugglers planned to move any more goods out of the warehouses, they must do so before the ship landed and the newly arrived East India officials could discover and stop the illicit trade. And when better than now, with the governor's troops occupying the waterfront? The smugglers wouldn't need mysterious lights to chase away witnesses.

An officer accosted Sano. "Early curfew in effect on the waterfront until further notice. Except for authorized personnel, everyone shall remain indoors between sunset and dawn."

Sano could see troops chasing peasants out of the streets. "I'm the shogun's representative," he countered angrily. "You don't command me."

"Go, or I'll arrest you," the officer said, unperturbed. He held his lantern up to Sano. "You're bleeding, in case you don't know."

Sano saw with alarm that his wound had bled through the bandage and onto the collar of his white under-kimono. He grew aware of a disturbing heat and pressure in his shoulder. To prevent the wound from festering, he needed immediate treatment. Afterward he might still catch the smugglers when they met their black market contacts to sell the goods. And he had a choice of suspects who might lead him to the rendezvous point: Iishino, Governor Nagai, Urabe, Abbot Liu Yun, and Chief Ohira.

Then, on his way home, Sano discovered further signs of how difficult continuing the investigation would be. Soldiers trailed him openly through the streets. He also sensed the presence of watchers he couldn't see. Reaching his mansion, he found troops loitering outside: The hunt for Hirata continued.

"Has there been any word from my retainer?" he asked when Old Carp met him in the corridor.

"I'm sorry, master," the servant mumbled, "but the soldiers almost caught him at the city treasurer's estate. He murdered a man while trying to escape. The troops have orders to kill him on sight."

Shock hit Sano like a thunderclap in both ears. "What on earth was Hirata doing at the treasurer's estate?"

"The police say he broke into the house to steal money so he could get out of town."

"Lies!" Sano knew better. Instead of trying to escape, Hirata was investigating their accusers. His inquiries must have led him to the Official Quarter, where he'd surely killed in self-defense. Sano's heart sickened as he watched the false charges multiply. Belatedly he noticed that Old Carp mumbled because his mouth was swollen. "What happened to you?" Sano asked.

Old Carp tried to smile, but winced instead. "Governor Nagai found out about how I tricked the spies by pretending I was you last night. Today he sent someone to teach me a lesson. But the beating wasn't too bad; Old Carp is tough. And a good joke like that was worth the price, yes?"

"No," Sano said, appalled because the servant had suffered on his account. And since he could no longer solicit Old Carp's help, how would he escape his watchers?

The desperate energy that had carried him through the day suddenly vanished. He felt weak from hunger, pain, and blood loss. Now that his enemies knew his arrest had not halted his investigation, they aimed to isolate him, to strip him of the power to exonerate himself and expose their crimes. Sano was utterly alone, virtually helpless. Yet even as he experienced the crushing black pressure of despair, his detective spirit rallied. A new plan took shape in his mind. However, he first had to restore his strength.

"I need more medicine and a fresh dressing for this wound," he told Old Carp. "Have the maids bring me a meal, heat the bath, and prepare my bed."

Soon Sano was fed, clean, and wore a new bandage on his shoulder. He retired to his bedchamber, where the futon, piled with soft quilts, offered an irresistible invitation to rest. But Sano feared sleep as much as he craved it.

Somewhere in the night was the assassin who'd shot him; he was surrounded by enemies. Sano dressed in fresh outdoor wear and refastened his swords at his waist. Eschewing the futon, he lay on the floor with his neck propped on a wooden headrest. Alert to the approach of danger, hand grasping his long sword, he skimmed the surface of sleep. But fatigue quickly pulled him into deep, dark oblivion.

HE WAS WALKING through a boundless forest of flowering cherry trees that gave off a peculiar acrid odor and crackling noise. Somewhere a temple bell tolled repeatedly, its sound loud and dissonant. In the distance stood a woman, arms waving in frantic agitation, pale kimono swirling in the hot, dry wind. Sano recognized Aoi, and his heart swelled with joy. He shouted her name, but the bell drowned out his voice. He ran toward her.

Then, as he drew near, he saw terror on Aoi's face and realized she wasn't beckoning, but waving him away. He couldn't hear her voice, but read the words her lips formed: *No! Danger. Run!* Sano ignored the warning. Reaching Aoi, he clasped her in his arms.

The moment they touched, she burst into flames. Her body, hair, and clothes dissolved in a hot, suffocating mass of light and smoke. Sano cried out, awakening with a start in his bedchamber. But the acrid odor remained; the crackling sound grew louder. The suffocating sensation didn't abate. Dense smoke and an eerie orange light filled the room. Coughs wracked Sano's chest; his eyes stung. This was no dream. The ringing bell was the fire alarm. The house was burning. Aoi's spirit had warned him.

Stumbling to his feet, Sano lurched across the room, coughing and gasping. He banged into walls and furniture before his groping hands found a door and opened it. A wave of heat struck him as he saw he'd mistaken an interior door for the one leading to the outer corridor and garden. Along the passage and in the room opposite his bedchamber, flames licked at walls and withered paper partitions. Billowing smoke forced corrosive fumes into Sano's lungs; his throat burned. Holding his sleeve over his nose and mouth, he ran back into the bedchamber, where the floor mats, painted mural, and paper windows blazed.

Suddenly the room's exterior wall crashed inward, and Sano saw flames leaping in the outer corridor. The crackling noise heightened to a roar, punctuated by thuds and crashes. He dared not negotiate the corridors, where the fire could trap him or falling timbers crush him to death. Shielding his head with his arms, he rushed through the inferno in the outer corridor. Intense heat seared his skin; the burning tatami charred his stockinged feet. His hem caught fire in a *woosh* of flame. The smoke blinded him. Then he burst through the ruined wall and into the blessedly cool, fresh night air. He fell into the garden and rolled to extinguish the flames that engulfed him.

"Fire!" he yelled, his voice hoarse from the smoke. A coughing fit overwhelmed him. Sitting up, he retched and spat. The mansion's roof blazed. Sparks flew upward like brilliant orange birds; sails of black smoke fanned the sky. "Help, fire!"

From outside the garden wall came shouts, running footsteps, and the insistent clang of the firebell. The Nagasaki fire brigade, clad in leather cloaks and visored helmets, burst through the gate. They conveyed buckets down a line from a well in the street, brought ladders, climbed to the roof, and splashed water on the burning thatch. With long picks, they pulled down the ruined mansion to keep the fire from spreading. The commander approached Sano.

"You're lucky to be alive," he said. "Better get out in the street, where it's safe. Here, I'll help you."

"The servants," Sano gasped, pointing toward the mansion's back wing, which was now consumed by flames. "We have to save them!"

He would have sped to the rescue, but the commander held him back. "It's too late. There's nothing anyone can do."

DAWN. THE RISING sun was a smear of orange in the vaporous sky, like a carp swimming in a murky pond. The fire was out, and the mansion's blackened skeleton stood amid a wet mass of soot, ashes, charred boards, and ruined furniture. From the wreckage of the servants' quarters, Sano and the fire brigade unearthed ten partially burnt but still recognizable corpses: cook, housekeeper, gardener, stableboy, five maids—and Old Carp. Mournfully Sano wrapped the servant's body in a cloth provided by a neighborhood shrine. He bent his head and murmured a prayer for Old Carp's soul. Then, as *eta* corpse handlers conveyed the dead to the city morgue, Sano collapsed wearily against the earthen wall.

His head and chest hurt; violent coughs brought up thick, salty phlegm. Raw, red burns on his arms and legs ached with a fierce heat. He was lucky to have survived Japan's most feared but all too common natural disaster, and for the first time thankful for Hirata's absence. Wherever he was, at least he'd not died in the fire. But pain and despair overwhelmed Sano as he tried to summon the energy to resume the fight against his enemies.

The fire brigade commander was walking through the ruins, muttering while he inspected them. A new sense of unease disturbed Sano. He rose and joined the commander.

"I've never known a natural fire to burn so hot and fast under these conditions," the commander said. "It rained most of yesterday; the moisture should have kept the flames from spreading. The weather was too warm for charcoal braziers. And I don't think the fire was caused by a lamp or candle accidentally left burning, either."

"Then it was arson?" Sano said.

"I'd stake my honor on it." The commander pointed upward. "Roof and ceilings totally destroyed. Only structural components left are interior ones." He kicked a pile of fallen beams and joists. "The fire moved down from the outside of the house to the inside, opposite the usual way. And look at this."

He picked up a charred plank and handed it to Sano, who noted the greasy residue on the unburnt portion. "Lamp oil," he said. His heart plummeted, and fury enveloped his spirit.

"Poured over the roof," the commander clarified, "then lit."

So the feared attack had come after all, though in a form Sano hadn't expected. The world darkened at the edges of his vision as the nightmare of his past investigations began again. Because of him, innocent people—including his only Nagasaki friend—had died. If he'd accepted Peony's confession, if he'd resigned himself to his fate after his arrest, they would be alive now. Who had done more harm: the murderer of Jan Spaen—or Sano? Beneath his ostensible quest for honor, Sano perceived another, less noble purpose, which he'd never before considered. Had a selfish desire to prove himself right—to triumph through his own moral superiority—caused eleven deaths and a possible war?

Sano's horrified guilt over his own motives turned to anger at the men who wanted him dead so badly that they didn't care who else they killed to make his death look accidental. He stalked out the front gate to the street. Just as he'd expected, the troops were gone. They'd probably left to let the arsonist do his work, then not returned because they'd assumed Sano would perish in the fire. Sano approached a crowd of curious onlookers.

"Were any of you around when the fire started?" he asked.

"I was," a young samurai volunteered. "I had firewatch duty last night." He pointed to a roofed wooden platform that rose on poles above the houses in the next block. "I saw the flames and rang the bell."

"Did you see anyone near the house then?"

The samurai nodded. "There was a man standing on the roof. When the flames went up, he jumped on top of the next house. I yelled at him to stop, but he ran away. By the time I climbed down from the tower and got over here, he was gone."

"What did he look like?" Sano asked.

"I was too far away to see him very well, but he wore a big hat and a short kimono."

And he must be fairly young and agile. It could not have been Governor Nagai, who would have delegated such dirty work. Though Abbot Liu Yun's age excluded him, Chief Ohira, Urabe, Interpreter Iishino, and the Deshima guards were possible culprits who would want to minimize the slim chance that Sano might be acquitted by the tribunal and convince the Edo authorities to investigate their affairs. Sano clenched his jaws in frustration. The tragedy had scarcely even narrowed down his original list of suspects.

Yet a cold, determined fury solidified like a layer of ice below the surface of Sano's anger. His enemies had made his work harder, but he would not give up. There was still the plan he'd formulated last night. He had more deaths to avenge now, and a guilty conscience to assuage.

If he lived long enough.

29

A SEARCH FOR better witnesses to the arson proved futile, but the god of luck did grant Sano two compensatory blessings. His money, sealed in a fireproof iron chest, had survived the fire. And when he left the site, no one followed: News of his survival had not yet reached his enemies. He hurried to take advantage of his temporary autonomy.

He gave his long sword to the street headman for safekeeping. In the merchant district, he replaced his burnt clothes with a short cotton kimono, wide straw hat, sandals, leggings to cover the bandages on his burns, and a baggy cloak to hide his short sword. At a ropemaker's, he bought a coil of straw cable and attached to it an iron hook purchased from a blacksmith. He tied the rope around his waist under his cloak, then headed for the waterfront.

A diminishing stream of evacuees made their way toward the hills; many shops were already closed, houses shuttered and empty. Sano surveyed the view and cursed under his breath. Troops still occupied the promenade, docks, and beach. Sentries still guarded the Deshima guardhouse and bridge; watchboats still circled the island. The evidence Sano needed to incriminate the smugglers and clear himself and Hirata was on Deshima. But how to get there?

Past Sano trudged water bearers, each with two wooden buckets suspended from a pole on his shoulder. Sano's interest roused as he watched the men fill the buckets at a well and carry them downhill. The morning was sultry, overcast, and windless; moisture from yesterday's rain steamed up from the earth. The water shimmered like colorless silk beneath the Dutch ship, Japanese war vessels, and patrol barges. The beat of the war drums continued, their relentless pulse underscoring the heat. Sano sweltered under his bulky clothing, but smiled when he saw the water bearers busily serving the thirsty troops. Hurrying over to the well, he approached a bearer who'd just obtained a refill.

"Give me your buckets," he said, drawing his sword.

The bearer gulped. "Yes, master!"

Sano shouldered the pole and hurried downhill, wincing under the awkward load. How did those fellows carry such heavy buckets all day long? He imitated the way they let the pole teeter so that the weight constantly shifted. Water sloshed from his buckets. A sore spot quickly formed on his shoulder. Sano reached the promenade breathless and panting.

"Water!" called a mounted soldier.

Sano hurried over. Keeping his face averted, he set down the buckets and filled the ladle. As he handed it up to the soldier, the horse suddenly reared. Water splashed the soldier's armor tunic.

"Clumsy oaf!" he said, cuffing Sano on the head.

Sano's samurai pride bristled at the insult. He stifled an angry retort, preserving his peasant disguise. "A thousand pardons, master," he said meekly.

Dispensing water to other troops, he moved down the promenade, but didn't see how he could sneak past the Deshima guards. His buckets were quickly emptying; soon he would have to go back to the well. Farther along the coast, past the buildings and docks, the shoreline was rocky and wooded. From there, he might sneak into the water. But he could never swim all the way to Deshima with his wounded shoulder, burns, and cumbersome gear. The watchboat sentries would spot him before he even got close. He had to find another way.

Then Sano saw a watchboat leave its post. The two-man crew rowed to the harbor patrol station and disembarked at the pier. A new crew took its place in the boat, rowed back to Deshima, and resumed the watch. Sano hurried onto the pier, as if to serve water to troops there. They were watching another boat approach and didn't notice him. The station shielded him from view of the soldiers on the promenade. Abandoning his buckets and pole, he shimmied down a piling and into the water. Its salty chill stung his burns. Quickly he removed his hat and cloak and stuffed them between the piling and a diagonal support beam. Then he gulped a deep breath, dived beneath the water under the pier, and swam toward another piling near where the boat would arrive.

The water was so murky he could barely see. Debris floated past him. His gear and clothing hampered his movements. Kicking and stroking strained his burned limbs and sore shoulder. His lungs demanded air. Just when he thought his chest would explode, his fingers touched slimy, algae-covered wood. He grabbed the piling and cautiously raised his head above water, trying to quiet his gasps.

The watchboat drew up parallel to the pier, almost within touching distance, the oarsman standing in the stern, his partner sitting behind the pointed prow that arched up from the water. Both wore arquebuses. Shivering, Sano watched the crew secure the boat, heard them greet the shore troops who helped them onto the pier. The replacement crew stepped aboard. Quickly Sano plunged underwater and swam under the boat. The dipping oar nearly hit him. The bow turned toward Deshima, and the boat's curved bottom began moving away. Still underwater, Sano rolled onto his back; kicking hard, he caught up with the boat and aligned himself along its length. He desperately craved air; he was drowning. The boat was moving too fast. Determination spurred him on. He grasped the prow and pulled himself up until his face just cleared the surface. The sea sucked at him as the boat picked up speed. Spitting water, he hung on, his nails digging into the rough wood.

"Something just hit the boat," Sano heard the man nearest him say.

The oar continued splashing. "Probably just trash," the other man said. "Harbor's filthy. Yesterday I saw four broken barrels, a dead dog, an old fishing net . . ."

While the litany droned on, Sano gasped and spewed and fought to maintain his grip. Twisting his neck, he saw that they were nearing the outer shore of Deshima, where two other watchboats floated outside the signposts. The men in them sat facing the harbor. Before Sano came within their range of vision, he let go and ducked underwater. When the boat passed over him, he grabbed the stern, letting it tow him.

The boat glided to a stop near the island's northwest corner. Cautiously Sano poked his head above the water and saw the crew sitting with their gazes turned seaward. Sano swam underwater toward Deshima, hoping the Dutch ship would hold their attention and the sound of waves and war drums mask any noises he made. Breathless and exhausted, he reached the island's rocky, vertical foundation. The fence rose high above him. Hurriedly he untied the rope around his waist, watching the sentries not twenty paces away. How much time before someone got bored and chanced to look behind him?

Half in, half out of the water, Sano leaned against the foundation and put his ear to the fence. He heard marching footsteps approach, pass, and recede: a guard, patrolling the perimeter. With no time to lose before the next inspection, Sano tossed the iron hook at the top of the fence. It struck with a loud thump, then clattered noisily onto the rocks, bringing the rope with it. Sano cursed under his breath; panic thrummed along his nerves as he glanced at the boat sentries . . .

. . . who remained immobile, facing out to sea. Praying for luck, Sano threw the hook again. This time it caught the fence and held securely. Bracing his feet against the island's foundation, he pulled his dripping self clear of the water, looking over his shoulder at the watchboats. Hand over hand he climbed up the fence. His feet scraped against the planks; he expected to hear an alarm rise from within the compound. When his head cleared the fence, he looked down into the narrow passage between the outer and inner fences.

It was empty, but Sano heard nearby voices. Briefly he contemplated the dire consequences of being caught trespassing on Deshima:

instant death. But he'd already breached island security, and the boat sentries would shoot if they saw him. He scrambled onto the top of the fence, wincing as the spikes jabbed him. Pulling the hook free, he dropped into the passage.

His feet hit the gravel with a loud crunch. Hastily he crammed the rope and hook inside his drenched kimono, then sped to the gate he remembered from his first visit. He cautiously opened it and looked inside.

In the barbarians' garden, three sentries sat playing cards, their backs to him. Smoke rose from their pipes. Tethered goats grazed; chickens scratched in the pen by the vegetable patch. Beyond stood the barbarians' houses. Sano slipped through the gate, closed it quietly, and sprinted across the garden. Ducking behind the goat shed, he studied the guards, who seemed unaware of anything amiss. The stairs to the balcony lay perhaps ten paces away. Then a clear remark emerged from the mutter of the guards' conversation:

"With all the extra troops on Deshima and all the barbarians locked up in the common room together, it's like a holiday for us regulars. We should have war more often."

Laughter followed; Sano's heart sank. How would he speak to Dr. Huygens in private, especially if the barbarians were under even heavier surveillance than usual? The task he must accomplish afterward also seemed impossible.

And how would he get off Deshima alive?

Sano thought of Hirata and Peony; of Old Carp and the other servants killed in the fire; of Kiyoshi, perhaps wrongfully condemned. He pictured Governor Nagai, Chief Ohira, Interpreter Iishino, Urabe, Abbot Liu Yun, and the barbarians, free to murder and smuggle again unless he stopped them. His particular anger at Dr. Huygens flared; his resolve hardened. Watching the sentries and keeping alert for others, Sano left his shelter and angled toward the gap between the houses. Through it he could see the street, the warehouse opposite, and the patrolling guards. Danger prickled his skin like the energy current before a lightning strike. Halfway there. Just ten paces to go . . .

Sano darted into the gap. He pressed himself against the wall and expelled the breath he'd been holding. Then he crept toward the street and cautiously peered up and down it.

Except for a sentry at each guardhouse, Deshima's security force was concentrated on the building that contained the common room, across the street and some fifty paces to Sano's right. There were ten men outside the door, three on the balcony, probably others at the rear. Could he create a diversion and draw the guards away so he could get inside to Dr. Huygens?

Then, looking down the street, Sano saw Nirin walk out of the doctor's surgery. Sano ducked back into the yard and hurried toward the surgery. A guard emerged from a building, and Sano darted behind a tree. At last he reached his destination. He peered through the window.

Inside, Dr. Huygens stood by the table where they'd examined Jan Spaen's corpse. Upon it slept a young man, covered with a quilt. A lone guard leaned against the wall, his back to the door. In an instant, Sano was in the surgery, his arm locked in a choke hold around the guard. The patient didn't awaken, but Dr. Huygens exclaimed in surprise.

"Quiet!" Sano rasped, straining to subdue his flailing, coughing captive. He applied more pressure to the guard's neck. The coughs turned to gasps; then the guard went limp and unconscious. Sano eased him to the floor, shut the door, then faced Huygens. "Why did you lie to me?"

Dr. Huygens didn't pretend to misunderstand. Behind his glasses, his eyes closed briefly as his shoulders heaved in a sigh of mingled sadness and relief. "I no want you think I kill Spaen," he said, adjusting the bandage on his patient's leg. "I afraid."

Sano remembered the calm detachment with which Huygens had examined Jan Spaen's corpse. At the funeral, when Huygens had said, "May all our sins be forgiven," he could have been praying for Spaen's soul—or asking absolution for his own sin of murdering Spaen. Had he helped Sano because he was a believer in justice, or to protect himself?

"You fought with Spaen before he died," Sano said. "About what?"

Huygens hesitated, but only long enough to draw Sano into the corner so their conversation wouldn't disturb the patient. Either he was unaware that Sano had lost authority on Deshima, or didn't care because he needed to confess. "I want leave East India Company; go home. Spaen no let me."

Then followed a tale of misspent youth and subsequent reform; of how Jan Spaen had gained power over and exploited Huygens. "I no mean kill Franz Tulp." Dr. Huygens's anguished eyes pleaded for Sano's belief. "I drunk; I mad. We fight. I hit too hard. He fall."

The doctor drew a long, shaky breath, as if experiencing anew the horror of that long-ago day. His red face was sweating profusely, his body odor pungent. Sano eyed the doors, waiting with controlled impatience for him to continue. "Then Jan Spaen come. He see Tulp's body, me with bloody pipe. I scared he call the, the—"

"The police," Sano said.

Huygens rushed on: "But Spaen say he help. We pick up body, carry away. I say, what if someone see us? Spaen say wait. Then horse cart come, fast. We throw body in front. Horses, cart, go over body. We run away. Hear cart stop, people shout: They think they kill Tulp."

And so, it seemed, did everyone else. Later Huygens had heard that the authorities had ruled Tulp's death an accident of the sort not uncommon to Dutch festivals: a drunken youth, crushed when he fell under a cart driven by more drunken youths. Huygens's fellow brawlers had kept silent for fear of punishment. He might have gotten away with murder, if not for Jan Spaen. Sano pitied Huygens, admiring his efforts to atone for the crime. His distaste for Spaen deepened. To solve the mystery of that cruel man's death, Sano had risked everything. But he couldn't let antipathy toward the murder victim affect his judgment. Nor could he excuse a suspect he liked.

"I'll ask you again," Sano said. "Where were you the night Spaen disappeared?"

Dr. Huygens took a step backward, but his eyes met Sano's bravely. "In my room; sleep. I no kill Spaen."

"Did you smuggle goods from the Deshima warehouse to a cove in the harbor?"

"I no smuggle. I no kill!"

"Did you plant the bullet in Spaen's body?"

"No! No!" Clumsily Huygens dropped to his knees before Sano, hands clasped in entreaty. "Friend," he said, weeping. "I sorry I no tell you Spaen hurt me. But I no kill. I know nothing of smuggling. Please, trust. Forgive."

Sano puffed out his breath in angry frustration. There was no physical evidence tying Huygens to Spaen's murder or the smuggling, yet Sano was now convinced of the doctor's guilt. Huygens had once killed a fellow student in a fit of drunken temper. If he hadn't really reformed, he could have done the same to Jan Spaen. His betrayal of Sano's trust finalized the case against him. Sano should never have trusted a barbarian; their worlds were too far apart, their values too different. The whole investigation was compromised, the evidence tainted. And unless Sano's next actions yielded good results, he would lose his life and honor.

"I have to go," he said.

He stripped off the unconscious guard's helmet, long sword, armor tunic, robe, and leg guards. He removed his own outer clothes and donned the stolen uniform, keeping his short sword. The guard was bigger than he, and the armor fit too loosely, but he needed the disguise. He crammed the inert body into an empty cupboard, threw his rope and hook in, and shut the door.

"If anyone comes, tell them the guard went outside," Sano told Dr. Huygens, who nodded as if eager to please. Then he slipped out the back door.

HIS FACE PARTIALLY hidden by the visor and side flaps of his stolen helmet, Sano crossed the yard. His heart tripped when the three guards outside the barbarians' house looked up at him. He nodded as he passed. They nodded in reply, then returned to their card game. Sano released his breath: the first obstacle cleared. Reaching the fence, he opened the gate and stepped into the perimeter passage, nerves taut.

Here lay the peril of a face-to-face confrontation with someone who could identify him as an imposter, while he was trapped between the fences. Would that he could subdue any passing patrol guards he met without adding murder to his list of crimes!

Sano hurried along the fan curve of the island. Now he heard brisk footsteps coming from behind. A blare of panic echoed in his head, and he quickened his steps. On his left appeared the gate he sought. Sano slipped through it and into the garden of the office compound. This was deserted; with the barbarians imprisoned indoors and all approaches to Deshima covered, the staff had relaxed security here. Beyond an ornamental pond and more trees, the chief's long, two-story house, with the thatched roof, large entry porch, and latticed balcony Sano remembered from his first visit, stood against the south wall. Along the west wall were the deputies' and interpreters' office cottages, the building where the Dutch sold their goods, the fireproof storehouses, and the stables. Sano detected no activity. When he noticed the barred windows of Ohira's house, his hopes dwindled, yet he saw an advantage to the situation. He might have trouble getting inside the house without being seen, but the presence of Ohira's staff might prove a boon rather than an obstacle.

Sano walked boldly up to the door, as would a guard on official business. He passed through the entry porch and into a dim, empty corridor with low ceiling, bare plank floor, and mullioned paper walls. From the first room to his right came the rustle of paper. Sano froze outside the door and listened.

The ceiling creaked above him: someone upstairs. But the first floor seemed vacant, except for this room. A furtive glance inside revealed a spacious office with a study niche on a raised platform at one end, furnished with a large desk and built-in shelves, iron chests, wooden cabinets and screens, and a row of smaller desks beside the windows. At one of these knelt a young samurai. His profile to Sano, he wrote on a scroll, frowning in concentration.

Remembering his past career as a clerk and scholar, Sano experienced a sharp pang of nostalgia. He steeled his heart against the youth who evoked those peaceful, bygone days. Drawing his short sword, he stepped through the door and closed it behind him. The clerk looked up. A cry of surprise died on his lips as Sano grabbed his collar and put the sword to his throat.

"Don't scream, or I'll kill you," Sano said in the clerk's ear.

Held immobile against Sano, the youth whimpered, "Yes, master." His upturned face was white; his eyes rolled. Sano could feel the thin body trembling. His own heart was racing. *Please let me not kill this innocent man!*

"The records of the goods brought to Japan by Director Spaen," Sano said, keeping his voice low, calm, and authoritative. As commanding officer of Deshima, Chief Ohira had the responsibility for keeping an inventory of Dutch imports. "Where are they?"

The clerk gulped. His rapid, panicky breaths sounded as loud as screams. Sano glanced toward the door, afraid the other staff members might hear. "Be quiet, and I won't hurt you." He pulled the blade back so it no longer touched the man's throat. "Show me the records, and I'll let you go."

"There. Over there . . ." The clerk's shaking hand pointed to the study niche, where a long scroll, covered with inked characters, lay open on Chief Ohira's desk.

"Is that all of them?"

"Yes. Yes!"

Still gripping the clerk tight, Sano sheathed his sword. Then he untied the clerk's sash, bound his ankles with one end, wrists with the other.

"No," moaned the clerk. "Please . . ."

Sano wadded a sheet of paper and stuffed it into the clerk's mouth, muffling his voice. He hurried over to Chief Ohira's desk and examined the scroll, which was dated two years ago. Chinese silk, British wool, and Indian cotton, he read; Cambodian deer hides; nutmeg from the Spice Islands; Dutch spyglasses . . . Each item was described in detail. But Sano was more interested in what was missing from the list. As he'd hoped, he found no mention of the firearms or clocks found in the smugglers' cave. And the scroll bore Chief Ohira's round, red personal seal—proof that he'd falsified the warehouse inventory, leaving out goods he knew would be sold illegally and thus never reported to Edo.

Elation surged in Sano as he rolled the scroll and tucked it under his loose-fitting armor tunic. This was the evidence he needed to convince the tribunal of his innocence; evidence that proved the smuggling had preceded his arrival in Nagasaki, and incriminated one of the chief witnesses against him.

Then, before he turned to leave, he saw on the desk a sheet of paper partially filled with characters: an unfinished copy of the inventory. From between entries Sano had already read, descriptions of the smugglers' loot leapt out at him. The paper was clean, white, and crisp; the calligraphy Ohira's. The chief, anticipating an audit of his records, had been preparing a new inventory that accounted for items missing from the original.

The placement of both lists, side by side and out in the open, intrigued Sano. Of course, with the whole Deshima staff in on the conspiracy, Ohira had no reason to hide compromising documents. But Sano glimpsed a deeper motive for Ohira's action—one he could exploit. He folded the page, tucked it inside his armor, and started to leave the room. The sound of the front door opening stopped him. Hurrying footsteps pounded the corridor. Sano whirled and ran for the window.

"There's a trespasser on the island!" shouted a familiar voice. "Everybody get out and search for him. Now!"

More footsteps; excited voices. "He knocked out the man who was guarding the barbarian doctor," Sano heard Nirin explain to someone. Desperately he rattled the window bars, which held firm. The office door flew open. Sano turned as Nirin burst into the room.

"Kenji, go to the mainland and fetch Chief Ohira immediately," the commander ordered. "Tell him—" His startled gaze took in the clerk, bound and gagged, and Sano at the window. Fury suffused his face. "You." He spoke on a disgusted laugh. "I might have known."

In a motion so fast that his image blurred, Nirin whipped his sword from its scabbard and lunged. The blade whistled through the air, straight toward Sano's neck. Sano had his stolen long sword ready, but its unfamiliar weight and grip disconcerted him. He almost failed to parry Nirin's stroke. Their blades met in a jarring clash of steel. Swinging his sword free, Sano tried a cross-body cut.

His blade glanced harmlessly off the commander's armor tunic. Nirin laughed and launched another assault. Sano, unaccustomed to fighting in armor, found himself at a serious disadvantage. He saw that Nirin was no better a swordsman than himself; his own helmet, tunic, and leg and arm guards shielded him. But this style of combat demanded a different strategy. All strikes must target an unprotected area of his opponent's body: face, neck, thighs, or upper arms. As Sano thrust and parried and circled, his wounded shoulder grew sore. The tunic chafed against the bandage. And he could tell that Nirin knew about his handicap.

The commander centered his attack on Sano's upper body, forcing him to fight with his sword raised, which strained the injury even more. Sano managed few counterstrokes while Nirin chased him around the room. He leapt backward over desks, bumped cabinets and screens. He heard shouts from the doorway. Clerks and guards burst into the room.

"Stand back," Nirin told them, slashing at Sano. "He's all mine."

Sano was gasping in pain, sweaty and panting with exertion. Warm blood trickled down his chest. Nirin, not even winded, closed in on him. Completely on the defensive now, Sano dodged and parried. His shoulder weakened. Nirin aimed a cut at Sano's neck. Their blades crossed, locking Sano's arm in a high, awkward twist. Pain shot from his shoulder to his hand. He let go the sword, and the spectators cheered. Nirin raised his weapon in both hands. Sano leapt backward just in time to avoid the slice. He drew his short sword, but with his reach reduced, he couldn't get close enough to Nirin to score a cut. The commander's longer, heavier sword battered his. If this continued, the fight was lost.

Ducking a swipe aimed to sever his head, Sano kicked a screen into Nirin's path. The commander stumbled, throwing out his arms to regain his balance. Sano didn't use the chance to slay his opponent: He needed Nirin alive. Darting behind the commander, Sano grabbed the back collar of Nirin's armor tunic and jerked him upright. He jammed his sword under the commander's right arm, with the tip of the blade touching the unprotected armpit.

"Drop your weapon!" he ordered.

Nirin went rigid. Slowly he turned to Sano, eyes sharp with terror and hatred. He opened his mouth to speak, but no sound emerged. Cries of dismay issued from the men at the door. When Sano repeated the order, Nirin dropped his blade.

"Now unsheathe the other one, and throw it over there," Sano said. "Good. Now fold your arms."

Nirin did, and his wide sleeve fell, hiding Sano's sword.

"Let him go," blurted a guard.

Ragged breaths tore Sano's chest as his body fought to restore its depleted energy. "We're going to walk off the island together," he said to Nirin. Holding the commander by the armor, Sano marched him toward the door. "Out of the way," Sano told the guards and clerks, "or he dies."

Mouths agape in shock, the men didn't budge. Sano thrust the blade upward, felt it bite flesh. Nirin flinched, croaking, "Do as he says."

The men sprang away from the door. Sano propelled Nirin down the corridor and out of the house. "Don't follow, or I'll kill him," Sano called over his shoulder, halting the guards' rush across the garden after them.

"If you think you can get away with this, you're crazy." Outrage and fear mingled in Nirin's voice. "There are troops all over the island. You'll never get past them."

Sano fought his own doubt. "Yes, I will, because you're going to help me." He kicked open the gate and shoved Nirin through. "Not one word, unless I tell you to speak." His heart seized when he saw guards swarming the street, hunting the trespasser.

"Over here!" Nirin called. "He's got me."

All heads turned toward them; all sound and motion stopped. Then came the outcry. Guards surrounded Sano and Nirin, swords drawn. Sano remembered a hostage incident he'd once resolved. Now *he* was the villain. A nightmarish sense of unreality fell over him.

"Let us through, or I'll kill him," he shouted.

He jerked his sword forward, exposing the hilt. The crowd quieted, looking to their leader for orders. Nirin sucked in his breath as the blade poked his armpit, then forced a laugh. "You can't kill me. You need me to escape. Don't listen to him. He's bluffing."

The crowd stirred, but Sano felt Nirin's uncertainty, and saw it on the other men's faces. He knew what they were thinking: Anyone mad enough to break into Deshima was mad enough to murder his hostage. Finally the crowd parted. Sano and Nirin proceeded, step by step, down the endless street.

"Where is Chief Ohira?" Sano asked Nirin.

The commander shot a venomous glance at Sano. "My superior's whereabouts are none of your business," he said as they neared the main gate. "I will tell you nothing. And you have to keep me alive to get past the bridge guards."

"Where is Ohira?" Sano jabbed Nirin again, provoking a stifled groan. After the bridge, he must pass the main guardhouse, the heavily occupied promenade, and the troops in town, but he would handle one thing at a time. "I'll hurt you if I must."

They reached the gate. "Open it!" Sano ordered the sentry. "And make sure no one follows us."

Nirin stiffened; sweat ran down his face. It was clear that he feared maiming more than death. He spoke through clenched teeth. "Do as he says."

The sentry opened the gate. Sano marched his prisoner onto the bridge. "Where is Ohira?"

"All right. All right!" Nirin was trembling now. "He said he was going to the Daikoku Shrine." At Sano's prompting, he gave the location. "What do you want with him?"

The truth about Spaen's murder and the smuggling operation, Sano thought. Chief Ohira's cooperation was the key to freedom for himself and Hirata.

As Sano and Nirin crossed the bridge, the sentries bowed to their commander, frowning at Sano. "Tell them I came to Deshima with your permission," Sano whispered, keeping the sword hidden beneath the commander's sleeve. "They're to make sure no one else leaves the island."

The commander repeated the lie in a thin voice so unlike his normal one that Sano feared his ploy would fail. He sensed Nirin's mind racing through possible strategies for escape, all of which led to his own death. When the sentries let him and Nirin pass, relief flooded him. They got through the guardhouse without the customary exit formalities. On the promenade, they blended with troops dressed in similar uniform.

"You won't get away with this, because I'm going to kill you," Nirin said, dragging his feet.

"Was it you who shot me?" Sano asked. "Did you burn my house?"

"No, but I wish I had, because then you'd be dead now!"

"Did you kill Jan Spaen or Peony?"

"No!"

Sano knew he couldn't restrain Nirin indefinitely. As they moved up the street past clusters of departing townspeople, he cast about for a way to shed his hostage without a fight to the death. Then he quickened his pace, forcing Nirin to walk faster.

"Where are you taking me?" Nirin demanded.

Sano marched the commander to the well at which he'd gotten the water buckets. "Out of the way," he ordered the bearers gathered around it. Then, to Nirin: "Jump in."

Struggling in Sano's grip, Nirin gave an incredulous laugh. "I will not. You're mad!"

Another jab with the sword, and he climbed onto the well's stone rim, cursing. A hard push from Sano sent him over the edge. He disappeared down the shaft, a long scream trailing after him. There was a splash as he hit the water. His terrified cries echoed from the depths of the well. "Help! Help!"

Citizens flocked to see who'd fallen into the well. Police came and shouted for rope, for strong men to help rescue the victim.

In the confusion, Sano slipped away before anyone could stop him, and headed for the Daikoku Shrine.

31

THE DAIKOKU SHRINE was located on a wooded slope near the edge of town, off the main highway leading beyond the hills. Between the double crossbeams of the torii gate, an engraved stone tablet bore the name of Daikoku, god of fortune.

Sano entered the gate along with a stream of peasant, merchant, and samurai families who had come to seek the god's blessing during the anticipated war. He climbed a flight of stone steps to the shrine precinct, a clearing sheltered by cypress trees. A flagstone path led to the main shrine building. Worshippers clustered around refreshment and souvenir stands. A stone statue of Daikoku, plump and smiling, carried a sack of treasure and the magic mallet with which he granted wishes. He sat upon two rice bales gnawed by carved rats—his earthly messengers—amid flowers and other offerings. Priests dressed in white robes and oblong black caps mingled with the crowd. The fresh mountain air carried the sweet, musky perfume of incense. Over the children's laughter, the clack of wooden soles, and chanted prayers, a bell rang, deep and clear. Above the city, the sun's rays pierced the clouds like spokes of a gleaming silver fan. As Sano washed his hands in the stone ritual basin, the tranquil atmosphere of the shrine lifted his spirits. His problems seemed remote; he could almost forget that he must cause immense suffering to the man he'd come to find.

Scanning the precinct, he saw Chief Ohira standing at a stall that sold lucky figures and candy, colorful strings of origami flying cranes, which signified longevity, and wooden prayer stakes. Alone, in his somber clothing, the chief looked out of place among the brightly dressed families. As Sano approached, Ohira bought a stake. He inked one of the brushes set out for the customers' use and wrote a prayer on the stake. Engrossed in the task, he didn't notice Sano come up beside him.

"Please protect us from evil, and replace our troubles with blessings," Sano read over the chief's shoulder. The names of Ohira's large family followed. It was a commonplace prayer, but poignant under the circumstances. Sano hated what he must do, but Chief Ohira had earned his own destiny.

Now Ohira looked up and saw Sano. "You again," he said wearily. "How dare you disturb me in a sacred place?" He seemed more gaunt than ever, as if his flesh had withered around a core of pain, all that was left of him. "What do you want? How did you find me?" Turning away, he walked to the statue of Daikoku.

Sano followed. "Your commander told me where you were."

Ohira's steps faltered. "You've been to Deshima? But how? . . . Your pass was revoked." He stared, then shook his head when Sano's appearance offered no clue.

Before coming to the shrine, Sano had discarded the stolen armor. His clothes had dried in the afternoon heat, and with his lone short sword at his waist, he looked like any ordinary low-rank samurai. Now he didn't waste time explaining his escapade to Ohira, who would find out soon enough anyway. The Deshima guards would report what he'd done. Troops would be searching for him. He must act fast.

"How I got to Deshima isn't important," Sano said. "It's what I found there that matters." He pulled the scroll and the unfinished copy out of his kimono. "The tribunal will be interested in these, don't you think?"

Recognition flared in Ohira's eyes. A shudder ran through him. Then he squatted and pushed his prayer stake into the ground amid others at the stone god's feet. His hands trembled.

"So I am in your power now," he said, despair reflected in the slump of his shoulders, the melancholy timbre of his voice. He touched the stake. "I've sent my prayers too late for them to do any good."

The moment seemed as fragile as a priceless porcelain tea bowl Sano had once used at an Edo Castle tea ceremony: thin, translucent, its surface crazed by the heat of the kiln. He took a deep breath, seeking the wisdom to handle the moment without damage. "Or maybe your prayers have already been answered," he said.

"What do you mean?" Ohira rose, avoiding Sano's gaze.

"You left these documents out in the open, as if you hoped someone would find them and punish you, although there was little chance of that on Deshima. You're not really sorry I found them." Sano tucked the scroll and copy back in his kimono. "The gods are wise. Sometimes they know and grant our deepest, most secret wishes."

Ohira emitted a humorless laugh. "Through you, the agent of my fate? Do you think I wish public disgrace and dishonorable death? I can assure you that's not the case."

He stalked down the path to the main shrine building, a wooden hut with a thatched roof and railed veranda, elevated on wooden posts and surrounded by a picket fence. Sano followed Ohira up the stone steps. "When your boyhood friends died, you swore to uphold the law and prevent others from committing crimes," he said, referring to the story Ohira had told him yesterday. "By breaking your vow, you destroyed your own honor. You couldn't openly confess and endanger your family, but you crave punishment." He paused as Ohira pulled the rope that hung from the eaves, ringing the bell to summon the god. Leaving their shoes outside the door, they entered the shrine. "And you can't bear to live while your son dies."

In the anteroom, daylight filtered through the door and window gratings, casting soft diamond patterns on the polished cypress floor. Sacred white paper plaits hung from the pillars. The walls were covered with gifts to the shrine: model ships, swords, houses. White curtains shrouded the doorway to the inner sanctuary, receptacle for the god. A calm hush pervaded the air, which smelled of incense, candles, and pine resin. Chief Ohira dropped to his knees before the curtains, head bowed in tacit acknowledgment of Sano's words. Sano knelt beside him. After a long moment, Chief Ohira spoke in a voice quiet with sad resignation.

"I compromised Deshima security and falsified the warehouse inventory on Governor Nagai's orders. I didn't want to, but what choice had I? A samurai must obey his superior."

In Bushido, obedience was the supreme virtue, which often conflicted with individual morality and the law. Sano, who understood the conflict all too well, realized that guilt and self-hatred had caused Ohira's physical infirmity, eroding body and spirit.

"Nagai said that if I refused," Ohira continued, "he would replace me with someone who would allow the smuggling. He threatened to withdraw his patronage of Kiyoshi." The chief's voice cracked in anguish; he turned to Sano, hand extended in a plea for understanding. "What was I to do?" Then the rush of emotion subsided. Ohira bent his head over his folded hands. "Now all is lost."

"It doesn't have to be," Sano said.

"What do you mean?" Ohira's voice held a glimmer of hope.

Sano had evidence; he had Ohira's confession, which the chief, in his eagerness for punishment, would repeat to the tribunal. But he wanted more.

"Kiyoshi can be saved." Sano hesitated, feeling a sudden unwelcome sense of identification with Jan Spaen. In view of what he meant to do, was he not also an exploiter of men? "Your son is not a smuggler or a murderer—his one crime was accusing me to protect you. If we can persuade him to tell the truth, he won't have to die."

Chief Ohira exhaled in a moan. "You don't know the whole story. And I can assure you that when you do, you won't be so willing to help Kiyoshi.

"I visited him in jail this morning. He was like a madman, but he regained his senses long enough to tell me everything. Two months ago, he chased the mysterious lights because a fortune-teller told him they were ghosts who could give him enough money so he could marry the girl he loves. Kiyoshi saw the lights go to Deshima and followed them to the cove, where he saw the smugglers. Later he overheard me telling the guards to relax Deshima security on nights when the smuggling occurred. He didn't know that Governor Nagai and other officials were involved. He assumed I commanded the ring myself. On the night of his arrest, he went to the cove to persuade me to give it up."

So it was his father whom Kiyoshi had gone to "stop" and "warn." Sano's guess was confirmed.

A mournful laugh caught in Ohira's throat. "My poor, devoted, naïve son. Yes, he protected me, but not just by lying. He began prowling the waterfront at night because he was afraid the police would catch me—how was he to know they were accomplices?" Ohira paused, as if gathering courage. "Kiyoshi fired arrows at anyone who went near the harbor."

"He shot me?" Sano said, amazed. Not Nirin or the Deshima guards, then; not an assassin sent by Chamberlain Yanagisawa. He'd guessed Kiyoshi's motive, but not how far the boy had gone to shield his father. Now his incoherent rambling made sense. He'd "placed personal interests above those of the shogun and nation" not by smuggling, but by protecting his family instead of reporting the crime. The "blood on his hands" was neither Jan Spaen's nor Peony's, but Sano's.

"I apologize for my son," Ohira said. "He intended no harm; he only meant to frighten you. When you wouldn't leave the harbor, he panicked. His shot went wild and hit you." The chief shook his head sadly. "But that's no excuse. He attacked a representative of the shogun, which is treason. Therefore he must be punished. As must I, and the rest of our family."

Sano felt no animosity toward the boy who'd almost killed him. He would have done the same to protect his own father. "When the judges learn of your crimes, they'll have no choice but to impose the death penalty," Sano said. "I can't save you—and you don't want that anyway, do you?" Ohira's silence was his affirmative. "But when I regain power, I'll persuade the *bakufu* to exempt your wife and younger children from punishment." He had done so for the families of other criminals, under special circumstances. "And Kiyoshi needn't die if I don't report what you've told me. Which I won't—if you'll help me."

Ohira stared, as though not daring to believe what he'd heard. "Of course. I'll do anything. Anything!"

"Tell me who killed Jan Spaen," Sano said, "and the names of all the smugglers."

"I don't know." Fresh despair deepened the lines in Ohira's face. "I wasn't there when Spaen died. I've never even been to that cove. My second watch commander piloted the boat." So it was Nirin whom Sano had followed across the harbor on the night of his arrest. "My job was to falsify the inventory, relax surveillance on Deshima, and supply manpower."

And to take the blame if anything went wrong, Sano thought as his hope of exposing the criminals faded. How efficient of Nagai to set up a scapegoat in advance!

"I don't know who the smugglers are, or who leads them," Ohira finished.

"But you must have communicated with them," Sano said, grasping for any possible clue.

"Anonymous messages arrived at my office in town. I never tried to trace them—I didn't want to know any more than necessary. And I destroyed every one."

Thus there was no written evidence against Governor Nagai, Interpreter Iishino, Urabe, or anyone except Ohira. But Sano refused to give up. "What exactly did these messages say?"

"The day and time of the smuggling. The place where my men should take the goods . . ." A grimace of revulsion twisted Ohira's lips, as if provoked by an unpleasant memory.

"What is it?" Sano asked.

"Another message came yesterday. My men are to transfer the rest of the illegal goods off the island tomorrow."

"Where?" Sano demanded. "When?"

If he could deliver the information to the tribunal judges, perhaps they would free him and pursue the real criminals. For the first time Sano felt success within his grasp. And maybe, when the smugglers were caught, he would learn who had killed Spaen and Peony and burned his house.

"The message said that a new rendezvous location must be arranged," Ohira said, "because the cove is sealed. I'm to await further instructions, which will arrive soon."

Soon enough to save himself, Sano wondered, and Hirata? Soon enough to deliver Spaen's killer to the Dutch captain and prevent a war?

Outside, wooden soles clattered up the shrine's steps, heralding the approach of worshippers. In the distance, the urgent pulse of the war drums continued. Sano rose to leave.

"Tell me the moment you hear," he said.

"Yes, of course. How shall I reach you?"

With his house ruined, the police surely looking for him, and nowhere to go, Sano said, "Can you suggest a quiet, discreet inn?"

"The Double Happiness." Ohira gave directions. "I'll send word to you there."

Before departing, Sano bowed to the inner sanctuary and placed a coin in the offertory box for good luck. Ohira remained kneeling, eyes closed in silent prayer. An unnatural serenity had fallen over him, lending a strange beauty to his ravaged face.

"Will you be all right?" Sano asked, concerned for the man whose destruction would clear a path toward the truth, and his own salvation.

The chief's voice sounded remote, preoccupied. "I shall just stay here awhile longer."

Guilt and pity gnawed at Sano; he felt no triumph over accomplishing this mission. Fervently he wished he was the sort of man who could have declined the investigation, or at least ended it before destroying Peony, Old Carp, and Ohira or endangering Hirata and the nation. His truth-seeking nature seemed a curse, the serving of his personal code of justice a cruel self-indulgence. Yet what could he do now but see the investigation through to the finish? And he still felt in his deepest soul that this was right. He must serve honor and accept his fate—just as Ohira had.

"I'm sorry," he said softly, but the chief gave no sign that he'd heard.

Sano left the shrine, intending to take shelter at the inn while waiting for Ohira's message. But when he stepped outside the torii gate, a premonition of danger stabbed him a moment before he spied its cause.

Down the highway past him marched a huge procession, led by footsoldiers carrying banners emblazoned with the Tokugawa crest. Mounted troops escorted three palanquins whose open windows framed solemn, elderly officials dressed in black ceremonial caps and robes. An army of servants and porters followed, carrying chests and bundles. Sano's throat constricted; dread sickened him.

The treason tribunal had arrived a day earlier than expected. Time had run out. And Sano had no chance to adjust his plans. From the direction of the city stampeded an angry horde of samurai: *Yoriki* Ota, in full battle uniform, riding a gaudily caparisoned steed; *doshin* brandishing *jitte;* police assistants carrying sticks, ropes, and ladders; mounted troops and footsoldiers; a drenched and furious Nirin.

"There he is!" shouted Nirin, who must have led the pack to the shrine. "Get him!"

The horde swept down upon Sano. The police stripped off his sword, bound his hands, and interlocked the ladders around him to form a cage.

"Your trial begins tomorrow morning," *Yoriki* Ota informed Sano with a triumphant leer. "Until then, you will enjoy the generous hospitality of Nagasaki Jail." He slapped the reins and motioned for his subordinates to follow. "Let's go!"

Caged like an animal, prodded by sticks, hounded by jeers, and ready to die of shame and despair, Sano began the long walk to Nagasaki Jail.

32

THE TREASON TRIBUNAL convened in the reception hall of the mansion where the three magistrates were staying. Bleak, early morning light barely penetrated the barred windows. Lanterns cast a sinister yellow glow over the magistrates, who wore black ceremonial robes and surcoats bearing the Tokugawa crest, black caps, and black-hilted swords, seated upon the dais. Court officials and secretaries knelt behind desks. Soldiers guarded the doors. Across a wall mural painted in murky colors, mounted archers hunted a tiger through a forest.

Sano, the accused, wearing a dirty muslin kimono, knelt on a straw mat before the dais on the *shirasu:* an area of floor covered with white sand, symbol of truth.

"The trial of *Sōsakan* Sano Ichirō is now in session," intoned the magistrate who occupied the center position on the dais, behind a low table piled with scrolls. About sixty years of age, he had a long, rectangular face with jutting chin and razor-edged cheekbones. His body was fit and strong, his posture erect. "Hearing this case are Magistrates Segawa Fumio of Hakata and Dazai Moriya of Kurume." He bowed to the men on either side of him; the secretaries recorded his words. From the hills above the city came the pounding of the war drums, like a monster's heartbeat. "And myself, in the capacity of supreme judge: Takeda Kenzan of Kumamoto."

Sano's throat clenched as he recognized the name. Takeda was famous for a conviction rate of nearly 100 percent, and for the harshness of his sentences. Of the other judges, Sano knew nothing. They represented his chief hope of acquittal, yet their impassive faces betrayed no mercy.

"The defendant is charged with six counts of treason," Supreme Judge Takeda said. "Operating a smuggling ring; persecuting Japanese citizens; procuring weapons from the Dutch; conspiring with them to overthrow the government; enlisting Chinese military support; and practicing Christianity."

As Sano prepared to refute the accusations and persuade the judges to let him catch the real criminals, his thoughts were clouded by pain, fatigue, and worry. He'd spent a hellish night in a filthy prison cell. The jailers had denied him food and water, while what seemed like every samurai in town had come to taunt the highest-ranking inmate Nagasaki Jail had ever housed. The trip to the courtroom had further taxed Sano's strength and wounded his pride. Guards had forced him to walk in the ladder cage past jeering crowds who hurled stones and garbage. His injured shoulder ached; his bruises throbbed; he stank, and knew his appearance would prejudice the judges as much as the lies told about him. Worst of all, the jailers had confiscated the stolen records from Deshima, leaving Sano no evidence for his defense.

"Additional charges against the defendant were brought by the Honorable Governor Nagai yesterday," Supreme Judge Takeda said. "Trespassing on Deshima and attacking the staff. Bribing the Dutch ship's crew." Takeda indicated the scrolls on the table. "We the judges have reviewed the witnesses' statements and deem them satisfactory. We hereby find the accused guilty of all the aforementioned crimes."

Staring in shock and disbelief, Sano demanded, "That's it?" He'd known his chances of fair treatment were slim; yet he hadn't expected such a perfunctory condemnation. "Don't the witnesses have to testify? Am I not even allowed to present my own defense?" Even the lowliest peasant usually had his say before the verdict was rendered, and the chance to face his accusers in court. "You can't be serious."

"No one gave you permission to speak," whined Judge Segawa, a wizened little man with a prissy mouth. He turned to Supreme Judge Takeda. "Let us pronounce the sentence and conclude this distasteful business as expediently as the Honorable Chamberlain Yanagisawa would wish."

Plump, bland Judge Dazai nodded. Sano lost all hope of finding allies in these men, who were obviously Yanagisawa's flunkies and sought to win the chamberlain's approbation by destroying him. But he wouldn't surrender without a fight.

"The charges are false," Sano said hotly. "The so-called witnesses have framed me to protect themselves." The judges frowned in wordless disapproval. Officials, secretaries, and guards watched with disdain. "I demand a chance to prove my innocence!"

After the echo of his voice faded, the ensuing silence lasted an eternity. Then Judge Segawa said, "This emotional outburst is extremely offensive. Takeda-*san*, I beg you to end these proceedings now."

But Supreme Judge Takeda's attention was focused on Sano; interest narrowed his eyes. "Due to the severity of the charges, I'll allow the accused to speak on his own behalf." To Sano, he said, "Go ahead."

Maybe Takeda was merely curious to hear what he would say. But Sano glimpsed in the supreme judge the type of official who wished to believe that everything the government did was right, so he could claim by virtue of association to a share of the honor. Thus he turned a blind eye to malfeasance in his colleagues. When enforcing laws, he erred on the side of harshness because he perceived any offense as a personal insult and preferred that the innocent occasionally be punished rather than the guilty ever go free. Hence, Supreme Judge Takeda had accepted the witnesses' testimony and assumed Sano's guilt. However, if Sano read Takeda right, the judge wouldn't be satisfied with punishing one man if there was a chance that other criminals might be caught. And by agreeing to listen, Takeda had demonstrated more independent spirit than his fellow judges.

Now Sano launched into the most eloquent, desperate speech of his life. He justified his misinterpreted actions. He mentioned his service record as proof of his loyalty and good character. He related Assistant Director deGraeff's, Dr. Huygens's, Abbot Liu Yun's, and Urabe's motives for killing Jan Spaen. He explained how he'd discovered the smuggling, and his case against the Deshima staff, and that Peony had surely died because of what she knew. Sano cited the burning of his house as evidence of a conspiracy against him—one that certainly included Nagasaki's all-knowing, all-powerful governor. Last, Sano told of the falsified records, Chief Ohira's confession, and his plan for capturing the real smugglers and exposing whoever had murdered Jan Spaen and Peony.

"Honorable Judges, I swear upon my honor that I have spoken the truth," Sano finished, hoarse and shaky from intense physical and mental exertion. "I beg you to believe me, and to dispense justice to the actual perpetrators of these heinous crimes!"

Officials and secretaries laid down their brushes; the guards stood like motionless shadows. Sano could tell by the judges' reflective expressions that they saw the logic in his statement and knew they couldn't shirk their professional responsibility by dismissing it outright. He felt a surge of premature elation.

Then Supreme Judge Takeda said, "Do you have the documents you mentioned?"

"No, Honorable Judge," Sano was forced to admit. "They were confiscated after my arrest."

Judge Segawa laughed, a shrill, nasty cackle. "More likely they never existed." He and Judge Dazai exchanged nods, their complacency restored, their goal of pleasing Chamberlain Yanagisawa within easy reach.

"But Ohira's confession will hold," Sano added hastily. "He wants to enforce the law. The disappearance of the records won't matter to him." Sano decided to worry about whether this was true if and when Supreme Judge Takeda agreed to cooperate. "Bring Ohira in. He should know by now when and where the smugglers plan to meet. Give me a chance, and I'll deliver them all to you."

Supreme Judge Takeda's thick brows drew together in a scowl. "You insult me, *Sōsakan* Sano, if you think I would act on unsubstantiated claims from someone with everything to gain by slandering other men. Do you take me for a fool?"

The other judges smirked. A sense of doom fell over Sano.

"The original verdict stands: guilty on all counts," Takeda said. "I will now pronounce the sentence.

"Sano Ichirō is denied the privilege of restoring his honor through ritual suicide. His head shall be severed at a public execution, and his remains displayed as a warning to potential traitors." Takeda clapped his hands twice.

Guards rushed over and seized Sano. "No," he cried. "I swear I'm telling the truth!"

This was a samurai's worst nightmare: to toil and sacrifice in loyal service to his lord, yet end his life in disgrace and dishonor. From the depths of Sano's soul exploded a fireball of anger at his accusers, at Chamberlain Yanagisawa and the entire corrupt *bakufu*. He kicked and flailed, scattering the white sand of truth. But the guards locked iron shackles around his wrists and ankles.

"Let me go. I'm innocent!"

Then, as the guards dragged him toward the door, it flew open. A running figure burst into the room, followed by a shouting, sword-waving mob. Shocked out of his pain, shame, and anger, Sano recognized the runner. "Hirata?" His heart swelled with joy, then contracted in horror. The soldiers would surely kill Hirata. "No!"

"*Sōsakan-sama.* Merciful gods, I'm not too late." Hirata fell to his knees before the dais and the surprised judges. He wore nothing but a loincloth. Dirt and sweat streaked his body. Most startling of all, he'd shaved his head. Bowing to the judges, he spoke in a breathless rush. "Honorable Judges, I've come to plead for my master's life. I beg your permission to prove his innocence."

As Sano watched helplessly, the mob surrounded Hirata. "This man got past us before we could stop him," said the commander. "My apologies for the interruption." To his men: "This is the fugitive traitor and murderer. Take him outside and kill him."

The soldiers hoisted Hirata's struggling body over their heads. "No!" Sano leapt to the rescue, but his captors jerked his chains. He fell with a crash. The guards carried Hirata past him.

"Wait." Supreme Judge Takeda's voice boomed from the dais, halting the soldiers' rush. "Bring him back."

"What? Why?" bleated Judge Segawa.

Takeda ignored him. The soldiers dumped Hirata facedown in front of the dais. Sano, lying on the floor in a tangle of iron, watched in puzzlement as the supreme judge studied Hirata. Takeda's strange expression offered no clue to his intentions.

"Sit up," Takeda ordered Hirata, who did. "Are you the man accused of abetting *Sōsakan* Sano's treason, breaking into the treasurer's mansion, and murdering a soldier?"

Hirata bowed. "Yes, but I'm innocent, and so is my master." His voice cracked; he cleared his throat and continued bravely, "Please forgive my intrusion, Honorable Judge, and please allow me to explain."

"In a moment." Supreme Judge Takeda regarded Hirata in apparent fascination. "I understand you've been in hiding. How have you occupied yourself during that time?"

Now Hirata's voice rang with ardent determination. "I've been gathering information about the men who have unjustly accused my master."

Sano closed his eyes briefly in despair. Even while a fugitive, Hirata had not abandoned the investigation, or his campaign to clear his master. For this steadfastness, Sano loved the foolhardy young warrior, his truest friend. But now they would die together, because it was obvious Hirata had brought no material evidence with him.

"Do you know that troops have been hunting you day and night, and that Governor Nagai has already condemned you to death?" asked Takeda.

"Yes, Honorable Judge." If Hirata felt any fear, Sano couldn't detect it in the straight line of his naked back, the proud lift of his shaven head.

"And still you risked your life to come here and speak on your master's behalf?"

"Yes, Honorable Judge."

A spasm of emotion tightened Supreme Judge Takeda's stern face. "*Inshōteki*—impressive," he murmured. He lifted his sleeve and wiped a tear from his eye. "A truer expression of Bushido than I ever hoped to see in this day and age."

As a historian, Sano knew how the Way of the Warrior had evolved in response to Japan's changing political climate. Peacetime lacked the clear-cut allegiances and rigorous austerity of war. Samurai owed conflicting loyalties to various superiors, patrons, and colleagues; myriad pleasures distracted them from duty; self-interest often prevailed over self-sacrifice. During the civil wars that had ended almost a century ago, samurai had gladly died in their lords' battles. Today there were few opportunities for glory—and fewer who sought them. Many samurai regretted Bushido's lost purity; evidently Supreme Judge Takeda was one of them.

"Such loyalty must be rewarded," he announced. After ordering the troops out of the room, he said to Hirata, "You may speak."

Hirata related an impassioned tale of posing as a police officer, conducting inquiries, and killing in self-defense. "Urabe has connections with gangsters. He has no one trustworthy to confirm his alibis for Spaen's murder, Peony's, or the smuggling. Interpreter Iishino spends more money than he earns on gifts for his superiors. How can he afford this, if not by crime?"

As Sano marveled at how much Hirata had accomplished, he watched the judges receive the news. Takeda's concentration never wavered from Hirata. The others barely hid their disapproval of their superior's weakness. And weakness it was, Sano knew from personal experience. Bushido, the foundation of a samurai's strength, was also his greatest vulnerability. Chamberlain Yanagisawa had used Sano's sense of honor against him, perpetuating schemes he couldn't thwart without violating its rigid code of conduct. Supreme Judge Takeda was harsh and unjust, but a display of loyalty moved him to bend the rules and open his mind. Sano's hopes burgeoned while Hirata continued.

"I disguised myself as an itinerant laborer and found work at the Half Moon Pleasure House. From the staff I learned that Iishino, *Yoriki* Ota, and Governor Nagai all attended a party there the night

Peony was murdered. I also found a teahouse proprietor who says Abbot Liu Yun regularly sneaks into the quarter disguised as a Japanese merchant. He was there that night, too.

"Honorable Judge, before you condemn my master, I beg you to conduct your own investigation of these men. Among them you'll find the real traitors."

Hirata bowed. Supreme Judge Takeda seemed lost in thought. Sano waited in an agony of suspense as the relentless war drums echoed the thudding of his heart.

Then Takeda said to the guards, "Bring *Sōsakan* Sano here."

The guards dragged Sano to the dais. The tight shackles had numbed his hands and feet, but he forgot physical discomfort as he knelt beside Hirata. The supreme judge's gaze bore into them. A steely vise of fear squeezed Sano's lungs; he felt Hirata's anxiety, too. With the discipline of his samurai training, he maintained a stoic facade while they awaited Supreme Judge Takeda's decision.

"*Sōsakan* Sano, your retainer's statement supports your claims, and his devotion speaks well of your character and his. Therefore, I grant you the chance to prove yourselves innocent."

The shock of reprieve overwhelmed Sano in a tidal wave of sensation: dizziness; ringing in his ears; a sudden loosening of tense muscles and release of trapped breath. He wanted to jump up and shout in joyous relief; he wanted to lie down and weep with gratitude. But honor and protocol required dignity.

"Thank you, Honorable Judge," Sano said quietly.

Then he turned to Hirata. One wordless glance mended the rift between them, cementing their bond. Sano realized how much he needed Hirata, and that he couldn't—and shouldn't—deny a fellow samurai the right to serve honor. Hirata's evidence had strengthened the case against their accusers, but it was his loyalty that had ultimately swayed Supreme Judge Takeda. To spurn such friendship might mean avoiding future pain, but also doomed Sano to constant loneliness, to losing battles he couldn't win alone. Then and there, Sano accepted Hirata as his true companion, in glory or disaster, honor or disgrace. This was the Way of the Warrior: absolute, eternal.

The tearful brightness of Hirata's eyes communicated his joy and understanding. He seemed radiant with an inner light, as if the outcome of the trial and Supreme Judge Takeda's praise of his loyalty had somehow validated his worth and brought him peace. Solemnly they bowed in mutual respect.

"This is an abuse of the law," Judge Segawa protested.

"Chamberlain Yanagisawa will not approve," Judge Dazai added.

As both men argued in favor of the original verdict and sentence, Sano guessed with a sinking heart that he and Hirata weren't safe yet.

"Honorable colleagues, do not forget that I command this tribunal," Supreme Judge Takeda said. "Your objections are duly noted, and dismissed."

Sano knew, however, that Takeda hadn't achieved his status by being gullible or ignoring the political realities of life in the *bakufu*, as his next words proved: "*Sōsakan* Sano, I shall personally oversee your dealings with the informant Chief Ohira, and accompany you to the smugglers' rendezvous. If you succeed in producing the criminals, the charges will be dropped.

"If you fail, the death sentence will be enforced—and extended to include not only both your entire families, but all your close associates as well. Keep this in mind while we carry out your scheme, *Sōsakan* Sano."

MIDNIGHT. FROM A high bluff beyond the edge of town, Sano looked down at Nagasaki. Darkness covered the city like a quilt upon a restless sleeper. The moon, a translucent white bubble caught in a net of cloud, illuminated warships, barges, and the Dutch vessel in the harbor. Torch flames streaked the waterfront and streets, where troops continued to patrol. Bonfires burned at clifftop fortresses. The war drums beat with increasing urgency. A palpable menace vibrated the warm night, deepening Sano's unease as he turned away from the view and faced his companions.

In a sheltering circle of pines, Hirata squatted motionless, alert for any approaching sound. Supreme Judge Takeda sat on a rock, arms folded, his face in shadow beneath his hat. Judges Segawa and Dazai huddled together, exuding impatience and disapproval.

"We've waited at least two hours, and still your informant has not arrived," Segawa complained. "You may as well give up, *Sōsakan* Sano."

"He'll come," Sano said with more conviction than he felt. Nervously he eyed Supreme Judge Takeda's four retainers, who surrounded the clearing. They were here to either help arrest the smugglers, or to take Sano and Hirata to jail if the plan failed. "Maybe he's having trouble getting out of town. But he'll be here soon."

When summoned to the courtroom—on the pretext of verifying his testimony—Chief Ohira had revealed where the smugglers planned to meet and agreed to take the tribunal there, but his manner had disturbed Sano. Kneeling before the dais, he'd seemed a shadow that might drift away at any moment. His eyes looked straight through everyone, betraying no recognition or emotion. Yet Sano had no choice but to trust Ohira. His life and Hirata's depended on catching the smugglers, to whom Ohira was the only link. To avoid arousing the suspicion of corrupt authorities, Chief Ohira had left the courtroom to go about his usual business until night came. He'd promised to send a servant who would lead them along a secret route to a hidden shelter from which he would take them to the smugglers' meeting place.

For the rest of the day, Sano, Hirata, and the tribunal had remained sequestered in the mansion, under the pretense of conducting a lengthy trial. For secrecy's sake, no one was allowed in or out. Upstairs, Takeda's retainers had guarded Sano and Hirata in case they tried to escape. Servants had bathed them and supplied food, clean clothes, and bedding. Hirata had slept, but Sano had been too tense to rest. He could hear Judges Segawa and Dazai arguing with Takeda. At the front gate, Governor Nagai's envoys frequently inquired about the progress of the trial. Sano watched through the window as Takeda's retainers sent them away with the message that the tribunal had not yet reached a decision. Time dragged; the day waned. Sano asked for news of the Dutch ship, and was unhappy to learn that it remained in the harbor, ready to attack. The long wait filled him with worry. Would his enemies guess the plan? Would Ohira renege on his promise?

Then, long after nightfall, Takeda's manservant entered, bearing two plain, dark cloaks and two sets of swords. "Master says to put these on. It's time."

Sano woke Hirata. They donned the garments and weapons. Takeda's retainers escorted them to the back door, where they found all three judges and Chief Ohira's elderly manservant.

"This is foolish," Judge Segawa said. He and Dazai glared at Sano. "Takeda-*san*, these criminals mean to kill us and escape."

Supreme Judge Takeda's eyes shone with a youthful adventurousness that had probably affected his decision. "My men will make sure they behave. Come."

Sano followed the servant out into the night, with Hirata behind him, the judges and four retainers trailing. Nagasaki, former haven of pirates, rebel conspiracies, and underground Christians, had not yielded all its secrets to Tokugawa law and order. The servant led Sano's party on foot along a circuitous route that only a longtime resident would know, down crooked alleys and through subterranean tunnels, over roofs and under bridges, along the river. They slipped right by patrolling troops. Moving steadily uphill, they left the city and entered the forest. Sano's trepidation gave way to heady excitement while he recalled the successful hunt for the body thieves.

But now, as the night wore on and Ohira still didn't come, Sano's worries revived. Judges Segawa and Dazai muttered angrily. The retainers edged closer to Sano and Hirata. Sano sensed Takeda's impatience; he saw his own doubt reflected in Hirata's eyes. Ghastly images flashed through his mind: a death march to the execution ground; himself and Hirata kneeling before the executioner's sword; troops herding their relatives and friends to the same fate.

Supreme Judge Takeda said, "We shall wait just a few moments more."

The war drums boomed. Smoke from the bonfires embittered the wind. Then Sano's extra sense roused to a faint disturbance of the atmosphere. His companions stirred, feeling the unseen presence, too. Without a sound, Chief Ohira appeared in the clearing. The moonlight emphasized his waxen pallor. His eyes were blank, sunken pools of darkness, as if filled with the night.

"Come," he said.

He turned and drifted through the forest. Sano, hurrying to keep the almost invisible figure in sight, felt as though he were following a ghost to some netherworld hell. A primitive fear awakened within him. Envisioning demons and monsters, he was glad of Hirata's solid presence beside him. Ohira alternately vanished in the shadows and reappeared, leading the way along forest trails so narrow and crooked they barely existed, up steep paths, and behind a waterfall's silvery curtain. Watchtowers loomed above them. The bonfires flared nearer, brighter. The air grew thinner and colder with increasing altitude, the wind sharper. Fatigue strained Sano's burned legs; his shoulder ached; he gasped for breath. On and up through the darkness they labored.

"A journey to nowhere, led by an idiot," Judge Segawa muttered. "Wait until Chamberlain Yanagisawa hears of this."

Suddenly they emerged onto open road. A high stone wall loomed up out of the night. Fierce dragons arched above the carved portals of a gate. Ohira led the party through this and into another world.

The forest had been razed and the ground leveled to create a large plaza open to the sky. Ornamental trees lined gravel paths. Flower beds surrounded rock gardens; frogs sang in a gleaming pond. Arrayed before Sano in imposing grandeur stood worship halls, pavilions, tall stone lanterns, a huge bell in an ornate wooden cage. On roofs, walls, and pillars, carved demons leered, their colors reduced to shades of gray by the moonlight. The pagoda rose like a sculptured shadow above Nagasaki's Chinese Temple: once the sacred domain of a thousand priests, now the lair of Abbot Liu Yun and the smuggling ring.

"I see no lights," Judge Segawa said. "The place looks deserted. Takeda-*san,* may we abandon this nonsense now?"

But Chief Ohira was moving down a path across the temple precinct. "Quiet," Sano warned. He and Hirata hurried after Ohira. The others trailed. When Ohira abruptly took cover behind a tree, Sano followed suit, motioning for the others to do the same.

Ahead stood the main worship hall, crowned with a snarling lion, the eaves of its massive tile roof upturned like demon wings, huge double doors shadowed by a deep veranda. In front paced a samurai, the silhouette of his swords clearly outlined against the white gravel path. From somewhere beyond him came thumps, scraping sounds, and muffled voices. Excitement sped Sano's pulse. He couldn't make out any words, but he recognized the now-familiar cadence of Dutch, mixed with Japanese. The smugglers must be bringing the goods now. Which barbarian had come with them?

Sano gestured for his companions to accompany him to the back of the worship hall, where the activity seemed centered. He'd taken several steps before noticing that Ohira hadn't moved. The other men, led by Hirata, ran across the garden and hid behind the bell cage. Casting an uneasy glance at the lookout, Sano signaled his party to wait. Then he ran back to Ohira.

"What's the matter?" he whispered.

"You don't need me anymore." Ohira turned his face away. "Go, and leave me in peace."

Sano couldn't let the chief stay here alone. Ohira was behaving so strangely; what if he warned the smugglers? "Come on," Sano said, dragging Ohira toward the others.

Moving from tree to rock, rock to statue, and skirting the pagoda, they circled the worship hall. Sano hung on to Ohira, who stumbled and lagged. The noises grew louder, and Sano heard snatches of talk: "Careful, now . . . don't drop it . . ." When they reached the back of the hall, they hid behind a pavilion with a thatched roof and lattice walls. Stone lanterns flared outside the hall's rear entrance. Two samurai, carrying between them a large wooden crate, staggered up the steps. Another stood on the veranda.

"Hurry up," he said. "We haven't got all night."

"Nirin," Hirata whispered.

The men carried the crate through the open doors and into the hall's brightly lit interior.

"I see I've not misjudged you, *Sōsakan* Sano," Judge Takeda said. His colleagues murmured a grudging assent. Takeda and the retainers drew their swords. "It will be our pleasure to help capture these criminals."

"Wait," Sano cautioned, seeing lights beyond the left side of the hall. Through a gate in the temple wall came a parade of samurai, some lugging crates, others holding torches. From the opposite direction, two more samurai led a group of cloaked, hatted men without swords. They all converged on the hall's entrance, where Nirin beckoned impatiently.

"Let them get inside," Sano whispered, counting at least ten samurai outside the hall. How many more were inside? The unarmed commoners might not pose much threat, but still his party was outnumbered. Sano doubted whether the smugglers would surrender any more easily than Miochin and the body thieves had. He expected Ohira to be useless in a battle, Judges Segawa and Dazai not much better. That left Takeda—an old man; Hirata—exhausted after three days as a fugitive; four retainers of questionable swordsmanship skill; and himself, with his wounds. The element of surprise was their only advantage.

The new arrivals entered the hall. Nirin followed, closing the door. One samurai remained on the veranda as a lookout. The chants of frogs and crickets filled the sudden hush. Sano said, "Takeda-*san,* you and I and two of your retainers will storm the door. Hirata, take the other two and go around front. Clear the entrance. Wait until you hear me, then come in."

Hirata and his team slipped away into the darkness. "What about us?" Judge Segawa said, cowering beside Dazai. "We don't want to go in there." Pointing to Chief Ohira, he added, "And what about him?"

Sano made a quick decision. "You stay here." He would have no time to defend them, and he didn't trust the chief not to sabotage the raid. "Make sure Ohira doesn't leave. And keep him quiet."

"How will we get past the sentry?" Takeda asked.

Sano picked up a rock. He heaved it into the darkness to the right of the hall, wincing at the pain in his shoulder. The rock landed with a clatter. This was the oldest trick in history, but it worked. The sentry turned toward the sound, then went to investigate. Sano crept out from behind the pavilion and followed.

In a garden, the sentry stood with his back to Sano, looking for the source of the noise. Sano stole up behind the sentry and clapped both hands hard against the man's ears. The sentry reeled, then collapsed, unconscious. Sano untied the man's sash, tore it into three lengths, then bound and gagged him. Hopefully Hirata was having similar luck with the sentry at the front door. Sano returned to Takeda.

"Let's go."

Keeping watch for more lookouts, Sano crossed the open space outside the worship hall. He tiptoed up the steps. The other men joined him on the veranda. He cracked open the heavy carved door and peered inside.

In the hall's vast interior, lanterns hung from the coffered ceiling. Their smoky golden light gleamed upon red-lacquered pillars, statues of scowling guardian deities, and brilliantly colored murals depicting a Chinese paradise of castles, lakes, and forests. Candles burned on the altar, where a many-armed Buddha sat enthroned amid gilt flames and sacred lotus. Twelve samurai, whom Sano recognized as Deshima guards, were prying the lids off four crates. The ten commoners had shed their hats and cloaks, revealing shaven heads, tattooed arms and legs: gangsters.

Nirin lifted items out of the crates for their inspection. "Spices. Silks. Medicines."

Sano didn't believe that Nirin, despite his air of authority, led the smuggling ring. He could see two men facing away from the door and partially hidden by the statue of an armored warrior. One wore the black hat of the Dutch, the other an ordinary Japanese wicker hat. *Turn around,* Sano urged silently. He knew the barbarian was Dr. Huygens; he just knew it. But who was the other man? Abbot Liu Yun?

Out of a niche in the hall moved a slight figure dressed in saffron robe and brocade stole. Hands tucked inside his flowing sleeves, Liu Yun silently watched the Dutchman.

Maybe the Japanese was Urabe, whom Hirata had linked with gangsters. Or Governor Nagai, not trusting his subordinates with the sale of the loot? But the barbarian's presence clued Sano to the man's identity.

"All right, we've seen enough," the lead gangster told Nirin. To his men, he said, "Close up those crates." Then he untied a bulky cloth pouch from his sash and offered it to Nirin.

"Pay the boss," Nirin said, pointing.

The Dutchman rose and walked around the crates. It was Assistant Director deGraeff. Sano felt a melting sensation of relief—his trust in the doctor hadn't been a mistake after all—and guilt, for wrongly suspecting his friend. Then the Japanese followed, and Sano's guess was confirmed.

Clutching a portable writing desk, the man jittered with nervous excitement; his toothy grin flashed. It was Interpreter Iishino, who spoke Dutch and whose presence was therefore required for negotiations with barbarians. The "boss"; leader of the smuggling ring.

"I'll take that," Iishino said. He put down the desk, a flat rectangular box with a hinged, sloping lid. Then he cupped his hands, gloating as the gangster poured gold coins into them. "Thank you, thank you." Kneeling, he counted the money into stacks on the floor. The gangsters repacked merchandise in the crates. Abbot Liu Yun, de Graeff, and the other Japanese lined up in front of Iishino.

"To Assistant Director deGraeff, for the goods he and Director Spaen so kindly imported," Iishino said, handing coins to deGraeff. He took brush, ink jar, and a small book from inside his desk and recorded the payment. "To Abbot Liu Yun, for the use of his temple, and for acting as liaison with the black market."

Keeping his right hand in his sleeve, Liu Yun took the money and stood beside deGraeff, who was counting his coins. Iishino continued doling out and recording payments. "To Commander Nirin and the Deshima guards for providing security and transport." The gangsters finished packing and sealing the crates; the last guard received his money. Iishino stoppered his ink jar. The smugglers' hierarchy was clear, though not the identity of Spaen's or Peony's murderer. But Sano must act before the smugglers and goods left the hall. He only hoped he'd given Hirata enough time to secure a position outside the front door.

"We'll go in now," Sano told Takeda.

He drew his sword, flung open the door, and burst into the hall. "Nobody move!" he shouted. "You're all under arrest!"

34

SILENCE DESCENDED UPON the hall as the smugglers stared at
Sano and his comrades in shocked dismay. Fragmented scenes coa-
lesced in Sano's vision: tiny Abbot Liu Yun and tall Assistant Director
deGraeff standing rigidly side by side; Nirin's fading smile; Interpreter
Iishino's stricken face; the Deshima guards clutching their money; a
glaring gangster, his arms blue with tattoos. Then chaos erupted.

"Run!" shouted the gangster chief.

His men bolted for the opposite door. At the same time, Hirata's
team burst through it, swords drawn, halting their flight. The Deshima
guards had started to follow the gangsters, but Nirin called, "Come
back, you cowards! Kill them, and we're safe!"

He drew his sword. His men faltered, then rallied around him, un-
sheathing their blades. With Nirin in the lead, they advanced on Sano
and Takeda. As Sano prepared for battle, he tried to watch everyone
at once. DeGraeff was running toward a side exit with Abbot Liu Yun
hurrying after him. Interpreter Iishino picked up his desk and fled.
Hirata's team faced off against the gangsters. One of them hurled a
knife, and the retainer on Hirata's left cried out and fell dead with the
blade sticking in his chest.

"Let the gangsters go!" Although Sano would have liked to arrest all parties to the smuggling, his small force couldn't handle everyone. "Catch Iishino, Liu Yun, and deGraeff!"

Nirin lunged, sword flashing. "Now you'll pay for throwing me down the well."

Sano parried while a tornado of blades churned around him. His counterattack merely slashed Nirin's sleeve. He dodged a cut aimed at his head, then whirled just in time to deflect slices from two Deshima guards. Takeda and his retainers fought the other ten. Energy poured from Sano's spiritual center, bringing with it a heightened awareness, an expanded vision. As he advanced and retreated, he saw Hirata chasing Liu Yun and the Dutchman. The abbot held a dagger in the hand he'd earlier kept hidden under his sleeve.

"Your partner killed my brother," he screamed, tearing after deGraeff. He must have been waiting for the right moment to attack, and the raid had spurred him to action. "Now you'll join Jan Spaen in death. Order will be restored to the universe—the I Ching does not lie. I shall have my revenge on you vile, mercenary Dutch at last!"

The terrified barbarian raced around the hall. Abbot Liu Yun shrieked curses in Chinese.

With a quick cut, Sano laid open a Deshima guard's throat. The man fell dead beside another slain by Takeda. Sano leapt over the bodies and continued battling Nirin and three other guards. One of Takeda's retainers cleaved a guard's skull, slashed another's chest, then took a fatal cut across the belly. The supreme judge fought expertly, but his garments hung in shreds, and cuts bled on his exposed legs. Sano felt his own strength diminishing, his reflexes slowing, and his sore shoulder leaking blood. He drew his short sword, fighting two-handed to parry strikes and reduce the stress on his injury.

Abbot Liu Yun cornered deGraeff against the altar, shrilling, "Die! Die!" and stabbing at deGraeff. The barbarian threw up his hands in self-defense. The dagger gashed his palms, then pierced his chest. DeGraeff screamed and fell. Hirata tried to pull Liu Yun away, but the abbot jumped on deGraeff and kept stabbing. Then deGraeff seized the dagger, and they grappled in a desperate struggle for its possession. Dutch and Chinese curses filled the hall.

Ducking a slash, Sano swung his blade in an arc and cut a guard's legs out from under him. As he rose, he saw deGraeff win control of the weapon and turn it on Abbot Liu Yun. Now the Chinese man's cries of agony drowned out the ring of blades. Two more guards replaced the fallen man. Sano took a cut to his thigh and stumbled. His opponents closed in for the kill.

Then a figure moved swiftly behind them. They both grunted; their faces went slack, and they fell forward. Blood poured from wounds across the backs of their necks. There stood Hirata, dripping sword raised.

"Liu Yun and the barbarian are killing each other," he told Sano. "Get Iishino. I'll handle this."

He joined Supreme Judge Takeda and two surviving retainers in the battle against Nirin and seven remaining guards. Sano hesitated, loath to abandon his allies. Then he looked around. Interpreter Iishino was nowhere in sight. Sano raced down the hall, past hulking statues and gleaming murals, fearing that the leader of the smuggling ring had escaped during the confusion. Then he spotted Iishino.

In a niche near the altar, the interpreter squatted beneath an arch of gilt flames, his desk in front of him. Anticipating a victory for his side, he'd apparently chosen this spot as a safe place from which to view the battle. He blanched when he spied Sano. Clutching his desk, he scooted farther back into the niche.

"*Sōsakan-sama*, this is not what you think." He flashed a sickly version of his grin. "I can explain everything, everything."

Sano stopped before the despicable man who had framed him and left his cohorts to fight alone. "Come here, Iishino." He wouldn't kill the interpreter, but oh, how he would enjoy seeing Iishino tried and executed.

Iishino flapped his hands. "Wait, wait. I am not one of them." His eyes darted with anxious cunning. "I—I discovered the smuggling and infiltrated the ring to learn who the criminals were. I was going to report them to the authorities in time to save you." Iishino smiled and bobbed his head. "It's the truth, I swear!"

"He's . . . lying."

The hoarse croak came from Abbot Liu Yun, who lay beside the altar. Blood from stab wounds on his torso stained his saffron robe crimson. His face was a mask of agony. Nearby, Assistant Director deGraeff lay dead, the dagger beside his hand. Liu Yun coughed, gasped, then continued:

"Iishino . . . started the smuggling. . . . Paid me to make the mysterious lights . . . and arrange contact with . . . black market. And he . . . killed Spaen. . . . I saw. He stole . . . my revenge. But the I Ching was right. I have crossed the abyss . . . and killed . . . my brother's Dutch murderer's comrade. Now I can die . . . in peace. Hsi! I join you now . . ."

His face relaxed; his eyes dulled. Sano marveled at the revenge lust that neither time, faith, nor reason could obliterate. Then he looked back at Iishino—and down the bore of a gun the interpreter aimed at him.

"Get away from me, get away!" Iishino quavered.

The tubular pistol with carved ivory grip and long metal barrel wobbled in his shaky hands. Sano had instinctively raised his swords to ward off the threat. Fear paralyzed him, even as he registered satisfaction at learning the identity of Spaen's killer. His lungs seemed made of iron, incapable of inhaling or exhaling air. He'd never faced a gun before, and his knowledge of firearms came from reading war manuals. Now he truly recognized the power of the foreign weapon. In a swordfight, he could have easily defeated Iishino. The gun made Sano the weaker of them.

"Drop your swords!" Iishino ordered.

The lid of his desk lay open; he'd taken the gun out while Sano was watching Abbot Liu Yun. Deploring his lack of foresight, Sano let both swords clatter to the floor. He'd known the smugglers had access to guns. He should have expected the cowardly Iishino to own one. He should have killed Iishino when he'd had the chance!

"Put the gun down, Iishino." Sano's voice sounded thin in his own ears. Hirata and Takeda were still battling Nirin and three guards; the other retainers lay dead. Now a core of angry determination hardened within Sano's fear. The venal, corrupt interpreter was a ruthless killer.

Sano refused to let him win. Though unarmed, he still had his wits to match against the interpreter's advantage. He stepped forward and said evenly, "My men will defeat yours. Kill me, and they'll be witnesses. You won't escape. So put the gun down."

As Iishino cowered in the niche, his gaze slid back and forth; his mouth worked. Yet he kept the gun aimed at Sano. With his left hand, he reached inside the desk and grabbed his account book—a narrow sheaf of paper bound in black silk and tied with scarlet cord. Tucking this in his sash, he stood. "Move, or I'll shoot!"

He thrust the gun forward in both hands. Sano leapt back. Iishino sidled out of the niche and toward the door. Sano eyed the gun's firing mechanism, a raised clamp holding a pointed flint that would ignite the powder when the trigger was pulled. "Guns aren't as reliable as swords, Iishino," Sano said. Swallowing panic, he followed the interpreter. "The powder may not light." It was a common problem. "And you only get one shot." Guns recoiled when fired; even at close range, the bullet could miss its target.

Iishino giggled. "This is a very superior gun. It belonged to Director Spaen. It fires every time, every time—he showed me. Don't come any closer, I'm warning you."

His voice had a hysterical pitch. The gun shook wildly. As Sano imagined death exploding from the barrel's round, black opening, his heart thudded. He hurried to calm the interpreter.

"Iishino, why did you smuggle?" he asked, knowing that criminals often liked to justify their actions.

"I had no choice, no choice." As Sano had hoped, Iishino's voice leveled; the gun steadied, and he slowed his backward flight to the door. "Governor Nagai made a secret deal with the barbarians. He told me to arrange everything." When Sano moved closer, he flinched. "Get away from me!"

Sano hastily obeyed. Iishino babbled, "How could I refuse Governor Nagai? I would lose my position. Besides, he pays me very well, and I need the money. It's very expensive to be always buying gifts for my superiors. It's not enough to do them services."

"Services like helping to frame me?" Sano interjected.

"Yes—I mean, no! Oh, but you wouldn't understand." Iishino grew angry and more agitated as he spoke. "You don't know what it is to be so lonely that you would do anything to be accepted. You're just like everyone else who shuns and ridicules me!"

Hastening to placate the interpreter, Sano saw a way to learn the motives behind the murders. "I do understand," he said. "I know how cruel people can be, no matter how hard we work or how much we deserve respect."

"Yes. Yes!" Responding to Sano's genuine sincerity, Iishino nodded vigorously.

Sano edged between the interpreter and the door. "Did Director Spaen also mistreat you? Is that why he died?"

Iishino's face crumpled. "I thought he was my friend." The gun dipped, and Sano wondered if he should grab it. No, not yet . . . "Oh, I know he was obligated to be polite to me—especially since I helped sell his private stock of goods. But he was always so nice that I thought he really liked me. I thought a barbarian could appreciate me the way my countrymen didn't. I was so happy," Iishino wailed.

He took a hand from the gun and wiped tears off his cheeks. Sano moved closer, summoning his nerve. "But then, that night at the cove, I realized I'd only been fooling myself," Iishino continued. "We'd just brought the boat into the cave—Spaen, Commander Nirin, and I. We were waiting for Liu Yun to bring the gangsters. I was so excited; I laughed and hugged Spaen and said, "We make the best partners in the world, you and I—though of course, you Dutch are not as smart as we Japanese."

Iishino smiled through his tears in remembered pleasure; he didn't seem to know he'd offended his "partner." Then his expression darkened, and he lifted the gun. "Spaen sneered at me, then said I was a piece of dung who wasn't fit to lick his shoes, and if not for the smuggling, he wouldn't have anything to do with me at all! I saw that our friendship was all in my imagination, my imagination. He scorned me—just like everyone else!

"I was hurt, then angry. To be rejected even by a barbarian!" Indignation flared in Iishino's eyes. "He was wearing his gun—I kept it in my office on Deshima, and let him have it for games with his whore, and whenever he left the island. When he turned away, I grabbed it and shot him."

Now Sano realized that all the complications of the murder case— Spaen's relationships with the other barbarians; Abbot Liu Yun's history; the intricacies of Dutch-Japanese foreign affairs; even the smuggling—had been peripheral to the crime. Director Spaen had died because of one man's basic human need for friendship, a motive that transcended cultural, political, and financial concerns. Sano pitied Iishino, with whom he felt a poignant kinship. His own background and nature had made him as much an outsider in the *bakufu* as Iishino. Had he cared more about the approval of others, he might have someday found himself in the same position: killing in revenge for one slight too many.

But hurt feelings didn't justify murder; pity must not obstruct justice. Sano eased nearer to Iishino. "What happened next?"

"Spaen fell. Commander Nirin shouted. I dropped the gun and bent over Spaen." As Iishino's gaze turned inward, Sano could almost see the scene reflected in his eyes. "There was so much blood. He didn't move, or answer when I called his name. I began to weep. I didn't mean to kill him, only to hurt him as he'd hurt me!

"Then Abbot Liu Yun was there. He said, 'Dump Spaen in the ocean and say he escaped from Deshima.' But Commander Nirin said, 'If his body washes ashore, everyone will see he was shot. The murder of a barbarian will bring Edo officials to investigate. The Deshima staff will be the obvious suspects, and Governor Nagai will sacrifice us to protect himself.'

"Abbot Liu Yun undressed Spaen and cut up the bullet wound with his knife. Then he began cursing and stabbing the body. He said he'd agreed to help with the smuggling so he could kill Spaen, and he was angry that someone else had beaten him to it. Commander Nirin pulled Liu Yun away and lifted Spaen into the boat. I took a crucifix that I'd planned to sell to the Christians and put it around Spaen's neck."

"So that if he was found, the authorities would think a Christian had killed him?" Sano asked quietly.

"No. So that my friend's spirit would have the blessing of his god."
A sob caught in Iishino's throat; the gun now pointed at the floor.

Soon, Sano thought. "And Peony? Why did you kill her?"

"One night when I was at the Half Moon Pleasure House, she stole
my account book. Later she tried to blackmail me. Spaen had told her
the book was a record of all the goods smuggled and everyone involved. She knew I dealt in Christian contraband, and when you told
her about the crucifix on Spaen's body, she guessed that I had killed
him. The night he disappeared, she saw me come to his room and lead
him away. If I didn't pay, she would send the book to Edo, and I would
be executed. She misled you by lying about Urabe being on Deshima
because she didn't want you to find out about me before I paid. But I
didn't have the money. So I killed her. I had no choice."

A weary desolation saturated Iishino's voice. He sank to his knees,
letting the gun dangle. "I never meant to hurt anyone. Things just . . .
happened."

"Such as when you burned my house?" Sano said, fitting the last
crime into the scheme of events.

Sadly Iishino nodded. "I wanted to make sure you would never expose my crimes to the Edo authorities. I had no choice, no choice."

Sano took one cautious step forward, then another, until he stood
within touching distance of Iishino. He noticed that Hirata and
Supreme Judge Takeda had reduced the opposition down to Nirin and
one guard. Their swords clashed with increasing ferocity as they circled and darted some twenty paces away. With luck, the battle could
end in victory for Sano's side. One grab, and the gun was his—

"Stop! Don't go in there!"

The cry from the door shattered Sano's concentration. Iishino's
head swiveled. They both stared as Chief Ohira walked into the hall.
Judges Segawa and Dazai followed, panting and flustered.

"He got away from us," Segawa whined.

Fearing that Ohira had come to aid the smugglers, Sano was puzzled yet relieved when the chief merely knelt by the door. But the interruption jarred Iishino out of his lethargy. He leapt to his feet and
poked the gun at Sano's face. "Get away!"

Sano sprang backward, heart in his throat. "Iishino," he began.

Iishino's eyes shone with renewed defiance. "You think you can trick me. But I'm too smart, too smart. You won't capture me, because I'm going to kill you!" His shaking finger touched the trigger.

Even as Sano stared at his own death, a terrible premonition wafted over him like a bad odor, taking his attention from Iishino. He looked toward the door and saw Chief Ohira draw his short sword. Judges Segawa and Dazai hovered behind him; the battle raged on.

"Ohira!" Sano shouted. "No!"

With an unearthly howl, Chief Ohira plunged the sword deep into his abdomen. Sano's samurai spirit applauded Ohira's decision, which precluded the disgrace of public execution and restored honor, but his conscience sickened over causing another death. He realized he'd thought he could somehow save the chief. But Sano couldn't succumb to guilt now; penance must wait. Iishino was watching Ohira's death agonies. Sano lunged. He locked one hand over the interpreter's, the other around the gun barrel.

"Let go, let go!" Iishino screamed.

As they struggled for control of the weapon, it wavered wildly in their joined grip, describing haphazard arcs in the air. The scrawny Iishino was stronger than Sano had expected—a bundle of wiry sinew and frenetic energy. He stomped and kicked with his wooden-soled shoes. Pain hobbled Sano's legs. Shrieking like a child throwing a tantrum, Iishino rammed his head into Sano's chest. Sano stumbled, trying to keep hold of the gun. Iishino spat in his eyes. Hot saliva blinded him. They whirled in a bizarre dance. Sano forced the gun upward, aiming at the ceiling. If he could discharge the bullet harm-lessly . . .

But Iishino's fingers covered the trigger guard. When Sano tried to push them away, the interpreter ducked his head and bit him on the forearm. Sano involuntarily relaxed his pressure on the gun. Iishino yanked it between them so that the barrel was directly in front of Sano's eyes.

"I'm going to kill you!" The interpreter spoke through teeth red with Sano's blood. "I hate you and everyone else. You made me a crim-inal!"

Straining and gasping, Sano tried to push the gun away, to wrench it from Iishino's hands. He slammed Iishino against a pillar. Still the interpreter didn't let go. The cold steel barrel grazed Sano's cheek. The gun held more terror for him than any blade, no matter how expertly wielded. Panic flooded his body and mind, banishing trained discipline as he fought. Iishino's hot, sweaty fingers clawed his hands, seeking the trigger. In desperation, Sano pulled the interpreter clear of the pillar. He locked his leg around Iishino's and yanked.

Iishino emitted a surprised yip and toppled backward. They crashed to the floor, Sano landing on top. The impact drove a bolt of pain into his injured shoulder. Now the gun was trapped between their chests, with Sano's weight immobilizing their locked hands and pinning Iishino down. Sano tried to shake the weapon and dislodge the flint. The interpreter jabbed bony knees against Sano, who lurched sideways to protect his groin. Over and over they rolled, their faces almost touching, the gun barrel separating their chins. Now Sano forgot his wish to see this murderer, traitor, and enemy formally tried and executed. To survive, he must kill Iishino.

A pillar halted their motion with a crash. Using all his strength, Sano heaved on the gun. Iishino's body came up with it. Sano shoved him down again, banging his head on the stone floor. Iishino's grip on the gun slackened. Sano jammed the barrel under his chin. Now Sano's finger was on the curved metal trigger. He squeezed.

The world exploded. The gun recoiled against Sano's chest with a stunning blow. His ears rang; acrid gunpowder smoke filled his lungs. Warm, wet blood covered his face, reddening his vision. He'd shot himself instead of Iishino!

Moaning, Sano scrambled off the interpreter. As his hands frantically probed his body for a wound, dizziness weakened him. He was dying . . . Then he felt hands on his shoulders, heard Hirata saying, "*Sōsakan-sama*, it's all right. Iishino is dead; so are Nirin and the guards. You're fine. It's over."

The news turned Sano's moans into the giddy laughter of relief. He wasn't shot; he would live. He'd won. Then he looked at Iishino. Laughter shriveled in his throat.

The interpreter lay motionless on his back, hands still clutching the gun. Below the left side of his jaw, a hole in his neck marked the bullet's entrance. The blood had soaked his clothes, the gun, his hands, the floor—and Sano. His toothy mouth gaped in a rictus of surprise; his eyes bulged with shock. The bullet had exited through his scalp in a spray of white bone fragments, pulpy, grayish brain tissue, and still more blood.

Supreme Judge Takeda stood beside Sano. "I'll send a report of today's events to Edo, stating that the tribunal declares you and your retainer innocent on all counts." The other judges murmured in grudging accord. "And you shall receive a reward for your heroic crusade against traitors who have undermined the shogun's authority."

The words impinged on Sano like discordant music. Slowly he rose and surveyed the twenty-one dead. Was it justice that had been served tonight—or his self-interest? Japan and the shogun's regime—both of which he'd grown to hate—or his own personal code of honor? Instead of triumph, Sano felt Iishino's blood on his skin, tasted its metallic salinity. Had he sought only justice, or revenge on his enemies? Had he selfishly sacrificed Peony, Ohira, and Old Carp to his own principles—to satisfy a craven need for adventure and moral superiority—as he had Aoi, the woman he couldn't stop loving? How could he go on without knowing the truth about himself?

"Come on, *sōsakan-sama*." Hirata took his arm. "Let's get out of here."

35

THE EIGHTH MONTH had arrived, bringing chill nights and clear, invigorating days. Through a sunny hilltop meadow of waving golden grasses, Sano strolled with Dr. Huygens. The autumn wind breathed a scent of frost and wood fires. Birds soared in the crystalline blue sky, lamenting summer's end with plaintive cries. Patches of scarlet, ocher, and brown wove through the green tapestry of the forests. The barbarian wore his black hat and cloak; he carried a large round basket. Nearby hovered the ten guards designated to escort the doctor on his official twice-yearly search for medicinal plants.

Stooping, Huygens picked a vine and whispered so the guards wouldn't hear him speak Japanese: "Good for burns." He smiled at Sano, putting the plant in his basket.

Sano tossed in a handful of the mint often prescribed by Japanese doctors. "Good for stomachache," he told Huygens.

In quiet harmony, they combed the meadow for remedies, exchanging medical lore. Fifteen days had passed since the raid on the Chinese temple. The morning after, Sano had gone to Deshima to inform the surviving Dutchmen of deGraeff's death and to apologize to

Dr. Huygens for wrongly suspecting him of murder. Later he and Supreme Judge Takeda had replaced the entire Deshima security staff with trustworthy men culled through intensive interviewing and evaluation of service records and character references. While Sano regretted the inevitable loss of crucial links in the Dutch-Japanese information network, he guessed that it would soon flourish again, though hopefully without violence. When his work was done, Sano, leery of more treason charges, had refrained from meeting Dr. Huygens again—until today.

Far below them lay the city, tranquil in the bright sunlight. The troops had left the streets; the war drums had ceased their call of doom. On the harbor's sparkling water floated a stately ship whose sail bore the Tokugawa crest. It had arrived yesterday, bearing a message from Edo: When the shogun had discovered Sano's absence, he'd overruled Chamberlain Yanagisawa's orders, commanding Sano to return home at once. Newly secure in Tokugawa Tsunayoshi's favor, knowing he would leave Nagasaki today, Sano had risked a last visit with his barbarian friend.

Dr. Huygens picked a mantis off a blade of grass and put it in a glass vial. "Take back to Amsterdam; show other doctors," he said.

He pantomimed viewing the creature through the magnifying device, and they laughed at the memory of Sano's encounter with barbarian science. As they hunted more specimens, Sano's gaze wandered down the harbor channel, where he saw the Dutch ship anchored beside the rocky outcrop of Takayama. Sails furled, dwarfed by the distance, it now seemed as harmless as a child's toy.

After the raid, Sano had brought Captain Oss the bodies of Interpreter Iishino and Abbot Liu Yun, who had killed Jan Spaen and Maarten deGraeff. Oss had retreated from the harbor. A few of the crew remained on board while the rest had accompanied the cargo to Deshima. The Dutch merchants had sold their goods. The new East India Company staff had taken up residence on the island. Now the ship awaited favorable winds for departure.

"Soon we go," Dr. Huygens said. "Home."

Home, to rebuild the life Jan Spaen had destroyed; to resume his medical practice and continuing effort to atone for his youthful crime. As Sano contemplated Huygens's long ocean journey, he thought how small his country was compared to the vast world beyond its shores. He realized that Japan couldn't hold the world at bay forever. The *bakufu's* policies provided a flimsy barrier. More foreigners would come—not just from the Netherlands, but also from many barbarian kingdoms—with superior ships and weapons, hungry for new trade and territory. Now Sano could see the shogun and the *bakufu* not as omnipotent tyrants, but as small men afraid of a future they couldn't control. Japan must eventually surrender its isolation, and what then?

Sano envisioned a day when barbarians would freely walk the streets of Japan's cities and his descendants travel to distant lands. Japanese and barbarians would speak one another's languages, share ideas. His adventurous spirit thrilled to the possibilities. But Sano could also imagine foreign warships attacking Japan; the boom of gunfire rocking sea and land; cities burning; the death of his people in wars more destructive than any before. Sano didn't know which vision would come to pass, but he realized how vulnerable Japan was, how fragile the culture that dominated and nurtured him. Even Bushido might not survive the onslaught of foreign influence.

Now Sano experienced a powerful surge of love for his imperiled country. Like a pure, clean spring, it washed away the bitter hatred with which his past ordeals had infected him. Perceiving the danger renewed his samurai will to defend to the death his lord—and, by extension, his homeland, his people, his way of life. He felt strong and exhilarated, as if he'd recovered from a long illness. The future seemed alive with promise, his purpose clear.

Soon Huygens's basket was full; in the harbor, Sano's ship waited. Shepherded by the guards, they walked downhill, through the city. Outside the Deshima gatehouse, they made their farewells.

"I wish you a safe journey and a happy, prosperous life," Sano said, bowing.

"You safe journey. Good luck, friend." The doctor extended his hands. At first Sano didn't understand the unfamiliar gesture. Then he clasped Huygens's hands in his own, pledging eternal friendship barbarian-style. And it seemed to Sano that by parting thus, they also wished both their nations a mutually beneficial journey into the future.

Sano walked down the promenade to the docks. Hirata and the crew were already on the ship with all the baggage and provisions for the journey. A ferryboat waited to convey Sano aboard; a crowd had gathered to watch the ship sail. From among the fishermen and samurai, an odd trio emerged and approached Sano: Junko, radiant in a red-and-white kimono, with her father and Kiyoshi.

The day after the raid, Sano had personally released the young samurai from Nagasaki Jail and taken him home. Kiyoshi had been unresponsive and incoherent then, but now Sano saw with relief that while he was still thin and pale, he seemed his normal self again.

"We want to pay our respects and wish you a good journey," Kiyoshi said gravely. He and his companions bowed.

The polite greeting worsened Sano's guilt. "Kiyoshi, about your father. I don't expect you to forgive me, but I offer my deepest apologies. If there's anything I can do—"

The youth's eyes darkened with pain, though not anger. "My father made his destiny before you even came to Nagasaki. What he did was wrong." Kiyoshi swallowed hard, then recovered control. "He restored our family's honor by taking his own life. His death wasn't your fault." Then Kiyoshi said in a happier tone, "We have good news: Junko and I are to be married. Our families have consented to the match."

The girl beamed. Urabe shrugged and said grumpily, "Oh well, filial loyalty is more important in a son-in-law than business talent—I guess. And he has good connections."

"Yes, he does." With concealed aversion, Sano recalled the reason for this. "My congratulations."

"A thousand thanks for making our marriage possible." Kiyoshi bowed again.

In an effort to compensate the Ohira family for their loss, Sano had excused Kiyoshi for shooting him and had also settled a large sum of money on the boy. Now he was glad to see that some good had come out of tragedy. As he watched Kiyoshi, Junko, and Urabe walk back toward town, Sano felt oddly at peace. By bringing the young couple together, he'd somehow laid to rest his futile love for Aoi. He was free, and ready for his own long-postponed marriage.

However, when Sano continued down the dock toward the waiting ferryboat, he met an immediate challenge to his new equilibrium. Governor Nagai, flanked by troops and officials, smiled and said, "Ah, *sōsakan-sama*. What a pity you must leave so soon. I regret that your stay in Nagasaki was less than pleasant. Perhaps you can someday visit again, under more favorable circumstances."

Anger heated Sano's blood. Such hypocrisy from the man who had engineered his troubles! He bared his teeth in a smile just as false as the governor's. "It pains me to leave," he said, imitating Nagai's bland tone. "The fact that the city remains in your capable hands is little consolation."

Governor Nagai had profited from the smuggling and let his minions suffer the consequences. Since all the witnesses to his involvement were dead and no other evidence existed, Sano had been unable to induce Supreme Judge Takeda to prosecute Nagai. The only possible threat to him was Kiyoshi, who might know more about the smuggling operation than he'd told his father. But Nagai had bought the young man's silence by restoring his protégé status. With this "connection," Kiyoshi and his new in-laws would prosper. The corrupt governor was safe.

"Yes. Well." Governor Nagai's eyes narrowed as he perceived the cut Sano had dealt him, but his manner remained affable, befitting a public appearance. "I'm honored by your praise of my hands—which will continue to control this administration for the foreseeable future." And there's nothing you can do about it, said his smirk.

With veiled mutual antagonism, they exchanged bows. As Sano climbed into the ferry, he said, "When I reach Edo, the shogun will hear about everything that happened."

Nagai chuckled. "I am sure he will. But perhaps you may wonder what happened to the smugglers' loot. As we speak, it is on its way to Chamberlain Yanagisawa. He will no doubt appreciate my generous tribute." With a triumphant smile, he turned and led away his entourage.

While the ferryman rowed Sano toward the ship, he gazed after Governor Nagai with grudging admiration. Trust the politically astute governor to protect himself! The lavish gift would improve his standing with Chamberlain Yanagisawa, who would in turn thwart any actions Sano took against Nagai. While Sano had brought a murderer to justice, closed down the smuggling ring, and saved himself and Hirata, he'd lost the final round of the battle. But the loss was yet another valuable lesson, which revealed new challenges in his vow to defend his homeland.

As a police detective, and later as the shogun's *sōsakan,* he'd approached every investigation like a soldier riding into battle. He'd thrown body and soul into a one-man crusade against corruption—a force as dangerous to Japan as any external threat. But one man couldn't purge the Tokugawa regime of evil any more than he could single-handedly repel a military invasion. To win, Sano must abandon the role of the lone soldier who would inevitably fall before the enemy host. He must become a general, marshalling allies and troops, building the power and influence he needed to defeat men like Governor Nagai. And it would be his ongoing challenge to understand his own motives. He must labor to align them with what was right and good; to differentiate the selfish impulses from the honorable; to minimize casualties in his search for truth and justice.

The ferry drew up to the ship, whose bold banners fluttered above the curved wooden hull and ornate lacquer-and-gilt cabin. Sailors dropped a ladder for Sano to climb; Hirata helped him onto the deck. At the captain's orders, the crew raised anchor. The sail billowed, and the ship moved down the harbor channel toward the open sea. Sano and Hirata stood in the stern, watching Nagasaki's docks, houses, and hills recede.

"I've never been so glad to leave a place," Hirata said fervently. He waved to the cheering crowd on shore. "I'd rather be seasick all the way home than stay here another moment."

"I agree," Sano said, though not only because of their bad experiences. Nagasaki, the trouble zone where Japan met the outside world, also represented the junction between his past and future. In leaving the city, he also left behind his political innocence, his mistakes, and his isolation for new allegiances and myriad new opportunities for success.

"What do you suppose has happened in Edo while we've been gone?" Hirata mused.

Sano smiled. "Your guess is as good as mine. But I do know that things will be different when I—" his eyes met Hirata's "—I mean, when *we* get back."

LAURA JOH ROWLAND, the granddaughter of Chinese and Korean immigrants, is the author of *Shinjū* and *Bundori*. She lives with her husband and three cats in New Orleans. *The Way of the Traitor* is her third novel.